Dear Mystery Reader:

Charles Knief, the award-winning author of DIAMOND HEAD, is back with SAND DOLLARS. Private eye John Caine, Knief's endlessly likable sleuth, is reeling from the tragedy of losing both his girlfriend and his beloved boat. Down in the dumps with nowhere to go, the retired U.S. Naval officer is called back into action when a wealthy San Diego woman needs him to track down the truth behind her husband's death.

His search for the truth leads him on a murderous tropical trail that takes him from Hawaii to California to Mexico. With justice hidden beneath the sultry south-of-the-border sun, Caine must keep his eyes open and antenna up for any clues that might lead him through the sex, sand, and speeding bullets to his final destination...the truth.

After you've read SAND DOLLARS, you'll have your bags packed and your sunblock ready and waiting for more fun in the sun with P.I. John Caine. Enjoy!

Yours in crime,

Joe Veltre

Joe Veltre
Associate Editor
St. Martin's Press DEAD LETTER Paperback Mysteries

Other titles from St. Martin's **Dead Letter** Mysteries

ON THIS ROCKNE by Ralph McInerny
AN UNHOLY ALLIANCE by Susanna Gregory
NO COLDER PLACE by S.J. Rozan
THE RIDDLE OF ST. LEONARD'S by Candace Robb
A MURDER IN MACEDON by Anna Apostolou
STRANGLED PROSE by Joan Hess
SLEEPING WITH THE CRAWFISH
by D.J. Donaldson
THE CLEVELAND LOCAL by Les Roberts
WHILE DROWNING IN THE DESERT
by Don Winslow
SEE NO EVIL by Eleanor Taylor Bland
CRACKER: ONE DAY A LEMMING WILL FLY
by Liz Holliday
QUAKER INDICTMENT by Irene Allen
BLACK AND BLUE by Ian Rankin
CRIME AFTER CRIME ed. by Joan Hess, Ed Gorman,
and Martin H. Greenberg
SAND DOLLARS by Charles Knief
THRONES, DOMINATIONS by Dorothy L. Sayers
and Jill Paton Walsh
AGATHA RAISIN AND THE WELLSPRING
OF DEATH by M.C. Beaton
THUNDER HORSE by Peter Bowen

Dead Letter is also proud to present these mystery classics by Ngaio Marsh

DEATH OF A FOOL
SCALES OF JUSTICE
SINGING IN THE SHROUDS
SPINSTERS IN JEOPARDY

“YOU CAN’T LEAVE NOW, CAINE.” HE COCKED THE REVOLVER.

I made sure I had my balance and could move when I needed to. Stevenson put both hands on the gun, aiming it straight-armed at my face. A .38 isn’t a large caliber, but it’s big enough. Six feet away and pointed at your head, the barrel looks enormous.

His hand shook as he pulled the trigger. I dove across the bed, rolling under the tongue of flame, landing on the balls of my feet. He fired again as I charged him. Something tugged at the collar of my jacket. I reached him as he fired the third bullet, kicked his feet out from under him, deflecting the gun with my elbow. Glass shattered in another room.

He still had the gun and the gun still had two rounds . . .

“Readers who miss John D. MacDonald’s Travis McGee will be pleased to meet John Caine . . .” —*Booklist*

“Rings with authenticity. Taut, tense, never a false note.”
—Robert B. Parker on *Diamond Head*

“A high-spirited, high-casualty tale.”
—*Kirkus Reviews* on *Diamond Head*

“Knief’s writing is smooth and seamless, and he’s concocted an involving plot to go with his likeable, attractive macho hero and exotic setting. The result: an action-packed, satisfying debut.” —*Booklist* on *Diamond Head*

Also by Charles Knief
from St. Martin's Paperbacks

Diamond Head

SAND DOLLARS

Charles Knief

St. Martin's Paperbacks

SAND DOLLARS

Library of Congress Catalog Card Number: 97-31638

ISBN: 0-312-96682-2

Printed in the United States of America

St. Martin's Press hardcover edition / April 1998
St. Martin's Paperbacks edition / February 1999

10 9 8 7 6 5 4 3 2 1

Édes Ildikémnek

Acknowledgements

The author wishes to thank the members of the San Diego Police Department's Special Intelligence Unit, Sergeant Manuel Rodriguez, Detective Fausto Gonzalez, and Detective Jesus Cesseña, who introduced me to the world of cross-border law enforcement, and who taught me how it works along The Line. San Diego is fortunate to have such men.

For her support and for sharing her wisdom, I cannot thank my aunt, Dorothy Harrell, enough. When she wrote her stories so long ago, she gave me permission to write my novels now. I can't say I wouldn't have written, but she made it so much easier.

Thanks have to go to Ruth Cavin, who always makes sense out of chaos, and who possesses the inerrant ability to find what must be fixed, and then gives her writers the tools to do the job.

I also owe a great debt to Jim Allen—friend, agent, and first-line editor with a nose for the right stuff. Thank you, Jim. You are a perfectionist's perfectionist, a cruel taskmaster, and I wouldn't have it any other way.

And for all those wonderful booksellers who made the selling of Diamond Head a much more pleasant experience than anticipated—especially Maggie Griffin and the gang at Partners & Crime, who became good friends and who gave Diamond Head the Nevermore (which is marginally better than the finger); Barbara Peters from The Poisoned Pen; Elizabeth and Maryelizabeth from Mysterious Galaxy; and because he generously loaned his name and temperament to one of the major characters of this book, Ed Thomas of Book

Carnival. We've seen you before, Ed, and we might see you again.

And of course there's my best friend, my confidant, my lover, my wife, Ildiko. I've been all over the world, but with you, sweetheart, life is finally a trip worth taking.

O Ku ke anoanu ia´u Kualono
He ano no ka po hane´e aku
He ano no ka po hane´e mai

He weliweli ka nu´u a ho´omoali
He weliweli a ka po hane´e aku

He `ili´ilihia na ka po he´e mai
He manu ke ha´i o Pulepule
O mihi i ke anuanu, huluhulu `ole
O mihi i ka welawela i ke´a´ahu´ole

O Hula ka makani kona hoa

A ka po he´enalu mai i hanau
Po-no

Fear falls upon me on the mountaintop
Fear of the passing night
Fear of the night approaching

Dread of the place of offering and the narrow trail
Dread of the receding night

Awe of the night approaching

Palatable is the sacrifice for supplication
Pitiful in the cold without covering
Pitiful in the heat without a garment
He goes naked on the way to Malama

The driving Hula wind his companion

Born in the time when men came from afar
Still it is night.

Reprinted by permission from *The Kumulipo,* Hawaiian Creation Chant, translated and edited by Martha Warren Beckwith (incomplete text).

1

"I didn't think you were gonna make it," Dennis Dillingham growled as I jumped aboard. Dennis captains and owns the *Mako,* making a living chartering out to dive shops in Waikiki. It's his business and I think it's his home. Dillingham's a small blond man with an enormous walrus mustache and skin that's similar in color and texture to an old baseball mitt. He's always barefoot, and I think he only owns one pair of faded green shorts. I've never seen him wear a shirt.

"Just got the call twenty minutes ago," I said, dropping my day pack on a berth cushion and changing into my wet suit. Tom Cotton, a shop owner and fellow divemaster in Waikiki, called and begged me to take his group, citing last-minute emergencies with his teenage daughter. It had happened often enough I didn't ask, just jumped in my Jeep and raced to the Waianae boat harbor. I don't charge him for my time when I cover him. It's more of a hobby.

"Tom brought your gear. Your group is over there." Dennis pointed to four Japanese men dressed in neon-yellow wet suits standing in a huddle at the stern, inspecting their equipment. "It ought to be easy keeping track of 'em in those outfits." Dennis shares my preference for dark-colored gear, the avoidance of bright and flashy colors, anything that might attract the attention of creatures in the water possessed of curiosity, hunger, and sharp teeth, a dangerous combination. My suit is dark blue and black. All the rest of my gear is black. I exchange my shiny stainless-steel Rolex for a black-plastic Casio when I go into the water. I carry two knives, a Phrobis and my Buckmaster, and a .44 Magnum bangstick.

No matter where I am, I like to be in contention for a spot at the top of the food chain.

"Thanks, Dennis." I studied my charges. Only four divers. They would be easily managed. I hoped they spoke English, and then realized they would have to. Tom's dive shop doesn't aggressively advertise for Japanese tourists. Some shops in Waikiki are nisei-owned and their instructors and divemasters all speak fluent Japanese. It's to everyone's advantage that they work that part of the market. We all want our guests to come back, and if tourist divers have a bad time due to anyone's ignorance, no one benefits. But Tom's a businessman. When the occasional foreign tourist finds him, he's always ready to make a sale or charter a dive.

I introduced myself to the four men and we sized each other up. There was some bowing and some shaking of hands, the usual mixing of the cultures. I bowed and they shook my hand. Everybody grinned.

I sensed the short, thickly built man with a gray brush cut was in charge, the head hotshot, surrounded by three junior hotshots, on a business-reward outing. I immediately liked the man. He was powerful, used to giving orders and having them obeyed, but he looked intently at me and listened to what I had to say. I was *sensei,* the teacher, and he was the pupil. I could tell why he had risen to the top.

I like the average Japanese tourist. Apart from the fact that the money they pumped into the economy spared Hawaii most of the effects of the latest worldwide recession, they are polite, well-mannered guests. They don't get drunk and throw furniture out of hotel windows. They don't drive down the streets of Honolulu at ninety miles an hour. If they are involved in a crime, they are usually the victims. They typically travel in groups, bring their families, spend copious amounts of money, take their hundreds of photographs, and return to Japan to be replaced by another group. They are quiet, generous, and interchangeable. They come, they spend, and they go home.

Veni, vidi, photi.

I came. I saw. I took a lot of pictures.

Everything this group wore was new. Brand-new. I would not have been surprised to find price tags attached. Tom must have been delighted to have these guys walk into his store. They sported about five thousand dollars' worth of gear.

Their certification cards all were current. Their equipment, right off the rack from Tom's shop, was correctly assembled. They listened to my briefing about the dive. They answered my questions intelligently. I was impressed with their depth of knowledge about diving in general, and about diving in Hawaii in particular.

I knew this would be an easy afternoon.

There were four divemasters aboard, each with three to five divers. The boat wasn't full. We would have room to spread out. I emphasized to my group the necessity of staying with me once we were on the wreck of the *Mahi.*

For a trained diver, the eight-hundred-ton minesweeper is an extraordinarily exciting experience. There are few chances to get into trouble. The water is clear, the current nearly nonexistent, and the fauna is, for the most part, friendly. But because fools are so ingenious that nothing is really foolproof, those few chances can be lethal. At nearly ninety feet, the *Mahi* is at the lower range of safe sport diving. My computer would tell me when it was time to rise. Failure to follow its calculations could result in a case of the bends, a painful, potentially crippling affliction. Worse, the interior of the hull is enclosed.

Unlike other ships that were sunk as artificial reefs, no large holes have been cut into the hull to allow access to the interior. The *Mahi* is intact. She has been down a long time and inside she is cold, dark, and full of accumulated silt. All her hatches are open. The unlimited visibility outside the ship lures some of the foolish to try the interior. With lights, the undisturbed water is at first crystal clear; it's similar to cave diving. What the uninitiated diver doesn't know is that while he's swimming through the still water inside the hull, his fins are kicking up a curtain of silt behind him, decreasing the visibility to zero. Any ship is a labyrinth of holds and passageways, each with several vertical ladders and horizontal ducts. Without an intimate knowledge of the ship, or without a guideline, a diver could run out of air before finding a way out. If he doesn't run out of air, he faces the danger of exceeding maximum bottom time, risking the bends. Invading old ships is a dangerous business.

I knew the *Mahi.* I'd been inside her more than thirty times. I knew human nature and understood that at least once, for whatever reason, one of my charges would decide to go exploring.

George, one of the other divemasters, had a group of three gung ho college boys from Southern California, smart-ass know-it-alls who were too busy trying to impress each other to listen to instructions. Watching them prepare their equipment, I concluded that even though they had certification cards, they didn't know what they were doing. Had they been mine, I would have canceled their tickets, refunded their money, and let them live. Unhappy is better than dead. But George has six children at home and augments his navy chief's pay with divemaster fees and tips; he probably thought it over too many times and decided they would change their attitudes when they got into the water.

Once on the bottom, their cocky look-Ma-no-hands attitudes got worse. I watched them as hard as I watched my own group, who followed me like baby ducks follow their mama. The kids refused to follow George and, after a brief tour of the upper decks of the *Mahi,* produced lights and plunged into the hull.

I turned my charges over to George and went, knowing they would get into trouble.

They did. A black wall of silted water hovered bulkhead to bulkhead, just inside a hatchway, evidence of their incursion.

After tying my guideline onto the ship's ladder and yanking it tight, I crept forward into the silt, feeling blindly along the companionway to one of the ship's holds. I didn't bother with a light.

The first diver found me within the first twenty feet.

When I touched him, he turned and ripped off my face mask in his panic. I put a headlock on him and dragged him toward the hatch. When we emerged from the silt into clear water, he tried to bolt for the surface. I collared him again, this time applying intense and specific pressure against one of his nerve trigger points, an experience so urgently painful it got his full and immediate attention. He stopped struggling and got quiet, the way people do when experiencing great pain, and I released the pressure, still keeping my fingers close to the spot in case he needed reminding. I brought him to another divemaster and signaled that this one had to go up. When I was certain he would do as he was told, I put my mask back on, cleared it, and went back in.

The other two were together and it took me a long time to find them. When I did, in relatively clear water at the dead end of a large ventilation duct that branched out into smaller ducts that were impossible for a tanked diver to get into, they weren't as panicky as their friend, probably because they could see, but they were anxious. The cloud of silt lay beyond the last bend in the duct and they had realized their problem and stayed put.

I tied them onto the guideline and had them hang on to my weight belt. We inched slowly into the silt, our only path to the surface the thin guideline. It took some time, longer than it should have taken. Halfway there, or where I believed was halfway there, the computer beeped its alarm, an urgent sound, demanding our immediate departure for the surface. All divers know that sound. The hand on my belt pulled me backward as one of the kids tried to get past. I blocked his path. We struggled briefly and suddenly I was fighting two terrified young men, each trying wildly to move ahead of me in the tight confines of the old duct.

This was not what I was trained to do. Killing them would have been easy. My problem was keeping them alive in spite of themselves.

As we fought, I kept moving forward, following the line. My bulk, increased by my tank and other equipment, prevented the boys from moving me out of the way. There just wasn't enough space. I used my fins to keep them back, roiling water at their faces.

The walls of the shaft opened into a bigger space. One of the youngsters slipped the line and eeled past me, kicking and gouging, an unseen, maniacal force. I got a hand on his gear, but he shook me loose. Then he was gone.

Some people seem determined, aimed at their own destruction like lemmings. There was nothing I could do for that one. I went back for the remaining diver, slowly feeling through the murky water, dependent entirely upon sense of touch, forcing my body to go through the motions and my mind to keep the terror down to manageable levels.

We found each other, outstretched fingers brushing in the dark.

Touch galvanized him. The kid's arms and legs climbed over me, punching me, kicking me, elbowing and kneeing me. It was like dancing with an octopus. I lost my mask. A knee to the jaw knocked my regulator loose. An elbow crashed against my temple. I saw stars.

I went for the pressure point I'd used on his companion but couldn't find it, the kid jumping around like he'd taken a big PCP hit, making it impossible to get my hands on him. I couldn't get him off me and I couldn't reach him. Every time I tried, he'd move away, out of reach.

I'd just exhaled when I lost my regulator and needed air. Fast. I couldn't see in the dark murky water, but black spots began appearing, overlaying the black in front of my eyes, and the roaring of blood in my ears got suddenly louder than the bubbles from our regulators.

We kept fighting and moving along the line and suddenly we were in a tightly enclosed space again. I grabbed the kid around his neck, cutting off blood supply to his brain. He went limp, stopped struggling, and for a moment I wondered if I'd killed him. I let up and he punched me, a weak and ineffective punch, but it made me smile.

Keeping his neck in the vise of my right arm, I reached behind me, feeling for one of the two regulators I use, found it, and shoved it in my mouth before the black spots entirely covered my vision.

Joni Mitchell was right when she wrote about not missing something until it's gone.

I located the line and hauled on it. Still tight. I began dragging the kid along with me. It took longer that way. He'd become passive in my grip, but I didn't trust his judgment enough to let him loose.

We followed two more turns and the computer beeped again. We had one minute to get out of the *Mahi* and begin our ascent.

I towed the kid along until the black became lighter and suddenly we were out of the blackness and into the blue-gray amphitheater of the Pacific.

George and the other two divemasters hovered above, guardian angels, there to lead us home.

I signaled with two fingers and turned the kid over to one of the other instructors.

George shook his head, holding up one.

Gathering my line, I went back in and they took the kid to the *Mako*.

He wasn't very far inside. I found him by accident, making the same wrong turn he had, just ten feet inside a dead end in an old service compartment. He'd cut his line to get free of me, but some of it dragged behind him, and I discovered it against the bulkhead and followed.

The young man had given up to his terror. I pulled on the rope and I felt something float toward me, bubbles erupting from a regulator, no fight left. Reaching out, I groped in the darkness until I grasped a hand that closed on mine. I squeezed and got no response other than the gentle pressure already there.

We went up together, rising slower than our bubbles, stopping at the forty-foot marker while I fed more information into the computer. We got lucky, just missing the painful hours in the hyperbaric chamber at the Barber's Point Coast Guard Station.

I checked his air. His tank was nearly depleted but I

judged we'd make it. I don't use much and had a reserve, but in his panic he had consumed more. We moved to the fifteen-foot bar hanging below the dive boat and held on to the white plastic pipe the way kids hold on to the crossbar on a roller coaster. I looked down and almost got vertigo, the water so clear I could pick out details of the *Mahi*'s upper decks seventy feet below. It was like hovering in the air above the ship. We hung under the *Mako* until my computer told us we'd purged the nitrogen from our systems. I shared my air for the last couple of minutes with the kid, using body language and hand signals to keep him from rising toward the light.

We finally broke the surface, returning to the air and the bright Hawaiian sunshine. The young men, white-faced and sober, kept silent as they boarded. That's what facing your mortality will do for you. I thought about yelling at them, but figured they'd had enough punishment. They were college kids. Maybe they were smart enough to have learned a lesson. If so, this experience would have been worth it.

I had my doubts, but it never hurt to hope.

Everyone else was back aboard the *Mako*. My group—now George's—watched me bring the boys aboard. They spoke rapid and quiet Japanese to one another all the way back to the harbor.

Dennis called me up to the pilothouse.

"Your nose is bleeding."

I wiped my upper lip. My fingers came away with bright blood. Dennis handed me a bandanna.

"Dumb shits," he said, his voice heavy with disgust. "They violate every goddamn rule, run from their divemaster, get themselves killed, and we get sued. Thanks, Caine."

"They looked like trouble."

"They look like shit now, but they'll be all right. Give them something to talk about when they get home." Dennis looked at me, squinting against the glare of the hot January sun glinting off the smooth Pacific swells. "You got a call on the ship-to-shore. Fella at the dock needs to speak with you pronto."

"He say his name?"

"J. Lawrence Tishman, attorney-at-law. What'd you do? Knock somebody up?"

I shook my head. "Can't. Had the operation."

"If your girlfriend ain't late, then it must be your car payment."

"Don't have one."

"Maybe your uncle died."

"Yeah. That must be it." The only uncle I had was named Sam. He'd be around long after I was gone.

"He's wearing a tan suit," Dennis added, wrinkle lines bunching up around his eyes.

"Suit? Like with a tie?"

"Must not be from around here."

I went back to check on my original group and to apologize for leaving them. I ignored the college boys. If they approached me, we'd talk. Without their initiative, I'd leave them alone.

"We understand," said the senior executive. "George showed us wonderful things."

"Thank you," I said, "for understanding."

"Thank you." The elder Japanese shook my hand and then bowed. It was more of a dip than a formal bow, reminding me that I was the lesser being. "We will do it again. With you."

I nodded.

"I'd be honored."

He handed me a roll of bills and bowed again. "A token of our appreciation."

I smiled and bowed and thanked the man again, my bow no deeper than his. When he rejoined his group, I went forward and glanced at the roll. Fifteen pictures of Benjamin Franklin looked back at me. Hundred-dollar bills. The ugly one. I found George and handed the roll to him.

"They already tipped me," he said.

"They tipped you again."

George nodded. He needed the money more than I did. "Thank you, John."

When the *Mako* docked and I finished putting the gear away, I looked for the tan suit. A small, slight man stood patiently near the bait tank wearing a beige suit and an expectant look, totally out of place on the boat dock, his pale, smooth, office-bound face scrunched up tight against the sunlight reflecting off the water.

"I'm John Caine," I said. "You are . . . ?"

"J. Lawrence Tishman." He handed me a card. Attorney-at-Law. Fort Street. Honolulu. "May I have a word with you?"

I shrugged, watching one of the college kids from the corner of my eye. He hesitated, hovering just within the range of hearing.

"My firm represents a group of real estate investors who believe the general partner guilty of stealing the funds. We'd like you to investigate."

I shook my head. "Sorry. Not interested."

"You are a licensed private detective, are you not?"

I nodded, wondering where this was heading.

"You were referred to us by one of the investors, one of the larger investors, a man named Choy. Mr. Choy indicated that he knew you."

That made me laugh. I couldn't help it. So Chawlie was complaining about someone stealing his funds? Maybe the old guy was starting into decline. "Sorry. I don't do that kind of work." They would want written reports, spreadsheets, invoices with receipts for expenses. There would be a 1099 in the mail next January.

J. Lawrence Tishman sniffed as if he'd suddenly smelled something foul. And at that moment I understood Chawlie had indulged himself at Mr. Tishman's expense. It had been a joke, typical of the man. Tishman knew it, too, and didn't want to be here, but his client had insisted, and when you work for someone like Chawlie, you do what you're told.

I glanced at the kid. He was still there, waiting. Whether or not he could hear our conversation wasn't important.

"There are other firms who'll do you a better job," I told the lawyer. "Tell Chawlie I was busy."

"Yes." Tishman smiled a small smile, glancing at the dive

boat. "I can see you're busy." He left, clearly not pleased, but obviously happy to be heading somewhere else.

"Mr. Caine?" The boy approached, hesitant.

"What is it?"

"I just wanted to thank you. What we did, it was my idea, and it was stupid."

Such honesty in the young should be rewarded. "You've done something most kids want to do, which is good, and you survived, and that's better."

"You're a detective?"

I nodded. "Sometimes."

"Like that guy on the old TV shows?"

"No. He was a lot better looking than me and a lot smarter. He lived in a mansion in Kahala. I just scuffle." I didn't even have a place to live any longer. I was bunking at one of the Waikiki hotels near the Ala Wai Canal until I could find another boat.

The kid looked embarrassed. He wanted to stay and he wanted to go. We had no mutual context with which to carry the conversation further. I let him off the hook.

"Thank you for coming to see me. I know what that cost you. You better go help your buddies get their gear off the boat now, don't you think?"

"Sure. Thank you, Mr. Caine." The kid offered his hand.

I took it, thinking that maybe the younger generation wasn't so bad, after all.

2

You're a cruel man, Chawlie."

The old man nodded agreement, his face unreadable in the fluorescent glare of the bare overhead lamp. He leaned back in his chair, meager weight against the orange plastic. Over his shoulder, a gecko scurried across the glass partition of his restaurant's foyer.

It was more than a month after the dive on the *Mahi* and I was leaving the Islands for a case on the Mainland. Chawlie had somehow discovered my intent and called, demanding an audience. I had been curious about Chawlie's ploy with the lawyer, but kept away from the old crook. Asking questions would have resulted in a blank stare. If he wanted to tell me, he'd tell me.

"You knew I wouldn't take that case," I said. "Mr. J. Lawrence Tishman went on an empty errand." I knew but didn't say that Chawlie would have sent the lawyer on a wild-goose chase for a reason known only to himself. Chawlie had used me, but he had his designs and they were none of my business.

"General partner stealing funds from investors. Stupid man. No finesse. Had a meeting of limited partners to decide what to do. They brought in haole lawyer, wanted to stir the shit. I biggest investor. Told them to hire private detective. Must hire only the best. You." A wizened finger pointed at my chest. "Knew you'd say no. Knew you'd be hard to find, too. Keep haole lawyer busy."

"While you handled the general partner."

Chawlie laughed, a cackling wheeze. "Handled him very much. Thanked him very much. Took my cut." He reached inside his sweater, brought out a thick wad of folding money and handed it to me. "Here's yours. For your trouble."

I took the money, putting it away without looking at it. I seldom have qualms taking money from Chawlie. He has so much. And he parts with it so seldom. And nearly everything he gets is tax free.

"So it was all for show."

Chawlie grinned. I've known him for as many years as I've lived in Hawaii and he's never changed. Maybe aged, but only a little. He's always been an ancient Chinese institution who owns restaurants and fishing fleets and construction companies and acres of land, as well as massage parlors and gambling dens, and he has legions of nephews to handle the details of his empire. Chawlie and I have history. He threatened to kill me a while back, but changed his mind and made three-quarters of a million dollars from the circumstances surrounding a personal tragedy.

"Haole lawyer confused, that's all."

And the subject closed.

"You find new boat yet?"

"No. Haven't looked."

"Still in that dump on Seaside?"

I nodded. Waikiki depressed me, closed me in, but I didn't have the urge to go out and search for a new home to replace *Duchess,* my boat of many years. She sank in a hurricane, along with all of my possessions. Living in a hotel was a temporary solution for an anachronistic vagabond, but I didn't yet have the urge to abandon that way of life.

Homeless but for the cash on hand, I'd gravitated to the beach. There was a lot of cash, so there was a lot of beach time. I'd made money after a personal tragedy, too. About the same amount as Chawlie. Maybe a little more.

Not worth the loss.

Not worth it at all, when I thought about it.

I tried not to think about it.

The Rainbow Marina was changing, too. That helped put me off finding a new boat. The navy was building a bridge to

Ford Island from Aiea, using the marina parking lot as a staging area. When it's finished, the new bridge will loom over my old slip. Construction would take more than a year, they said, peace and quiet a thing of the past, sacrificed to progress. Or, as in this case, to access.

And so I put off the move and stayed away from Pearl Harbor. If I found a boat, I'd have to find a new place to dock. Somewhere peaceful, away from traffic and the crowds and the construction. Somewhere on the windward side of the island.

But I wasn't ready.

I'd originally planned to head for California after the events of the previous year, but that ambition died gradually into inertia when I returned to Honolulu and found myself settling into a high-rise hotel room on a side street across from a pair of motion picture theaters. I lived a day at a time, content to watch the tides change and tread the sandy beaches, giving time a chance to heal minor physical and major emotional wounds.

I survived the Christmas season, not venturing far from my hotel room except to run or work out at Duke's Gym or accomplish the occasional errand. The holidays can be cruel when you're suddenly uprooted from your accustomed environs, your life shattered. The forced good cheer of the season too quickly brings up the gag reflex, so I hid from the world until the first week of January, when I felt it safe enough to come out.

So when I got a letter from a Mainland banker, the envelope containing a small retainer in the form of a cashier's check and airplane tickets along with a request to fly to San Diego, there was little holding me. A phone call to the banker solved the mystery of the connection. I don't know that many bankers. I know none on the Mainland. I don't advertise my services, even when I need the work.

The woman's son had been one of the boys I'd rescued from the *Mahi,* the one who had thanked me. He'd apparently related everything, including the fact of my profession, overheard during my conversation with J. Lawrence Tishman. His mother had checked me out, and liked what she'd heard. Her client needed an outside expert, someone who knew boats. Most important, the detective had to be a fresh pair of eyes, someone who could pick out the forest from the trees.

It intrigued me and I agreed to meet her and her client in San Diego.

San Diego had been an unrealized destination for years, a place where intention and destination never seemed to converge. Self-absorption is only one of my minor vices, and here was the excuse I needed to get off the beach. Max was there. So was the admiral. And California was a good place to buy a boat.

"This case in California. How long it take you?" Chawlie leaned forward, his voice a raspy whisper. When he does that, I almost expect him to call me Grasshopper.

"I don't know what it is yet. You have something?"

"No, no, no," said the old man. "Just think it would be good for you. Keep you busy."

"You want me out of the Islands?"

"Nothing like that. You are wasting your life here. You don't do anything. You need a cause. Without a cause, you cease to exist."

That was as close Chawlie had ever come to saying he cared about me.

"Flight's out tonight. Taking the red-eye to LAX, then renting a car and driving down the coast. Haven't seen California for years. I'll enjoy the drive."

Chawlie shook his head. "Going to LA? Taking your cash?"

"Why?" Chawlie held the bulk of my cash in his vault. It was safer than a bank, and he had no reporting requirements to some faceless bureaucrat who had my best interests at heart.

"You buy new boat. Not good for you to live in hotel. You're a waterman, not a tourist."

"I'd thought about it."

"LA's a hard place."

"They're a bunch of psychos, but I'm just passing through."

"You're going, you're buying new boat, you're taking cash money, you're in California. You better bring gun."

Chawlie wanted something. He wanted me gone, away from my normal haunts. Maybe someday I'd discover the reason, but most likely I'd live my life in ignorance.

That was okay.

I was used to it.

3

I was early for the meeting at Mr. A's, a glass-enveloped steakhouse atop one of San Diego's downtown buildings, but the clients were already there. They had been for a while and were more than a couple of drinks ahead by the time I arrived.

When I mentioned the banker's name, the maître d' swept a menu from his podium and held it above his head like a banner as he led me through the dining room. Eyes followed our procession, eyes belonging to a well-dressed crowd, the business and political class of the city. I was glad I'd worn a suit and tie.

Two women sat near a window, deep in conversation. A good-looking brunette and a petite blonde occupied a booth, stemmed glasses of white wine in front of them, the bottle on the table. San Diego's harbor spread below them like a kingdom at their feet, the sun descending toward the long, low hump of the Point Loma peninsula beyond.

Both women interrupted their discussion at my approach, the blonde extending her hand in the gracious and formal European tradition. I shook it. Maybe I should have kissed it, but I'd never learned the etiquette of hand kissing and decided to stay with what I knew. "Claire Peters," she said, her voice low, pleasant to listen to, her eyes alert, but not friendly.

"John Caine."

The brunette shook my hand firmly with an old-boy shake, the business grip. This would be the banker.

"Mr. Caine, I'm Barbara Klein. Thank you for answering my call for help."

"You went a long way for it. Don't they have any PI's in California? Or are they all in Hollywood?"

She smiled but it wasn't convincing. Even though I was invited, there was an exclusivity to this gathering, a female-only ambience that made me the automatic outsider. They were both powerful, successful women. I was the beach bum from out of state. And a male. It was as wrong as a woman in a barbershop.

A waiter filled my glass as I sat. I took a sip of the wine, a California chardonnay. It had the rich, oaky flavor that I liked.

Barbara Klein looked me straight in the eye, the way they teach you at all those good management schools. It matched her grip. She wore an olive suit with a white silk blouse that billowed at the neck. A large diamond ring graced her right hand, the way divorced women wear them when they like the ring but no longer love the circumstances of its acquisition. Her left hand sported no jewelry of any kind.

"We've spoken on the telephone so many times I feel I know you, Mr. Caine," Barbara Klein said. "You were a little unkind in your description of yourself, however."

"I said I'm a big old ugly man with a beard."

"You should have said rugged. Ugly is a little harsh."

"Maybe a little."

"He's self-effacing. He doesn't mean it." Claire Peters looked at me without interest. She was pleasant, but distant. I was hired help. The meeting was some kind of requirement. She didn't want to be here and she didn't want to meet me.

Claire Peters looked to be in her mid-thirties, but these days who can tell? The air near her held a light, sensuous scent. Her body, finely toned, had all the right curves in all the right places. Her hair, cut short at the nape of her neck, would have looked mannish on some women; on her it was totally feminine, complementing high cheekbones and the flawless complexion of a professional model. She wore a simple black dress with a modest black shirt jacket that had probably set her back a thousand dollars. The triple-choker strands of pearls at her throat looked real, as did the gold Cartier casually entwined with the diamond tennis bracelet. The skirt was just short enough to display trim, athletic legs. I could picture her running up and down a tennis court, smashing the overhead shot into the distant corner, just out of her opponent's reach.

"I'm pleased to meet you, Mrs. Peters," I said. "I don't know if I can help, but I'm here to listen."

"What do you know?"

"Only what Ms. Klein told me. Your husband died in a boating accident several months ago and there are some questions about the circumstances of his death. The accident happened in Mexico, which complicates everything."

"You've never heard of my husband?"

"I'm afraid not. Ms. Klein—"

"Barbara."

"Barbara told me that Paul Peters was successful in business. Beyond that, I'm ignorant."

She considered my statement. "He's ignorant. That's like he's ugly. Where did you get him?" She spoke to Barbara Klein as if I were somewhere else. I took another sip of wine.

"He saved my son's life." Barbara gave a fairly accurate description of the events on the *Mahi,* and of my other capabilities. She really had checked me out and knew my record. Someone must have tapped her into Kimo's line, because she knew about my military background, too.

"Is that about it, Mr. Caine?"

"I think you left out the part where I leap tall buildings with a single bound."

Claire Peters examined me, this time with interest. "Perhaps you're just about perfect. Do you carry a gun, Mr. Caine? Don't people like you carry guns?"

I shook my head. "People like me need guns if they make a lot of mistakes. I try not to get into situations where a gun is necessary."

"Barbara said you were smart. I need someone with brains. I don't need a thug." She appraised me briefly, a clinical appraisal, intense and specific. "You're big enough. Imposing. Rugged, actually. If things were to get rough, you look as if you wouldn't run away."

"I won't run away," I said, "as long as there's a reason to be here."

The corners of her mouth turned up in amusement. It was almost a smile. She turned to her banker. "He'll do, if you still think I need a detective."

Barbara nodded. "I'm being promoted to the San Francisco office," she said to me, then turned to Claire. "I won't be around to watch out for you. You need adequate representation, dear, and you've not been getting it."

"Joe's a good lawyer."

"Joe's a tax consultant. He's over his head. You know that."

Claire nodded.

"Well, I'll leave you two alone. I've got to get home." Barbara Klein rose from the table, her mission accomplished. "David's going back to Berkeley tomorrow, so I want to spend some time with him before he goes. Oh, Mr. Caine." She turned to me, her dark eyes penetrating. "I know David thanked you for what you did, but I feel I owe you a mother's appreciation. It was because of that, plus the other things I found out about you, that you're here. Yes, we have private investigators in California. Good ones, too. But you saved my son. And the way you went back into that ship made me know you are the kind of man Claire needs now. If she trusts you, she will tell you all the facts and"—she faced Claire—"if she knows what's good for her, she'll trust you." She turned back to me. I stood and shook her hand. "I'll meet you in Joe's office in the morning. In the meantime here's my card. If you need anything."

We watched her leave, taking the check, the full-service banker. And one hell of a woman. When she left, the room seemed empty. Claire and I sat next to each other in the booth, silently sipping our wine. When she didn't say anything, I did.

"When was the accident?"

"Two months ago. The *Santa Clara,* that was our boat,

blew up at a fuel dock in Ensenada, about a hundred miles south of here. It burned to the waterline. They were able to recover only some charred remains they identified as Paul. We buried what was left of him."

"Death certificate?"

"Of course. Joe, he's the family lawyer, he has all that. Tell me again. You've never heard of Paul Peters or Petersoft?"

"I beg your pardon?"

"Petersoft, Limited. My husband wrote software. We started the company in our apartment, then took it public. Now it's listed on the NASDAQ. We moved the corporate offices to La Jolla two years ago. We bought the property for cash. Paul and I made a lot of money in a very short time. Now that he's gone, I guess I'm the president."

"You *guess* you're the president?"

"That's part of the problem. Some of the stockholders have filed suit trying to block my appointment. Joe will tell you all the details tomorrow. If you want the job?" She said it with a rising inflection, as if it were a question.

"I don't understand what you want me to do."

She sipped her wine. It was a healthy sip. She set the glass down, patted her lips with her napkin, replaced it in her lap, and adjusted the corners so they matched. "Barbara said to trust you," she said.

"Paul was the president and CEO of Petersoft. He was a genius. I know that sounds trite, but in his case it was true. He was simply one of the smartest people I've ever known. We were married for fifteen years. At first we were very poor and we stayed that way for a long, long time." She looked me in the eyes. It was a pleasant experience, but disturbing, too. The blue irises were now the color of ice. "Long enough," she continued, my mind racing to catch up, "to appreciate the difference.

"Paul had a plan. He knew exactly what he wanted. He wrote his first commercial software program soon after we got married. Then he hit it big with his relational database with a graphical interface. He wrote it originally for a Macintosh platform, but Microsoft Windows made it possible to adapt it to other hardware. One of the biggest software companies picked it up. He never looked back after that."

She took another sip, another big one. So did I, unwilling to admit I had no comprehension of what she had just said.

"I know I'm not getting to the point and I appreciate your not pushing me," she said, looking at the top of the table. She smoothed a wrinkle in the tablecloth with her fingers until it was gone. Behind her, the sky turned orange as the sun hid beyond a band of clouds near the horizon. It cast a soft glow over her features.

"I handled the marketing and the operations, but Paul handled the creative aspects and the money. He was old-fashioned, I guess. He liked for the *man* to handle the *money*." Her voice took on a hard edge when she said those words in the same sentence.

"After Paul's death, Joe—he handles both our personal and corporate finances—discovered that for an eight-month period, Paul had systematically looted money from the accounts, transferring sums to a bank down in the Cayman Islands. By the time of his accident, he had transferred seven million dollars down there.

"Those banks, they're like the Swiss, except more secretive. We don't know for sure, but the money was probably moved somewhere else. It's vanished. Barbara investigated as far as she could and she says it was 'bounced' to a bank in another country so we can't trace it or recover it. It's just gone."

"Seven million dollars."

She nodded. "There's just enough left to pay the corporate taxes and close the company. Petersoft is just a shell without my husband. The life insurance the company had on Paul and the cash on hand will just about cover the debts. It's like he planned it to the penny. Almost.

"Financially, I'm okay. For the moment. I've got money of my own, a house in Point Loma that's clear-titled and a condo in Park City. We have a place in Maui, too. Joe says I'm going to have trouble with the IRS over the missing money from the joint accounts and there's an SEC investigation. I may have to give up the condos, but he thinks I can keep the house. I may have to pay taxes on money I don't have."

"Anything else?"

"He's alive." She said it matter-of-factly, as if it were of no consequence, as if its telling was a generally accepted truth, like gravity.

"You know that?"

She drained the rest of the glass. A waiter appeared and refilled it, killing the bottle. "Thank you, Hector. Another one, please."

"Yes, madam."

"Are you going to eat?"

"Why?"

"At the rate you're going, you're going to get drunk."

"Good." She sat back, squaring her shoulders, and stared at me in naked challenge, the kind of stare that would start a fight out on the street.

Okay, I thought. She wasn't my business. And sometimes getting drunk isn't such a bad idea. This couldn't be easy. "He's alive?"

"I saw him. A friend of mine came down from Newport Beach last month to drag me away from the details of trying to put my life back together. The devil's in the details, you know. Sometimes they just overwhelm you."

"They can do that," I agreed, remembering how hard it was to get through the first few months after Kate died.

"Edith said there was a little resort near Rosarito Beach. Caters to us rich gringos. She was right. We played golf. We played tennis. Men tried to pick us up. It was exactly what I needed.

"On our last night there we went to dinner at a place just below Rosarito. Calafia. It's kind of a hotel and restaurant, right on the top of the cliffs above the ocean.

"We had a good time. We had lobster and good Mexican wine. We laughed a lot. I decided my life probably wasn't over, after all. When we were ready to leave, Edith had to go to the ladies' room.

"This place sells T-shirts and I decided to buy one to remember the trip. You know, a kind of commemoration of Claire Peters coming back to life. The gift shop is right there, next to the entry. I had just decided on the one with the Mexican flag on it when he walked in.

"I sensed something and turned around and there he was. I spoke his name. He ignored me and went back outside. I called to him, but he didn't respond. I ran after him. When I got outside, he'd disappeared. He must have run." She took another sip of the wine. Watching her in the waning light of a winter's evening, I wondered what it was that made the man run from her.

"You've got to understand Calafia. It's a warren of little cobblestone streets and alleys running in all directions. He could have gone anywhere."

"You're certain it was your husband?"

"I could not mistake the man I lived with for fifteen years!" She looked around, startled by her own outburst. Heads turned in our direction. I smiled and nodded to them and they went back to their conversations.

"He'd lost weight," she continued, quietly. "He was very tan. Like you. He was wearing clothes I'd never seen before. But it was Paul."

"What was he wearing?"

"Jeans and a cheap plaid shirt. Work clothes. Paul wore a white shirt and tie everywhere, except on the boat. And then only a polo shirt and khaki slacks or Bermuda shorts. No blue jeans. No plaid. Nothing cheap. Not ever. Not even when we didn't have money. He had changed, but he was still Paul."

"What did you do next?"

"We went home that night. The next day I called Joe."

"What did he do?"

"He called the police. When nothing happened, he called them again. They told him they were trying, but the Mexican police refused to reopen the case.

"I pushed him into doing something else. We needed someone who could cross borders without asking permission. He came up with nothing. He says he's working on something, but he's vague and mysterious about it. He's the expert. He should know what to do, but he doesn't seem to. I'm frustrated. This is out of my expertise.

"I told Barbara about it. She told me she knew someone and insisted that I meet you. I didn't know who or what you were until we were introduced. If I was rude in any way, I apologize."

"What do you want out of this?"

The question troubled her. It was visible in her face that she had considered the ramifications of finding her husband alive, if it was her husband, and if he was alive, and she didn't like her conclusions.

"I'm hurt and confused. If I've been duped, I want to know why. The money's secondary. It would make things easier, to get the money back, but what I really want is the truth."

"The truth is usually painful."

"Not knowing is worse. Right now I feel foolish and stupid. I don't like feeling foolish and stupid. I'm not used to it and I have no intention of doing so." She took another long drink of the wine, holding my gaze over the rim of the glass. "Will you do it, Mr. Caine?"

Behind her, bright white lights illuminated the office buildings at the city's center, traced the shoreline of the harbor, and outlined the sensual, curving bridge to Coronado. Powerful lights on North Island silhouetted the aircraft carriers at the quay. Far out in the Pacific the sun had set, leaving a thin, pale line of orange painted on the black, cold backdrop of the winter sky.

"I'll do it," I said.

She smiled. It was a dazzling smile, bright enough to dim the lights across the bay.

"Then we'd better order dinner. You were right about getting drunk. Even then," she said, "you may have to drive me home."

4

"You got her approval, all right." Joseph Stevenson, Esquire, was not what I expected. Six foot three, 250 pounds of big bones and muscle, he could have been a defensive end for the Chargers as easily as a tax lawyer, except he was beyond his playing years, beginning, like many ex-athletes, to go to seed. Excess flesh bulged above his collar and rolled around his waist, but I still wouldn't have wanted to get past him on the gridiron.

Barbara Klein and I sat in the office of Stevenson and Stapleton, a plush enclave near the top of one of the skyscrapers I'd seen last night from the restaurant. Framed photographs of sports heroes posing with the lawyer and autographed footballs and baseball bats covered every vertical and horizontal surface in the room. It looked like a fanatic's garage sale.

"You took her home last night?"

"Give him a break, Joe," Barbara said. "She'd had more chardonnay than the law allows."

Stevenson ignored her. "You're driving her car?"

"I left the rental at the restaurant and turned it in this morning. She told me to take Paul's Range Rover. She said I could use it instead of a rental to save expenses."

"You could stay at her house, too. That'd save money."

"Mr. Caine is not moving in on the widow, Joe. This is strictly business. Why don't you turn off your testosterone and help him do what your client wanted you to do?"

He nodded. He wasn't satisfied, but he would accept it. He had to. "He's not licensed in California."

"That's okay," said Barbara, pressing. "I checked the law. Technically, he'll work for you. Realistically, he works for Mrs. Peters. You both do."

Stevenson sighed. "She called me this morning and told me what a gentleman you were last night. She instructed me to hire you. So you're hired."

"I'm an employee?"

"A ten-ninety-nine consultant. Fees and expenses. And the per diem, as discussed."

"And the money?"

"Five thousand dollars against per diem and expenses. Keep track. Your fee will come at the end."

It was as expected. I nodded and he handed me a pale green check stapled to a thick manila envelope.

"Files and reports are in there. Everything I've got. Names, dates, places. Any questions?"

"Do you think she saw Paul Peters?"

Joseph Stevenson leaned back in his leather captain's chair, steepled his fingers in front of his chin, and closed his eyes. I waited for the solemn pronouncement that was certain to follow.

"I don't know," he said.

I waited for more. Outside, an airliner made its landing approach to Lindbergh Field, passing below the floor where Stevenson and Stapleton had an office. It was weird, watching the airplane from above.

"Do you think it was Paul Peters?"

Stevenson shook his head slowly from side to side, his eyes still closed as if he were trying to picture something in his mind, the reception eluding him.

"Oh, come on, Joe," said Barbara, her voice sharp. "Tell him what you really think."

He opened his eyes and glared at her, opened his mouth to retort, then shut it again, visibly rethinking the entire situation and his position in it.

"She wants him to be alive," he said, softly but pedantically, as if he were explaining a complicated formula to a child. "I understand that and I understand why. But the Mexican coroner compared the dental records I supplied. I know they were Paul's, because I drove them down myself. The coroner said there was no doubt after a police investigation. He issued a death certificate. No foul play suspected. It was an accident, pure and simple. Some gas fumes in the bilge, a little spark, and boom. Nothing tricky about that."

Stevenson looked at me as if he'd said something significant. If he did, I'd missed it.

"I told Paul to replace those gasoline engines, but he liked the speed that diesels couldn't give him."

"Did he know a lot about boats?"

"Power Squadron all the way. Safety-minded. Never had a bit of trouble."

"Turn on the bilge blowers before he started the engines?"

"Like he was a religious fanatic. Same way he flew. Went through the checklist every time.

"Look," he said. "Paul Peters was damned smart and he was an anal-retentive, obsessive-compulsive bastard when it came to things that had to be done, the same way a good surgeon is. If it has to be done, and if it has to be done in a certain way, Paul Peters would do it exactly as specified. I was his tax attorney. If a report was due IRS by February fifteenth, it had to be in at eight A.M., February fifteenth. He knew how to play the game the way it was supposed to be played. And he never took chances."

I nodded encouragement.

"So if he liked gasoline engines because of their pickup, I never worried about him. Compared to Paul Peters, the Coast Guard is slack. He never once bent the rules."

"Until he blew himself all over downtown Ensenada."

"You know boats?"

I nodded.

"Then you know they can turn on you, just like a woman can turn on you. Any number of little things could have happened."

To her credit, Barbara Klein didn't explode, but she gave me a compelling look, rolling her eyes. I'd never known a boat or a woman to turn that wasn't abused or neglected, but I kept silent. It was more important that I learn about Joe Stevenson's views of the universe.

"Exactly what did happen down there?"

Stevenson shrugged. "I don't know. There wasn't much left of the *Santa Clara*. The Mexicans put it down to misadventure. An accident. The explosion was so large the exact cause will never be known."

"Insurance company interested?"

"The boat was self-insured, so there was no insurance company asking questions. As for life insurance, it looks like they'll pay off without much of an investigation."

"So who did she see?"

"Yeah, Joe. Who did she see?"

"Barbara, I'm not going to fight with you."

"Just answer the man's question," she said. I was getting used to being talked about as if I were an inanimate object. Stevenson looked at me and rolled his eyes. Maybe it was a California thing. He expected me to come to his aid in male solidarity. I remained impassive. If they were going to talk about me as if I were insensate, I could at least play the part.

"A lot of men look like Paul. And to listen to Claire, this guy was skinny. Paul had put on weight over the last couple of years, all that sitting around the office trying to make the company run and dream up new software at the same time. He had a lot of stress. He didn't exercise." Stevenson's hands smoothed the silk tie over his own budding paunch.

"She swears it was her husband."

"Did he acknowledge her? Did he turn his head when she called his name? No. Claire says he ignored her, as if she were calling to someone else. He was a genius in his own way, but he was a computer wizard, not an actor. He would have turned his head if he heard his name called."

"So it wasn't Peters."

"No, Mr. Caine. I'm satisfied that Paul is dead. The problem is the missing money."

"Seven million dollars."

"The Internal Revenue Service is screaming. They're threatening to bring in the FBI. The state of California is ready to seize everything Claire has. I'm holding them back, but I don't know how long I can do that. SEC and California are both launching investigations into the disappearance of corporate funds. There may be criminal charges. Those people don't believe she's as innocent as she claims. There's one shareholder lawsuit already. Another one will probably be filed within a few weeks.

"This is a mess. If we can at least trace where the money went, I might get them off her back. There's a meeting with the IRS in two weeks. If I just walk in there and say, 'Well, gee, guys. I dunno,' they'll crucify me. And her. These people are sharks. Do you have any idea what it's like, swimming with sharks?"

"Claire wants to find out who the man in Mexico was, Joe."

"I know, Barbara. We've got two jobs."

"They're related."

"Since she likes your Mr. Caine so well, he can keep her happy." He turned to me. "Go down to Ensenada and look at the pier where Paul died. Talk with Teniente José Enrique de la Peña of the Mexican Judicial Police. Go down to Calafia and chase ghosts. Spend the woman's money. Meanwhile, I'll chase the funds because that's the heart of the matter."

Barbara rose abruptly. For a minute she looked as if she might do violence. "I'll be downstairs," she said after a long moment, her voice almost a growl.

Stevenson watched her leave. "I hired an ex–Treasury agent," he continued, "who used to specialize in that kind of thing. He's one of the best there is. We'll work that side of the street. You work yours."

The meaning was clear. He objected to my presence. He didn't dare cross the widow Peters, but he didn't have to like me. He would provide the barest help and cooperation, if that.

"And one more thing. Claire's vulnerable right now. She doesn't need you trying to get into her bed. You understand that?"

"I understand, Mr. Stevenson."

"Fine. That's fine. You do your part and I'll do mine. It'll be a kind of contest."

"Well, I've got one thing going for me that you don't," I said, getting up and walking toward the door, following Barbara Klein.

"What's that?"

"I believe her."

5

Barbara met me at the elevator. It came as I joined her and we walked right in, no time for conversation. Two elderly women occupied the car, so we descended in silence. I felt an intense gaze and glanced down into a pair of round, highly magnified eyes framed by gold rims and wispy gray hair. The woman studied me intently. I smiled, trying to look friendly.

"Are you one of those football players?" she asked in a tremulous voice.

"No, ma'am. I'm too old and too small. Those guys are all a lot bigger."

She lowered her stare. "They must be giants," she confided to her companion.

The doors opened and Barbara and I waited for the two women. I went ahead and opened the exit doors for them and we followed them into the bright sunshine.

"I'm sorry," Barbara said once we were alone on the way to the car. "I don't like the man. I don't understand how Paul and Claire could do business with him."

"He's not honest?"

"Oh, I don't know. I think he's ineffective, all bluster and no depth. He promises more than he can deliver, and, you know, his stance on women! He talks like he just fell from a tree!

"Claire knows how I feel, but he continues to represent her. Even now." She put her hand on my arm. "Let's forget about Joe. You had to meet him. Now forget him. You're here because he's been unable to get off the dime. The only time you've got to see him is when you need more money."

"Thank you."

"Don't thank me. Claire's my very good friend and she's been through a very rough time. I wasn't the one watching their funds, and even if I had been, it may not have made a difference. There are all kinds of reasons why an account can gradually decrease over a period of time. As long as there's operating capital plus a reserve, we usually ask no questions. I won't be around now. She needs someone in her corner and when I leave, there's no one else."

We arrived at a new black two-seater Mercedes that chirped when she squeezed her key chain. I opened her door.

"Oh, Claire told me about last night. She apparently tried to make a pass at you."

"Or two. Or three."

"She can be insistent. Don't feel that she's some virginal . . . never mind. You were a gentleman. I don't believe there are many like you anymore."

"Never kept count." I closed her door after she swept her legs into the car. Nice legs. Long. She rolled down her window and smiled at me behind dark sunglasses.

"I'll be at the four-one-five number if you need anything. Or if Mr. Macho makes too much trouble for you to handle. But I have a feeling you won't call. You seem fairly self-sufficient."

"Fairly," I admitted, stepping back from the curb and watching her drive away.

I walked back to my car, dodging panhandlers, and sat in the leather driver's seat of the Range Rover. It was time to decide where to start. If Peters really did die in Mexico, the Mexican *policía* would be the logical place. I took out the file and leafed through it until I found Teniente José Enrique de la Peña's telephone number.

The cellular telephone was in a padded leather box between the seats, the speaker and the microphone in the sun visor. I punched in the numbers.

My call was answered at once. I started talking but realized I'd reached a voice-mail beeper and waited until the gruff Latin voice finished his instruction and the familiar tone sounded, then punched in the number of the Range

Rover's cellular phone and hit the pound sign. A recorded voice thanked me in Spanish and I disconnected.

The phone rang immediately.

"Lieutenant de la Peña?"

"No, this is Claire. Already working, I see."

"Gotta start somewhere."

"How was the meeting?"

"Interesting."

There was silence; then she said, "Thank you, again, for last night. I'm sorry about . . . I'm not . . . it's not like that."

"You've been under stress—"

"No excuses. I'm sorry. I apologized. I did not make an excuse. The proper response is, 'You are forgiven.' "

"You are forgiven."

"Thank you. Can you come over here? I've been thinking, and you need to know some things I didn't tell you last night. Things I'm sure Joe didn't tell you."

"I'm on the way."

"Thank you, Mr. Caine."

"It's John."

I took the long route to Point Loma, cruising the wide highway squeezed between the harbor and the airport, hoping de la Peña would return my call. The winter sun was bright, but the light felt both weaker and harsher than my gentle Hawaiian sun. Otherwise, San Diego and Honolulu were similar cities. Of the two, San Diego was possibly the more lovely.

De la Peña hadn't called by the time I pulled the Range Rover into the circular drive in front of the Peters mansion, perched on a hill overlooking the harbor, a Spanish mission-style estate with a rolling front lawn that could have provided enough lots for an entire subdivision.

Juanita, the housekeeper whose help I'd enlisted the night before in prying the merry widow from her BMW and into the house, appeared at the door. A huge smile lit her face when she saw me. I wondered if she was remembering my comic attempts to get out the door with my virtue intact.

"Good morning, Meester Caine. Mees Claire said to poot you in the den." She smiled all the way, and the last thing I saw of her was a wide, white-toothed smile as she backed out of the room and closed the door.

Claire had had too many bottles of chardonnay, and she was what you might have called amorous to the extreme. When I got out of the house, I had felt both relieved and disappointed in my fierce moral strength.

"You could have had her, boy," my evil side said, leering all the way back to the hotel.

"And it would have been wrong," preached the little angel on my right shoulder.

"Maybe," said the devil on my left, "but it sure would have been fun."

"But you don't get anywhere schtupping the boss lady," I said.

"I beg your pardon?"

Claire entered the den dressed for tennis, all in white except for a flaming strip of color integrating both the top and the skirt, some designer's idea of what the tennis set wore this year. The short, pleated skirt showed off her legs. I judged them magnificent, on a scale of one to ten, about a ten and a half. She had good shoulders, too, the kind professional players develop after years of practice.

"I was having a conversation with myself," I said. "Regretting my actions of last night."

"But you were a gentlemen."

"Exactly."

She laughed, a good, hearty laugh, straight from the belly. "And now you regret it?"

I shook my head. "Only partly. I don't go around—"

"Schtupping the boss lady?" Claire's eyes sparkled with amusement.

"You heard that?"

"Just that."

"Yeah. It's bad for business. But it may have been nice, in other circumstances."

She nodded, looking at the floor, avoiding my eyes. "You

don't hurt my ego," she said quietly. "But thanks again. It would have been wrong."

She walked across the room, trailing her finger along the back of a leather couch. It would have been an incredibly sensual act except for the fact that my sensual receptors were deadened and the red-alert signals were going off in my brain. When she reached the opposite side of the room, she turned and looked at me with the same direct, challenging stare she had used the night before. "I don't know you very well, Mr. Caine, but I feel as if I can trust you. Well, aside from your belated admission, I know I can. It was important last night, what you did. Or what you didn't do."

She crossed her arms beneath her breasts. I tried not to stare. "Juanita told me some of it this morning. At first I was ashamed of myself, and then I thought, what the hell. It might make it easier for him to believe me."

"I do believe you."

"Joe doesn't."

"I know."

She blinked. "He told you that?"

"Not in so many words, but he made it clear he thinks I am superfluous."

"Are you?" Once again that open stare accompanied the challenge. This woman reminded me of Kate in many ways.

"Not if you're telling the truth."

She nodded. "That son of a bitch."

"He thinks you know more than you're telling him. He didn't say that, either, but I understood that he's going through the motions with you."

"I felt that," she said, biting her lower lip. "You really think I'm not lying?"

"Why would you?"

She thought about it, uncrossing her arms and then re-crossing them again. "Yeah. You're right. What motive would I have?"

"If you'd planned this with your husband, if the two of you set out to loot your own accounts and run away, there's no reason to fake it. Cash in and get out. A lot of people do that. If you did do it, why broadcast that he's still alive? It has no logic."

"Put that way, it doesn't. But the IRS and the state of California apparently don't think that way."

"Linear thinking is not a bureaucrat's greatest attribute, Mrs. Peters."

"Call me Claire." She leaned against the back of the leather couch, hiking the tennis skirt up a few inches, exposing more of a tanned, firm thigh. I stared her right in the eye. "And Joe doesn't believe me," she said, matching my stare.

"Apparently not."

"I wonder why. It seems like he's always been a friend. I thought he was my friend."

I decided not to mention Barbara's opinion. "How long have you known him?"

"Paul met him five years ago at a tax seminar, just after the company started growing. Joe represents a lot of sports people and Paul was always attracted to that kind of thing. Although he couldn't play the games, he loved to watch. Joe represented something glamorous to Paul. He introduced us to quarterbacks and boxers, all kinds of people you read about on the sports page. He used to play for Pittsburgh."

"Not the Chargers?"

"No. He played two years for the Steelers and then quit. Some kind of broken something in his leg that made them cut him. So he went to law school and specialized in tax law for rich athletes. He moved to San Diego when Tyrone Crenshaw took him on as a client."

"I'm sorry, I don't know Tyrone Crenshaw."

"Where've you been?"

"Hawaii. And I don't follow professional sports."

"Tyrone Crenshaw came out of the slums and was the number-one draft pick six or seven years ago. He signed a multiyear, multimillion-dollar contract and did well for the first season. Then he dropped out. He just quit. He didn't show up for training. Blamed it on drugs, blamed it on his manager, blamed it on everyone but himself. He committed suicide about a year later. Hung himself in a cheap hotel room downtown. He was broke.

"No one could understand how a bright young man could spend all that money so fast. Joe did what he could for him and for his family. He paid for the funeral out of his own pocket, I heard. Everyone believes that all the money went to cocaine."

"This happen while Joe was watching your finances?"

"No. It was before."

"Any other clients of his have problems?"

"What an odd question. Of course not."

"Just covering the bases. It wouldn't be the first time a lawyer skipped out with the funds."

She shook her head. "That would have been impossible. Joe's a good friend. Besides, there's no way he could get his hands on any of our money. He was an adviser, nothing more. None of the funds went through his accounts."

Her eyes flashed. When she was angry, they seemed to turn from blue to a pale emerald green. "Just because you don't think he needs you is no reason to attack him!"

Here was a boundary I was not supposed to cross. I raised my hands in surrender. "I'm just asking questions. That's why you hired me."

She shook her head again. "No. That's not why I hired you. I hired you to find my husband and to find out why he took the money!"

"Whoa! I didn't come here to fight with you. You said there were things I needed to know."

"Well, now I'm not so sure!" The emerald gaze was forceful enough to sting all the way across the room. I was glad I wasn't close. I might have been burned.

"Okay," I said. "You decide. But decide right now, because if you don't like the way I work, you can fire me. I haven't cashed your check."

"Wait a minute, wait a minute, this is getting us nowhere." She uncrossed her arms and looked down at the tops of her Nikes. I waited, standing fifteen feet away, but feeling her heat. I hated the fact that she felt so alone.

"Thank you," she said after a minute. "I had to get control of myself. I hate losing my temper."

"Me, too."

"But you didn't. You were, once again, a perfect gentleman."

"Don't you just hate that?"

Despite the emotions boiling within, she smiled, a kind of forlorn and ragged smile, but genuine. "Yeah. It could give me a case, wondering about you."

"So where do we go from here?"

"Come on," she said, walking across the room and taking my arm. "There are some things I need to show you. After that, I'll stop interfering with what you're doing. But you really can't start a serious investigation without knowing these things."

She tugged me toward the door. "You've been acting like one, so I'll treat you like one."

"Like one what?"

"A priest. You are so uninvolved and distant. I need to make a full confession," she said. "And you're Father John."

She led me out of the den to the hallway, pulling me upstairs.

6

"This was his bedroom." Claire Peters pushed me into something that might have been put together by the set designer for *Out of Africa*. Decorated in dark woods and rich, brown leathers, it was masculine-macho, the kind of bedroom you might expect to see in the home of a man unsure of what he was, or of a child pretending to be a big-game hunter. A child with an unlimited allowance.

Half-closed wooden shutters blocked out bright sunlight. Green tropical plants shaded the glass, giving the impression the room was somewhere in the middle of a dark jungle.

The head of a magnificent male lion dominated the far wall, surrounded by the heads of other trophy cats and game animals. A zebra skin was artfully thrown across the bed, and a tiger skin lay diagonally across the plank floor, green glass eyes tracking us as we entered.

They reminded me of Claire's eyes.

"You didn't sleep here."

She barked a harsh, brittle laugh. "Not once."

In an alcove, unseen from the door, were half a dozen Nautilus machines. The latest models.

"He use these much?" I asked, remembering what Stevenson had told me about Peters's physical condition.

"Only at first. It was his passion for a while. To get in shape. But he lost interest. That was about the same time he started taking all those vitamins and herbal remedies." Claire's eyes closed, while she peered into the past. "Now Juanita dusts them every day. That's the only activity they get."

A gun cabinet stood against the wall next to the lion. "Did he shoot these?" I asked, pointing toward the animal heads.

Claire shook her head. "No. He bought them from an estate sale. He bought the guns, too, but he never fired them. It was all part of the look, I guess."

I opened the cabinet. "May I?"

She shrugged.

I took from the rack a short, double-barreled rifle that looked like a shotgun, but the walls of the stubby barrels were thicker. I opened it. It was a .505 Gibbs, an elephant gun, guaranteed to drop anything that walked on any number of legs on any continent. It had been well used and well maintained. I'd never fired one. Never wanted to. The kick from this thing would be punishing.

I replaced the Gibbs and picked up a long, scoped rifle, something I was more familiar with, a Remington 700 ADL in 7mm Magnum, bolt-action with a variable scope. Not an elephant rifle, but still a lot of gun. I used to be fairly good with one of these back in the bad old days when I'd been assigned as a sniper in some rotten, stench-filled jungle half a world away. Holding the weapon brought back memories I'd have rather kept buried. I put both the rifle and the memories away and closed the cabinet. All the other rifles and shotguns looked new.

"He never fired any of these?"

She shook her head. "Not to my knowledge. He had some pistols, too. A twenty-two he took with him on the boat and a thirty-eight he kept here, but I don't think he ever fired a gun in his life. It just made him happy to have them, so I thought, good for him. I was a good wife."

"You sound wistful."

"Just resigned, I guess."

"Why did you show me all this?"

"Until we came to this house, we were a couple. Even the first few years here I could count on Paul to be there for me. In the middle of the night if I couldn't sleep, he'd rub my back, like you would a baby, and gentle me back to sleep. He was my husband and I believed he would do anything for me."

She shifted her gaze toward the Nautilus machines and wrinkled her brow.

"About a year ago," she continued, "all that changed. I know exactly when it was. Just before Christmas. He went out of town to a seminar on real estate investment and when he came back, he was different."

She turned those green eyes on me, that confrontational look returning.

"Put on your priest's hat, because you need to hear this. It's embarrassing, but I think it's important for you to know. Our life together, including our sex life, was better than good for all the years of our marriage. It was everything that it should have been, or so I thought. I was happy, fulfilled, and I thought he was, too. Until last year. Then it just turned off like a light switch. I didn't know if it was me that turned him off, or if someone else turned him on better, but when he came back from Palm Desert, he was a different person.

"That's when he redecorated this room. That's when he bought all this Hemingway crap and those machines."

I watched her eyes. She was getting angry relating the betrayal.

"Hold on a minute," I said. "Did you discuss this with him?"

"Of course. I'm not stupid. I didn't need to find any notes or lipstick on his collar or long blond hair on his coat to know what was happening. We'd been married nearly fifteen years and I thought, at first, that it was just a fling.

"I mean, we had so much together. He was my best friend! We didn't even have other friends, we were so involved with each other. And then this! It threw me off balance. I wasn't sure what was wrong for a while, but I did press him.

"When he hired this sweet young man to come in and change his home office into another bedroom, I thought maybe he'd had a sea change, that maybe it wasn't another woman after all. But that didn't seem to be the case.

"After he decorated the place and moved out of our bedroom, I fought back the only way I knew how. We went to Europe for what was supposed to be a month. It lasted only a week. It was the worst week of my life, until recently.

"We didn't fight. It was worse. He ignored me. In every hotel room we had separate beds.

"One night I slipped in beside him and tried to get him to make love to me. He recoiled from my touch! Like I had a disease or something! It was too much. I dressed and went downstairs and sat in the lobby until the sun came up. We checked out later that morning, flew home, and never spoke of it again.

"When we got back, I decided to make my own life, apart from Paul. I still loved him, and I really didn't have any proof that he was doing anything wrong. He was always cordial, never mean or nasty. But he wouldn't sleep with me. There was nothing I could do about that, so I had to make a decision. I didn't divorce him. Nothing changed in the business. I wanted to give him some time to see how it would work out.

"Now I know that a month or two after we returned from Europe, he started moving money out of our accounts.

"And now, a year later, he's gone."

Dappled light coming through the half-closed shutters played across her features. As she related her story, her body became more and more rigid. She stood near the window, arms wrapped around herself in a tight embrace. She looked like a painting of a beautiful, suffering woman, something from the Middle Ages, when suffering was equated with a high morality. Well, maybe some things don't change. "Why tell me this?"

"You don't seem judgmental. You seem aloof, apart from everything. And despite what I said earlier, I can't really trust Joe. He was Paul's friend. I have no one."

"Do you think Joe helped Paul disappear?"

She wrinkled her brow. "Joe is too ethical, and I don't think he could really keep that kind of a secret. No. I think he was taken in by Paul, too.

"Remember, Paul is smart. Very smart. If he wanted to pull something like this, he would do it and not have to involve anyone else."

"Except?"

"There was an except?"

"You know there was, the way you said it."

She sighed. "Okay. I'll say it. There was another woman. There has to be."

"You know who she is?"

She shook her head. "I don't have a clue. There's this void where my heart used to be. I'm mourning him, but I'm so angry I can't think deeply about it. I saw him! He's alive! That was no mistake! And I can't think of any reason why he'd leave me unless it was for another woman."

"And you want to find out why he left. That's the most important thing."

She looked at me as if I were some special kind of idiot. "No. Regardless of what I said last night, the most important thing is the money. I need it back. The company needs it back. That was my company, too. I helped build it, right alongside him. If the son of a bitch stole it, I want it back. And while you're getting it back, you can find out where he is and why he did it."

7

It is exactly five miles between the Intercontinental Marina and Spanish Landing, a tiny park wedged between the harbor and the highway. A fast, flat run, ten miles out and back. A stiff breeze blowing in off the harbor chilled me, but five minutes into the run I was glad I'd left my sweatshirt in the hotel.

Despite the wind, I was running effortlessly. A little before Paul Peters disappeared, I'd been shot in the right thigh pursuing a serial killer in Honolulu. I lost my boat, my only home for over a decade, and most of my possessions, but those were unimportant compared to the loss of Kate Alapai, a woman I discovered too late that I loved, and who in turn had loved me.

Now I was back in the best physical condition possible for a man my age. It felt good to be nimble again. Several times in my life I'd been close to death; too often I'd seen those whom I loved die. Survival had given me a deep appreciation of life and the joy of living it. In Hawaii I am a rainbow junkie and enjoy nothing more than watching them float along the green slopes of the Ko'olau Mountains. I can watch them for hours. Nothing else gives me the same kind of peace. Here, with the weak winter California sun reflecting brightly off the surface of San Diego Harbor and the tall, graceful buildings beside it, I got a similar infusion of harmony.

Heading along the Embarcadero toward downtown with the wind at my back, I reviewed why I was here. Barbara Klein said it best: Claire Peters needed someone on her side. I knew nothing of the abilities of the local police and had my doubts about Stevenson's agenda. I told myself she had no one else.

I was new in town, didn't know the layout, didn't know the players, had no contacts, and wasn't certain why I'd been hired from so far away. Teniente José Enrique de la Peña wasn't returning my pages. I wanted to visit Petersoft, Ltd., after leaving Claire's house, but there was some kind of audit going on and the acting manager couldn't be bothered. Claire told me she'd handle it and get back to me. So far, I'd done nothing but bother the widow and annoy her attorney.

With nothing to do, I ran, amused at the job I'd been talked into accepting.

I finished my run along the wide promenade at the rear of the hotel and walked by the marina to warm down. A wizened, suntanned boat salesman dressed in clothes as wildly colored as a Third World postage stamp leaned crepey bare forearms on the teak railing of a million-dollar motor yacht, the old boat the marina sales office.

Seeing the yachts reminded me of that other thing I had come here to accomplish. *Duchess,* my home for more than a decade, lay at the bottom of the Pacific, sunk by hubris and a hurricane. Living on land made me itchy, the feeling of something solid beneath my feet unwelcome.

I'd lived aboard boats for most of my adult life. The illusion of freedom, the idea that you could slip the restraints of civilization and sail out to sea as easily as untying the dock lines—that illusion is addictive. I liked having the option. Somehow, it had become a part of being John Caine. Chawlie's assessment had been on target. I still thought of myself as a boat person, even though I had no boat.

Self-mockery can last only so long. Pulse and breathing under control, I approached the salesman.

"Nice marina," I said.

"Finest harbor on the coast, friend." He looked at me with interest, predatory instincts alerted. About sixty years old, he looked ninety, with a nut-brown face from years spent in the sun, creases and lines superimposed over the wrinkles, a budding basal-cell carcinoma on the bridge of his nose. "Staying at the hotel?"

I nodded.

"You in the market for a boat?"

"One of the reasons I'm here."

He brightened at my reply. "Jack Kinsman," he said, extending his hand over the railing. He had to stretch and I had to reach over the shore rail to take it, but we managed. "What are you looking for?"

"Ketch. Sixty feet or so. Diesel engine. Rigged for long-range cruising."

"Got nothing like that here, friend, but there's a Sparkman and Stephens on the market. Built in nineteen thirty-eight. It's a sixty-four-footer, and it's a schooner, not a ketch. You have any objection to a wooden hull?"

"Prefer it to Tupperware," I said.

He laughed, a generation of whiskey and unfiltered cigarettes degrading it into a coughing fit. "Don't get many like you," he said when he recovered. "Live aboard?"

I nodded, smiling back. "Can I see it?"

Kinsman shook his head. "Yes and no. Have to arrange it in advance. Belongs to a man who wants to sell it, but he's picky about when he shows it. You ready to buy now? Or just looking?"

"I'm serious. With cash."

"How can I reach you?"

I gave him my room number and the cellular phone in Peters's Range Rover. He gave me his card. I was certain I'd hear from him.

The hotel had a gym and I spent another hour there earning my standard daily rate, then went up to my room to shower and change. There were no messages. I ordered room-service coffee and croissants and took a quick, hot navy shower. By the time the knock came, I was dressed, sitting by the window, looking at the hundreds of yachts tied to their moorings fifteen stories below.

When the server was gone, I went back to the easy chair by the window and made my daily round of telephone calls.

"Admiral MacGruder's office," said the young male voice on the other end of my first call. "Please be advised this is not a secure line. Yeoman Becker speaking. How may I help you, sir?"

"My name is John Caine. I'm looking for Chief White."

"Would that be Senior Chief White, sir?"

"Big fella. Vile temper. Sits around, coasting toward retirement. That Senior Chief White."

"The chief is unavailable at this time, sir. May I direct your call to his voice mail?"

I sighed. Voice mail had invaded the SEALS. I hated voice mail. "Please, Mr. Becker," I said. "And thank you."

"You're welcome, sir."

I left my whereabouts on Max's voice mailbox. I wouldn't call him again. If he came back from wherever he was, he'd call. Knowing Max, he was off somewhere furthering the policies of the United States of America. I remembered something I'd recently seen on CNN, an item about American troops in a place that was cold and snowy and nasty and filled with people who were friendly to neither Americans nor each other. If he was there, I'd be long gone before he was available again.

The file didn't contain the names or phone numbers of the police officers who had handled the case on this side of the border. I called Information for the business number of the San Diego Police Department, dialed it, and explained what I wanted to a succession of very bright, very eager people, none of whom seemed able to help me. I gave up and telephoned Stevenson. When I told him what I wanted, he seemed confused.

"I don't understand," he said. "Everything I have is in that file. You say it's not there?"

"Nope," I said. "Everything but. No names. No numbers."

"Then I must have it here. I'll have to look. Can I call you back?"

"I'm in my hotel room, playing phone tag. Call me when you remember the name, or when you find the phone number."

He promised to do so and hung up. Odd, I thought. That was odd. He seemed such a put-together guy. I didn't like him because something in me didn't trust him. But he did seem as if he could find his way around a legal file. Or at least write down the telephone numbers of the people connected to a case.

A second attempt proved successful. Starting over at the main switchboard, I found a young woman who knew exactly what I wanted and with whom I had to speak. She gave me the number of the Southern Division, an outlying police station near the Mexican border. I was to ask for Sergeant Esparza. He was in command of one of the teams in the Special Intelligence Division, handling the cross-border problems and liaising with the Mexican police. If anyone knew how to contact Teniente de la Peña, it would be Sergeant Gregorio Esparza.

One more phone call and I was speaking with Sergeant Esparza himself.

"Can you come down tomorrow?" he asked. "I'm kind of busy right now, but I'd be happy to help tomorrow morning. Nine o'clock?"

"Where are you, exactly?"

"You know San Diego?"

"Used to be stationed here, but it's changed."

"Mexico is still south, though. Take I-Five south to the Fourteenth Street turnoff. Take that east for two miles. We're right there. Just give your name to the desk sergeant. Uh, what is your name again?"

"Caine. John Caine."

"You got anybody I can call that'll speak for you? Or would you prefer I see what NCIC can spit out?"

"Help yourself. But there's a couple of people at the Honolulu Police Department who can tell you about me. Try Lieutenant Kahanamoku, of Homicide."

"Kahaka what?"

I spelled it for him, dug deeply into my memory and pulled out Kimo's direct number. "Call him."

"I don't know that I have the budget to call Hawaii. You got anybody closer?"

"Nope. Everybody I knew here is long gone." There was an admiral in Coronado, but I hadn't even asked for him when I called Max, and I wondered why.

"Too bad. I'll do something. What are they, three hours behind us?"

"Two now. Three when you go on daylight saving time."

"Thanks. See you tomorrow."

My last call was to de la Peña's pager, knowing it was a wasted effort, but doing it for no other reason than to torment the bastard.

8

You have to understand that in Mexico everything has its price. You can pay for something to happen, or you can pay for something *not* to happen." Sergeant Gregorio Esparza was a slender man in his mid-thirties, but looked even younger. With his rimless glasses and his Timberlines and Dockers, he looked more like a college student than a cop. Only the stainless-steel 9mm on his left hip confused the image.

We were sitting in an interview room, a tiny cubicle at the back of the small concrete bunker that served as the Southern Division police station. There were no windows and only the one door, and although the walls had an attractive vinyl wallpaper and the desktop was covered with a deep-green plastic laminate, I was glad I could get up and walk out at any time.

"*La mordida,*" he continued. "The bite is the law of the land. It's a Third World country. It's not like here."

I nodded. I knew how Third World countries operated.

"A man secures a position in law enforcement, he's supposed to provide his own equipment. Even his own supplies. So how else is he supposed to make things work?"

I understood what Sergeant Esparza was telling me. He was not defending Mexico's system. He was merely explaining how business was transacted.

"So you think the scenario I outlined would be feasible?" I asked. "A person could go down there, blow up his boat, and arrange to have the authorities confirm that he was dead? Even issue a death certificate?"

"Is that what you think happened?"

"If Paul Peters is alive, that's a reasonable explanation."

Esparza shook his head. "It's possible. We haven't had much contact with the family. I never heard about the wife claiming she saw him at Calafia."

That didn't square with Stevenson's version of the facts. I filed it for future reference.

"The family attorney, Stevenson. Did he help much?"

"Not much. Our team handled most of the details. He provided dental records, wrote a few checks to bring the remains back. We took the dental records down to Ensenada. They were a match." He smiled. "At least that's what the coroner said."

I nodded. That version wasn't in Stevenson's story, either. "What about Teniente José Enrique de la Peña?"

Esparza shook his head. "He doesn't know you. He doesn't recognize your telephone number. That's why he won't return your calls. If you were to go down there alone, he wouldn't see you."

"Why not?"

"It's a culture of 'I'll do for you if you can do for me,' " he said. "They work with us because we're *norteamericano* cops, because we represent power. But mostly they work with us because we can do things for them that they can't do for themselves. Some of them are real professionals, they're just handicapped by the system. We can provide backup for them. We cooperate on finding criminals that flee to the United States. There's a lot we can do for them, so they work with us.

"As far as cooperation at this level, there's no problem. It's on their own turf that things get nasty.

"Did you know, for example, that the Mexican government will not allow police officers to carry their own guns? They insist that they only carry issue weapons. So what happens? The government has about half as many guns as they have police officers. They get to the end of the supply and say, 'Well, sorry about that. Don't go out alone. Just partner with an officer who is armed.' Of course, the street cops, they say 'Fuck that,' and carry their own, even though they're in violation of the law. That's where it starts.

"There are many layers of police in Baja, too. There's the *federales,* based in Mexico City. There's the state judicial police, and there's the *municipales* and the *judiciales,* judicial police from each city. It gets confusing if you try to sort it out. Sometimes they can't.

"Remember in nineteen ninety-three when Colosio, the presidential candidate, was assassinated in Tijuana? After it happened—that afternoon—the state judicial police surrounded the *federales* in their own building and laid siege. No shots were fired, but it came close. Very, very close. The thinking, I'm told, was that Colosio had been murdered by the federals. This was right after that Catholic cardinal was shot at the Tijuana airport. No one was ever arrested for that, but the *federales* were suspected."

"And?"

"And so people like Teniente José Enrique de la Peña are in business. There is no real leadership from above. His position is not civil service. It's patronage, depending upon those above him, those with whom he has influence. He doesn't know how long he'll be in power, because it depends on many things, most of which are out of his control. So he gets what he can as he can. If you don't have anything to offer, you'll hit a stone wall. Or worse."

"So either they won't talk to me, or they'll do what?"

"Seven million dollars is a powerful argument. If somebody did make a deal with Peters and his death was rigged, and then you come down without cover of authority asking all kinds of questions, your presence might be interpreted as a threat. Threats get neutralized."

"They'd try to kill me."

"How would you like to spend the rest of your life in La Mesa prison? It could happen. Or they'd kill you, which might be better."

"How do you suggest I go about meeting de la Peña?"

"My team is heading down to Ensenada in a couple of days. Come along. We'll introduce you to some people who may be able to help. Get you started in the right direction. Open a few doors. And if there is anything to it, our introducing you will give you some small protection. Not much, but it might make somebody think twice about killing you if you annoy them."

"I'm good at annoying people."

"Then let me know every time you go down alone."

"You're serious."

"Uh-huh." Sergeant Esparza stood up. Our interview was over. "I'll call you when I know when we're going, but it looks like Thursday. Can I reach you at your hotel?"

"Yes. I appreciate it, Sergeant." I got up and went to the door.

"No hay de qué," he said. "And by the way, that lieutenant in Honolulu said to keep a close eye on you. He said you could be a loose cannon."

"I do what I can."

"He told me a little about you. What you did last year. What you used to be. That's why you're getting the cooperation, you know. We wouldn't do this for just anyone."

"I appreciate it."

"Think nothing of it. Just don't make me have to arrest you. He said that's possible, too." Sergeant Esparza held out his hand at the door. He was still smiling, but his eyes were hard. I wondered what else Kimo had told him.

"I'll remember that," I said, shaking his hand.

Outside, the winter sun was covered by low gray clouds that threatened rain. The temperature had dropped while I was inside. I walked to the Range Rover, wishing I had a jacket, and wishing that I knew what Stevenson had really done. If I had my choice of the two wishes, I'd take the jacket. I knew I'd find out about Stevenson. Even if it took a year, working my standard daily rate.

I decided to drive to his office and ask him about the number for Sergeant Esparza. He had not called me back as he had promised, and now there were a couple of other questions that deserved answers. Not that I would ask. It was too early for that. But I could work around them and see if he would get nervous or defensive.

His office was downtown, in a high-rise among the cluster of high-rises that huddled together like a stand of trees on a prairie. I found a parking place on a side street, fed the meter, and walked the two short blocks to the entrance of Stevenson's building.

Standing across the street waiting for the light to turn, I saw Stevenson emerge from a side entrance accompanied by a young Latino male. The kid looked to be in his late teens, dressed in baggy pants and a bulky plaid shirt, the gangster uniform. His hair was buzz cut, the way they do it in boot camp and jail, cut so short he was nearly bald.

The kid was too small to be a sports hero, except maybe a jockey, and too young to be an ex–Treasury agent. He looked dangerous. I wondered what was going on. Stevenson, I noted, treated the young man with deference, as if he were the supplicant and the kid the lawyer.

Lacking explanation, but possessed of curiosity, I followed them to a deli, where they went inside and sat at a table near the big glass windows. The kid kept a busy eye on the crowds passing the restaurant, and seemed only half interested in what the lawyer was saying. Stevenson was animated in his conversation, using elaborate hand gestures and pointing toward the table with a stiff forefinger, careful not to point directly at the kid.

I stayed as long as I could, until the kid looked at me twice with those hard, flat eyes. The second time, our eyes made contact. I broke off the staring contest, not wanting to arouse his suspicion, and walked away. I didn't look back until I was around the corner and he could no longer ensnare me with the cold, bleak stare of a pitiless monster.

9

The only message waiting for me when I returned to the hotel was from Jack Kinsman. The owner of the schooner was willing to show it on Thursday. I called Kinsman, told him I wasn't available Thursday, and asked him to arrange something for the afternoon. The salesman grumbled a phlegmy baritone in my ear, telling me he'd try.

While I waited, I looked out my window at the gray skies, following them until they met the monochromatic horizon of the Pacific. Somewhere out there was where I felt comfortable. Somewhere out there was what passed as home. I pictured the clear blue skies over my island, and the impossibly green mountains with their leis of cloud over the peaks. Soon, I promised myself. As soon as this was over. I'd go home.

Sometimes you don't know where you belong until you leave it.

It hadn't been in my plans before. There had been no plan after San Diego. I'd been willing to go wherever the urge took me. The Mainland sounded like a place I'd wanted to visit after Kate's death made Oahu impossible. Everywhere I looked, every place I visited, reminded me of her. It ripped open the scabs on my heart each day the sun rose over the Ko'olau Mountains. Honolulu is a big city, but it's on a small island in the middle of a big sea. I needed to get away from all of it for a while.

Now Hawaii was calling. Now I wanted to go home. And I would. Once this was over.

Sometimes investigations take off on their own, needing only a slight nudge to set them off like rockets. This one was hard to start. I saw several paths, all leading to Mexico, all with signs that warned against going down alone. I'd hit a stone wall, I'd been warned, or the wall would hit me. Sergeant Esparza's trip was two days off. I wanted to visit Petersoft, but with some kind of official investigation going on, it was explained to me that my presence was not desired at this time.

Lacking other leads, lacking any other way to get to the truth, I would have to sit and wait. I wasn't any good sitting and waiting, even earning a standard daily rate.

Kinsman called me back and told me to pick him up. The owner had agreed to meet us if we could come right now.

I put on a long-sleeved denim shirt over my polo. I was learning that Southern California could get chilly, despite what the local chamber of commerce would tell you. The emergency-exit stairs at the end of the hall spilled out across from the marina sales office and I enjoyed the exercise.

Kinsman was dressed as an aging peacock again, this time in a black-and-green aloha shirt covered by a bright yellow duffel coat with red piping. He looked like a hot dog gone bad. He followed me around the grounds of the hotel to the parking garage, smoking the butt end of one cigarette and lighting another before we got inside the structure. He puffed four or five times on the new cigarette before I opened his door, then tossed it away.

"You know where the San Diego Yacht Club is?"

"Shelter Island, right?"

"That's the place." He settled back, fumbling in his pockets. "You mind if I smoke?"

"I don't mind," I said, "but the owner might."

He nodded. "Smoke Nazis. These people are all turning into Smoke Nazis." He rolled down the window. "You mind if I flick my ash out the window? That way, no one will know."

"Fine with me."

"That's the truth," Kinsman continued. "We're all second-class citizens these days. First they took the ads off the television. Then they kicked us out of places where smoking was accepted. Used to have our own sections, then the do-gooders came around and forced us out altogether. Now they're kicking us out of the bars! Like if you valued your health you would be in a bar in the first place.

"A man can't have a smoke indoors anymore. If he wants to indulge in a perfectly legal habit, he's got to go outside and risk pneumonia. Damned Smoke Nazis. Pretty soon they'll make it illegal to smoke in your own home."

"Tell me," I said, "about the schooner."

"You know Sparkman and Stephens?"

I nodded. "Local firm. Built classics about half a century ago, didn't they?"

"Yeah. Absolutely beautiful craft. Built most of their hulls back in the thirties. Closed the yard because of the war, the Big One. Vanderbilts had a sloop, so did the Du Ponts. Bunch of movie stars had 'em, too. A Sparkman and Stephens is like a Rolls-Royce, it's about as good as it gets."

"What about the owner?"

"Owner wants to meet you. His name's Ashton. Supposed to be an old California family, but I never heard of 'em. Boat's been in the family since it was built. Old family. Old money. But nobody sails anymore, I guess. And this thing's a classic. Classics take more work just to keep them afloat. And a lot of dough."

Kinsman leaned out the window and took a long drag on the cigarette. The windstream nearly blew the cigarette out, but he puffed on it hard and the little orange tip glowed brightly. He had the technique. He'd done this before.

"The owner wants to make sure you've got the money and the know-how to keep it up, I guess," he said, once he'd finished that round of inhaling. His sparse hair, blown back, exposed a high, wrinkled forehead liberally covered with liver spots.

He spent the rest of the drive with the window down, inhaling inside the car and exhaling with his head out the window like a happy Labrador puppy. The cold wind bit into my shoulders but I didn't complain. A man needs his vices. Sometimes they're all he has. I had enough of my own that I didn't dare criticize another's.

The yacht club's gate guard checked our names and waved us through, pointing out a parking spot. Kinsman seemed familiar with the grounds and led me to one of the docks behind the clubhouse. I hadn't been to the club since the late sixties, when I sailed Sabots as a guest of a girl whose family belonged. Very few memories of that decade remained, replaced by other, less-pleasant recollections of other times in other places.

Most of the yachts were gleaming white, trophies of successful lives in the business arena, court cases won, or gallbladders removed. They had a kind of bland similarity, with names like *Mama's Mink* or *Jury Rig,* names with no romance or imagination. The yacht at the end of the dock had a black hull topped by a mahogany railing, her wooden masts raked at the perfect angle to catch the slightest breeze, yet stout enough to withstand the strongest gale. Her name was *Olympia.* She was truly magnificent.

The owner led us through a tour above and below. Four staterooms plus a chart room, now an electronic navigation and communications shack that would put the United States Navy to shame. GPS, loran, radar, satellite telephone, she had everything necessary to navigate and communicate. Refitted engines and a five–kva generator filled the engine compartment. A new stainless-steel galley featured a microwave convection oven and a double-compartment sink. And throughout, teak, mahogany, and brass covered everything like a pasha's palace. I fell in love.

"The family is asking two hundred fifty thousand for her," said Ashton, a big, florid man, wedged tightly into a boating outfit that was expensive, but old. He'd had these clothes for a long time and either could not afford to buy new when he'd gained the weight or didn't care how he looked. "At that price, it's a steal."

I agreed, but said nothing. I looked at Kinsman and cocked an eyebrow. "What do you think?"

"If you want it, we'll have to get a survey done," he said. He knew. Years of sales had made him sensitive to the lust he must have seen on my face. "Of course, the price seems steep for the market these days." He turned to the owner. "It's a buyer's market right now, Mr. Ashton. My client here has the cash, but he doesn't want to throw it away unnecessarily. I'm sure you understand that, sir."

"I'm in the banking business," said Ashton. "We take money seriously. That's why the price is set so low. This is a very expensive vessel to maintain. No one in the family uses it any longer. We've decided to sell it. Reluctantly."

"Of course," said Kinsman. "We'll get back to you today or tomorrow."

"It might be sold by then."

"That would be too bad," said Kinsman. "But that's life. We'll pay for a survey, if you'll arrange it."

The banker nodded. "I don't see how that can hurt. If you prefer, you can use your own marine surveyor. I'll let the guest-relations people know."

"And then we'll contact you, once we've read the report."

"That seems fair."

We shook hands and, after a last glance at the *Olympia*, left the yacht club. Kinsman rolled down his window and lit another cigarette.

"I want you to offer two hundred," I said, louder than I wanted, but necessary because of the wind and the traffic noise. "Cash."

"Right. Cashier's check, wire transfer."

"No. Cash."

Kinsman brought his face into the car, his cigarette bobbing up and down as he stared at me. "You some kind of drug dealer?"

"No. I just have the money in cash. The man's a banker. He'll know how to get rid of it. And this way he can declare it any way he wishes."

"But there's records, transfers, bills of sale. Things like that."

"All based on what he claims the price of the sale is."

Kinsman nodded.

"So if I pay him two hundred thousand for the boat, he can

say he got one fifty, one sixty. Maybe even less, depending on his greed."

"And he pockets the rest."

"He look like the most honest man you've ever met?"

Kinsman chuckled, stuck his head out the window, took a deep drag on the cigarette, coughed twice, and pulled his head back in. "I think we can do some business, Mr. Caine," he said. "I like the way you think."

"You think we'll get the boat?"

"I'll work this guy the way a whore plays a sailor with a hard-on. He'll want it so bad he'll sell out his own mother. Which, come to think of it, he'd be doing, if she's still alive."

"Get that survey tomorrow, if you can. I'll be out of town on Thursday, but let's do this Friday."

"And you got the money?"

"I have it," I said.

"Where you can get to it fast?"

I nodded.

"I'll make sure that survey happens. Call me when you get back on Thursday, or on Friday morning. We'll wrap it up then."

"And your commission?"

"Comes out of his cut," said Kinsman, adding more wrinkles to his permanently furrowed brow. "Which will go down if he lowers the official price."

"I'll make up the balance to you. In cash."

"Just what I wanted to hear. It's nice doing business with a gentleman. Don't see many of them these days."

"We're a dying breed," I said.

"Just don't become extinct before Friday."

10

I skipped running the Embarcadero and spent slave time in the hotel gym instead, content to stay inside. The promise of rain had been fulfilled with a vengeance. Heavy showers pounded the streets and buildings, washing the beggars away to wherever they went when they weren't pressing tourists for coin.

I ate dinner in one of the hotel dining rooms facing the harbor. There was no sunset, just a gradual fading of the day until only the powerful quay lights of North Island pierced the black.

My mood was as dark as the sky. I should have felt celebratory. I'd found *Duchess*'s replacement. *Olympia* would be a comfortable home. While I was working out in the gym, Jack Kinsman had left a message that the owner had accepted my offer, contingent upon the survey. That was no surprise. I'd never known a banker who didn't know what to do with cash.

A couple in the booth across from me caught my eye. They weren't young, but they were obviously in the throes of that first, startling gasp of a new relationship. They were too sophisticated to paw each other in public, but in their own way they let it show. I envied them.

The sound of the rain against the windows ebbed for a moment, then renewed its energy, lashing the building and rattling the glazing. People looked up from their conversations, glancing at the wall of glass and then at each other, and smiled reassurance before returning to their tasks.

Everybody had somebody except me.

I killed the glass of merlot, my only one for the evening. I didn't feel like drinking, didn't appreciate good food or good wine; I found that all tastes were reduced to that of ash. I dropped some bills on the table and went up to my room.

The light on the phone was blinking. Claire Peters had left a voice-mail message that she was scared, that someone was lurking around the house and she felt she needed protection. I flashed for an outside line and called her.

"Peters residence. Juanita speakeeeng."

"This is John Caine—"

"Oh, jess, Meester Caine. Please hold for the lady." There was a murmur, as if a hand had gone over the mouthpiece, then Claire's voice.

"John. Are you at the hotel?"

"I got your message," I said. "What happened?"

"We've had a prowler. Someone came into the backyard."

"Are you all right?"

"They're gone, I think. But we would both feel better if you would come over."

"Of course. Fifteen minutes."

"Faster, if you can."

I hung up and retrieved my briefcase from under the bed, worked the combination lock and opened it. Nestled between banded stacks of hundred-dollar bills, secure in its holster, lay my Colt .45 Gold Cup and five eight-shot magazines loaded with Black Talon hollow-points. The lady said she was frightened. A prowler, she said. Someone lurking outside.

I thought about it for a full ten count, then closed and relocked the briefcase and shoved it back under the bed. She already had an arsenal over there. If firearms were necessary, and I had no reason to believe they were, there was enough firepower at the house to bring down a couple of Bradley Fighting Vehicles. And it would be convenient to keep my ace in the hole.

Ignoring the elevators, I ran down the fire stairs to the garage level, got into Paul Peters's Range Rover, and made it to Point Loma in less than ten minutes. The fury of the storm helped. Traffic was almost nonexistent. Few people, it seemed, wanted to test their abilities in this weather. It was a good night to stay home.

If you had one.

11

Juanita opened the door before I reached the porch. "I was waiting for joo," she said. "Looking through the door." She closed the door and locked it. I didn't see it at first, but when she locked the dead bolt, her hand gripped a blue-steel revolver.

"What happened?"

"Mees Claire, she say somebody outside. In the backyard. I look out. There was nobody. Then she say other side, by the tennis court. I go look out that window. There was nobody. It start to rain hard, so I can't see nothing else."

"Did you call the police?"

Juanita shook her head. "There was nobody there. But Mees Claire, she still say there was somebody. I don't know. She call joo. Then you call back and she go up to her room and lock the door."

I looked at her hand. She carried the revolver with her forefinger outside the trigger guard, a sign she either didn't know anything about firearms, or that she did and was very, very careful. She glanced down at the gun.

"In my country," she said, "we had visitors in the night sometimes. *Patrullas Muertes*. Death patrols. We learned we must protect ourselves. My husband, the death squad come for him one night. He never come back. I had to leave the country and come here."

"I'm sorry, Juanita."

"Me too," she said, her voice singsong. "It's supposed to be better there now, but I don't know. Mees Claire, she is very good to me. And I cannot leave her now."

"Take me to her, please."

"You go upstairs. I wait down here."

Juanita, the survivor, the brave little guard at the gate. I nodded. "Come get me if you see or hear anything," I said. "And call the police. Please."

She pressed her lips together into a tight line. "I do not like the police."

"It's not like in El Salvador. They're here to protect you, not to kill you."

She shrugged, as if I didn't know what I was talking about and she had no argument to convince me of my naïveté. I turned and went up the stairs. Of the eight doors opening to the landing, only one was closed. I knocked.

Metal slid against metal as the door opened about an inch. Claire Peters peered through the crack, one emerald eye poised over a 12-gauge muzzle. The eye blinked once, and then the door swung wide. I watched the shotgun lower slowly until it pointed toward the floor. Claire wore what looked like a powder-blue sweat suit, except it was made of a feather-light cashmere.

"You were safe," I said, edging past the gun.

"I thought so. But it's nice to see you anyway." She let me slide past into the room. Her bedroom. "Come in."

"I'm in."

"I noticed."

"You, ah, know how to use that thing?"

"I shoot skeet."

"Handy thing to know if a skeet ever breaks into your house."

"Have to be tiny things, skeet. I'm loaded with number six." She moved to the window overlooking the backyard. "Someone was out there. I looked and saw someone looking in, toward the house."

"Did he . . . was it a he?"

"Of course it was a he. Who would send a woman to scare me?"

I'd known some women who would scare Rambo, but I let that alone. "What did he look like?"

"Dark. Wearing dark clothes. It was before it started raining hard. Right at dusk. I couldn't make out any features, but he was standing next to the avocado tree."

"How big was he?"

She shook her head. "I couldn't tell. It was just a glimpse. Then I ducked away from the window and called Juanita."

I went to the window. Nothing was visible in the dark beyond the blazing white pool of lights over the tennis court. "Do you have lights for the grounds?"

"Only the court lights. There's the lights that shine up the trunks of the trees, but that's just for landscaping. We rarely used the backyard after dark."

"Is there a gate from the alley?"

"Yes. Back near the garages. But it's always locked."

"So what happened?"

"Juanita looked but said she saw no one. When she came back, I turned on the tennis-court lights and saw him again. Just for a split second, because when the lights came on, he ran."

"Which way?"

"Back toward the garages."

"Do you have a flashlight?"

"Juanita does."

"You staying up here?"

"I'll come down now. This is the best place to watch the whole backyard."

"Juanita is a good guard. She let me in. She was watching the front of the house, waiting for me. She was carrying a thirty-eight."

Claire's eyes went wide. "She had a gun?"

"And she was going to stand there and protect you with it until I arrived. Whatever you're paying her, give that woman a raise."

She nodded. "I will."

Claire followed me down the stairs. Juanita was no longer in the entry and we found her in the kitchen, humming tunelessly, taking a tray of cookies from the oven. There was no sign of the gun. She smiled her wide, white-toothed smile when she saw us, a study in contrast to our previous encounter.

"Could I borrow your flashlight?" I asked.

She nodded. "Here," she said, wiping a hand on her apron and reaching into a drawer, handing me one of those black-aluminum five-battery flashlights that cops carry, the kind that could be useful as a club.

I stepped outside. The rain had stopped, but the trees dripped heavy drops of water and the gutter drains rumbled, a staccato drumming, covering any noise I might make. Or noise anyone else would make.

I went directly across the broad, sloping lawn to the bushy avocado tree and shone the light on the ground near its trunk. It had rained so hard that any tracks might have disappeared, but the intruder was sloppy, or unlucky, and there must have already been mud from recent irrigation. Near the redwood fence were two impressions of a hard landing.

I studied the footprints. People tend to land with their feet shoulder-width apart. It's instinctive, not something we have to learn, although the paratroops spend a great deal of time teaching us to do things that way. Whether this guy had training or not, his feet landed about eighteen to twenty inches apart, center to center. That made him narrow shouldered. The ovoid craters were not too deep, either, telling me the intruder was not heavy. I had the impression of a slight, small person. A female, or a young slender male.

Like the young gangster I saw with Stevenson.

That was a path I didn't want to travel down just yet, but I filed it away for future reference.

The remainder of the footprints tracked across the lawn toward the tennis court. I followed them to the bright white lights and noted the clumps of earth littering an otherwise immaculate green surface.

So Claire had seen someone out here. It was not her imagination.

It would be handy for her husband if she made a report of a prowler, or several reports, and have the police find nothing. It would make her sound like a hysterical woman, seeing things in the dark. It could cloud the credibility of her claim of seeing her husband in Mexico.

Was that the basis of this exercise? Or was there something else?

Whatever it was, and whoever it was, it was over for tonight. As I started back across the lawn, the clouds opened up again and poured on me. By the time I reached the patio, I was soaked to the skin.

Juanita let me in.

"Mees Claire wants to see you."

"I'm a little wet," I said, handing her the flashlight.

"There's clothes from the meester. He was about your size. Maybe shorter. If the lady say it okay for you, I'll get some, if you want."

I thanked her and she went off, happy to be busy. It is a good self-defense, being busy. It keeps your mind off other things. Uncomfortable things, dangerous things, lurking out there in the dark. Things that may come to your door one night and take your husband away from you so you'll never see him alive again. Or, as it was for me, things that took place faster than you could react, taking the woman you loved away from you forever, leaving you in a hospital waiting room, waiting for someone to tell you that there was no hope, no chance for her ever to come back.

"Here you are," she said, returning to the kitchen with her arms full of khaki trousers, polo shirts, and sweaters. "Mees Claire say you can have whatever you want. Meester not coming back, I think." She handed me the stack of clothing and two big bath towels. "There is a bathroom in there," she said, pointing to the service entrance off the kitchen. "You shower and change."

I thanked her and went to change. When I came back, wearing khaki Dockers and a loden-green pullover, Juanita was taking another batch of cookies from the oven. The room smelled of flour and warm cookie dough.

"The pants are too short!" Juanita laughed. The waistline was fine, but Paul Peters had been some four inches shorter than I. "Otherwise you look nice. Mees Claire wants to see you. She is in her room." Her eyes had a sparkle I hadn't seen since the night she helped me get the lady into her own bed, alone.

With kitchen sounds behind me, I raced up the stairs in my bare feet. A Mozart symphony drifted down the stairs to greet me, the string section sawing away for dear life, overpowering the rest of the orchestra, just the way old Amadeus intended. For a guy so good with the keyboard, he did tend to favor the strings.

I knocked on her bedroom door.

"The door is open." Claire's voice came from the end of the hall, from the library. I followed the voice to the library and poked my head around the corner.

"Come in," she said. Claire was seated at the end of a leather couch, facing a fireplace with a cheery little fire going. The room could have easily been part of an English castle. It had a warm, welcoming feeling.

"Come. Sit." She patted the leather beside her. She was still wearing the cashmere sweat suit. It clung to her body. Her nipples were erect.

I sat on a leather easy chair across from her. "This is comfortable. Thank you."

"You're a lot taller than Paul," she said, staring at my bare feet. "Would you care for a glass of wine?" She had a bottle opened beside her.

"No. Thank you."

"Are you saying that because you think I drink too much and you wish to discourage me?"

"No. I just don't care for any right now. I understand it may be rude to refuse, that the appropriate response would be to have accepted the drink, then casually sip it to make it last. But I don't want to lie to you. I figure we can be friends if we won't lie to each other."

She stared at me as if she had never heard such a concept. Then she smiled.

"I want to thank you for coming so quickly. You don't know how much better I feel now that you're here."

"There was someone outside," I said.

"I know. Didn't you believe me?"

"I just wanted you to know that the physical evidence supports you. I think someone wanted you to panic and call the cops, and they would not be able to find anyone. There are traces that someone had been out there, but when and under what circumstances are questionable. I'm on your side. The police are skeptical.

"Make a couple of calls like that and they'll put you down as a nutcase. And then no one will believe your story of seeing your husband in Mexico. He's dead. That's that. Anything else is just a hysterical widow who's been left with a lot of debts. Poor woman. Could happen to anybody. End of story."

She leaned forward toward me, enhancing the intimacy. She knew something about violating space. "You think that's what happened? You think someone's trying to make me crazy?"

"I think it's possible somebody wants to make you look crazy," I said. "Or there's another possibility."

"What's that?"

"It was just a prowler. Some kid on a thrill trip, or maybe a burglar who ran off when he found someone home."

"That doesn't make sense. Lights were on upstairs and down. And why go to the tennis court?"

I nodded. She was right.

"I want you to stay the night, John. I would feel so much better if you were here."

"Okay." I had been expecting that, and would have asked if she hadn't.

"You're the only one I can trust."

"Me and Juanita."

She smiled. "Yes. I hadn't expected her to do that."

"Do you know anything about her?"

"Just a little. Enough."

"Where did she get the gun?"

"It was Paul's. He kept it in his room. She put it back after. I checked."

Brave. Determined. Neat, too. The perfect housekeeper. "You are in no danger with Juanita around."

"Yes. I know," said Claire.

"Of course"—I glanced at the shotgun, where it leaned against the wall—"you seem to be able to take care of yourself, too."

"I'm fairly well protected in the event of a skeet invasion."

"I can't be a bodyguard and investigate your husband's disappearance, too."

"Maybe you can hire some help. How much would that cost?"

"I'll make some calls tomorrow, look around. I'll come up with somebody."

"And in the meantime?"

"Have Juanita make up one of the spare bedrooms. I'm ready to turn in."

12

The storm continued through the night and hung on with the rising of the dawn. I spent a warm, comfortable night burrowed under borrowed down, sleeping the sleep of the blessed. Not even dreams disturbed my peace. When I woke, the light coming through the windows was murky gray, an analogue to the sound of the rain hitting the roof and dripping from the eaves. I rolled out of bed, surprised how cold it was in San Diego.

I showered and dressed in the husband's clothes, conscious of what the widow Peters might be trying to do, yet willing to accept the gifts. When I went downstairs, Juanita had breakfast waiting, a plate of sausage and scrambled eggs mixed with a fiery red sauce that looked homemade.

"Good morning!" she said. Some people's cheerfulness in the morning was forced. Juanita's was genuine. Like many people who had lived on the edge, she seemed to take each day of life as a gift.

"Good morning, Juanita. Is everything all right?"

"Oh, jess. Mees Claire is still asleep. She sleep late most mornings now. Not like before."

I assumed that meant before her husband's death.

"Does she go into the office?"

"No. Not now. There is not much to do these days, I hear."

"Who runs the company?"

"Guy named Adrian. I don't know his last name. He's there every day. He's a young guy. But things are pretty slow. Joo want juice?"

"No, thank you. Can you ask Mrs. Peters to give him a call this morning? I want to go to the office and look around. I couldn't yesterday."

"The audit?"

"That's what they told me." Of course Juanita would know. She operated in the center of the Peters household universe and everything was discussed in front of her as if she wasn't there.

"It's over. I hear Mees Claire talking last night on the telephone. Just before the prowler. There's plenty trouble, no?"

"Sounds like it," I said.

"Qué lástima," she said, shaking her head slowly. "Mees Claire doesn't need any more trouble. She is a good person." Juanita looked at me, as if I had answers. I didn't have any. I didn't even know the questions. When I didn't respond, she continued. "Okay, I'll tell her. Where will joo be?"

"Out," I said, instantly regretting the abruptness of my reply, knowing it came from my impotence. My plans were simple. I would go back to the hotel and call Sergeant Esparza. "Why don't I go out there now if the audit is over. That way they can call you and get permission while I'm there."

"Okay. Mees Claire will be awake by then."

I ate the rest of my breakfast in silence. Juanita busied herself with laundry and other chores. When I finished, I took my dishes to the sink, rinsed them, and put them into the dishwasher. Juanita came in carrying my clothes. They were folded into a neat, compact stack a marine drill instructor would applaud.

"Here are your clothes, and here is a jacket belonged to Meester Peters. It might fit joo, jess?" It was a brown-suede jacket with Thinsulate lining. I tried it on. Although extra large, it fit a little tight in the shoulders, but well enough, and it would keep off the rain and the chill.

"Gracias, Juanita."

"De nada," she said, automatically answering in Spanish. Then she giggled. "Oh, joo speak e-Spanish very good!"

"I speak the accent without a trace of the language," I said.

She screwed up her little face and burst out laughing. "Joo are a funny man, Meester Caine. Joo make me laugh."

"And you are a good woman, Juanita. Keep Mrs. Peters safe, and call me if anything happens."

"And I'll let Mees Claire know they will call from the office."

"Thank you very much."

I changed back into my own slacks before I went out to the car, the husband's high-water pants uncomfortable in both their appearance and their symbolism.

The Range Rover was where I parked it the night before but there was something different about it. Sometime during the night someone had run a sharp edge down both sides of the body and had written something on the hood. I stared at the highly stylized markings, recognizing them as similar to gang graffiti, trying to decipher them until they made sense. The writing was in Spanish. *"Mate lo,"* I said aloud, reading the tortured characters. "Kill it." It also meant "Kill him."

I got down on my hands and knees and looked under the body, then opened the hood and searched the engine compartment. I checked the wiring for the ignition, following it from the key switch through the fire wall into the electrical system. The battery wires betrayed nothing out of the ordinary. Nothing was out of place. Unless someone was world class, there was no bomb on the Range Rover.

But I still felt the adrenaline flow and my butt pucker involuntarily when I turned the key and the engine kicked over.

So our visitor hadn't gone. He was still around after I arrived. And he was bragging about it. There was ego involved.

I smiled. That was something I could use.

On the way out to Petersoft, Ltd., I tried Sergeant Esparza. He was in.

"Good morning, Sergeant. Are we still on for tomorrow?"

"Unless something strange comes up today." I could hear men laughing in the background, an explosive male baritone of testosterone and camaraderie. Someone slapped a desk with the palm of a hand. It didn't sound angry. " 'Course, strange things come up every day around here." There was another round of laughter in the background, Esparza playing the room.

"Do you know any ex-cops who are available to work bodyguard? I need a couple of men. Experienced guys."

"You want someone who's worked bodyguard. Not just some retired stiff off patrol."

"That's what I need."

"Sure. You got a pen?"

I fished around, found a Mont Blanc in the inside pocket of Peters's jacket, Jack Kinsman's business card in my wallet. "Okay," I said. "Name and number?"

"Ed Thomas. He's a retired detective sergeant. Used to work SWAT, too. Has his own license and I know he takes bodyguard jobs. He can get a couple of guys, too. They all carry. They're all ex-cops. Thomas is picky about who hires on with him, so you'll get a good team. Tell him Greg Esparza gave you his name." He gave me the phone numbers for Thomas, both cellular and office.

"I'll tell him," I said. "And I'll see you tomorrow morning."

"Meet us at eight-thirty. They have very strict laws in Mexico, so don't bring your roscoe."

"My what?"

"Your gun."

"I don't carry a gun."

"Uh-huh. Sure. Just don't bring it."

I thanked him again and phoned Thomas. He was in his office and agreed to meet me at the marina for lunch. I told him how to recognize me. He told me he'd find me by asking the hostess.

Smart man.

13

Petersoft, Ltd., occupied a three-story concrete building along Torrey Pines Road between the UCSD campus and the Salk Institute. The building didn't look as if it had been constructed from the ground up. It appeared to have landed after a voyage through deep space. The windows looked strange, long thin vertical lines with no apparent conscious spacing, their meaning obscure until I recognized the pattern: bar code, spelling out some formula or name or something in light and space and concrete. The asphalt parking lot, as big as a football stadium and hidden from Torrey Pines Road by landscaped berms, was nearly empty.

I parked the Range Rover in a spot near the entry. The front door was locked. I peered through the glass. The first floor was as deserted as the parking lot. A hand-lettered sign instructed visitors to go around the back.

Rain was still falling hard, but I walked along the pathway next to the building. Thick landscaping covered the grounds and the trees offered some meager protection, but by the time I made the rear of the building, the rain had soaked my head and shoulders, and I began to wonder if Peters had left a hat around, too.

An open door and metal stairs were my reward. I followed the stairs to the second level, opened the fire door, and found people.

A pretty blonde in her early twenties wearing 501's and a bulky white pullover sat hunched over a workstation near the door. She ignored me and continued peering at the screen in a nearsighted way that made me wonder why she didn't wear glasses.

"Excuse me," I said. "Can you tell me where I can find Adrian?"

"He's in the lab," she said, not looking away from her task. She pointed toward the other end of the building. It was a crooked point, but I followed her finger and found a glass enclosure in one of the corners.

"Thanks," I said.

There was no reply.

I made my way through a half-abandoned landscape of workstations and empty cubicles. Wastebaskets overflowed and trash littered the floor as if people had moved out in a hurry, and the ones who remained didn't give a damn about the mess. It reminded me of the old proverb: something like "Why worry about your haircut when you're about to lose your head."

Two people occupied the lab, looking at some papers laid out on a desk. Both were young. Both male.

"Excuse me," I said again. "Is there an Adrian here?"

"That's me." One of the men focused his attention on me. He was tall, nearly my height, with high cheekbones and clear gray eyes. He wore his blond hair longish, swept over the back of his head like a lion's mane. When he looked at me, there was little interest.

"I'm John Caine."

"Claire called. She said to give you whatever you needed. What do you need?"

"I don't know," I said. "But I'd like to see Mr. Peters's desk."

"His office is upstairs. I'll take you." He spoke quietly to the other young man, who nodded and folded the papers they had been scanning and went out the door.

"Come on," Adrian said to me. "We'll take the stairs. The elevator's out."

I followed him up the fire stairs to the third floor. In the corner of the building, with windows facing both the Pacific and the groves of eucalyptus trees lining Torrey Pines Road, was an all-glass enclosure. Even the door was glass. Adrian unlocked the door and stepped aside.

"I'll be downstairs. You need anything, come get me." His hostility covered him like a blanket.

Not knowing what I'm looking for is standard for me, but

I know what I want after I've found it. There was nothing here but more questions.

I sat in Paul Peters's leather chair, my feet on his desk, and gazed through the glass wall at the empty executive floor. He had been king of all he surveyed. His domain, now crashed and burned, was another victim of the accident. Or whatever it was.

Were I Paul Peters, with a beautiful and loving wife and a successful company, a life I had carved from nothing at all with my own two hands and intelligence, why would I want to leave all this? Why would I subject my friends and employees and family to the stress of dealing with the mess I left behind? Ego had to be involved. What would make a man abandon all this, including this monument to his ego?

What had Claire said about another woman? A year ago, last December, Paul Peters had attended a seminar in real estate investment. In Palm Desert. There would be records. There would be expenses. He would have been given a notebook, a syllabus, handouts. There would be hotel bills, airplane tickets, expense-account vouchers, possibly a list of attendees. Of course the company would have paid for it. Why have your own company if you don't use it?

In the third drawer of his credenza I found a collection of leather desk-model Day-Timer notebooks. In the book for the previous year, in the month of December, I found a notation about the seminar. December twelfth through the sixteenth. Desert Hot Springs Resort. Room 1651. There were four telephone numbers scratched on the page under the notation. I took out my notebook, which today was Jack Kinsman's business card, and copied the numbers.

That was the solitary clue. There were no Polaroid photographs of a young vixen wearing only a lewd smile, no hidden notebooks, no agendas of trysts. I spent an hour making certain there were no more leads before I gave up. It was almost time to meet Ed Thomas.

I went downstairs and found Adrian drinking coffee, leaning against the top of a partition, talking quietly with the same young man who had been in the lab.

"I'm through," I said.

"Okay. You lock it up?"

"I didn't have the key."

"Okay. I'll do it." He made it sound as if I'd put him out.

"Did Paul Peters carry a personal Day-Timer?"

"Yes."

"Do you know where it is?"

"No."

"Would he have kept it here?"

"I don't know."

"Can you find out who gave the real estate investment seminar in Palm Desert that Mr. Peters went to in December of last year? And can you get me a copy of his expense account? All receipts?"

"Sure. When do you want it?"

"Friday okay?"

"I can do that."

"Can you get me a list of people who attended?"

"I can try."

"How many people went through his office since he, uh, died?"

"You. Me. Mrs. Peters. Mr. Stevenson. And those guys from the government yesterday."

"The audit?"

He nodded. "They tore the place apart. They asked me the same questions, except for that investment seminar stuff. They wanted everything."

"IRS?"

"I don't know. Just the government."

"No one else?"

"No."

"Thanks for your help."

"Sure."

"I'll call you if I think of anything else."

"Okay."

Feeling like a blabbermouth, I fled down the stairs and braved the elements back to the Range Rover. I had the glimmering of an idea, but I wasn't sure where it would go.

Just like all my other ones.

14

Ed Thomas was a big man in his late sixties with white hair thinning on top and a white mustache and goatee that made him look like a fit Kentucky colonel. He wore a double-breasted blue blazer and an open-necked blue shirt over tan trousers with knife-edge creases. His boots were polished to a high sheen. His gun was barely noticeable, riding high on his right hip.

"You're Caine?"

I stood up and shook his hand. He had a firm grip. It gave me hope.

"You're Thomas?"

"Esparza gave you my number?"

"Yeah. He said you were good."

"Probably wants a cut. I trained him when he first came on, my last year. He's a good officer. Lots of potential there. Maybe someday he'll be chief."

"He said you're a private detective and that you knew protection."

He nodded. "You need bodyguard work?"

I explained the problem and explained the client, which in most cases amounted to the same thing. In this instance it was beginning to look like the family lawyer might be a part of the problem. I explained that, too. Thomas nodded understanding when I laid out the deal. Something about him reminded me of Obi Wan Kenobe, but taller and with less hair.

"Heard about Peters. It was all over the papers when it happened. Thought it was just an accident."

"Maybe. The wife doesn't think so."

"I guess not."

"Can you do it?"

"Two men can cover sixteen hours. You'll cover the other eight?"

"I don't want to do it that way. I'm following something and I don't want to be tied to a schedule." I also didn't want to be available when the widow Peters had a few drinks and became amorous. There was no telling how long my willpower would last. It was getting more difficult as time went on. "But she should be okay during the day," I continued. "She seems to be afraid of the dark."

Thomas snorted. "Aren't we all?"

We agreed on a daily rate for the two shifts. Ed said he'd man the graveyard shift himself, and he had a good man, retired San Diego PD, ex-SWAT, who could work early evening to midnight. He assured me that between the two of them there wouldn't be any trouble they couldn't handle.

"Prowlers, you say? You want us armed?"

"Yes."

"Side arms and shotguns?"

"Whatever you think appropriate. I'm not going to tell you how to do your job."

He squinted at me. "Well, you're a rare son of a bitch. I thought everybody was an expert on everything these days."

"When can you start?"

"We'll both be there tonight. You got the address?"

I wrote it on a napkin and handed it to him.

He looked at the address, brought it closer to his face so he could read it, and snorted again. "Fancy neighborhood. You know who lives across the street?"

"The governor?"

"Close. Her royal highness, the mayor." He stood up, pocketing the napkin. "A bigger pain in the ass you'll never meet. I know we were supposed to have lunch, but I'd better start setting this up. You don't mind, do you?"

"Not at all, Ed. I'll see you tonight. About five?"

"Tell the lady not to worry. Ed and Hatley will be there."

15

She surveyed beautiful. Got 'em to expedite, since you're in such a hurry. Got a little dry rot in the bilge, but nothing to worry about. You'd expect that in a wooden boat. New engines. The latest electronics. New generator. New hull paint. She's in better shape than when she was first launched." Jack Kinsman, the boat salesman, was happy with the report. It meant no delay in the completion of the sale, which meant no delay in receipt of his commission. "Wanna come sign the papers now?"

"No," I said. I was standing naked at the window, dripping water on Intercontinental's carpet fifteen floors above his floating sales office. It was still raining hard along the waterfront.

On the television across the room, the weatherman admitted he really didn't know when the rain was going to end. It was an El Niño year and San Diego, it seemed, was in the path of something called a storm track. Another gully washer was on its way, currently pouring on the good folks in Seattle, but it would be here in a day or two. In the meantime, the present deluge had backed up an emergency storm drain, filling the basement apartment of a woman confined to a wheelchair, drowning her while her husband was at work. The public-works spokesman said he couldn't understand it; everything worked fine all summer.

"I'm sorry, Jack. Can't make it this afternoon. Let's leave it for Friday as we'd planned." I lusted for the *Olympia*, couldn't wait to own her. But I had a standard daily rate to earn, and things were getting interesting.

Kinsman called when I was fresh out of the shower. I had

run again despite the rain and worked out hard at the hotel gym when I returned. I compromised and took the elevator to my room, ordered room-service coffee and pastries, and then hit the shower.

I'd just hung up and was toweling dry when the knock came at the door.

"Just a minute," I called, wrapping the towel around my waist. I opened the door a crack. "I'm just out of the shower. Can you leave it at the door?"

"Of course, sir. Can you sign for it?" A pale white hand thickly covered with blond hairs pushed the invoice and a pen through the crack. I added a fifteen-percent tip, scribbled my signature, and pushed it back. "Thank you, sir," said the voice in the corridor.

Still wearing only a towel, I counted to ten and opened the door, looked both ways to make certain the hall was deserted, picked up the tray, and shut the door. I carried the tray to the little table and sat in the easy chair near the window, poured some coffee into a china cup. Rain spattered against the glass. Ah, the joys of casual dining.

There was another knock at the door.

"Who is it?" I called from my chair. I wasn't expecting anyone and wasn't inclined to move. My body was a little stiff from all the recent exercise.

"Room service."

It was a different voice. Another pot of coffee? More pastries?

"Already got it," I said, still not moving, except to take a bite from one of the bear claws.

"There was a screwup on your order," said the voice outside. "I'm here to make it right."

Curiosity got the better of me. This wasn't the same kid who delivered the tray. This voice was crude, untutored. A street voice, not what I was used to in this hotel.

"Just a second," I said, getting up and securing the towel around my waist. It was my intention to open the door a crack and send him on his way.

It didn't happen that way.

I turned the lock and the door imploded at me, the leading edge hitting me between the eyes like the blade of an ax. I bounced off the mirrored closet door behind me. As I rebounded, a fist hit me square on the point of my chin.

Shooting stars and comets filled my head. Another powerful blow struck me in the stomach. I doubled over, gasping for breath. He hit me again. The mirrored door broke and I went backward through the glass and fiberboard into the closet. I lay on the carpet, naked and bleeding, unable to breathe. Voices filtered through red haze at the edge of consciousness.

Somebody kicked me in the ribs. I didn't respond.

"He's done," said the same voice.

He was right. After getting hit by a bunch of fists and a door, I was done.

"Where's the money?"

"He can't help you. Get his wallet!" Someone closed the door to the corridor.

I was aware of two young men, hinky and nervous, yelling at each other. It upset me that they were yelling, offending my sense of professionalism.

Somewhere in the back of my mind, somewhere deep inside where I keep the rational side of my thought processes, I was reminded that I wasn't supposed to root for these guys. I wasn't on their side.

I opened my eyes, careful not to attract attention.

The two young thieves, opening drawers and dumping my clothing on the carpet, were a nightmare Laurel and Hardy. One was tall and thin, emaciated like a junkie, the other short and powerfully built. Both were totally bald, shaved heads glistening like oiled bowling balls.

The taller one picked up Paul Peters's leather jacket and pulled out my wallet, fanned through it to verify its contents, and stuck it in his hip pocket. The short, thickly muscled Hardy, who reminded me of a fireplug, took the wallet away from the junkie.

"I'll keep it," he said. There was no objection from the tall bandit. Fireplug retrieved my Rolex from the cabinet top, then got down on his hands and knees and looked under the bed.

"What's this?" He pulled my Halliburton briefcase into the light.

Most of the five thousand dollars Stevenson had given me for expenses was in the wallet along with my credit cards and other identification. That was an acceptable loss. The briefcase containing the quarter million to purchase *Olympia* was not.

I watched them try to open the combination lock. And I waited. The longer I lay there, the better I felt. The haziness began fading and my thinking became less fuzzy, slowly coalescing as the situation focused. I ignored the pain. It was insignificant. My body was tight. My heartbeat slowed to its normal sixty beats per minute, a steady pumping of the fluids. I became calm.

I was a carnivore, lying in wait for prey.

And they had to pass me to get to the door.

"What the fuck?" Fireplug was on his knees, my briefcase in front of him, the combination lock giving him trouble.

"What's that?" The junkie reacted to a noise, a door slamming somewhere down the corridor. His eyes were wide and white around the pupils. His hands shook.

"It's nothin'," said Fireplug.

"I'm outta here!" The skinny junkie took two steps toward me and I came up off the floor and grabbed him by the throat and the testicles, using his momentum to pick him up over my head and swing him around in a full circle like kids playing airplanes. Fireplug turned just as I unloaded his partner on top of him, swinging him down in an arc that brought both men together with as much force as I could muster.

The tall one's body covered the little guy and didn't move. Fireplug squirmed out from under and produced a butterfly knife, which he held in front of him, aimed at my navel. I spread my arms wide, anticipating the quick stab. If he was trained, I'd have some problems. If he handled a knife like O. J., I'd be all right. I had about eight inches in height and probably a foot of reach on him. No matter what, he wasn't leaving with that briefcase.

"Get out of my way!" The fireplug's voice cracked. It wasn't so much a command as a plea.

I shook my head, grinning. It must have given him pause. A big old white dude, naked and bleeding but still standing, still blocking his way to freedom, still challenging his authority even though he had the knife, and grinning like this was going to be fun.

"I'll cut your little white dick off, you don't move, muthafucka."

"Your move, asshole," I said quietly. "You came in here, you bought the whole thing."

Confusion crossed his face. He had the weapon. I was the one who was supposed to be afraid. I was just some old tourist, easy pickings. Things weren't going according to plan.

He made a feint toward my face. I went in under it, got his elbow in my right hand, his wrist in my left, and yanked backward with everything I had.

He screamed as the tendons separated.

He dropped the knife.

I kicked his leading shin, connecting with the ball of my foot, and he went down.

He lay where he fell, curled in a fetal position against the bed. I picked up the knife, found my soggy sweatpants where I'd dropped them and pulled them on, chancing a quick glance in the mirror. My face and back were covered with blood. I traced a finger over my forehead and found a deep cut between my eyebrows, souvenir of the edge of the door. Something stuck me in my back, causing sharp pain whenever I moved.

The two on the floor lay still. I poked their buttocks with my toe. I was not gentle.

"Hey!" Fireplug was conscious, still curled into a ball, holding his maimed right arm.

"Give me my stuff and get out of here," I said.

"Fuck you," said Fireplug, sniffing, his breath coming in quick pants. "You fucked me up."

"Probably," I said. "You'll probably lose most of the use of that arm." That was exactly what I'd intended.

"Fuck you!"

"Suit yourself. Give me my watch and my wallet and get up and walk out of here. I won't call the cops. I won't call Security. You get a free ride. Continue to argue with me and the fight hasn't ended yet. You'll leave through the window over there. Your choice."

For the first time, the little guy really looked at me. He knew I wasn't lying. "What about him?"

"If you can take him with you, he can go, too. Just make sure you're only taking what you brought with you. I'll keep the knife."

He shook his head as if none of this were real, then rolled to the side, nearly made it to his knees, found himself off balance, and fell heavily onto his injured arm. He whimpered when he hit the floor, but he didn't cry out. He was almost as tough as he thought he was.

"Help me," he said.

"Nope. You're on your own. My watch, please, and my wallet."

"In my pocket."

"Take them out and hand them to me."

He struggled with his left hand, but managed to pull out my old stainless-steel Rolex Submariner and my wallet. He handed them over. I expected him to do something stupid, but he'd learned something in this room, and he wasn't about to go over the line again.

I checked my watch and slipped it on my wrist. I'd bought it in Hong Kong on an R and R during the Great Southeast Asian War Games and had worn it without pause ever since. It kept passable time and because of its history, was one of the few possessions I really cared about. This young man was not the first to try to take it away from me.

"Get your buddy," I said.

He looked down at the limp form at his feet. "I can't. He's too heavy."

"Oh, come on," I said. My voice had taken on a friendly tone, almost like the chiding of a favorite uncle. "You're a big boy. You work on those muscles. Lift weights. You can do it."

"He's dead."

I reached down and felt the carotid along the neck. The pulse was strong, his breathing regular. "No he's not. He's just resting. Now pick him up!" The last I shouted in a parade-ground bark.

Fireplug grabbed his partner and pulled him to his feet. The junkie's eyes fluttered open. He looked around, not comprehending where he was. "Wha's happening?" he asked.

"You're going home, son," I said. "You've had a bad day."

"Yes," he said. He spoke as if he had seriously considered the word and found it profound. "I believe I have."

"You gonna open the door?" Fireplug had his hand full trying to stand and support his partner at the same time. Another obstacle, like the door, seemed more than difficult. Well, that was the idea.

"Nope. No help. That's the deal. You can do it."

Fireplug struggled with his partner, finally getting him to stand on his own. The junkie didn't actually stand. Fireplug just leaned him against the wall, pinning him there with his body. It was the only way he could get the door open. They shuffled into the corridor.

Before he closed the door behind him, Fireplug turned and glared at me, his anger coming back, bringing some courage with it.

"I sure hope I see you somewhere," he said.

"You better hope you don't," I said. "That's the other part of the deal."

"What's that?"

"I see you anywhere near this hotel again, you're going off the roof."

16

It took me longer to get dressed and out of the hotel than I anticipated and I arrived at Claire's house long after my appointment with Ed Thomas.

Most of my injuries were superficial, but I had a sliver of glass wedged between my shoulder blades that I could not reach no matter how I tried. I didn't want to involve the hotel. Security was already in a snit.

In order to explain the mess in the room, I reported that I'd lost my balance and had fallen through the mirrored door. That was the truth, but it wasn't the whole truth and nothing but the truth, and the woman in the blue blazer didn't believe it for a minute. In the end it didn't take much to convince her. I was a guest, after all, and if a guest said he just lost his balance and fell over, then okay, it happens all the time. Sorry about that.

There was nothing she could do. She was too bright not to notice the cut on my forehead but she didn't mention it. I'd refused medical treatment, signed a release that the hotel was not at fault in any way, refused a voucher for a free meal in the hotel's restaurant. I even offered to pay for the damage.

"That won't be necessary, Mr. Caine," she said. "You're certain there's nothing we can do for you?" She had to ask that question. Her report would go to the general manager.

"Nothing. I'm sorry about the door. It was my fault."

"You didn't have a fight in here, did you?"

"Why?"

"We spoke with two men in the lobby about ten minutes before you called. They had both been injured. One severely. Their injuries looked as if they'd been fighting."

"Two men?"

She nodded. "Said they'd fallen on the quay wall and got lost and were cutting through the hotel grounds to get back to Harbor Drive. My boss recognized one of them from a previous incident. They're strong-arm robbery types. The guest opens the door and they push their way in, beat the hell out of the guest, rob him, and leave. We called the police but we couldn't detain them. No reason to. No guest had complained." She looked me directly in the eye when she said that, almost a sneer on her face.

"Did they knock on your door?"

I shook my head. "Do I look that stupid? Open a door in a big-city hotel without knowing who was out there?"

"People do that when they're on vacation, Mr. Caine. People get relaxed. They make mistakes."

"Sorry. Didn't happen."

She frowned. "Well, I can't make you say something you don't want to say. You look like you've been in a fight. They look like they've been in a fight. You can't get into trouble. You were the victim. If you were robbed, you should report it."

I pulled out my wallet, showed her my watch. "See. Everything's all here."

She sighed. "Okay. You fell through the door. That's what you want, that's what I'll write in my report. I sure wish you'd change your mind."

"You really think they tried to rob me?"

"Do I look stupid?" She smiled. It was a conspiratorial smile, just between the two of us, letting me know she knew but didn't really care. The guest wasn't going to sue.

I smiled back. "No, ma'am. You do not."

She took my signed release, started to say something else, but pursed her lips together as if she'd decided not to waste more time or breath. We both knew she'd tried her best, and we both knew I wouldn't cooperate. I'd made a deal with those two, and I would stick with it, regardless of the circumstances. I didn't think they'd be too active for a while, and my civic conscience was clear. They'd probably had more punishment this afternoon than the court system would give them in a year, and it didn't cost the taxpayers anything at all.

As I showed her out, she turned and looked at the room once more, at the broken glass in the closet and its proximity to the door, at my forehead and its vertical gash. She took it all in, shook her head, and left.

The sliver of glass was biting into my flesh and still bled freely. I'd wrapped one of the hotel towels under my shirt and could feel that it was already saturated. I went into the bathroom, stripped off my jacket and shirt and the bloody towel, wrapped the remaining clean towel around me, and pulled my clothes back on. I rinsed out the bloody towel and hung it over the tub.

Before I left the room I reached under the bed and pulled out my briefcase. After the incident I no longer felt safe keeping it in the hotel. It was secure only when it was with me. I took it along, thinking to have Juanita stash it at the house. I knew I could trust her.

I had to hunch over the steering wheel on the drive to Point Loma to keep the glass shard from moving around. The rain kept coming down in sheets, decreasing visibility and giving me an excuse to drive slowly. By the time I arrived at Claire's house, I was over an hour late.

An elderly pickup truck sat in the driveway, looking out of place. I parked behind it and made a dash for the house. Juanita opened the big oak door before I got to the porch, almost as if she had extrasensory perception. She grimaced when she saw my face, but said nothing. My forehead felt hot and swollen around the injury.

"It is raining," she said. "And you are all wet again. Let me take your coat."

I nodded, shrugging out of the sodden leather jacket. When I did, I heard her gasp.

"You are bleeding here, too!"

"Had an accident," I said.

"What happened?" Ed Thomas came into the entry from the kitchen, trailed by another man.

"Tell you later. Can you get a piece of glass out of my back? I'd appreciate it." I set down my briefcase, and had some trouble straightening up again after I set it down. The glass rode with the muscle one way and cut the other.

"Come in here," said Ed. "The light's better." I followed him into the kitchen. I stayed stooped over.

"Take off your shirt and lean over the sink there." I did. The towel dropped to the floor. Juanita picked it up and said something in Spanish too fast to understand.

"Juanita, you got some pliers?" Thomas asked. "Needle-nose would be good."

Juanita took the towel and hurried from the room.

"What happened? You looked okay when I saw you this afternoon. Who needs the bodyguard? You or the lady?"

"Long story, Ed. Where is Claire?"

"Upstairs. On the phone. Something to do with her company. Juanita let us in. You called her, I guess, or she probably would have shot us. She made us show our badges and ID before she unlocked the door. When she did, she was carrying a piece."

"You guys are her backup," I said.

"This hurt?" Ed wiggled the glass back and forth with the tip of his finger.

"Yes."

"Good."

Juanita returned with needle-nose pliers. When Ed tried and failed to grasp the sliver, complaining about his vision, she took over. She was not afraid to dig the tips of the tool into my back to get purchase on the glass and she tugged it out of the wound the first time.

"That's a big one," said Ed. Juanita held it up for me to examine as if it were a trophy I should be proud of. It didn't look as big as it felt.

Juanita poured something on my back. It was cold and I could feel it bubble inside the wound.

"Stay that way for a minute, Meester Caine." Juanita patted my back with a cloth, wiping the blood from my skin. "I'll get you a bandage and another shirt." It would be another of Peters's shirts, I thought. I was cutting deeply into his wardrobe. The thought troubled me until I thought about it some more. Peters wouldn't be coming back, no matter how this thing settled out. He was either the ex-husband or the dead husband. Claire knew that from the moment she had seen him in Mexico. I might have been the only one who had thought about him as Claire's husband.

"Mr. Caine, I'd like you to meet Hatley Farrell. He's retired San Diego PD. Best man for this kind of thing."

"Pleased to meet you," I said, turning my head toward a compact, balding man dressed in rumpled khaki trousers and an old blue sweatshirt. What little hair he had was snow white. A pair of thick horn-rimmed glasses perched on his nose. He looked to be in his late seventies, a benign presence, like someone's favorite grandfather.

"How long have you been retired, Mr. Farrell?"

"Twenty-two years."

"Hatley was SWAT commander," said Thomas. "I've used him for years. Good man."

I nodded, thinking I'd either hired the Gray Panthers or the striking arm of the AARP. Thomas told me the man had been retired, but he'd neglected to tell me how long. This was the guy who was supposed to work evening to midnight. Claire now had two grandfathers and a maid guarding her. But then, she did have the skeet gun.

Juanita returned with the bandages and another shirt. I dressed and she bandaged my forehead. I had to sit in a chair and slump low so she could reach.

"What does the other guy look like?" Thomas grinned at me. My wounds weren't serious and he knew it now and could joke about it.

"You don't want to know."

"Connected to this?"

"I doubt it. Just a misunderstanding at the hotel. That's why I was late."

"You feel up to giving us a rundown on this case?"

"Sure." I told them everything I knew and suspected about the previous night. I told them about the attorney and his young gangster companion so they would have a feeling for the opposition, if in fact that was the source, and if there really was an opposition. I told them about Peters's death, and the missing millions, and his wife seeing him alive after he'd been cremated. I left nothing out. They were both cops. They'd both been in situations like this before and probably had over seventy years of combined experience between them. I needed their experience as much as their presence.

"It could have been just some kid," said Thomas.

"Not with the graffiti on the car." Farrell shook his head. "That was a warning. And the fact that the kid didn't leave when the maid went out. Even after you arrived. A casual prowler or a Peeping Tom would have been long gone."

"You're talking as if the kid in the backyard and the kid with the lawyer were the same," I said.

Juanita finished dressing my wound and I sat up. I could see my reflection in one of the windows. A white bandage decorated the center of my forehead. Already a drop of blood leaked through. It looked like a target.

Farrell peered at me through thick lenses. "You think?"

"I'm keeping my options open. He's my employer."

Thomas smirked. "That's right. He's paying you."

I nodded. "He's paying you, too. Mrs. Peters is his client. Ultimately the money is coming from her, but he's your boss, and it's always a good idea not to screw with your boss unless you've got a real good reason."

"So we look for a kid, a gangster," said Thomas. "We look for low-rider cars because that's what they drive. Or stolen muscle cars. That's what they use when they drive-by. And we wait."

"That's what you do. And if Mrs. Peters sees something, or thinks she sees something, check it out. But don't get into trouble."

Farrell chuckled. "I've been in trouble my whole life."

"You armed?"

"Shotguns and side arms," said Thomas. "Big flashlights tonight. Hatley wants to rig up temporary lights in the backyard with motion sensors, something to give us an edge if somebody calls."

"Do it. If it ever stops raining."

"Sunny Southern California."

"Yeah. Maybe Seattle slipped south or something. I don't remember it raining this much when I was stationed here."

"You were in the navy here?" Farrell squinted at me. He had baby-blue eyes like Paul Newman's, startlingly young in the old, weathered face, except Farrell's eyes were cold. Killer eyes.

"Naval Amfib Base, Coronado. Couple of times in the seventies and the early eighties."

"I ever arrest you?"

"Never been arrested in this country, Mr. Farrell," I replied. "Nothing that ever stuck, anyway."

17

"Meester Caine, Mees Claire wants to see you." Juanita wore a worried expression. She knew Claire would react when she saw me.

Claire had endured some great stresses over the past several months. Her habit of taking a drink before turning in or even getting slightly sloppy might or might not have been something she did before I knew her. I wasn't the one to judge. Like Old Blue Eyes, I was a firm believer in whatever it takes to get you through the night.

I saw her as coping well. Before me, only Barbara had believed her. There were even indications that her trusted legal adviser might have set her up, betrayals piling upon betrayals.

And there were those missing seven million dollars, and a company she'd built, fallen into ruins.

On reflection, had those same blows fallen on me, one right after another, I'm not sure how I would have reacted. Probably grabbed the skeet gun and holed up in the bedroom.

"Oh, my God!" Claire said when she saw me, her face pale. "Juanita said you'd been stabbed."

"I fell through a looking glass. Like Alice. I met the Mad Hatter and his faithful Indian companion Tonto."

Claire stared blankly.

"Juanita took a piece of glass from my back. I couldn't reach it. It was an accident."

"That's not what Juanita said. She told me you'd been attacked at your hotel." I winced. Juanita had been there when I'd briefed Thomas and Farrell. I wondered what else she'd said, but I didn't worry. She wouldn't say anything to Claire that would intentionally upset her. She had to tell her boss something about my injuries because they were impossible to ignore, but I was confident she wouldn't report my suspicions about Stevenson.

"It was just a simple tourist mugging," I said. "It wasn't related to you. A couple of guys picked my room out of a thousand others, probably because they saw room service deliver and knew someone was there."

Her eyes told me she didn't believe me.

"It was random, Claire. Like getting hit by lightning."

"Do you feel okay?" she asked. "Would you like a brandy?" She had a snifter next to her with only a swish of amber liquid at the bottom. A crystal decanter and an empty snifter sat next to hers.

"That sounds fine. Thank you."

She smiled. "I didn't think you wanted to drink with me."

"I just didn't want to drink that night. It didn't matter if I didn't drink alone, or with someone."

Claire turned the snifter on its side and poured the brandy until it reached the brim, righted the glass, and handed it to me. She had done this before.

"Cheers."

"And all the ships at sea," I agreed. I sipped the brandy and immediately regretted it. The alcohol discovered a cut in my mouth I hadn't been aware of and it burned until the brandy numbed it. I took another sip, a small one. It didn't hurt as much.

"So how are you? I hope you're better than you look."

"I usually am," I said. That was the whole truth. There wasn't much pain, nothing a couple of aspirin couldn't cover.

"Those men downstairs," said Claire. "They're so, so old. Are you sure they can do the job?"

"They were recommended by the police department. They're both ex-cops. They're both armed. They've done this before."

"But," she said, "they don't look like they could run very far or very fast."

"If they're guarding you, you don't want them to run."

She nodded, a point conceded. "All right. I'll take your word for it. You spoke to them?"

"They know what's happening and they know how to handle the situation. You're in no danger."

She looked out the window as if to assure herself of my honesty. It was black outside, reminding me of the other thing I wanted to tell her.

"They want to install temporary lights in the backyard. With motion sensors. Leave the switch on and if something moves across their field, the lights will come on. It will give you some control over what you can see out there, and it will discourage a repetition of last night."

"Okay. If you think it would help." The tone of her voice was flat.

"I think it would be best."

"Then fine. Let them do it." She said it as if it were a favor she was doing them, allowing them to work on her house. "John," she said, "I want you to move out of the hotel. I thought about it last night, but I didn't say anything and thought I'd better think about it some more. Now with this mugging, I think we'd both be better off if you were to stay here until this thing is over."

I was happy at the hotel, but the prowler changed the equation. A while back I was in the wrong place at the wrong time and a woman was killed because of it. I wanted to be here if something were to happen again. The only thing I feared was losing my privacy. I needed a place to get away and think. I could insist on that when I needed it, and I could use *Olympia* once the paperwork was done.

"Okay," I said.

I wondered what Stevenson would do when he heard it. Not much, I guessed, since the client was paying the bills. He didn't want me moving in on her. He had warned me about that. Was that what I was doing?

"Stay here tonight," she said, "and you can check out tomorrow morning."

"Okay."

"You went to the office today?"

"I met Adrian. He seems angry."

"He was working under one of the finest minds in the business. Now he's presiding over the funeral of what would have been a great company."

"Who does he blame?"

"Me, I guess. He idolized Paul. He had dozens of offers when he graduated from Cal Tech. He came to Petersoft for only one reason. Paul. He's very bright. Now he doesn't know what's going to happen. Yesterday, federal investigators were there. There's talk that they're going to indict me."

"What's your attorney say?"

"He says wait and see."

That didn't sound like advice I'd want to take, considering the consequences. She needed a criminal attorney, a good one, and she needed one now.

"That's all he said?"

"He believes he and his ex–Treasury agent are closing in on the money. That will take the pressure off me if they can recover it."

I almost asked her if she believed that, but I didn't. I wondered if there really was an ex–Treasury agent. That would be something I could find out. If he lied about that, the rest would follow.

I switched the conversation back to Adrian. "Adrian is going to get Paul's Day-Timers for last December. Do you have his pocket ones here at the house?"

"He used an electronic one. It had everything in it. I'm not sure, but I think it might be here. No. He had it on him when he—when the explosion occurred." She stuttered the last phrase, and I wondered if she had started questioning what she had seen.

"I'm going to Ensenada with the police in the morning," I said. "Finally going to Mexico."

She nodded. "You're going to look at Calafia?"

"And the fuel dock. And I might speak with Teniente de la Peña, for what it's worth."

"Be back before dark, John. I know these guys are supposed to be good, but they're old."

"If we're lucky, we all get that way."

"And if we're not?"

"Then we find out what comes next," I said, thinking about Kate and a green cliff face on the north shore of a beautiful tropical island in the middle of the Pacific.

18

"So what happened to you?" It was becoming a tedious question. Sergeant Gregorio Esparza was only the latest to ask, and he didn't particularly care. To him it was just conversation.

With me in the shotgun seat of an unmarked car in the parking lot of the Southern Division station, we waited for Ambrosio Rodriguez and Manuel Menchaca, the two other members of the team, killing time by getting to know each other. The storm continued and we passed the time talking and listening to the radio. During the news, the weatherman said he was going to the zoo to investigate a report that the keepers were loading pairs of animals on a big boat that they'd built in the parking lot.

"I met a couple of your Welcome Wagon ladies yesterday. They wanted to give me some lasting memories of your fair city. They wanted donations, of course."

"They get anything?"

"They got hurt," I said, and gave him the short version.

"City should give you a medal," he said. He was about say something else when a new black pickup truck skidded into the parking lot and did a three-sixty, disappearing in rooster tails of rainwater.

"That's Ambrosio," said Esparza. "Manny's with him."

The truck halted, then backed into the space next to ours. Two men jumped out.

"Here," Esparza said, handing me his stainless-steel automatic in a black-nylon pancake holster. "Give him this." I rolled down my window. A Hispanic man with a fierce bandito mustache and wearing a waterproof windbreaker with the hood up approached the car. When he leaned in, I handed him the pistol.

"What's this? You greet me with a gun in your hand?"

"I've been told that's the safest way," I replied, watching the mustache levitate as he smiled.

"Ambrosio Rodriguez," said Esparza, making the introduction, "this is John Caine, the private eye I told you about."

"Oh, yeah? The guy from Hawaii? Pleased to meet you." We shook hands through the window. He had a strong grip, but not punishing. He was letting me know I was all right, a member of the club. "Let me put this away," he said, referring to the automatic. "You got anything on you? Any weapons?"

"Just a Buck knife," I said.

"That's not a weapon."

"You'd be surprised."

"Whatever. What happened to you?"

"Ran into a door."

Esparza laughed and Ambrosio disappeared. The rain continued falling, sheeting the windshield. Visibility was dismal and dropped even more when heavy gusts of wind increased the velocity of the rain.

"Let's go, amigo!" Both rear doors opened and the two men jumped in. "Man, it's raining out there!" Ambrosio slammed his door. "This is Manny Menchaca. He's a little wet. He's been climbing trees."

The other policeman was trying to dry his long black hair by slicking it back with his hands like squeezing a sponge. Water poured down his back. His jacket was soaked through, the leather saturated as if he'd been out in the elements for hours.

"Nice to meet you," said Manny. "We had a couple of errands to run this morning. Sorry we're late."

"We got her!" Ambrosio said, smiling. "Snapped her picture!"

"Three rolls," added Manny. "It was raining so hard she never knew we were there." There was pride in his voice. "We were in a tree across the street. Nobody even looked."

"Got tape, too?" Esparza was grinning.

"Yep. Audio's shitty. The rain is background. Just about all white noise. But she's on there. Got her doing the dirty deed. Red-handed. If it ain't all it should be, maybe the lab can clean it up."

Esparza backed out of the space and squinted ahead. The windshield wipers weren't keeping up with the deluge. He was a very cautious driver. He slowly pulled into traffic and I wondered if we might reach our destination before nightfall.

"We've been working on a sensitive investigation," Esparza explained. "A local politician with her hand out. Last night Manny heard rumors of a payoff. A where and a when. Came from a good source inside her office. Not only is she dishonest, she's a bitch, too. It'll make some people very happy to see her go down. Guess it was worth standing around for a couple of hours in the rain."

"Says the man who spent the morning in the office," said Manny, grinning.

"Fuckin' A, man," Ambrosio said.

"Rank still has some privileges." Esparza grinned, watching the road ahead and keeping a death grip on the wheel.

"Where we going?"

"Ensenada, Manny." Esparza glanced at me, then turned his attention back to the road. "We've got a stolen truck report. Guy said it was stolen out of his driveway. Not unusual for this border town." He eased the big Chevrolet onto the freeway, toward Mexico. Traffic was heavy but he found a spot and slipped in. "Ambrosio here, he finds out the same truck was involved in a rollover in Mexico and totaled the day it was supposed to be stolen from San Diego. American insurance isn't any good down there. This guy can't collect. So Ambrosio thinks, well, maybe the guy doesn't want to be out twenty thousand dollars or so, so he reports it stolen. He's got a nasty, suspicious mind, does Ambrosio."

"Yeah. Spent too much time dealing with the public."

"Ambrosio checks. Yep, *federales* have a report. And they have a name and a photograph of the guy who was driving, on account of he was arrested. That's standard if you get into an accident, you know, whether you have insurance or not. You get into a fender bender, you go to jail in Mexico. If someone's injured, even if it's you, it's a felony without insurance. Only your friendly insurance agent can get you out.

"Maybe this guy doesn't have Mexican insurance, so he sees some way to get out of it, get his investment back. Maybe he's greedy. Maybe just stupid. No matter. We're going to spend fifteen minutes with the *policía federales del caminos* and then come back and put the cuffs on this guy for insurance fraud. That's a felony up here."

"And that's what you do?"

"Sometimes. Sometimes other things."

"Yeah," said Manny, "like hanging around in a tree during the mother of all thunderstorms."

"We're mostly liaison between Mexico and San Diego. Sometimes we work with the feds, too, but—"

"But we try not to," Ambrosio added.

"—but we spend most of our time assisting the Mexican police, either up here or down there, and having them assist us when we've got something going down there."

"Like this insurance fraud."

"Like that." Esparza began slowing as we approached the border. In the median, a sign proclaimed GUNS ARE ILLEGAL IN MEXICO.

"We were in Anaheim yesterday, taking a couple of the federal judicial police up there to find one of their bad guys."

"Found him, too." Ambrosio's bandito mustache rose a couple of notches as he smiled again.

"Yeah. That was satisfying."

"What was he wanted for?"

"Murder. Killed his girlfriend and her parents. Then went north."

"Oh." It gave me a different perspective, hearing this. You hear about people committing crimes north of the border and heading south. It was like looking into a mirror. I'd never thought about it working the other way. Also, the specter of Mexican law enforcement crossing north to our side wasn't something I'd considered before.

"Kid thought that once he was up here, he could disappear."

"Dumb shit thought all Mexicans look alike to the gringos." Ambrosio laughed.

"He didn't count on Ambrosio."

"Nobody looks alike. He stood out like a sore eye," said Ambrosio in an exaggerated accent, happy at the memory.

We crossed the border. It wasn't much of a ceremony. Two men in a toll booth waved us through. Behind them, out in the elements without cover, stood Mexican military units, soldiers armed with automatic rifles that they tried to keep dry by hiding them under olive-drab ponchos, barrels pointed toward the ground.

"The army guards the border?"

"They have a new president," said Esparza. "He's trying to make it look like they care about what happens on the border. Maybe he does. Things like that happen, sometimes."

He took the four-lane highway that ran parallel to the border. Just a few feet to the north a steel fence stood, marking, I supposed, the exact geographical location of the beginning of United States soil. The fence had many holes under it, dug into the soft tan mud. Beyond the fence, pale green pickup trucks sat at intervals of a hundred yards, American border patrol, waiting for the night.

On this side of the fence hundreds of campesinos from the fields, and the poor from the cities, men and women and children, gathered, in clusters, waiting to try for it, hoping for a better life. They, too, were waiting for the night. They huddled in the rain, with no shelter and nowhere else to go.

"Tell us again about this dead man the wife saw walking around." Ambrosio leaned over the seat and poked Esparza on the shoulder. "This that yachtsman who blew himself up a few months back?"

"That's the one."

"His wife thinks he faked his death and skipped with seven million dollars," I said. "She was convinced he was dead until she saw him at Calafia."

"Better than a divorce in California," said Ambrosio. "Seven million. Gotta admire a guy for that."

"You should know," said Manny.

"Cost me half my pension. Fucking bitch."

"So there's a problem," I said. "There was a body. A coroner issued a death certificate."

"And if he's alive," Ambrosio grinned, the mustache bobbing, "then who was the body?"

I nodded. "They found human remains in the ruins of the boat which they identified through dental records the family attorney brought down."

"No he didn't," said Esparza.

"He didn't?"

"I told you the other day. He gave them to me. I remember when he brought them in. We took them down and turned them over to the coroner."

"Oh, yeah," said Ambrosio. "I remember that."

"Do you recall the name of the dentist?"

"I don't have to. I made a copy." Esparza smiled at me briefly before turning his attention back to the road. The rain was not letting up on either of the two Californias. It had been one continuous drenching without ceasing for three days. The radio reported mud slides in Malibu and Laguna Beach, north of San Diego. Mexico, though a different country, was closer than Malibu or Laguna Beach. There had been no news about conditions on this side of the border.

"So she sees this guy. He takes off. That's it?" Ambrosio was still turning it over.

"That's it."

"So he's not dead."

"Doesn't look that way," I said.

"Looks like we might have a homicide, Sergeant."

Esparza nodded. "Caine here is going to follow up. We're going to introduce him around. Try to keep him out of trouble."

"That's good."

"And he's going to let us know what he finds out."

"That's good."

"Aren't you, Caine?"

I nodded. Why not? "Did Stevenson call you after his client saw her husband down there?"

"No. He may have called Mexico directly. He had some kind of relationship with de la Peña, *el jéfe* from Ensenada Homicide. He didn't call me."

Here was another inconsistency that bothered me about Stevenson. He either forgot the facts, or intentionally blurred them.

"And Caine here is going to do something else for us," said Esparza.

I glanced at him and then stared out the window. The road along the coast was densely populated with incomplete concrete structures and rickety wood-framed houses that looked as if they could stand some more work to make them stable. There were no trees. Nothing moved except an old dog trotting along the side of the road, tongue lolling, oblivious of the rain.

"He's going to buy us lunch when we get to Calafia."

"Lobster," said Ambrosio. "I always like their lobster."

19

The three cops did not order lobster, although they kept the threat hanging over me until the waiter came and everyone ordered fish tacos. I waited until they ordered their drinks, not knowing if a beer or two was acceptable this far from the flagpole. When they ordered coffee I made it unanimous, reflecting on the changes over the last twenty years.

Even ten years ago there would have been no question about a beer. One or two beers in Mexico would have been accepted, maybe even expected. Now it's an acknowledged fact that nobody drinks on the job except politicians, the same ones who make the rules for everybody else.

Calafia was exactly as Claire described it. A warren of little cobblestone streets going off in all directions. The restaurant gift shop was near the entry doors, the rest rooms across the hall. I looked outside, studying the layout. In the dark a man had many avenues of escape, any number of places to hide. Once Claire got over her shock, she went after him, but by then it was too late. He had vanished.

My acceptance of her story was stronger now that I had been here. Too many details fit too well to make it anything other than believable. I'm not naive; I try to be intellectually honest and thought I'd given her a fair hearing. I wondered if Stevenson and the others who acted as if they did not believe her had given her the same courtesy.

That's why I was here. That's why I took her case in the first place.

On impulse, I purchased a T-shirt with the Mexican flag on its chest. Claire was a small woman. I bought her an extra large. She could sleep in it. If she didn't like it, she could give it to Juanita.

"Seen enough here?" Esparza and his team were good men and hadn't pushed me, but they had a schedule to keep.

"I'll come back on my own in a day or two," I said. "There's nothing but more questions."

Esparza nodded. "Isn't that always the case?"

Ambrosio and Manny came out of the room marked HOMBRES, each doing a little dance in time with the canned salsa music.

"Are you ready to see Teniente José Enrique de la Peña?" Esparza had his hands on his hips.

"Sí, mi sargento," said Ambrosio. "And we are to stop at the Hotel El Mirador?"

"The fuel dock."

"We'll hit that next. It's just down the road a few miles."

"That's where the accident happened?" I asked. That was the one place I needed to spend some time. There would be witnesses.

"Yeah. Not much to see. I think the hull is still there, burned to the waterline."

"I want to see that," I said.

"Okay."

We hesitated at the double front doors. It was still raining and none of us wanted to make the dash to the car.

"You go, *mi sargento,*" said Ambrosio. "You are our leader. We, your humble servants, shall follow. Besides, you got the keys."

"RHIP," added Manny.

Esparza nodded and ran to the sedan. When he got the car doors unlocked, we followed, which would have been helpful had he not locked the doors again just as we got to the car. He sat behind foggy glass, laughing at us until Ambrosio and Manny stalked back to the restaurant and stood under the overhang. I followed. They refused to go back to the car until Esparza got out, walked back to the restaurant, and apologized.

"Worked," said Ambrosio to Manny, with a sly grin. "Made the boss get wet all over again."

We drove by the Hotel El Mirador but the rain came down so hard it didn't make sense to get out of the car. A burned-out boat hull lay on its side on the concrete at the far side of the marina like a beached whale. Few things are sadder than a boat out of water.

I debated getting out of the car to inspect the wreck, but decided I couldn't ignore the rain enough to learn anything; I'd spend too much time and energy trying to keep dry. At least I knew where the hull was and could return when it stopped raining.

I looked around. Buildings surrounded the marina and the fuel dock. If a bomb had been aboard, someone could easily have set it off by a radio transmitter, watching from one of the many windows. That told me nothing. It would take a bomb expert to find traces of bomb material in the hull, presuming it was there, and assuming the evidence had not been accidentally or intentionally removed since the explosion.

"Let's go," I said to Esparza. "I've seen all I can see now."

Ambrosio made his stop at the Baja California headquarters of the Federal Highway Patrol, a single-story concrete-block structure on the waterfront in Ensenada. We waited while he went inside and got what he wanted, returning ten minutes later with photocopies of the booking statement and the accident report, both confirming that the same man who had reported the truck stolen in the United States had also wrecked it in Mexico.

Our last stop was on the south side of Ensenada, near the industrial district. Sergeant Esparza had made an appointment with Teniente de la Peña, who waited for us in his office.

De la Peña was a bully, a large man in his mid-forties with big shoulders and a self-satisfied belly that obscured his gun belt. In his dark khaki uniform he presented an imposing figure, which he knew and used to his advantage, giving the impression of power and brute force.

He looked like a man who would do exactly what he wanted, when he wanted, looked like a man who could make something happen. Or keep something from happening.

De la Peña spoke no English, or at least that was the impression he wished us to have. The interview was conducted in Spanish, Sergeant Esparza acting as my translator. I'd grown up on the Mexican border and was conversant, though rusty, but I didn't want de la Peña to have complete knowledge of my abilities, either.

The conversation didn't go well. Most of my questions were shunted aside. Many of his answers were *"No sé":* "I don't know," or "I don't remember"—a handy device to stonewall without getting caught in a lie that could trip you up later. When it became obvious even to me that the exercise was futile, I told Esparza I had no more questions. De la Peña stood and ushered us out of his office like a waiter with a poor-tipping guest. He shook the three policemen's hands, but ignored mine.

"He's hiding something," Esparza observed, once we were back in the car, cutting across town toward the docks and the Tijuana highway. "You really annoyed him," he added.

"Told you I was good at it."

"Didn't know how good."

"Did we accomplish anything?"

Esparza thought about it, squinting through the windshield. "It depends on how you view your objective. If you merely wanted information, you failed. If you accept the fact that his obvious refusal to discuss the incident is, in itself, information, then you did learn something. Which is it? And was it worth the trip? Only you can answer that."

"What do you think?"

"He's lying. I learned something, too, this afternoon. This wasn't just a waste of time for the department."

"What was that?"

"I can't trust that guy."

"That's the kind you bet your life on sometimes," I said.

Esparza nodded. "Promise me something, Caine."

"Sure."

"Check in with me before you head down here alone. Somebody should know when and where you're going, and when you expect to come back."

"You think it's that serious?"

"I think that Teniente José Enrique de la Peña wants to put you out of business. I think that the good *teniente* thinks you could unravel his whole operation if you're unchecked."

"I think that you should follow up as soon as possible," said Ambrosio from the backseat, his voice uncharacteristically quiet. "I was watching him. He was so uncomfortable talking about this he's going to take some immediate steps to close some doors."

"What do you mean?"

"If I was that yachtsman? And I was hiding out down here and de la Peña knows where I am? I'd start looking for another hiding place. De la Peña looked like he might shut everything down."

"Yeah?"

"He look like a guy who'd hesitate to kill a dead man?"

We rode in silence for the next seventy miles, the landscape obscured by the monotony of the rain. All I saw were black hills and poverty, and an occasional glimpse of a gray dark ocean.

Someone's beeper went off. All three cops glanced down at their belts. Esparza stared so long I nearly grabbed the steering wheel as the car drifted toward the oncoming lane.

"It's the boss," he said.

"We're close enough to the border. Try it."

"You do it. I'm kind of busy."

Ambrosio leaned over the seat, grabbed the handset from the dash. When he got through, he started the conversation in a loud voice, then got suddenly quiet. He looked at me. "He's here," he said. I kept silent. Something had happened and I'd find out soon enough. "Hey, Sergeant. How long before we hit the border?"

Esparza scanned the road ahead. "Twenty minutes, give or take. We might save some time through Otay Mesa."

"Go through Otay, Sergeant."

Esparza nodded.

"Twenty minutes to the line," said Ambrosio into the handset. "Another thirty minutes after that. We can push it, maybe make it faster, but figure an hour with everything. Okay. See you there." He hung up the phone and looked at me. "Sergeant, that was the lieutenant. Our plans have changed. We're going to Point Loma once we cross the border. No stops. Not even for our weapons. We're to report to Homicide once we get there."

"What happened?"

"Caine's been guarding this yachtsman's widow. Hired a couple of ex-cops to cover it while he's gone. They had a shooting today. Lots of noise. Coroner's there. The mayor complained. She lives across the street, you know."

"Who's hurt?"

"Don't know. There's at least one guy down."

"Dead?"

"They don't send the coroner for minor wounds."

"How's the widow?" I couldn't stop the question.. It just spilled out of my mouth.

Ambrosio shook his head. "The lieutenant didn't say. We'll find out soon enough. All he said was, it was some guy. That make you feel any better?"

It didn't and he knew it, but he tried to make it sound better.

"You hire Ed like I suggested?" Esparza asked.

"Yes. He brought in a guy named Farrell to help out. Farrell was supposed to come on about four, so most likely he was there."

"Hatley Farrell?"

"That's the name. You know him?"

Esparza smiled. "Toughest cop San Diego ever had. Put nine men down in thirty years. A real Dirty Harry."

The Hatley Farrell I'd met was a little guy, but I didn't forget his eyes.

"If anyone is dead, it's the bad guy. Farrell must be close to eighty by now, but last I heard, he could still hit the ten ring with that cannon of his. You know, Farrell's the only guy I ever met carries a forty-one Magnum. Got special permission from the chief. Damned cannon. Four-inch barrel. Magna-ported. Customized. He's the last of the real *pistoleros*."

"Hey," said Ambrosio.

"Okay. One of the last," said Esparza, "but you're not an ace and Farrell is. The point is"—Esparza looked at me—"that he may be slowing down some, but Farrell is a dead shot. He's also no virgin. If there's shooting to be done, Farrell will do it. Your people are all right. That's a promise."

"Hey," said Ambrosio. "You think de la Peña set this up? How long ago we talk to him? Two hours? All he had to do was pick up the phone and place the order. It goes down while we're slipping and sliding up the Baja coast. By the time we're home, it's over."

"Except for Farrell."

"Yeah. And all that."

And John Caine was somewhere else when they tried to kill her. Some bodyguard. Mr. Ineffective.

Feeling helpless, I slumped in the passenger seat and sat as still as possible, trying to force my heart rate back to normal and trying to stop the adrenaline flooding my arteries.

20

It was dark by the time we arrived. Blue, red, and amber emergency beacons blinked on and off, a festival of light. News vans and official vehicles blocked the street in front of Claire's estate. The blue-white glare of camera crews illuminated the house from the sidewalk.

A female police officer guarded the driveway, standing in the rain under a bright yellow slicker, trying to keep dry, reminding me of the Mexican troops at the border. The cop raised her hand to stop our car and went to the driver's side.

Esparza rolled down the window and flashed his badge. She waved us through. Rain was still falling and her long fingernails shone like rubies reflected in the car lights.

Inside the gate, another officer directed us to the rear of the house. Lights burned in every room, as if Claire were hosting a vast party. We ran through the rain to the kitchen entrance. Esparza showed his badge at the door and we were admitted.

The kitchen was crowded but I could see Ed Thomas towering above everyone else in the room. Claire sat at the oak table, Juanita next to her, holding a handkerchief to her mouth. Farrell sat in the corner, conferring with two detectives. Claire saw me enter and tried to smile. It was that same brave smile I'd seen before, ragged, but still there.

My heartbeat began to slow for the first time since we'd crossed the border.

A big Latino policeman stood over Juanita, speaking in low tones. When I came closer, I recognized the Spanish. He had looked up when we entered and acknowledged Ambrosio with a sharp nod. Ambrosio went by me and patted him on the back.

"Ambrosio," said the big cop. "Heard you were in Mexico."

"Just got back, amigo. What you got?"

"Two punks broke in. Broad daylight, right across the street from Her Honor's house. Both had SMG's."

"That right? Submachine guns?"

"Mac-11's. Forty-fives. Like in the movies. Shot the shit out of the place."

"Hey over there!" An authoritative voice from the corner boomed over the buzz of conversation in the room. The voice belonged to a tall man with a glare to match. He was one of the two cops interviewing Farrell. "You got anything to say, take it outside. Otherwise, keep doing what you're supposed to be doing. If you're not supposed to be here, get out."

"See you around, Ambrosio," the detective said, then turned back to Juanita.

Ambrosio looked at me and grinned sheepishly and shuffled out of the kitchen. I followed him.

The living room had its own crowd, most of them gathered near the French door to the backyard. Chunks of plaster and dusty lath littered the hardwood floors near the entry corridor. A staggered line of bullet holes stitched across one wall, continuing to the ceiling.

A corpse lay on its back, surrounded by blood and broken glass, one leg stretched out straight, the other bent at the knee. A shaven, stubbled head faced the room. Both eyes were closed, the mouth slack.

Just outside the open door another body lay crumpled on the tiles. Blood pooled under it; some of it had collected in the grout lines and run down the slope to the edge of the steps, where the rain thinned it to a pale pink.

Both bodies looked impossibly young.

I bent forward and took a close look. Each chest had three entry wounds centered, holes so close together I could have covered them with the palm of my hand.

Two ugly black submachine guns lay on a table, MAC-11's, a powerful, reliable weapon good for close work, if you knew that it tended to pull up and to the left and you practiced with it. With a thirty-round magazine in .45 ACP, a MAC-11 could lay down some impressive firepower. I looked again at the line of bullet holes on the opposite wall. It climbed to the left from its point of origin. There was only one short line on the wall.

"What do you think?" Ambrosio said.

"This was some serious shooting," I said. "Whoever put these guys down didn't miss."

He nodded. "This ain't stunt work."

Esparza and Manny joined us.

"Captain decided we didn't need to be here after all. He thought Caine here might know something, but I told him he was with us, down in Mexico. We've got to go," said Esparza, shaking my hand. He looked at the two boys on the floor. "I'm glad it wasn't worse."

"It's better than I feared."

"Yeah. Sometimes it is," he said. "When you go back to Mexico, let me know first. I'll try to keep an eye on you, if I can."

"Thanks. Good luck."

"You, too, Caine. You're the one who needs it." He handed me the plastic bag with the T-shirt I'd purchased in Calafia. "You left this in the car."

"Thanks."

They left me standing there, holding the bag. I stared at the corpse. It looked familiar. All dead bodies do. I'd seen more than my share in my time. More than I cared to see. There is a kinship in what Will Durant called The Great Certainty.

"How was Mexico?"

Ed Thomas stood behind me. "It was quiet," I said. "This your work?"

Thomas shook his head. "Farrell. He was in the kitchen drinking cocoa with the housekeeper when he heard glass breaking. He unholstered his revolver and came into the living room and found these two just inside the door here. He gave them the standard warning, told them to put down their weapons. You know the drill. Fools. All they saw was a little old man with a big old gun. Then they made a fatal mistake. They pointed their guns at him. One opened up. Hat returned fire." Thomas shook his head sadly. "They brought it on themselves. It was a righteous shooting, no matter how it looks. Nobody is going to argue he used excessive force."

"Why would that be an issue?" I asked.

"These were kids. Look at them." I did, getting close to the bodies again. "How old would you say they were?" Thomas asked.

"Eighteen or nineteen," I said, after I examined their faces. They were both thin, and they both had some facial growth, but it was sparse. Both were Hispanic males, so alike they could have been brothers, and probably were.

"Try fifteen or sixteen. They're babies. Farrell can't believe he shot two kids."

"He upset about that?"

"He isn't happy about it, but they caused their own deaths. If he didn't kill them, they would have killed him. He just can't believe they were armed with that kind of firepower. These are gangsters. They may never have had much of a chance to be anything else, but that doesn't matter now." Thomas looked at me. "They came to kill everyone in the house. These boys were hired guns."

"We better get Claire and Juanita out of here."

Thomas nodded. "That's just what I was thinking. We'll take them to a hotel tonight, somewhere bright and safe. Then we can figure out where they'll be anonymous and secure."

"You have anyplace in mind?"

"I know some safe houses, but it would be better if they're out of the city."

I knew where I'd put them, after I closed the deal. "I've got an idea," I said, and told him about *Olympia.*

Thomas smiled. "I like that," he said. Then he frowned. "You've got another problem."

"Claire?"

"Related. She insisted on calling that lawyer. He's on his way over here. Wants to fire you. Insists he can do a better job. Got me on the line and ragged me about ensuring Mrs.

Peters's safety. Wanted a complete account of what happened, and where you were when it all went down, and how much money was I costing, blah, blah, blah. I took about two minutes of his shit before I told him to go fuck himself."

"So he's coming over?"

"Yeah. Sorry."

"Is Claire free to go?"

"The detectives are done with her. They're still questioning Juanita."

"Can you get her for me?"

Thomas smiled again. "You want to get her out of here before that lawyer comes over. You don't want him influencing her. You devious bastard."

"Just cowardly."

"I'll get the lady. Take her to a hotel, anyplace, just so she's gone by the time shit-for-brains shows up. I'll bring Juanita once everything is settled here."

"What about the house?"

"Farrell will stay," said Thomas. "He likes the place. He told me to tell you he's sorry he messed it up."

"I won't take her back to the hotel at the marina. Stevenson will probably figure I'd go there. Where do you suggest?"

"Someplace quiet, where there's a lot of other hotels." He thought a minute. "Mission Valley. Hotel Circle. There's a Marriott. It's quiet. Check in under my name." He handed me his American Express card. "I'll add it to your bill."

21

Before I answered the knock on the hotel-room door this time, I looked through the viewing port. Ed Thomas's face peered back at me, so I opened the door.

"Everything okay?" Thomas resembled a cat with canary feathers clinging to its mouth.

"Come in, Ed," I answered. "Hello, Juanita."

The housekeeper nodded, but kept her head down. Her eyes were red from crying. She clutched a handkerchief and a fabric bag in her hands and shuffled in behind the private detective.

"Claire's next door," I said. "She's upset, but she's all right. She didn't like being forced out of her home."

Thomas looked around the room and the interconnecting doors. Mine stood open against the wall. "Nice suite. Top floor," he said. "That's the last time I lend you my credit card."

"Took the back six rooms on this floor, closest to the stairwell. They had some vacancies, so it worked out." I handed him the keys. "Take your pick. The two across the hall and the one the other side of Claire's are vacant. Put Juanita in one. That makes two empty. It should cause confusion if anyone finds out where we are."

"You do know security."

"That's my business, Ed. It's what I do."

"You still let me do things my way."

I shrugged.

"By the way," Ed said, "we're fired. Stevenson showed up before the cops were through with Juanita. He told me that you, me, all of us, we're fired. Gave me a letter."

I stuck out my hand.

"Lost it."

"You wouldn't go home, anyway," I said.

"Would you?"

"Not now."

"I don't know what you did in Mexico, Caine, but something is shaking."

"Somebody got stupid. Cops get anything we need to know about?"

"The dead guys weren't local. They rushed their prints through the system and came up with zilch. Theory among the muck-a-mucks is that they were brought in from Mexico just for this job."

"Hired assassins."

"Didn't need to be a rocket scientist to figure that out, but it's nice to be validated."

"Why don't you let Juanita get settled, then we'll talk."

"If you don't mind, I'm turning in, too. Been a busy day, and I missed my hot milk."

"Farrell okay?"

"He's fine. He went home, but he'll come back tomorrow, when everyone is gone. Chances are nothing's going to happen tonight and he told me he's pretty tired."

"Thank him for me. He did a good job."

Thomas frowned. "He killed two people."

"And did a damn good job doing it. Better them than him, Juanita, and Claire. Good night, Ed. I'll see you in the morning. Good night, Juanita."

"Good night, Meester Caine." She stared at the floor when she replied, her voice subdued.

I watched while Ed opened her door across the corridor and went in to check for boogeymen. When he came out and handed her the key, she accepted it with a placidity I found disturbing. I'd thought Juanita was the strong one, the survivor. I saw her as the cheerful trooper, the defender at the gate. I'd taken her cheerfulness and her courage for granted, thinking they would always be there for her.

Evidently the evening's events had been far too similar to

others in her life. When death hits too close to home, and there's no chance to jump back into one's defense mechanisms, then dealing with it is the only thing one can do.

In the end, we all have to deal with it, one way or the other.

I waited until I heard the locks set in place before closing my door.

I lay on the bed and turned on the television. CNN reported that a mysterious band of commandos had attacked something, somewhere in the Mediterranean, putting a terrorist out of business, a terrorist who had blown up a United States military installation. They had come in the night from the sea in small boats, hitting their target so quickly the local authorities could not react fast enough. By the time the police arrived, the commandos were long gone and the terrorist, whom the reporter always identified as "the suspected terrorist," had been turned into hamburger. No one else had been injured.

The reporter, a jowly British gentleman who looked as if he hadn't had a bowel movement in decades, sniffed that the commandos' suspected country of origin was the United States. The tone of his voice held a whiff of condemnation as if it were okay for people with a grudge and an ax to grind to maim and murder innocent civilians, but reprisal was just not fair; not a viewpoint I could share.

The story depressed me further. I wondered if Max had been involved.

In my years in uniform I'd hunted terrorists with Max, but those were the days of the cold war, and there were other considerations that kept us from acting. Terrorism had been largely supported by the Soviet Union, one of the major powers Washington didn't want to upset. We saw the Soviet army up close, every time we crossed the Iron Curtain. The old Soviet Union was nothing more than an overgrown Third World country with nuclear weapons. It may have had millions of men in uniform, but as a military force it was a joke, effective only against unarmed civilians and ragtag bands of revolutionaries.

Washington didn't see it that way, of course. My team found Ilyich Ramirez Sanchez, whom the news media had dubbed Carlos the Jackal, twice, once in the Middle East, once in Eastern Europe. He was the pudgy little Marxist, a son of a Venezuelan dentist, who gave Western Europe and the Middle East a run for its money back in the seventies. He'd hit and run—run back to behind the Iron Curtain—killing a policeman or two here, an innocent in a stroller there, an OPEC minister over there. The newspeople saw something magical in Sanchez. They canonized him, created the myth of the European gunslinger.

We could have knocked him off either time, could have reached right out and taken him as easily as we snapped his photograph. We wanted to. Dearly. But Washington, fearing something that wasn't fearsome, would not give us the green light. We had to be content to watch him strut like a peacock, convinced of his invulnerability and his place in history, just another dumb son of a bitch who thought it creative tossing hand grenades into crowded shopping malls.

It wasn't until after the fall of the Berlin Wall that Sanchez was arrested and jailed.

Max had been with me both times. He'd weathered the changes while I got out after Granada, having lost more friends to politics and stupidity than I could stomach. I wondered if he was content with the way things had turned out.

The connecting door opened and I shut off the television. Claire came in and sat on the side of the bed. She wore the Calafia T-shirt I'd bought her. Her legs were bare underneath.

"Are we safe?"

"As long as no one knows where we are."

"I'm not used to violence. I've never experienced anything like this. People invading my home. It's unthinkable."

"It's not real. It's the kind of thing you see on television. And then it comes into your living room."

"I don't watch those kinds of shows. Never did. I don't go to those kinds of movies, either. I'd always believed that if you bring violence into your life, it will follow."

"And now you're not so sure."

She placed her fingers on her temples. "I don't know what to think. I can't sleep. I'm getting a headache. I get migraines and I feel one coming on."

"You get pinched nerves in your back?"

She nodded.

"Frozen shoulder?"

"How did you know?"

"Lie down on the bed."

Claire looked at me, her expression unreadable.

"It's not like that," I said. "*Lomi Lomi* is Hawaiian massage. There's a woman in Kauai who taught me. It won't hurt and it might help."

"You're a full-service detective."

"Just doing my best."

I got off the bed. Claire retained that same enigmatic expression. Then she nodded and slowly pulled the T-shirt over her head, lay down on the bed, and rolled onto her stomach. She had worn nothing under the T-shirt. She neither flaunted her body nor tried to hide it.

My mouth went dry.

I went into the bathroom and took a small bottle of oil from my kit. Claire lay on the bed, her eyes closed, a neutral expression on her face. The skin of her back was smooth and tan, the muscles bunched and hard. I rubbed the oil lightly onto her skin and on my forearms.

"That smells good," she said.

"Kukui oil. From a tree that grows in Hawaii. It's essential to *Lomi Lomi,* if you want to do it right." Starting at the small of her back, my fingers searched her muscles, looking for telltale knobs of cramped muscle tissue.

"Ouch."

"Patience. You've got quite a crop of knots here."

"I get those. Always have."

"When you are tense."

"Yes."

"That may be what causes your migraines. The muscles knot up, then get worse and pull on the connective tissue. I'm going to loosen them. When we're done, you'll find those muscles attach to your skull behind your ears. That's where your migraines start. We'll take those knots and push them out through your neck."

"Ohhh."

"That hurt?"

"Noooo. That feels so good."

"These aren't so bad. We can get to most of these." My fingers searched the muscles in her back, probing the ridges and the valleys. When they discovered a knot, they pushed and kneaded and manipulated the knots and the muscles, dissolving the large ones and moving the small ones from the back up toward the neck.

Claire smiled, her eyes closed, her face visible in profile. Her body was compact and powerful, her golden skin flawless. I closed my eyes, letting my fingers explore and heal, allowing them sole access. I told myself I was here only to heal. My fingers listened to the rhythm of her body, followed wherever the pain could be stopped. I put those other thoughts away for another time.

"Umm." I opened my eyes. Claire's face held a beatific expression.

"Umm is better than ouch," I said.

"Umm," she repeated.

I worked on her for over an hour, pushing one knot after another up through her shoulder blades. Finally, I pushed out the knots from her shoulders and neck. When I rolled my forearms up and down her back, the muscles were soft and supple.

"Where have you been all my life?" she asked lazily. "My headache is gone. I feel wonderful."

"Kauai has some of the best body workers and teachers in the world."

"They must be, if they taught you."

"Can you sleep?"

"I think so," she said. "Oh. What are you doing?"

"Your feet. It'll relax you. Make you sleep." I poured more oil on the soles of her feet and massaged them until she snored softly. Her face was peaceful, as if she hadn't a care in the world.

I covered her and turned out the light. Then I took my shaving kit and my briefcase and went into the other room to sleep.

22

Friar's Road had, I guessed, been named for the Spanish Franciscans who established the first string of missions up and down the coast of what is now California. About five miles from the hotel is the first one, Mission San Diego de Alcala. I ran down Friar's Road to the mission and back, twice passing the mammoth concrete stadium where the Chargers and the Padres play. I don't know where they got the name Chargers, but I was willing to bet the Padres were also named after those same Catholic missionaries.

Maybe they should change the football team's name to the Priests. Maybe they already thought about it and decided it wouldn't help.

The days of downpour had ended and the sky was blue and vacant, as if no rain ever fell on this corner of the country. It felt good to be out from under the clouds again. My running improved when I didn't have to buck a headwind full of rain.

The Mission Valley Marriott sits back about two hundred yards south of Friar's Road. I jogged into the parking lot beside the hotel and found Ed Thomas leaning against his truck, drinking coffee from a paper cup and letting the early morning sun warm his balding head.

"When you're ready," he said, "I'll drive you down to pick up your car."

"Needed to go for a run."

"I stopped by your room. Mrs. Peters told me to go away."

"Have some breakfast while I shower."

"I'll put it on the card." Thomas turned and tossed the coffee into some bushes near the pavement. His manner was brusque, even rude.

I wondered about Ed's behavior during the ride in the elevator up to my room. I didn't really know him, but he seemed the kind of man that if something bothered him, it would come out.

Claire was still sleeping when I picked up my roll bag. I tiptoed quietly toward the bathroom.

"John?"

"I'm just getting my stuff. Stay in bed."

"I'm up," she said, rolling over. She stretched beneath the blankets. "I feel marvelous. No headache."

"Sleep all right?"

"All night long. I must have drifted off while you did my feet." She hugged herself, and discovered she was naked. "You covered me."

I nodded.

"So you've seen it all."

"Only the back, but what I've seen is lovely."

"Always the gentleman. Even when the lady practically throws herself at you."

"Is that what you did?"

"Some guys would have thought so."

"We don't belong together, Claire. You should know that. I wouldn't be good for you. Especially now."

"You mean if I were to roll out of the covers and invite you in, you wouldn't?" She lowered the blankets to a dangerous level, about half a millimeter above her nipples.

"No," I said. "Not now. It would complicate things."

"I wouldn't want to be a complication," she said, her voice heavy with sarcasm as she dropped the blanket.

"That's not helping, Claire."

"Who're you? Saint John?"

"Father John, remember? You called me that."

"I wanted you to know about the situation. I wanted you to know about Paul's infidelities, because it seemed to be the only motive he could have."

I stared at her. She was beautiful. Some women look wonderful in clothes, but when they lose the outer coverings, they don't live up to the advance billing. Claire was one of the few who looked better without clothes. "I'm not made of stone, Claire. Cover up."

"You're turning me down?"

I nodded.

"Why?"

"We need to focus. Someone tried to take your life last night. It was a serious attempt. Whether you know it or not, you're on the run. You can't go back to your home. Not right now. You can't live the life you were used to living. You're a target. Hatley and Ed are here to protect you. And I'm here to find out who is targeting you and why." I felt no need to tell her that my emotional life was deadened and that the only way I knew how to keep the pain away was to keep it dulled. It was too soon to try again.

"And then?"

"And then eliminate the threat."

She studied my face. "You'd do that."

"Without hesitation. And as pleasant as the view is, please cover it up."

"I feel like a fool."

"Don't, Claire. It isn't personal."

"God, you are focused."

"I'll make you a deal. When all this is over, I can take you to Hawaii. I know beaches where you can get an all-over tan, where you wouldn't see another person, where waterfalls spill onto the beach and you can take a freshwater shower after getting out of the surf. If we get your money back. Maybe then. If you're no longer in danger. If the offer still stands." I was surprised how easily the lie tripped off my tongue.

She considered my suggestion, pulling the covers up to her chin. "I think I might take you up on that. After this is over I'd like you to take me to Hawaii."

"It's a deal. Right now I'm going to shower. Ed and I will pick up the Range Rover. Then I'm going to get you a place to stay. We can't stay here. Those newspeople will find you and then everyone will know."

"You think they would try here?"

"If they know where you are, they might. That's why nobody should know but Thomas and Farrell. Nobody else. You are news in this town right now, and reporters are out looking for you. Fortunately, every miracle is only good for three days. By Sunday your story will be stale and they'll find something else to feed on. Until then, you need to stay out of sight to stay alive."

"Those boys were going to kill me."

"Everyone in the house. You. Juanita. Everyone. Farrell stopped them the only way they could be stopped."

"I should be frightened," she said, "but somehow I've never felt safer in my life."

"Be a rabbit. Hide in your hole now. Later, when we've got it all together, we'll come out."

"What happened in Mexico yesterday?"

"First the good news. I annoyed somebody with something to hide. He overreacted."

"That's the good news?"

"Your story holds up. I don't know why they panicked, but they did. Score one for our side. The next time I go down there, they'll be waiting. Maybe then I can find your husband."

"What's the bad news?"

"There isn't any. Now let me take a shower. You can go into your own room while I'm in there. Okay?"

I didn't wait for her answer. And when I closed the door to the bathroom, I locked it.

The remainder of that Friday was so busy it blurred. Thomas first took me to Petersoft. I telephoned Adrian and he told me he'd found the material I'd asked for. He also instructed me to hurry. He had put Petersoft, Ltd., on a four-day work week due to the current economic situation, and he wanted to go home.

After Petersoft, Thomas drove me down to the Intercontinental Marina, where I checked out of my room. The manager came out of his office when I identified myself to the desk clerk. He solicitously inquired about my well-being. My bill, he said, had been comped as a result of what he called "that unfortunate situation" of the other evening.

Never having looked a gift horse in the mouth, I thanked him and picked up the remainder of my clothes. Thomas and I were out of there in ten minutes. We left my bags in Thomas's pickup and walked over to the harbor side of the hotel, where Ashton, the banker, and Jack Kinsman waited for me to close the deal on *Olympia.*

Kinsman had the papers ready and the three of us met the banker in the sales manager's private office. The fat man seemed to swell when I opened the briefcase and counted out the money. The presence of the pistol didn't seem to faze him. He was so focused on the hundred-dollar bills piling up on the desk he was oblivious of the gun.

I caught Thomas's eye once during the meeting. He saw the money and the .45, and waggled a finger at me, as if I were a naughty boy.

The transaction took nearly half an hour. Even with a cash deal, the federal government and the state of California and several other bureaucracies had some form to sign or other ways and means of letting us know they had a claim on some portion of either the boat or the money. By the time we were done, my writing hand was sore. The banker immediately excused himself and left, leaving Ed and me and Jack Kinsman sitting in the main cabin of the yacht-turned-sales-office.

"Congratulations, Mr. Caine," said Kinsman, lighting a cigarette, his first since the transaction started. "You are now the sole owner of a classic sailing vessel. I hope you enjoy it."

"And I hope you enjoy this," I said, slipping a thick wad of folded notes into his palm. "You did a good job. You must have done this before."

Kinsman chuckled, examined the bills, and chuckled again before putting them away. "Always like doing business with a gentleman," he said. "Can I get the documentation done for you? It'll take about a month. All part of the service."

"Please. Make the home port Pearl Harbor."

"That's not a city. How about Honolulu?"

"Just make it Pearl Harbor. That's her home port. The Rainbow Marina, Pearl Harbor, Hawaii."

"Want to change the name?"

"No. It's bad luck, changing the name. And I like her the way she is." Ashton had agreed that the name went with the yacht, and it had become a part of the deal.

"I know, but I had to ask. Here's her keys. Here's your guest pass for the yacht club." Kinsman slipped them to me over the desk. "Ashton arranged for you to open a tab there. You've got credit. His guest. Stay as long as you wish. His family still owns the slip, but he says they've no plans to fill it at the present time."

"That's fine. Thank you."

"You need anything else, you let me know."

I thanked him again and Thomas and I next went to the Southwest Division police station to pick up the Range Rover. Then we split up.

"I'll get Juanita and Claire. You run by the house and pick up the stuff we talked about. I'll meet you in two hours back at the boat."

"I haven't seen that much cash money in years," said Thomas. "Not since I busted a cocaine dealer in Rancho Santa Fe."

"That's honest money. Compensation for the loss of my old boat."

"That's your safe house?"

"It is not a public place. People who work at the yacht club are relatively closemouthed about what they see and hear. They have to be if they want to keep their jobs. There's four of us. There are four staterooms. It's big enough so we won't get on each other's nerves. And if we feel threatened, we can sail away. Go to another port or just stay out of sight of land for a while."

Thomas looked at his list. "You really think we're going to need these long guns?"

"I don't know. Bring them anyway. And as much ammunition as you can carry. It's just a precaution, but nobody ever died from being too prepared."

He nodded. He liked that. "Did you tell Mrs. Peters that her lawyer fired us?"

"Not yet," I said. "We haven't really talked."

"I understand."

I didn't like the way he said that. "What's that supposed to mean?"

"She spent the night in your room?"

"And I slept in hers. Where's this going?"

"Your business, Caine, but sometimes it's difficult to remain objective when you're fucking the client." He looked away from me, watching the distant line of cars streaming toward Mexico. "If you're hired to protect her, it's even worse. Clouds your judgment. Slows your hand."

I started to open my mouth to protest, then closed it again. It could have gone that way. I was sure that was Claire's intent. But it hadn't.

"You are right," I said. "It is none of your business. So why bring it up?"

"I'm not like you, Caine. I don't have a quarter million in cash to carry around in a briefcase. I work for a living. This and my pension is all I've got."

"You'll get paid, Ed. Even if I have to pay you myself."

"Talk to the lady. I'll put you on my payroll this time."

"What is your problem?"

"I got to thinking about this whole thing after the shooting. Here I am involved in a little gang war, people getting shot right and left, and I don't have a contract with anybody. And the only person who has any money here is the target. It doesn't make good business sense. I mean, I guess you can afford to work for free if the client dies, but I can't. Now do you understand?"

"Sure. I'll talk to her. Get her a contract, the standard form. She'll hire you."

"Got one right here. Give it to her." He handed me a sealed envelope, the kind with the clear window for the addressee. I could see Claire's name and address typed on a form inside.

"Okay, Ed."

"I'm not like you, Caine. I can't take these kinds of cases just because it feels good. I'm no Don Quixote. I'm a mercenary."

23

I found Claire near the hotel pool on the sundeck, one level below the lobby. She was dressed in another cashmere sweat suit, a pink one this time, sprawled on a chaise longue, trying to catch some of the sun's warmth. Huge black sunglasses obscured her face. Her poise surprised me. Out in the open, surrounded by who knows what, after the previous night's events, I'd expected her to stay in her room as I'd requested. But she didn't. I had the feeling she would do as she pleased regardless of the circumstances.

She waved when she saw me. I went down the concrete steps, watching the railings and the entries.

"Everything okay?" she asked casually, as if she were on vacation instead of hiding from people who were trying to kill her. Even with two bodies in her living room, she seemed to have a sense of unreality about the danger she was in.

"Ready to move?"

"You got us a place." She had a cool, detached manner, with no hint of her earlier playfulness.

"My boat. It's at the San Diego Yacht Club. We can stay there at least a week."

She looked at me, another appraisal, her head tilted sideways, squinting into the sun. "I'm packed," she said. "I was just waiting for you. Juanita is upstairs in her room. Last night was hard on her."

"I know," I said. Claire told me she knew of Juanita's history. Having a shooting in one's home after something like that can shift the boundaries of how one defines security. For her, the big house on the hill in Point Loma had always been safe haven. Money, the money behind the house, that was safe, too. Although Juanita was not the owner of the house or the money, she was a part of it, and the safety extended to her. Now the house and her security had been violated. She had to come to grips with it in her own way.

Everybody needed security. And the thought led me to the other question: Ed Thomas's problem.

"Stevenson came to the house last night after we left," I said. Claire took off her sunglasses and looked at me again, squinting. "He gave Ed a letter, discharging me—and Ed and Farrell, all of us—from your service. I decided not to bother you with it last night, and you really weren't conscious this morning, but it's something that has to be dealt with. Something else that has to be dealt with."

"He fired you and you brought me here?"

"Yes. You are safe here."

"I understand that. You knew you had been fired? All of you? And still you risked your lives for me?"

"Sometimes it isn't about money," I said, wondering if maybe Thomas wasn't right again. "And sometimes it is. We don't take an oath to fight to the death. Ed is a little nervous. He'd like a contract. If you'll sign it."

"You said you wouldn't run away," she said, "if there was a reason to be here. You meant that."

"I did."

She leveled that stare at me again, the challenging one she'd first turned on me in the restaurant. "Do you have a copy of this contract Ed Thomas wants me to sign?"

I pulled it from the pocket of her husband's jacket. She glanced through it and signed it at the bottom. "I guess this means you don't want me communicating with Joe," she said.

"Not until this is over."

"You think he has something to do with it."

"I honestly don't know what to think."

"I understand why Thomas wanted that signed," she said. "And I don't blame him. In his shoes, I'd want the same thing. Why aren't you so interested in getting something on paper?"

"A contract is just words, Claire. It's only good if you don't trust the other party."

"Or if you don't think the other party is going to live long. So you can collect from her estate."

"Well . . ."

"Don't start bullshitting me now, John. I appreciate honest answers."

"Those are his feelings, Claire."

"But they're not yours."

"No, they're not. To him, this is strictly business."

She studied my face for a few moments. "There are implications there I find fascinating."

"Don't worry about me," I said, searching the surrounding deck. "It's my job to worry about you."

"That's all you're doing?"

"Sure. Let's get Juanita and get going."

"Can we stop at the airport?"

"Why?"

She looked at her watch. "Barbara's plane lands in an hour. She insisted after I told her what happened."

I shrugged. It wasn't unexpected that Claire would call her, nor was it a surprise that Barbara would come. It might even keep Claire off the phone.

"More the merrier," I said, surprising myself at the thrill of anticipation that went through me at the possibility of seeing the banker again.

We met Barbara at the Southwest terminal at Lindbergh Field. Dressed for traveling in Eddie Bauer's best, carrying a single bag, she seemed to bring the sun out from behind the clouds. Seeing her made me warm inside, a strange feeling I didn't recognize at first until it came back suddenly: happiness. I couldn't explain it. Feelings like that didn't need explanation. Under the circumstances, I sought none; they wouldn't be explored, either.

"Are you sure you're all right?" Barbara kept asking Claire. "Those men were sent to kill you?"

"That's what John said. And Ed Thomas. If it wasn't for Hatley, we'd all be dead now."

"Then we owe you and your associates a debt of gratitude," Barbara said, smiling at me the way I could get used to being smiled at.

I shook off that kind of thought. It could only fuzz my thinking, and with two fresh bodies in the picture, fuzzy thinking would inevitably lead to more.

"And how are you, John? You seem to be holding up after all that excitement."

"I wasn't there," I said. "It happened while I was in Mexico."

"Lucky for you," she said, winking. "I think Mr. Farrell handled things splendidly. You didn't need to be there."

"But . . ." I was about to say I wished I could have been there, and that was true, but admitting that in front of someone like Barbara seemed difficult. It was something most women would not understand.

"You were about to say you wished you had been, weren't you?"

"Yes."

"Can't blame you, considering what you are." She patted my cheek. "I'm sure you've had your chance."

I smiled, uncertain as to her reference. How much detail had Claire passed on during their conversation? I mentally shrugged, deciding it didn't much matter. We arrived at the yacht club and I took her bag and two of Claire's and led the way down to the boat.

"I've had my chance," I said. "Most likely will again."

"It wouldn't be right, a man like you, if you didn't regret not being there. Still, I'm happy you were in another country when it happened. And Mr. Farrell didn't need your help, now did he?"

"No. He's a legend, I'm told. One of the last of the great gunfighters."

She nodded. "I'm not surprised. It becomes you, you know. You're the kind of man a woman secretly wants to know. You're different than most other men, all animus, thoroughly existential and elemental. There aren't many men like you and Mr. Farrell and Ed—"

"That's for sure. Here's your bags," said Thomas, dropping the last load.

"Thanks, Ed," I said. "I was going to help, but got caught up in the conversation."

"Sure. You ladies need anything else? No? You're staying put, Caine? You're not going anywhere?"

I nodded.

"Then I'm going home. See you in the morning."

Ed went home and I spent the rest of the day getting Barbara, Juanita, and Claire settled and exploring my new boat.

It was strange to me, too. *Olympia* was new territory. I was her owner, yet I had no knowledge of her. I felt I was spending my wedding night with a chaperon. A crowd of chaperons. An association with a boat is similar to a relationship with a lover. You have to know her moods, her eccentricities. You need privacy with your lover to establish an intimacy. It's difficult, on that first night, to be with a lover if you share the bed with three other people.

That's what it was like, but we managed. I explored *Olympia* as well as I could while the others bedded down in their staterooms, staying up late to have my private time with her, exploring her hidden places, running my hand over smooth texture, letting my eyes rove wherever they wished. She was beautifully made.

I knew I had found a home.

24

"Are you sure you can get the address from your computer?" I asked. "Just by typing in the phone number?"

Adrian and I sat at the long table in Petersoft's conference room. We'd taken over the entire room, spreading papers and computer equipment over the table. I felt like an archaeologist invading a lost civilization. It was Saturday morning and corporate headquarters was vacant as a tomb. But some things were better. I was getting more cooperation than I'd received on my first visit.

"That's easy," said Adrian. "They're a database on CD-ROM. Give me the number and I can access the billing address and the party to whom it's billed. Or do it the other way, give me the address and I can give you the telephone number. It's based on Paul's relational database. Put the information in as lists, or, in this case, import existing data lists, and you can bring it up any way you want."

I'd finally gone through the material Adrian had given me, including the corporate phone-billing records. If I were looking into the background of anyone other than Peters, I'd have given up. The phones weren't identified to a specific workstation except for Peters's own private line. There were thousands of individual calls. Peters's private phone didn't go through the central computer, so it had a separate bill. Since he was the subject, I'd concentrated on his bills.

The number of calls was still voluminous. Adrian had agreed to meet me at the office to help me sort them out. He'd already eliminated the routine numbers of the company's suppliers and merchants. That left about eighty numbers that weren't identifiable. Quite a list, I thought.

"Tell me the number, I'll see if I can identify it."

I read the first one, area code first.

Adrian typed it into his laptop. "Taurus Industries," he read from the screen. "1443 Stanford Street, Denver, Colorado."

"What do they do?"

"I don't know, but it sounds familiar. They may have been trying to sell us something. How many times does it appear?"

"Twice more. That's all."

"That would be about right. I don't think there's anything to that one."

"Okay. Here's another one." I read him the number from the local 619 area code. It matched one of the numbers I'd found in his Day-Timer.

"It's a pet shop in North Park. I remember that. He was thinking about a puppy or something. It was supposed to be a surprise for Claire for Christmas. Then something happened, and he changed his mind."

We went through the list, one by one, until we came to the end. We had seven private residences we couldn't identify except as to name, and the names were unfamiliar to Adrian. That included four of the Day-Timer numbers.

"Thank you for coming in on Saturday," I said. "I'll run these down the old-fashioned way."

"Go knocking on doors?"

"Yep. It's the only way sometimes. But you've helped. This would have taken me weeks."

"No problem." He started packing his computer away. "Anything else you need, just call me. I owe you an apology, anyway."

"You don't have to."

"I didn't mean to be rude the other day. There was a lot going on. We've got this terrific new product and we're just that close to getting it on the market, but nobody will take us seriously. It's a combination of hardware and software, something new to the company, but we can't get it off the ground. Suppliers have been stiffed, so they won't give us any more credit. Production's in the toilet."

He closed and opened his fists, flexing his hands. "If we only had the money to operate, we could make much, much more. This is a winner. But we can't get anyone to talk to us."

I looked around the room. On the paneled walls were framed software packages Petersoft, Ltd., sold to the public, and commendations from various federal agencies for software sold to the government. Petersoft had been a going concern. Now this young man was trying to hold it together. He was even looking to the future.

"Just tell me," he said. "Are you going to get the money back from Paul? The rumor is he's still alive, that he ran away with the money."

"I don't know if there's any money left, and I don't know for sure that Paul has it. But I'll find him if he's still alive. It's what I do. And I'm good at it. People just don't disappear. They leave traces. Everywhere I go, I find tracks."

"You learn anything today?"

"About computers? Yes. I've never messed with them much before. That stuff's pretty handy. Will you show me how to get into it?"

"Sure. And if you think this stuff is good, wait until you get on the Net." He shook his head sadly. "If you don't come up with the money pretty fast, I'll have some heavy time on my hands." Adrian zipped the leather case around his laptop. It made a fairly small package. "I'll be happy to show you. I even think Paul's computer is still here. You want to look through it?"

"Sure."

"Come on. It should be in his office."

We went up the fire escape to the third floor and Adrian swore halfway up the stairs and started running. Alarmed, I followed.

"God damn it!"

"What is it?"

"I'm stupid! Paul had everything on his computer! He had a data management program that kept track of everything he did. It worked with his electronic Day-Timer! All the answers to your questions are in there!"

He unlocked the glass door and ran to Peters's desk. He opened all the drawers, but they were empty.

"Oh, shit. Those fucking feds must have taken it."

"IRS?"

"Whoever. When they were here. They must have taken his laptop."

I nodded. "Well, good try, but no loss. I've still got those addresses."

"What if the answer's not there?"

"We'll think of something else," I said, although I didn't know what.

"I'm calling those feds first thing Monday morning. I want that computer back."

"Don't lose sleep over it."

"They didn't leave a receipt. Aren't they supposed to leave a receipt?"

"You have a business card?"

"In my desk."

We jogged back down the stairs to his cubicle. His desk was piled high with papers, stacks leaning one way or the other. He rummaged through his pencil drawer. "I keep all my cards filed here." Business cards were in no particular order, just thrown into the drawer. He picked up a stack and looked through them. When he couldn't find what he was looking for, he tossed them onto the chaos on his desk and went for another one.

"Here," he said, after the fourth handful of cards. "I found it." He handed me a white card with blue printing. It said OFFICE OF AUDIT MANAGEMENT. The great seal of the United States and a Washington, D.C., address and telephone number and the name BRADLEY JACOBY, AUDITOR were also imprinted on the card. I'd never heard of the Office of Audit Management. I had my doubts whether there even was an Office of Audit Management. And I'd never heard of even the most grasping of bureaucrats failing to leave a receipt. I mean, it was one more piece of paper, wasn't it?

"Impressive. I'll bet if you call that number, you'll get the Agriculture Department, or some such. But they'll never have heard of the Office of Audit Management or Bradley Jacoby, Auditor."

"You saying it's a phony?"

"Yes."

"Then who was it?"

"Somebody like me, except smarter and a little more devious. Somebody looking for Paul Peters. And his missing seven million dollars."

Adrian suddenly snapped his fingers and said, "Phone Home."

"What?" I wondered if Adrian was having had delusions of *E.T.*

"Phone Home. All of the company laptops have the Phone Home program. Laptops are easily stolen. Leave it in your car, set it down in a busy restaurant or airport, look the other way for a heartbeat, and it's gone. These things cost nearly six thousand dollars apiece, the ones we use, and the deductible is way up, so we found this little program and loaded it in all the company laptops."

"What's it do?"

"The computer automatically calls the monitoring company once a week if it is hooked to a modem. If the telephone system has caller ID blocking, it turns it off, makes the call silently, without the modem noise, without turning on the computer, without alerting anybody. It tells the monitoring company where it is by identifying the telephone number it's using. Then it turns the caller ID blocking back on and shuts down."

"What will that do?"

"Identifies the phone number it's calling from. You just saw it. From that, we can get the exact address."

I liked the thought of that, kidnapped computers calling home, turning in their captors.

"I'll call the monitoring company. If whoever-it-is hooks up the modem, we'll know who has it for sure."

"I'll still use the old-fashioned method, if you don't mind."

"Go ahead. But if it takes more than three or four days, the computer will beat you."

"I'm used to it," I said. "Phone home. 'Help me! I've been kidnapped!' " I pictured a computer late at night sneaking its way through a darkened house to a telephone and whispering into the line. "I like that."

25

You might think that Saturday would be a good day to find people at home, but it wasn't proving to be the case. After days of rain, with unblemished blue skies and warmer temperatures, people were out of their homes, doing whatever it was that made their lives worth living.

I visited five of the seven addresses and found them occupied, but locked and empty, their residents taken leave in pursuit of happiness. Wherever they had gone, and whatever they pursued, their neighbors had evidently followed. Maybe it was a group thing. Five stops, five blanks. Like Schwarzenegger and MacArthur, I vowed to return.

The sixth stop, vacant, with a FOR LEASE sign on the door, was a split-level duplex in the Hillcrest district, an artsy-craftsy neighborhood of shops and restaurants and restored older buildings bordering the vast, green expanse of Balboa Park. According to Adrian's computer program, the departed tenant had been one Lorena Garcia.

The place interested me because there had been daily telephone calls to this address from Peters's private line beginning the December before he "died," sometimes three to four calls a day. There had also been a cellular phone number listed to TopProp, Inc., of San Diego, a now-defunct real estate investment company, with a similar frequency of calls. Pacific Bell had no forwarding number for TopProp. According to the young man at the telephone company, there was no forwarding number for Ms. Garcia, either. Adrian told me he had never heard of TopProp or Lorena Garcia.

The apartment above the Garcia place had a sundeck. Music boomed from an open door. I climbed the wooden stairs to the second level and introduced myself to the two young men sunning themselves on plush, padded chaise longues. They wore matching bikini briefs, their bodies glistening with oil.

"Good afternoon," I said.

"Are you here for the Jehovah's Witnesses? Because if you are, you're just wasting your time." The young man closer to the railing removed his sunglasses and peered up at me. "And ours."

"Maybe he's a Mormon," said his companion.

"No. They dress better. They always wear *ties.*"

"Yes. *Hideous* ones."

"I'm looking for the woman who lived downstairs," I said.

"Lorena? She's gone. Split."

"When was that?"

"Who are you, anyway?" asked the one who had removed his sunglasses. "And what happened to your face?"

"My name's John Caine. I'm a private detective." I didn't answer the second question, not knowing how these two would take the answer.

"You mean like Marlowe?"

"Or Spenser, with an S?"

"He couldn't be a private detective," said the first man. "He doesn't have the name of a seventeenth-century English poet."

"He's biblical, though. Didn't you hear? He's Cain?"

"Is that the mark of Cain?"

I took out my license and showed it to them. "Hawaii? Oh, like Magnum! I love Hawaii. Dig Me Beach at Ka'anapali and all that."

They were having fun at my expense and there was no harm in it. I stood there, enjoying the sun and the gentle breeze that flowed from the park onto their little sundeck, and waited them out.

"We went to Hawaii last year. It was marvelous!"

"My name's John."

"I'm Tim. This is Jim. Jim and Tim."

"Do you by chance know where Ms. Garcia moved to?"

"*Ms.* Garcia is it? You are so politically *correct,* aren't you?"

"Guess so," I said. "I was trying to be polite. Do you know where she is, or not?"

"You don't have to be snotty."

"Sorry."

"Now ask me again."

"Do you know where Ms. Garcia moved to?"

"No. She didn't tell us. She paid her rent right through to the end of the month, but she moved out early," said Tim.

"It was only a couple of days. You make it sound as if we got a whole *month* out of her," said Jim.

"Okay. But she was a good tenant. Never complained."

"She was never here."

"Even better," said Tim.

"Well, she was here," continued Jim, "but we never saw her. I think she worked out of her apartment. Something to do with real estate."

"Do you remember the company she worked for?"

"No," Tim said, "but she gave me a brochure once. I think it's in the kitchen mess drawer."

"I cleaned that out. If it was in there, I threw it away."

"Why would you do that? Now this man *needs* it."

"Somebody has to clean up around here. You never do."

"I'll go look." Tim got out of his chaise longue and padded into the kitchen. "I want another Snapple, anyway. Would you like something, Mr. Caine?"

"No, thank you. But if you could find that brochure, it would help."

"I'm looking, I'm looking." He disappeared inside, waving his arms. Jim and I stared at each other.

"You straights find us bizarre, don't you?"

"That's your goal, isn't it?"

"What do you mean by that?"

"I mean you no harm, you mean me no harm. We're all just getting by. You guys put on this outrageous act for me so I won't get too close."

He nodded. "That's about right."

"If I get too close, you're afraid I'll judge you."

"Won't you?"

I shook my head. "You don't know anything about me and I don't know anything about you, your character, your principles. How could I be judgmental?"

"I don't know. How could you?"

"Can't. And it's a waste of time, anyway."

"Like the Jehovah's Witnesses."

"Or the Mormons."

"No sense of style there."

"Cheap bicycles."

He laughed. "*Hideous* ties!"

"What are you guys doing?" Tim returned, some papers in his hand.

"Mr. Caine here and I are discussing philosophy and theology. We agree on almost everything," said Jim.

"What's the secret?" asked Tim. "Jim and I can't seem to agree on anything."

"That's because we're too close," Jim laughed. "Oh, we get so very close."

"I found the brochure. She was selling shares in resort properties. I don't know why I forgot that. Remember when we went to one of her presentations?"

"I do now. It was lame."

"It sounded good at first, but when Jim ran the numbers, it came up as a horrible investment. We politely told her thanks, but no thanks. You'd have to be a lunatic to invest in something like that." He handed me an expensive, glossy foldout for a Palm Desert Resort. It lauded the pleasures of condominium resort living.

"Thank you," I said.

"We own rental property here in San Diego," said Tim. "Where we can keep an eye on it. That's our retirement fund."

"There was something strange about this thing, too," said Jim. "Do you remember what it was?"

"I'm trying to recall. Other than the food, which was horrible. I know! All of the investors were men! There were no women. We were the only ones there who kind of stood out."

"Stood out?"

"The sales staff were all women. Lorena was just one of the salespeople. There were two or three others, and they only brought men."

"Yeah. We were the only ones there who weren't interested, if you know what I mean."

"No."

"They were using *sex* to sell the properties. We saw some vigorous sales techniques that night. It was a *seduction,* not a sales pitch. The salesgirls, if you'll pardon my lapse into the unpolitic, were more like hookers. It didn't take long for us to realize we'd been invited by mistake."

I looked on the back of the brochure. TopProp's name and address were printed on the back, along with another telephone number.

"Thanks, guys. I appreciate it."

"You didn't tell us why you're looking for Lorena. Did she do anything wrong?"

"I don't know," I said. "It depends on how far she went to make a sale, I guess."

26

The address, when I found it near the airport not far from the duplex, proved to be a strip mall private post office, a narrow little shop squeezed between a pizza parlor and a frame store.

The man behind the counter might have been a retired postal worker. He oozed officiousness and hostility.

"I don't talk about my customers," he told me in response to my first question, hairy, meaty forearms leaning against the counter. "You a cop?"

"No."

"Then fuck off."

I left. Before I did I glanced at TopProp's box number and saw edges of envelopes through the little glass window in its door. The box wasn't stuffed, as if it had been abandoned, but it looked full enough to tell me it was due a visit soon.

Since I didn't have any other leads, there was only one thing to do. After I cleared the final address, I'd stake out the postal store.

From the Range Rover I called the last telephone number and spoke with a Mrs. Sandoval. She remembered speaking with Paul Peters a year ago. She was a dog breeder in Linda Vista, and Mr. Peters had purchased a puppy from her and never picked it up. She later sent him a refund check, minus expenses, and she never heard from him again. Encouraged, I called the others on the list. They all were home, and they all had reasons why they had spoken to Peters.

One was a former employee of Petersoft, a programmer who had been laid off by the cuts after Peters's disappearance, and she wasn't amused by my call. She told me she hoped the company would go belly-up, just like its president.

That left only one lead from the telephone bills. And I was sitting on it.

I went into the pizza parlor, ordered a large pepperoni and a large iced tea to go, went back to the parking lot and watched the customers of the postal store. I'd parked far enough away that the owner couldn't see me from inside, yet close enough to watch the door. I didn't know what I was looking for, but I figured if I watched long enough, something would happen.

It was kind of a tenuous thread, but when you're desperate, a thread tends to look like a hawser.

Jim and Tim had provided me with a description of Lorena Garcia. She was, from their point of view, sensual and hot, a Latin lovely. Slim, with large breasts that were so improbable they shouted "surgical implants," as Tim had described them. She tended to dress conservatively. Jim said that meant she didn't decorate her dress with bottle caps. Tim said she dressed in a business suit during the day, and comfortable, stylish clothes after work. From Tim I got the idea of a classy, style-conscious lady. Claire's darker counterpart.

No one of that description arrived by six o'clock, when the store closed for the day. I started the Range Rover's engine when the last customer left and the owner locked the door.

Sundays, the postal store didn't open until eleven, so at dawn I ran south from the yacht club along Rosecrans Avenue, down the residential side all the way to the submarine base at the end. A uniformed guard stopped me for identification at the front gate, and when I took the chain from around my neck and handed my retired-officer's identification to him, he compared my clean-shaven photo with my bearded face, scrutinized me, made a decision, saluted, and allowed me to continue.

The road ran another two miles to the end of the peninsula. The submarine base lined the harbor side of Point Loma, stretching along the foot of the tan cliffs below residential property. I ran past the McDonald's and the little submariners' chapel to the officers' club at the end of the point, where San Diego's harbor meets the Pacific Ocean. I circled the club and then headed out at a leisurely jog.

There are no boomers in San Diego. This submarine base is home port to attack subs. I counted twelve at dockside, the largest number I'd ever seen together at one time. Must be a part of the peace dividend, I thought, or there just wasn't much for them to do anymore. I'd heard that Moscow had abandoned its missile boat program, and the rumors were that China didn't really have nuclear subs. Good. It wouldn't hurt my feelings if they all stayed in port.

I'd been a surface sailor, with an inbred mistrust of submarines. In my time in the SEALS I'd been a passenger in subs several times, but I never got used to it. It wasn't one of my favorite means of transportation. Still, I was glad we'd had ours.

I wasn't convinced we didn't need them, regardless of what the politicians said. Of course, it had been decades since I'd taken what any politician said about anything at face value.

From the headquarters building the road climbs into the hills before it drops back down to the gate. I hadn't run this road in twenty years, and I wasn't in the same shape I had been in twenty years before, but I could still make it to the top and puff down the other side. Old age wasn't creeping up on me too fast. From the summit I could almost see the yacht club where *Olympia* docked.

When I returned to my boat, I found Ed Thomas perched on the fantail, awaiting my return. He had a shotgun across his lap, partially covered by a colorful beach towel. He looked a little wired, but he was holding up.

He'd informed me the night before that the yacht club was too close to the house, and he felt uncomfortable about the placement of the boat. I went below and grabbed my jacket. When I returned topside I handed him the contract Claire had signed.

"That what you wanted?" I asked.

"Yes. Thank you."

"I might need your help," I said.

"Name it."

I told him about the audit, how it didn't sound like a real government investigation. I asked him to run down the agency and see if there really was a Bradley Jacoby or an Office of Audit Management.

When I went below again I found Barbara, Claire, and Juanita making breakfast from the stock of groceries Thomas had brought from the house. Claire gave me a quick smile, then turned back to her chores. Juanita smiled, showing me her gums. Barbara hugged me, then waved me off.

"You are all sweaty," she said, making a face.

"I get that way," I said. "Excuse me." I wove my way between the three women. On the way by, Claire handed me a glass of orange juice. There was a twinkle in her eye I hadn't seen before.

"It's good to see you are back, Juanita," I said.

"I've been here," she said. "Oh. Oh, that."

"Yeah. Oh, that."

After breakfast and a shower, I returned to my stakeout, cooped up in a car on one of those Southern California postcard days that lavished its beauty on others and wasted it on me. From ten minutes to eleven until after dusk, I sat and watched people come and go. None of them matched the woman's description.

When I returned to the boat, I could tell that my boarders were uncomfortable in their confinement. Barbara and Claire had played three sets of tennis, but had not left the yacht club. Thomas reported he'd had no luck trying to trace the Office of Audit Management. No one had ever heard of them. Likewise, his sources in the federal government had never heard of a Bradley Jacoby.

I took that as an answer and wondered if the laptop had phoned home yet.

I dispatched Ed to the house for a report from Farrell, and asked him to bring him over. Knowing we would be at risk, but feeling the risk was worth it, we all went to dinner at one of the Mexican restaurants in historic Old Town.

San Diego began in Old Town about the time Jefferson

and the others signed the Declaration of Independence. It was in Spanish hands then, an extension of Old Mexico. Some of the original buildings remained, now restored as restaurants. The entire district had the frantic feeling I felt in Waikiki, as if I knew I was supposed to have fun but I didn't know why.

We took advantage of the change of weather and sat outside, but close to the space heaters. The Mexican food was good; the margaritas were even better. I sipped mine and wondered where Paul Peters was, if he was anywhere, and where Lorena Garcia was and how she fit into the picture, and I wondered where the seven million dollars had gone, and if she had anything to do with it.

It seemed to fit. Claire told me she felt there was another woman. And when I had sat in Peters's executive chair at his abandoned desk, it was the only thing that seemed to make any sense. Yet even that wasn't enough of an explanation to warrant his behavior.

Yet, I reminded myself, we weren't talking about mental logic here. We were talking about penile logic. The two seldom have anything to do with one another.

What was that old joke? Why do we men name our penises? Because we hate having a stranger make all our decisions for us. In my life I'd been guilty of that a time or two, so I wasn't qualified to judge Peters.

Call it empathetic understanding.

Farrell reported he had mended the door and had started repairing the bullet holes in the plaster. By the time Claire and Juanita came home, the house would be patched and painted, good as new. He also planned to install permanent lights in the backyard, controlled by motion sensors and switches in both the master bedroom and the kitchen.

Claire took my arm as we strolled to the car behind Barbara and Juanita.

"You don't tell me what you're doing, but you seem to be doing a lot of it," she said.

"I'm watching a place. That's all. It's not much, but it might be something. And watching it takes all my time."

"I didn't want you to run away from me. I thought that's what you were doing."

"No. I'm just working."

"I spoke to Joe today. I told him that you weren't fired."

"When did you speak with him?"

"I called him today. From my cellular. It's digital. It can't be traced, and I didn't tell him where I was. I'm not stupid."

"I never thought you were," I said, relieved. "What did he say?"

"I told him you were hiding me, and although it didn't reflect on him, you didn't want him to know where because he didn't have a need to know. I told him I was safe and that if it turned out otherwise, I'd call him."

"And?"

"And he said many things. Most of the things he said were 'Where are you?' and 'What is Caine doing?' and the like. He pressured me. I had to remind him that he worked for me, not the other way around."

"And he accepted it?"

"I asked him how his investigation was going, the one with the ex–Treasury agent tracing the money. He told me he had some promising leads. I asked him what they were, and he said he couldn't tell me just yet."

"Have you received any bills from the ex–Treasury agent?"

"No."

"You probably won't."

"You think he's lying?"

"I don't know, Claire. I don't trust Stevenson."

"He said the same thing about you. You don't tell me what you're doing, either."

There was silence between us for a long moment. We reached the Range Rover and I unlocked it and helped her in. Barbara climbed into the backseat. Something in me wanted to reverse their positions, and I wondered where that came from.

"Do you trust Thomas? Do you trust Farrell?"

"Yes. Of course. Hatley saved my life."

"Then do you trust me?"

"I never said I didn't. I just said Joe doesn't trust you."

"Oh."

"You know, John Caine, for a smart man, you can be kind of stupid sometimes."

"I'm just another human being," I said, "crushed by my limitations."

27

The clouds came back the next morning, threatening rain, then fulfilled the threat and drenched San Diego again. After a perfect weekend, the start of the workweek heralded more days of downpour. According to my friend on the radio, it was the same storm that had soaked Seattle, then San Francisco, then Los Angeles. Now it was here.

I was back in the parking lot across from the pizza parlor. The rain provided good cover. I could watch, warm and dry in the Range Rover as people fled from their cars into the strip-mall shops. The only ones who went out were those with a mission. No one else would have wanted to brave the elements.

While waiting for something to happen, I did isometric exercises with the steering wheel and the dashboard. I don't know if they helped, but my arms and shoulders felt pumped. I'd also purloined a tennis ball from Claire's sports bag, left on the settee in *Olympia*'s lounge, and I squeezed it to pass the time. One hundred with the right hand, one hundred with the left, then switch again.

Squeezing tennis balls and pushing and pulling the steering wheel and listening to talk radio were about the only things I had to pass the time. I didn't want to eat more pizza. A caller to a local station wanted the National Guard to shoot illegal aliens as they crossed the border. Another guy wanted to plant land mines on our side. The host exhibited about the same amount of humanity, talking of tanks and troops to defend our borders as if the country were being invaded. I thought of the men and women and children I had seen huddled in the rain on the other side of the steel fence, waiting for the dark and a chance to cross to the promised land. In a way, it was an invasion of sorts. I also recalled the indiscriminate, impersonal, and deadly damage that land mines do. I was aware there was a problem here, but the locals seemed rather harsh, and I wondered how the new migrants affected them. I had no answers. I wondered if there were any answers.

I was on my sixty-third set of tennis-ball squeezes when a familiar figure parked a white Chevrolet Blazer two parking spaces away from the Range Rover. I recognized him immediately, although his presence came as a shock, instantly coalescing all my thoughts and suspicions into a single theory. Coincidence was an interesting idea, but I rejected it. The circle, if it was a circle, had nearly closed.

The young gangster who had broken bread with Stevenson, so many days before, the one I'd seen from across the street, the one whose dead eyes I'd never forget, got out of the Blazer and casually strolled across the parking lot as if it would be a sin against nature to acknowledge the rain. His stride was languid. The elements were there only for other people. They had no effect on him.

He reminded me of that old dog down in Baja, lolling along the roadside, ignoring the rain.

I remained poised behind the wheel, watching him enter the post-office store. He was there for only a few minutes before he came out again, shielding a stack of manila and white envelopes beneath his plaid overshirt.

When he climbed back into his Blazer and drove out of the parking lot, I followed.

There was a freeway on-ramp two blocks from the mail drop and he gunned the Blazer. The Range Rover had no trouble keeping up. I kept my lights off, the better to blend with the gray background. Traffic was light, but there were plenty of trucks and high-sided vehicles rolling, and I didn't think he could pick me out of the background even if he looked. We went south on the interstate through San Diego's downtown, then toward Mexico, which I assumed was his destination, until he turned off the freeway while passing through Chula Vista, a little border bedroom community that was almost, but not quite, rural.

I dropped back about a quarter mile because there was sparse traffic on the quiet country road, the Blazer barely visible in the rain, except for its taillights. When he braked and turned, it was easy to see, and I noted the road he had taken.

He had made it so easy I almost followed after him, but something in the layout of the surroundings made me drive by the intersection. It didn't look like a place where two cars could travel unnoticed, so I got cautious. As I passed, in my peripheral vision I saw the Blazer, parked, facing the road.

It pulled out and sped off, back the way we'd come. I watched him disappear in my rearview mirror as the highway dipped below the horizon.

Decision time. Was he aware that I had been following him? Or was this a standard precaution?

My hands and feet made the decision before my conscious thought, and I surprised myself when I turned off the road into a tract of new houses, a single urban block of two-story stucco dwellings sandwiched between muddy dairy fields and a cemetery. I turned the Range Rover around in the middle of the block and parked at the curb, facing the highway, mimicking the gangster's earlier maneuver.

I'd stopped in front of a house with tricycles and Big Wheels scattered across the front yard. Curtains parted at the big front window and two small faces peered at me through the rain.

I was doing the only thing I could do. If I turned and followed him, he would be certain to see me. If he was doing what I thought he was doing, he would double back again and I could pick him up once more. It was the lesser of two evils. Did I want him to discover my interest? Or was it better to lose him this time and go back to staking out the postal store in a different car and pick him up later? Next time use two or three cars linked by radios or cellulars. Do it right.

Down the block, the Blazer crossed my field of vision, traveling in its original direction. He'd doubled back. I pulled away from the curb.

If he thought he was being followed, he didn't act like it. This time he went in a beeline to a two-story apartment building in the old section of Chula Vista. Iron bars covered every window on the structure, even those high off the ground, and bars and wire mesh blocked entry to the interior courtyard. Black, green, and red graffiti crawled across the stucco, a spray-painted conversation of lasting importance and bewildering reason.

The gangster double-parked and went inside, showing no fear of parking tickets, car thieves, or arguments from the owners of the cars he blocked. I waited halfway down the street, next to a fire hydrant.

This was his lair. I felt it. I was willing to bet the two young men who died in Claire's home had been dispatched from this place. What connection this kid had with TopProp, or Lorena Garcia, or Teniente de la Peña, or Joseph Stevenson wasn't clear just yet, but it would be. What had been theory before was now fact. They were all related, one way or the other. And Paul Peters and his seven million dollars could not be far away.

An idea that had been floating in the back of my mind suddenly came to the surface. I reached for the telephone and punched in the numbers.

"Esparza."

"This is John Caine."

"How are you holding up?"

"Fine, thanks. I wondered if you could look something up for me. An old suicide, a closed case."

"How old and who?"

"Tyrone Crenshaw. He hanged himself in a downtown day-rate hotel several years ago."

"I know the guy. He was that running back the Chargers drafted the year they could really have used a running back. He started off great, then fell into coke and meth and heroin and whatever else he could sniff or shoot up or smoke. Went through almost a million dollars before he exploded. That one?"

"That's the one," I confirmed. "Could you let me see the file?"

"It's closed, so I don't think it would hurt. It's probably buried somewhere, but it'll be microfiched or scanned or something. When do you need it?"

"ASAP," I said. Down the street, the young gangster had come out of the building with three of his companions. They were getting in the Blazer. It was raining harder now, but each young man was taking great pains to ignore it.

"Come by later today. I'll see what I can do."

"Could you do one more thing for me?"

"Why not? You're not even a taxpayer in this state."

"Could you look up the owner of a building if I gave you the address?"

"Sure. Got any pants need pressing? Windows need washing? My wife takes in laundry. My cousin does odd jobs."

I gave him the address of the gang building. "This is related to your case," I said. The Blazer started from the curb. I waited for a passing pickup truck and then followed.

"What case?" Esparza asked.

"That homicide, and those two assassins at the Peters estate last week."

"That's not my case. What homicide?"

The Blazer blasted through a red light. Traffic was still insubstantial. I slowed, looked both ways, and went through, too.

"I have reason to believe that Paul Peters is still alive, or at least was alive after the coroner issued a death certificate. If that is true, then there's a presumption that he staged the explosion to clear his paperwork. If that was the case, then the body—if there really was a body, and the Mexican coroner says there was—could be a murder victim. That would make it a conspiracy to commit murder. And that's under your jurisdiction."

"Uh-huh," he said. "And who would this body have been?"

The Blazer got onto an on-ramp of another freeway, heading south.

"I don't know," I said, "but if I were you, I'd at least take a look at missing-person reports around the time of the explosion."

I followed the gangsters through raw agricultural land and onto the interstate. The freeway was on a raised berm, twenty feet or so above the fields; it was like traveling on a narrow island above a green sea. A yellow sign warned that the freeway would end in two and a half miles. There was a green sign ahead, but I couldn't read it yet. Traffic up ahead was slowing.

"How come you're so helpful all of a sudden?"

"That shooting the other night focused me," I said. "Now I'm following somebody who may make everything clear."

"Who're you following?"

I came upon the green sign and I smiled. Traffic had come to a near stop, just creeping along. I could see the barriers and the soldiers at the checkpoint ahead.

"Doesn't matter now, but remember when you said the next time I go into Mexico I'd better check in with you?"

"Yeah. Why?"

"I'll be there in about ninety seconds," I said, watching while two cars ahead, the white Chevy Blazer drove across the border into Tijuana.

28

Avenida Revolución bisects Tijuana the way a coroner's scalpel bisects a corpse. From the U.S. border to the foothills, Revolution Avenue runs through every neighborhood in the city. I followed the Blazer as it wandered through all of them.

Commercial and residential areas flowed together without pause, mixing interchangeably, becoming a homogenized conglomerate. Residential structures varied from squat, brightly hued concrete blocks to barely habitable hovels made of discarded lumber, glass, and cardboard. The shack communities spread from the road into the surrounding hills like a plague, with an order and organization that was truly unique. Winding lanes, too narrow for anything other than foot traffic, wandered away from the vehicle thoroughfare like lost children.

The concentration of shacks didn't thin as they reached the highest elevations; they stopped abruptly as the neighborhood changed from dirt poor to filthy rich. Hovels leaned against a walled estate near the top of the hill, its masonry integrated as a part of their structure. Every lot beyond that was spacious and fortified, the street resembling a crowded collection of tiny feudal castles.

I was on foreign soil now, so my natural caution increased a few notches. Not all the way to paranoia, but just below, closer to anxious fearfulness. That felt comfortable. It suited the circumstances.

Thankful for the rain, I dropped back even farther behind the Blazer. The rain made the afternoon darker. I kept my lights off, trying to be inconspicuous on the well-traveled streets of an alien nation. Even with my caution and precautions, I got caught off guard when the Blazer stopped in the middle of the street without signaling, angling off to one side. The maneuver forced me to stop behind it. The gangster had stopped at an intersection, near the entry gate of a corner house, positioned so that it was impossible to drive around him.

I shifted into reverse and glanced in the rearview mirror. No one blocked my way. I kept my foot on the brake. The occupants of the Blazer seemed oblivious of my presence.

A wrought-iron gate opened slowly near the front of the Chevy. When it was open, the Blazer drove inside the courtyard of the house. After a five-second delay, the gate closed again. I shifted back into first gear and drove on, not wanting to draw attention to the Range Rover, and found a parking spot around the corner.

I couldn't see the entry from the front seat, so I got out and walked to the opposite side of the street and stood against the wall. It wasn't a satisfactory position. Walls topped with shards of broken glass fronted every estate. No cover existed on either street. No portals existed to give me shelter from the elements. A lone pedestrian standing in the rain and watching a house was too conspicuous. No conceivable story could cover that circumstance other than the obvious. I returned to the Range Rover to think it over.

Another four-wheel-drive vehicle of similar coloring drove slowly past. The driver didn't even glance in my direction. That inspired me to reposition the car so I could see the entry. The Range Rover was natural camouflage in this kind of neighborhood, where a sixty-thousand-dollar truck was standard household equipment. I could be a friend of a neighbor, waiting for the occupant to return. I could be a family member from up *norte.* Any logical reason could explain my presence. As long as I didn't overstay my welcome.

Content that I was safe and dry, I found the tennis ball and a good Mexican music station and watched the entrance to the estate.

It didn't take long. The electric gate opened and the Chevy Blazer backed part of the way into the street. The young man whom I had seen first with Joseph Stevenson and then at the postal store in San Diego was at the wheel, and he seemed to be arguing with someone out of sight, in the courtyard behind the wall. Through the open window he gesticulated wildly, his face contorted and ugly.

I rolled my window down and strained to hear. The young man's voice carried across the street, despite the pounding of the rain. Though I couldn't make out any of his words, there was passion in his argument. He was not happy. Answering him, still out of sight, was the voice of a woman, a relatively young woman.

The Blazer jerked into the street. The woman followed from behind the wall, trailing along the driver's side. She looked to be pleading with the gangster, her hands opened in supplication.

She wore designer jeans and a loose cable-knit sweater, her long hair piled on top of her head like a disheveled turban. She filled the sweater and the jeans admirably. And she matched Tim and Jim's description of Lorena Garcia.

Whatever she said to the young man, it calmed him. He shook his head. She spoke to him again. He shook his head again, but it wasn't the same. The violence had fled from him.

He reached for her and she patted his hand. He shook his head and a smile crossed his face for the first time. The woman took his hand and tenderly kissed it, caressing her face with the fingers and palm. When his fingers brushed her lips, she kissed them, gently and individually. The young man's face softened, and the hand, which had been a fist, relaxed.

He said something I couldn't hear, and then rolled up his window. The woman's clothing had become wet and clung to her figure, the sweater molded against her breasts. Her hair had come undone and now lay limply down her back and across her shoulders.

The Blazer backed until it was clear of the sidewalk, straightened so it was pointing in the direction it had come, then took off, the tires spinning on the rain-soaked street.

The woman stood in the driveway watching the white car with the big chrome wheels until it disappeared down the hill toward the slums.

Wanting to get a good look at her face, I pulled from the curb and drove slowly past.

She turned just as I passed her driveway and walked toward the gate. It was disappointing that I couldn't see her face up close, but the rest of the view was wonderful.

I drove down the hill, no longer interested in the itinerary of the gangster. I had found something much more fascinating.

Some women are not quite beautiful and yet extraordinarily attractive to men. I don't know if it's pheromones, but I have noted that certain women who are not necessarily beautiful, but who have *it,* whatever *it* is, will almost always draw the attentions of men. Perhaps it is availability worn like an invisible poster. We can be drawn almost uncontrollably, as if hypnotized. And some women, no matter how good-looking, no matter how seductively dressed, cannot capture male attention no matter what they do. It might be chemistry, but I don't profess to know the specifics. All I know is that this one had it. Even in the rain. Even thirty feet away. Even after a public and passionate argument with a gangster. Even soaking wet.

Especially soaking wet.

If Paul Peters were to desert the lovely and intelligent Mrs. Peters, this one had the equipment, the chemistry, and the talent to force the issue.

The seduction reportedly occurred at Palm Desert, a winter resort where people from Southern California go to relax. A man alone, in a beautiful and romantic setting, might succumb to the seduction of a woman like Lorena Garcia if she were to focus her exclusive attentions on him. I could see how Paul Peters might fall victim to her charms.

But it would have only been a weekend thing, unworthy of throwing away a good marriage. Something else was at work here and I didn't know what it was.

It was still raining, but the day had turned out to be a fine one. I had a chain from Stevenson to a gang-banger to a cutout mail drop, and from there to the gang-banger again and hence to the girl. It wasn't exactly a full circle, but in my mind's eye I pictured Paul Peters as a planet, with all those people circling him like so many moons. There was a connection. There had to be. I would have to think on it.

At the bottom of the hill I pointed the Range Rover back toward the border, but not before I stopped and bought a hundred dollars' worth of Cohiba Esplendidos, eight inches of pure Cuban cigars.

That was five.

It had been a long time since I'd smoked a good cigar. The Cubans still made the finest, regardless of how they screwed up everything else on their little island. I lit one and smoked it as I drove. It helped me think. I was still smoking and thinking as I passed through the international border. I took the Esplendido out of my mouth to tell the customs officer that I had nothing to declare.

Well, that was true, as far as it went. I hadn't thought long enough to make any declaration worth mentioning.

But I knew I was on the right path.

29

The rain stopped and the clouds blew away, leaving behind a chilled but clear evening and the promise of a fair morning. Slanting sunlight reflected brightly off rain pools puddling the docks.

I sat on the stern rail of the *Olympia,* smoking my second Cuban cigar and thinking about my next move. It seemed a wasteful extravagance to smoke forty dollars' worth of Esplendidos in a single afternoon. On the other hand, it wasn't as if I'd never get a chance to buy another one. I knew I was going to pass that little tobacco shop tomorrow and every day after that until Lorena Garcia came out and I could follow her.

Following the woman seemed the only thing to do. I couldn't think of another angle. Anything else would be counterproductive. Stakeouts and tailing were my least favorite investigative techniques, but they were paying off in this case. Besides, how many of us, other than the Kennedys, ever get to do what we want all the time?

"Are you always this chummy?"

I turned. Behind me, Barbara Klein leaned against the cabin wall. She looked good, wearing a gray Banana Republic sweatshirt and Tommy Hilfigers. I had thought her hair was brown, but the afternoon sun caught highlights of red and auburn, and myriad colors in between.

"It's too crowded below," I said. "I needed air. And I needed to think. How are you holding up?"

"We get to play a lot of canasta," she said, a little ruefully. "I may never play canasta again, after this."

"Days get a little long when it rains," I said.

"You could say that. You're gone all the time. You don't know what it's like here."

I could picture it. Confinement is never attractive to an active person. But it was keeping them all alive.

"How's Claire?"

"Claire's starting to get on . . ." Barbara shook the hair from her eyes, covering an abrupt change of mind. "She's fine."

"How are you and she getting along with Ed?"

"He's distant, but that's just Ed, I think. He comes and goes. When he goes, Mr. Farrell is here. They never leave us alone. And Ed always has that shotgun with him."

"Two armed and dangerous grandfathers. Or great-grandfathers. I think Farrell has two or three great-grandchildren."

She shivered. "Yeah. The Over the Hill Gang."

"Not quite over the hill."

A flight of brown pelicans glided over the marina in V formation, wing tip to wing tip. They changed direction, riding unseen air currents, without apparent communication. I watched, fascinated. The last time I'd been here, brown pelicans were an endangered species, their eggs destroyed by pesticides. Now the big seabirds were common again along the coast. They must have done some prodigious mating while I was gone.

Good for them.

"Juanita seems better than when I got here," Barbara said. I nodded agreement. At dinner, the little housekeeper's smile had been back in place.

"She's getting over what happened at the house. I think she feels safe with you and Ed around, and she really likes Mr. Farrell. He treats her like a daughter."

I nodded. I'd noticed that, too.

"We're just bored, but we're not complaining. Still, I wonder when this will be over."

"I think it will be over soon," I said. "A week. No more."

Her eyes widened. "You mean that?"

"We're making progress." I had no absolute proof of

Lorena Garcia's participation. Only a feeling. Except that feeling buzzed like a bad transformer.

"You think you know where the money is?"

I shook my head. "Not even close. But I may be close to someone who does."

"I spoke with Joe today. He said Claire was just wasting her money hiring you. He was emphatic. He said Claire doesn't have much money left, the company isn't making any, and if the government seizes her assets, she won't have anything left at all."

"That true?"

She nodded. "She's fine for a while, unless they start taking her apart. And it could happen any time. If they do, she won't have anything to pay you with."

"Or him."

"He mentioned that, too."

"He ask where she is?"

"Uh-huh. I didn't tell him."

"Good."

She studied my face. "You have more than just one reason for saying that, don't you?"

"Yeah."

"And you don't want to tell me, do you?"

"No."

"No? Or not yet?"

"Not yet."

"I can live with that," she said. "It makes me trust you."

"Why?"

"You're protecting Claire from something. You can confide in me, you know, but if you don't feel comfortable with that, I understand. But I know that you're keeping your thoughts to yourself so you don't hurt anybody."

"Wow," I said. "You're good."

"You're protecting Claire because it's about Paul, and you don't want to hurt her any more than Paul already did. Isn't that it?"

I said nothing. I didn't need to.

"You've found the other woman, haven't you?"

I looked toward the entrance of the harbor where Point Loma met the Pacific. Someday soon I'd take *Olympia* out there and head home. I wished I could go right now.

"Aren't you glad this rain is finally over?" I asked.

She slugged me in the arm. "Okay," she said. "You've got your reasons. But you just confirmed what I already knew. And," she said, bringing her face close to mine, "what Claire already knows, too."

"I don't have anything," I said. "But I think I have a link with a woman who may or may not have been with Paul. It seems likely. I can't prove it. Not even to myself."

"And so you're watching her."

"And so I'm watching her. And there's something else. She may be tied to Claire's attorney."

"How do you know?"

"Wheels within wheels. They are all tied together somehow. I don't know how, but they are. I've got the end of a string and I'm pulling it until it all unravels. So far I found one end tied to Stevenson and one end tangled around a woman in Tijuana who fits the description of a woman in San Diego who might have been involved with Claire's husband. It's nothing, yet it's something." I was not going to tell her about the gang kid. I had no idea how he fit, and I didn't want to scare her. The implications of his presence after the shooting in Claire's living room were scary, even for me.

"That's what you've been doing? Following people?" She moved close to me. I found it pleasant, not something I wanted to avoid.

"That's all," I said, listening to my voice as if it belonged to someone else. "Sitting and watching and waiting for something to happen. And when it does, I follow to see where they go. It's not as interesting as canasta, but I get to listen to talk radio, and I get to see some interesting landscape I'd probably never see otherwise."

Barbara's hands closed on my forearms. I could almost feel her heat through the leather.

"And tomorrow," I continued, "I'm planting myself near

the woman's house. When she comes out, I'm going to follow her."

She stepped away and stared at me, giving me the hard look. "If you find the money, I don't want you to tell Stevenson."

"That never entered my mind," I said. In fact, I'd already thought to ask Ed Thomas for the name of another attorney. Maybe two, a tax attorney and one who sues other lawyers. Set one shark on another. Play a little game of "Let's You and Him Fight."

"I came up to see how you were. You seemed so distant during dinner, I thought something was wrong. I feel better now, after our talk. And I really needed the air, too. Claire was getting on my nerves."

"I thought you were friends."

"She can wear thin, even so. We're all confined in a tight space where personality conflicts magnify. Here, give me a hand." She climbed onto the transom and sat beside me, hooking her feet inside the railing. "Claire sometimes acts like a spoiled child. She's had it very good for a long, long time, and she expects that her money and her position will continue. She doesn't hear the pounding at the gate.

"She's in a position where she could lose everything. Claire's a tough woman. She's weathered this whole thing with Paul. She was the one who asked me to find somebody like you. I didn't force her. Yet, just before you got to the restaurant, she wanted to leave. Sometimes I think she really doesn't want to know the truth."

I nodded, but kept silent, listening intently.

"I've never trusted Stevenson. Now you tell me he might be involved. That would not surprise me, but it would Claire, and it would devastate her right now."

"How?"

Barbara shook her head. "I'm not supposed to know, but Claire and Stevenson had an affair about a year ago, about the time that Paul began distancing himself from her. It may have started earlier, but it continued until Paul's disappearance. Then they broke it off. Suddenly. I don't know which of them did it, but there was some pain.

"Don't you see? Every man she's been in contact with lately has betrayed her. First Paul, then Joe. And there's you."

"Me?"

"She told me about your relaxation technique the other night, your *Lomi Lomi* massage? And she told me you've turned her down twice now. That's a record for Claire. She's not used to it. You've become a target, Mr. Caine. The more you turn her down, the more attractive you become."

"I didn't do it for that reason."

"That may be true, but it doesn't change Claire."

"You don't know much about me," I told her softly, bordering on a subject I did not want to revisit, yet plunging ahead. Somehow, it was the right place and the right time and the right woman. "About a year ago I was in love. I lost my Kate a few months before Claire lost her husband. She's still with me, most nights. I don't think I could do Claire, or anybody else, any good until she leaves, you know?"

"I didn't know," she said.

"It's okay. It happened so fast, the love and then the death, there wasn't the time to enjoy the good before the bad took its place. I wasn't in the right place to help her, and when I was in the right place, it was the wrong time. Too little, too late, that was my curse."

"Claire said you'd offered to take her to Hawaii."

"That's right. Letting her down easy."

"She'll never go with you."

"I sincerely hope she doesn't," I said. "But if she wants to come, I've made the offer. It's up to her."

Barbara looked at me in a way I'd come to know: She cocked her head and stared when she didn't get the answer she expected, as if turning her head would bring her a new perspective, a different dimension of empathy. "It's up to her," she said, the sentence ending in a flat monotone, although it was a question and not the flat declarative statement it resembled.

"He said, hoping she will not take him up on it," I laughed, hoping she would get the joke.

"Claire's a good person. I'm not disloyal. But I thought I should warn you." Barbara's face was turned toward mine, our shoulders touching. I could feel her body heat through my jacket and her sweatshirt and it was a pleasant touch, something I had missed.

Then she leaned over and kissed me. I guess it was supposed to be a sisterly kind of kiss, but our mouths found each other and suddenly I was kissing and being kissed back by a healthy, passionate woman. It was the kind of kiss that makes your toes curl. She put her arms around me and I enfolded her into an embrace, her body molding its way into mine as if the molecules of her flesh knew exactly where they belonged.

We parted, breathless, and stared at each other.

"Wow," I said.

"Wow, too," she said.

"You'd better get below while you still can."

She nodded. "You think your Kate would approve?"

"I think so."

"So where does this leave us?"

"Nowhere. Until this thing is done."

"I thought you'd say that," she said, kissing me again, a gentle kiss this time, on the cheek above my beard. "You've got some white ones in there, Mister Caine," she said, running her fingertips through the bristled hair on my chin. It tingled where she touched me.

"I'm leaving tomorrow. Flying back to San Francisco. Got to go back to work. I just wanted to get to know you a little better."

"Did you succeed?"

She nodded. "Yeah. Better than I thought I would."

Then she went below again, leaving me alone in the last moments of the sunset.

I found my cigar. It had gone out. I dug around in my pockets until I found my lighter and set fire to it again, turning it all the way around until it was perfectly lit.

My God, Caine, I thought. You are one dim-witted bastard. Life just isn't long enough to turn down a woman like that. Under any circumstances. You'll be dead someday and then who'll know? Who will care?

But as I puffed away on the Cohiba Esplendido, the little voice in the back of my head told me that I would know when it was time. And in its way, it would be another betrayal of Claire. Not that I wanted to go to bed with her—well, that wasn't true, either, but I knew that wouldn't happen—but it would be, in essence, another betrayal, an insinuation between myself, her protector, and her best friend.

Better to stay aloof from the fray.

I had no one to answer to but myself. Sometimes it's hard.

And sometimes it's even harder.

This was one of the hardest of all.

I remained on deck until the sun slipped over the Point Loma peninsula and the evening breezes came up and chilled me, even through Paul Peters's leather jacket with the Thinsulate lining. I didn't go below until the cigar had burned all the way down, and I probably broke all sorts of environmental laws when I tossed the butt into San Diego Harbor.

In my life I've learned many lessons, but one stands out above all the others: Most of the time doing the right thing is a thankless chore, and all the time it's a monumental pain in the ass.

30

I crossed the border at five the next morning, full of purpose and hot coffee. When the sun rose two hours later, I was settled inside the Range Rover, parked at the curb between two other luxury cars about a hundred yards south of the estate. It looked different in the sunshine. The whole street looked better. What had been gray the day before was now vibrant. Even the walls were pretty. Vines and other tropicals covered some of them, giving the street a hanging-garden effect. I liked that. The greenery covered some of the broken glass.

No one bothered me. The street could have been populated, but I saw few people. In comparison to the crowded avenues of the poor, it was deserted.

It was purely a guess, but I thought the woman in the estate would come out this morning. The sky was blue after nearly a week of rain. Today was a day to play, or to work, if one worked.

It was a good guess. At eight-fifteen the electric gates opened. I started the Range Rover's engine and waited.

A blue BMW convertible, a Z3, the same model and color as the one from the James Bond film, backed out of the courtyard and headed north, down the hill toward Tijuana. I followed. As I passed the estate, the gates slowly closed. Before they shut all the way, I got another glimpse inside. All I could see were red Mexican paver tiles and white stucco walls.

I kept the Range Rover over a hundred yards back until we reached the high-traffic area. She turned on Revolución and followed it until she turned on Internacional, a four-lane highway that ran parallel with the border, the same road Esparza had taken. I remembered that it ran near the bullring and then turned south, where it became the toll road to Ensenada.

I kept close behind the Beemer, about three cars back, unconcerned that the driver could pick me out of traffic. Her car was low to the ground, and I was up high and could see over the top of the cars ahead. Traffic thinned after Rosarito Beach, however, so I gave her a longer lead. The blue convertible was easy to spot, even when it hit 180 kilometers per hour. Peters's car had no trouble keeping up and it felt good to let the Range Rover push its upper limits. After bumping along in second gear, it felt as good as stretching my legs.

I fell behind when we reached the coastal mountains, where the road twisted and turned through the narrow passes. Cliffs on the western edge of the road fell half a thousand feet to the Pacific below, giving me reason for caution that the young woman in the low two-seater didn't seem to have. When we came out of the last pass, she was long gone. I used the straightaway to try to catch her, but she had vanished.

When I reached the northern suburbs of Ensenada, I realized I'd lost her, so I turned around and headed north again. Logic dictated that she wouldn't travel faster than road conditions permitted. She didn't seem stupid. She must have turned off the road soon after leaving the mountains. With that in mind, I drove slowly, watching both sides of the road for a sign.

Three kilometers below the final pass I found it. It wasn't a sign from heaven, it was one that said RESORT TIME SHARE PROPERTIES. Under that, TOP PROPERTIES, S.A. stood out in bold red lettering. Parked behind a small stone building with a lot of glass and a waterfall artfully falling in front of the entry was the blue BMW roadster. I drove into the crushed-gravel lot, parked next to the Beemer, and got out.

I stretched my legs and put on my jacket. Then I thought about it and took it off and stowed it under the seat. If this was the woman Paul Peters had an affair with, she could recognize the jacket. I knew I had taken a chance with the Range Rover, but there are so many of them in Southern California it would not be remarkable to see another one the same color.

But if I came in wearing an expensive suede jacket the same cut and style and color that belonged to her former lover, she would know.

Shivering a little, I hurried to the front door. When I opened it, a little bell tinkled on a string, just like an old-fashioned general store you'd see in the movies.

She sat behind a big oak desk, looking through some paperwork, when I entered. When she glanced up and saw me, her face became radiant, as if I were her long-lost twin brother she hadn't seen since the womb. I don't know how she did it, but she also managed to convey the impression that she'd like to screw my legs off.

"Hello!" she said. "Welcome to Baja Dunes. I am Elena. How may I help you?" Her voice had a lilt and a slight inflection, the only trace of an accent. She wore a conservative business suit that modestly bared only a tiny portion of cleavage but made me wonder what she looked like unrestrained by cloth and latex. She was using a different name, but it was Lorena Garcia. It had to be. Once again Tim and Jim were correct in their reportage.

"I was out for a drive and saw your sign. You're selling time shares in a resort?"

"Come over here," she said, indicating a table in the middle of the room. That's what she said. Those were the words she used. It sounded like she really said, "Come over here and take off your clothes." "We have a scale model of the development."

I joined her at the table and saw a model of a blue glass harbor bordered by a green golf course in what looked like a ravine. On the tops of the hills surrounding the golf course and the harbor were tiny white structures, snaking along the natural shape of the hillside in sinuous curves.

Other, larger buildings surrounded by walls occupied the peninsula between the harbor and the ocean, estates with private gardens. Sand dunes ranged behind the condominiums and the golf course, sheltering the community from intrusion. She took pains to point that out. The community was private and isolated. Just the thing for the upwardly mobile.

"That's nice," I said, impressed. It was an excellent design.

"Here is the hotel," she said, pointing out the largest structure, straddling the south side of the sand spit, occupying the entire peninsula. "A big American company just bought that. They're planning on two hundred rooms. Not so big it would draw crowds, but big enough to help with the expense of the golf course and the harbor."

"Nice," I said.

"They will have, of course, two gourmet restaurants. We expect them to have a French chef and an internationally qualified sommelier."

"How nice," I said, starting to sound like a parrot with a limited vocabulary.

"Are you interested in a condominium or a detached house?"

"A condo would be nice," I said.

"On the beach or on the mountain?"

Those hills looked like the ones above my head. Hardly mountains. "I'd like the beach."

"You look like a beach guy," she said, as if that were the most peachy thing she'd ever heard. "This one's available." She pointed to an end unit near the harbor, quoted me a price, and told me what I would get for the money.

"Sounds like a good deal," I said. And it did. Almost too good. "When would it be ready?"

"Construction is going on now. We're dredging the harbor first." She flicked her lovely dark eyes toward the boom of a huge dredging barge looming in the middle of a lagoon behind us. There didn't appear to be much activity.

"Once that is finished, we will start the roads and the infrastructure."

"And how long will it take for construction?"

"About six months," she said.

It would take six months just to dredge a harbor the size of the one in the model. And that was if people were working. I looked outside. No one appeared to be there.

"Can I take a look around?"

"No. I am sorry. It's a construction site. Too dangerous."

"Okay. Do you have anything else to show me?"

"No. I am sorry. We shall be building the models soon. Perhaps you would like to come back?"

"Perhaps. Do you have a card?"

"Certainly, Mister . . ."

"Caine. John Caine. I'm just visiting, but I'd love to see it when it's complete."

She handed me a business card, but suddenly something in her manner turned ice-cold, like the mention of my name flicked her off like a switch. She knew my name. She'd heard it before.

"Thank you. Now if you will excuse me, Mr. Caine, I have some other appointments."

I looked around the sales office. It was vacant, but for the two of us.

"Okay, Ms. Garcia," I said.

"Gonzales."

"I beg your pardon." I looked at the card she had given me. It read Elena Gonzales, Sales Manager. "I can't read all that well without my glasses. I could have sworn it said Garcia."

"No," she said, carefully enunciating each word. "It doesn't. My name is Gonzales."

"Well, then, thank you."

"Have a nice day," she said. She didn't say it like she meant that, either.

I climbed back into the Range Rover and drove down the sandy road through some scrub trees and brush to a padlocked chain-link gate. The lock was rusty. So was the fence, which extended in both directions and appeared to enclose the entire harbor. What I could see of the dredging machine looked rusted and ill-used.

I turned around and headed back toward the Ensenada–Tijuana Highway. As I passed the big window of the sales office, I saw her at her desk. She was on the phone, speaking passionately, her free hand a closed fist.

31

An hour later I was ten feet down off the top of the ridge, just south of the harbor, lying in damp nettled scrub watching the activity below. There wasn't any.

The dredging machine floated on pontoon barges in the middle of a lagoon. Two areas of sandy beach on the north shore appeared to have been dredged a long time ago. New foliage grew along the edge of the sandpiles.

The lagoon, a shallow bay at the end of a long, wide river canyon with two black mesas off to the east, was one of those natural, brackish backwaters that exist at regular intervals along the California coast. Even though we are two countries, the geography has been here longer than the political entities and knows no boundaries. Geologically, the northern end of Baja California is identical to the southern end of California. This place could have been Carlsbad or Encinitas, or Malibu.

Tall stands of grass and reeds bordered the edges of the lagoon. Beyond that, the sand dunes went on up the beach for miles, disappearing into the coastal mist. Bare postage-stamp concrete slabs, nearly covered by encroaching dunes, sat back from the water. They were old, still bearing the pattern of vinyl asbestos tile, the remains of a fish camp. That and the ancient dredging machine were the only evidence of human habitation. Tall birds, snowy white egrets with long, graceful necks, waded in the shallows. Seagulls swooped in and out, going about their business in their loud, frenetic way.

A pleasant breeze flowed down from the mountains through the canyon. The sun felt warm against my back. I had the same feeling that Brigham Young must have had when he first saw the basin of the Great Salt Lake. This is the place.

When I was certain the place was deserted, I began moving down the hillside. Mindful of the sign at the border, I had no weapon other than my Buck knife. Aware of the existence of young men armed with submachine guns, I moved cautiously, the way they'd trained me so long ago. I didn't like the odds. And didn't old Sun-tzu say the best way to win a war is not to fight one in the first place? Having participated in more than a few wars myself, I was a firm believer in that kind of sentiment.

If only they would let me.

It took me half an hour to descend the hill in stealth. No one accosted me. Besides the birds, the only living thing I saw was a ground squirrel that stared at me briefly and fled chittering into the underbrush. When I reached the sandy dunes, I moved faster through the ravines, keeping my head below the ridge tops.

Up close, the old dredging machine looked even worse, covered with rust, missing cables and secondary booms, derelict. A vacant space existed where the engine should have been, the whole thing, as I suspected, a prop for the sales office back at the road.

I visited the concrete slabs. Partially covered by intruding sand, they were old, rusting anchor bolts protruding every foot or so, stained and chipped from decades of hard use. Once upon a time the place had been a fish camp. Someone must have purchased the property and torn down the shacks and built the sales office. They may even have had excellent intentions at first. But the enterprise somehow degenerated into a scam, just another way of extracting another Yankee dollar.

Was this all it was? Did Paul Peters sacrifice his company, and his marriage, and even his life, for this?

The lagoon was lovely with the bright, clear sky reflecting off its surface. From here the hills above did, indeed, look like mountains from the shore. Over the sand spit, the big blue Pacific Ocean stretched to infinity. The breeze I had felt on the hill also eddied across the lagoon, ruffling my hair. Although I preferred it the way it was, I could picture the possibilities. And I could see how someone could become addicted to the idea, especially when Lorena Garcia (or was it Elena Gonzales?) turned on the sexual heat. Add steamy sex to a beautiful setting and you might have a winner.

But that didn't answer the basic question. Peters was smart enough to have balanced an affair with his business and his marriage if that was what he wanted. He could have had it all. The sad truth is that many men do it. Why would he throw away everything, even to the extent of looting his personal and corporate accounts? His were the actions of hate, not love. He could not have ruined the people he loved any more thoroughly if that had been his stated intent.

The recent rains had washed the sand away from a corner of one of the slabs and I sat on it to think about the problem. After all those days under cold gray skies, the sun felt good on my face. I picked up some sand and ran it between my fingers.

Unless one is hopelessly mentally ill, there is logic to everyone's actions. That's the premise I was forced to use, but I couldn't see the logic here. If I knew the reason Paul Peters did what he did, I might deduce the wheres and the hows. I had the feeling I was in the middle of the answer, yet it somehow eluded me.

I felt I was pushing my luck, sitting out in the open. The peacefulness of the locale had lulled me into a false sense of security. I stood and started toward the ocean. Something solid just below the sand caught my toe and I sprawled across the old slab.

I got up on all fours and brushed the sand from whatever it was I'd tripped over. It was another slab, buried more deeply than the others, near the surface only because the sand had been washed away by the recent heavy rains. I brushed more sand away. It was newer, inexpertly finished. Why, I wondered, would anyone put a slab there, then bury it?

I removed my jacket and cleaned off the cement until I

had an outline. It looked like a cap slab, about four feet wide by five feet long, recently poured, the concrete still curing. The other slabs were more than fifty years old, but this one didn't belong.

It could have been a grave, but I tended to doubt it.

Then I knew.

I covered the slab again and took some reeds and brushed my handprints away. They would be gone in a day or so, anyway. This beach sand had the consistency of sugar and didn't accept much of an impression.

When I'd hidden the slab to my satisfaction, I retreated along my original route. I watched the Range Rover from cover to make sure there was no sign of anyone near it, not approaching until I was certain. Then I drove back to the highway and headed south.

In fifteen minutes I reached Ensenada. It took me another half hour to find a store that sold the tools I wanted. Within an hour, I was back at the beach.

Stripped to the waist, I worked for two solid hours. Even though the concrete was green and relatively soft, concrete is still concrete, and using hand tools is not the easiest way to get through twelve inches of the stuff. I was just thankful there were no rebars or mesh in the mix.

By the time I'd broken through, the sun was angled in the west, and I put my shirt and jacket back on, chilled by the cold wind that swept in off the sea.

Two metal footlockers, heavy and sodden, lay like buried treasure beneath the sand. I dragged them out, one by one, and carted them a hundred yards into the dunes and reburied them. The sun was nearly set by the time I finished, giving me only one last chance to triangulate the location with nearby monuments.

For added insurance, I paced off the position in two directions. The boxes were metal. If I couldn't remember, at least I could use a detector to find them. They were heavy, and had a lot of mass. It wouldn't be too difficult.

In the meantime, I was the only one in the world who knew where they were.

Satisfied, I returned to the lagoon and swept the area clean of my activity. When I finished, it was pitch-dark, and I had to feel my way up the mountain and down the other side to get to the Range Rover.

In an hour I arrived at the Otay Mesa border crossing, where a hefty young woman dressed like a forest ranger ordered me to pull into a covered area and wait until they searched the car. I was instructed not to use my cellular telephone. An armed guard watched me. I waited thirty minutes, watching the guard watching me. While I waited, I smoked one of the last of my Esplendidos.

When they did search, they opened everything, including the spare tire. Finally, they brought in a dog. When that didn't work, an older, gray-haired border guard took me into the station, where I was strip-searched. He looked like retirement was only a few months away. His eyes had that tired, used-up look, as if they had seen everything a pair of eyes could see in one lifetime.

Two men went through my belongings. When they went through my clothing, they found my remaining Cohiba in my jacket and confiscated it.

"It is a violation of federal law, Mr. Caine," said the gray-haired officer, "to bring products of the Republic of Cuba into this country."

He waited for an answer. I just looked at him.

"I have the authority to confiscate your vehicle, too."

I didn't say anything.

"What do you have to say for yourself?"

"Am I," I asked, "to be shot at dawn?"

"This is a very serious violation of the law."

"Yeah, and John Kennedy bought twelve hundred cases of Cuban cigars just before he ordered the ban."

"I've heard that before," he said tiredly. "Get dressed, Mr. Caine. Go home."

"Why did you do this?"

He shook his head. "I shouldn't tell you, but you've been had. We were waiting for you. Had a tip you were carrying drugs. It came from a normally reliable source." It was evident the gray-haired officer didn't like his job some of the time. Nobody does, when he discovers he's been used.

"Mexican law-enforcement officer?"

"No comment."

"Teniente José Enrique de la Peña?"

"He has something on you?"

"I annoyed him," I said.

"Then you better watch out. If you go back, you might just stay on that side of the border."

"Thank you," I said. "You're the second one to give me that same advice."

"If I were you," said the old border guard, "I'd take it."

32

The key to the whole mess was now in my hands and I didn't want to waste it. It was obvious that Lorena Garcia–Elena Gonzales or whoever told de la Peña about me and he had, once again, overreacted. To me, it was good news. I'd lost a cigar, but gained a clue. It confirmed the closing of the circle.

I punched the numbers on the car phone. It was dark, but not yet five o'clock, and I hoped people would still be working.

"Esparza."

"This is Caine, back from Mexico. Had no trouble until I got back to the good old USA." I described my detention.

"Border weenies apologize?"

"One guy did, his way."

"They stop us from time to time. Don't take it personally."

"They got a tip from a Mexican law-enforcement officer."

"De la Peña?"

"Apparently. Customs was waiting for me. Tore my car apart. Even got strip-searched. De la Peña told them I had dope."

"I can see why they'd want to search."

"You find out about that address?"

"I sure did. Property's owned by a Delaware Corporation. Stevenson and Stapleton handled the transaction. Their address was all over the paperwork at county records."

"Thank you. You know what that means?"

"I was certain you would tell me."

"Means Stevenson is in this."

"In what?"

"Tomorrow. Give me until tomorrow. Then I can tell you."

"Well, I don't really have anything else to do right now. The president's coming out here in a couple of weeks to press the flesh, so I've got eighteen or thirty Secret Service agents hanging off the edge of my desk, but that doesn't add much to my workload, plus I've got sixty or seventy other major crimes I'm working. I guess I can wait until tomorrow, considering I'm not working on this as a crime in the first place."

"Oh, it's a crime."

"Thanks."

"Think of it as job security."

"I worry about running out of things to do."

"I'll call you."

"I'll wait breathlessly."

I'd forgotten to ask about Tyrone Crenshaw, and Esparza hadn't volunteered the information. It would have to wait. I hung up and punched in a new set of numbers.

"Law offices of Stevenson and Stapleton. How may I direct your call?" The receptionist's voice, quiet and peaceful like an FM classical music station announcer, had a slight British accent. I wondered if it was real.

"This is John Caine. I'd like to speak with Mr. Stevenson."

"Would Mr. Stevenson know what this is regarding, Mr. Caine?"

"I doubt it," I said.

"I beg your pardon?"

"Our mutual client is Mrs. Claire Peters."

"Oh, certainly. One moment, please."

She put me on hold. I listened to Kenny Rogers for five seconds, an oldie, something from the seventies, bringing back pleasant memories that vanished when Stevenson picked up the line.

"I'll give you thirty seconds to tell me where you've got Claire Peters."

"That's not a professional way to open a conversation between colleagues."

"Caine! Where the hell are you?"

"Heading north on I-Five," I said, "approaching downtown."

"You kidnapped my client!"

"She's hiding. You know why."

There was silence on the line. I moved over a couple of lanes. The Balboa Park exit was getting closer.

"I'm not certain I like the implications of that remark."

"I'm not certain I give a shit. Like 'em or don't, it stands. I'm hiding Mrs. Peters from everyone. You, too, Joe, until I know who can be trusted and who cannot. You lied to me more than once. I'm not sure you can be trusted."

"That suggests I might have had something to do with the break-in. Am I included in your list of suspects?"

"Don't know. Can't take the risk."

There was more silence. He was thinking, digesting what I had said. The only thing he had now was my legal status. If he was involved, he'd bring that in. I took the freeway exit and went up the long, shallow grade toward Sixth Street.

"I fired you. You're no longer on this case."

"There's a licensed PI working for Mrs. Peters. I'm affiliated with him."

"I see."

"No, Joe, you don't. You're missing the obvious."

"And that is?"

"How is your ex–Treasury agent getting along? Has he found the money yet?"

"You are no longer involved. I cannot divulge information that belongs to my client. That would be unethical."

"Claire called you yesterday. She asked the same question."

"I refuse to discuss my client's situation with you."

"I'll bet he doesn't exist. Does he exist?"

"I'm hanging up. You should find your own attorney. You've gone too far."

"If you were going to hang up, you would have done it. And it's privileged communication, Counselor. You and me. Nothing actionable about that. You hired me to find the money. I did."

"What?"

"I found the money. Couldn't find the husband, but I found the money."

"You've got it?"

"Nope. But I know where it is."

"No!"

"Yep. And I know about you and your friends. What are you going to do now?"

More silence. He hadn't been prepared for this. I turned left on Sixth Street and drove down the hill into the grove of skyscrapers that was San Diego's financial district.

"I don't believe you."

"That so bad? The guy from out of town breaks the case in a week? You find that so hard to believe?"

"It's . . ." Miracles sometimes do happen. How often is it when a lawyer can't think of something to say?

I stopped in a yellow zone across from Stevenson's building, wedging the Range Rover between UPS and FedEx delivery vans. The brightly lit exit from the underground parking garage was about twenty yards south on the other side of the street, giving me an unobstructed view.

"You haven't been truthful with the police," I said. "You'll probably have a lot more to say once we've spoken with them."

"What do you mean?"

"Tyrone Crenshaw, for one. Remember him? Your old client? The police might want to reopen the case. Call it what it really was. Seems there was a sultry Latin lady seen coming out of his hotel room just before he committed suicide. The police couldn't put two and two together back then because they didn't have the whole picture. They will now. They may want to talk with you."

"That's absurd!"

"There may be a few more, too, depending on what they find. You've been a busy boy, Joey."

"You fantasize."

He hung up. Well, there are ways of learning things by hard work and sweat, and then there's the direct route, tell your subject what you believe to be the truth as if it were fact and see where it gets you. Of course, it's an all-or-nothing technique. It can be pretty embarrassing when you're wrong.

If I was wrong, Stevenson would stay in his office, make some phone calls, file some legal action against me, get a restraining order, drop the system on top of me like a hammer hitting an anvil. If I was wrong, that would be the right thing to do. If I was right, he would be coming out of the underground parking garage any time.

Norm had told me the other night that Stevenson drove a big gold Lexus sedan. There were a lot of luxury cars in the financial district, but few gold ones, and even fewer gold Lexus sedans. There was a chance I'd miss him, but it was the only thing I had and it seemed worth the effort.

Six minutes after he hung up, a top-of-the-line gold Lexus exited the building into Sixth Street and busted a red light heading south. I hadn't planned on that, so I pulled out, waited briefly for traffic to clear, and followed him across.

Satisfaction bloomed. It's good to be right once in a while.

I got close enough to confirm that it was the lawyer and drifted back again. No sense spooking him. So far my plan was working. I wished I knew where it was going from here. I hadn't thought that far ahead. I only knew that the more you stirred the muck, the more stuff floated to the surface. Stevenson, it seemed, was floating merrily along.

The Lexus got onto the southbound interstate toward Mexico, stayed on the freeway all the way to Chula Vista, and exited on a familiar off-ramp. It wasn't the smartest thing to do, but it was predictable. That helped, because I could follow at a discreet distance.

The gold sedan turned exactly where it was supposed to and stopped in front of the apartment where the gang-bangers lived. I remained at the end of the street and watched the lawyer get out and run to the gate. It was locked, the place deserted. He banged on the wrought-iron bars but no one answered. Shaking his head, he returned to his car.

I thought I heard the power locks engage from half a block away.

Stevenson gave me everything I needed to know. Somehow, Paul Peters had fallen victim to a honey trap. The attorney was the finger man. He would find the targets, even warehouse them as clients for years before siccing the lovely Latin lady on them. She was the bait. I didn't know how yet, but she wooed the target away from wife and family, getting him to cash out huge sums of money, betraying trust, responsibility, and wedding vows all at the same time. If the victim got out of line, there were the enforcers. How de la Peña fit into the picture, I didn't know, but since they worked both sides of the border, they would need protection in Mexico. I had seen de la Peña as the master of the play. Seen through a different lens now, he was only a minor player.

The lawyer held the other keys. He was the front man. He would know everything there was to know. There were two ways of getting that information. I could turn over what I knew to the police, they would question him with an attorney present, and he would deny everything and be released. The cops might or might not investigate further. I tended to doubt it. Stevenson would scream foul and sue everyone involved. It would accomplish nothing.

There was another way.

The Lexus passed me at a good rate of speed. I turned around and followed.

This time he led me to a place that used to be known as Logan Heights but nowadays the local paper hinted at a cultural change and referred to the area as Barrio Logan. On a narrow side street, Stevenson stopped at a wood-framed house that had been converted into a duplex. Three young black men sat on the front porch, one with a full cast on his right arm from wrist to shoulder. When he stood to talk to Stevenson, he was shorter in stature than his companions. I knew who he was.

I noted the address and wrote it down on a receipt I found in my pocket. The odds were that the lawyer owned this place, too.

The door opened and the junkie, the taller of the two thieves I'd thrown out of my room, came out and stood watching Stevenson as if he were an exhibit in the zoo. Well, what do you know? Reunion day.

Stevenson did the gang handshakes as if he were an honorary honky member. So he had a brown gang and a black one, too. Good to know multiculturalism had reached the criminal class. I guess he thought it was a boon to the community to spread opportunity around like that.

The lawyer conferred with the young men, reached into his coat, and handed one of them something that looked like folded bills. He repeated the fanciful handshakes and hurried to his car.

That presented me with a conundrum: Follow Stevenson or find out what the gangsters would do? I chose the gangbangers because they presented a more immediate danger.

I knew I could find the lawyer when I needed him.

33

Surveilling the gang was about as exciting as watching concrete harden. I expected them to go somewhere and do something after Stevenson left. They didn't. They kept busy sitting on the porch doing nothing. They were excellent at doing nothing. They elaborated on all the themes.

The longer I sat and watched them, the more conspicuous I became. A big, white, bearded honky in a new four-wheel-drive luxury car stood out in this neighborhood, and it wasn't long before I had a visitor.

He was polite. He used his knuckle to tap on the window.

I rolled it down.

"You a cop?" A big man in a clean white T-shirt and designer jeans. He wore no belt, didn't need one. He was about my age, but harder, his upper body sharply defined beneath the light cotton.

"No."

"What you want wit' those boys?"

"No offense, sir," I said, acting on instinct, "but is this any of your business?" He wasn't bracing me for sport. His demeanor was of a man who seriously wanted information. There was something paternalistic about him.

"This my neighborhood. It all be my business." He fixed me with a hard stare.

"I'm going to do this carefully, so you don't think I'm going for a weapon," I said, reaching into my jacket. I pulled out my Hawaii investigator's license and held it up so he could see it. He held out his hand but I shook my head. "Read it from there."

"You a cop."

"Not like that. Those boys are involved in a case I'm investigating. They've just made contact with a suspect I was following. The man paid them. I wanted to see what they would do for the money."

"You don't know what you doin', do you?"

"That's often the case."

He shook his head, as if he had just discovered a new strain of stupidity. "You know those boys?"

"I met two of them."

"You know those boys?"

"I know what they're about," I said, hoping he wouldn't repeat the question again.

"You know those boys," he said. "They be bad boys. They don't like you, just because you different."

"How," I asked, "am I different?"

"You white."

"Oh."

"You say you met two? Which two?"

"I gave the broken elbow to the short one."

"That was you? You that white tourist they tried to rob at the hotel?"

"You know about that?"

"Man, they tol' everybody. Course I know about that." He pointed to my forehead. "They give you that?"

"Yes."

"That all they do?"

"Yes."

"I bet they got lucky, getting that far with you. You look tough."

"I was surprised to see them," I said.

"They be more surprised, they see you."

"You think I should leave?"

"Let's you and me go talk wit' them."

"What?"

"Come on. This be my neighborhood. They respect me. They respect you a little, too, I think. Let's go talk wit' them. You can ask the questions you want."

"Who," I asked, "are you?"

"Name's Lucius, but everybody call me Lucifer."

"That's because . . ."

"Because I'm baaaad. Those boys, they won't hassle you, you wit' me."

I got out of the car. I was about to lock it, but I saw Lucius watching and smiling and decided that as long as I was under his flag, the Range Rover would be safe. If he decided I was no longer worthy of his protection, it wouldn't matter if I locked it or not.

"You smart man," he said. "You know things."

"Thank you, Lucius."

"Call me Lucifer."

"Not if my life depended on it."

He chuckled. "May come to that."

The four young men saw us coming and their postures changed to poses. I realized there was a certain amount of calculation going on. If Lucius was as bad as he said, they would want to impress, yet at the same time they would not want to appear weak. And then there was me.

They already knew everything they needed to know about me.

I saw the moment the little fireplug recognized me. His expression went unreadable, but he blinked, caught himself, and looked stonier.

"This be Caine," said Lucius. "He a private detective, come all the way from Hawaii to talk wit' you. What you boys done to make that happen?"

"We ain't done nothing, Lucifer," said one of the boys I didn't know. The taller of the two who had been in my hotel room stared, his mouth slack, as if trying to put me into some frame of context. The fireplug wore an expression that reminded me of a deer caught in headlights.

"Now he say he knows you, Tyrell."

"We met," Fireplug mumbled, looking at a crack in the sidewalk as if he wished he could squeeze down into it and disappear.

"This that man that break your arm?"

"Uh-huh."

"He pretty tough, fighting you and your brother."

"Uh-huh."

"You think you pretty tough, too?"

"Uh-huh."

"I think you pretty tough. I also think you pretty stupid. What you take money for?"

"I didn't take no money."

"From Joseph Stevenson. A lawyer," I added, my only contribution. Lucius glared at me. He didn't need my help.

"She-it, man. You take money from a honky lawyer?"

Fireplug didn't say anything. He stared at the sidewalk. Lucius grabbed him behind the neck and straightened his posture. "You take money from a honky lawyer? Huh? What you trying to do?"

"I didn't take no money."

"Empty your pockets!"

"Wha?"

"Empty your pockets! I wanna see what's in your pockets!"

"Oh, man, I—"

The punch didn't travel far, probably less than a foot, but it hit the boy on the point of his chin and laid him out on the grass. He didn't move. His immobilized arm lay on the sidewalk. I wasn't sure, but I thought his elbow hit the concrete when he fell.

"Anybody else want to tell me they didn't take no money from a honky lawyer?"

None of the boys responded. On closer inspection, I realized they *were* just boys, not yet out of their teens. The only time I'd seen any of them before had been a time of intense stress. You don't always make the best observations in times of intense stress. I started feeling a little guilty about the punishment I'd inflicted, until I felt the bump on my forehead.

Tyrell stirred. He opened his eyes.

"You gonna help me now?" Lucius stood over the kid, his body poised to help or to punish.

"Uh-huh."

Lucius extended his hand and hauled the boy to his feet. "Show me the money," he said. Tyrell complied. Lucius took the wad of bills and counted it. "There's a thousand dollars here. What that white man want you to do with a thousand dollars?"

When there was no response, Lucius closed his fist. The kid flinched. "He want us to burn a house down tonight."

"Ah, hell." Lucius looked at me, his expression bleak. "You know which house they gonna burn down?"

"Yes," I said. "They would all have been killed. The place is rigged with lights on motion sensors. There's a gunman staying there, a killer, not just a watchman. They never would have made it across the yard before he cut them down."

Lucius shook his head in disbelief, then turned back toward the four boys. "Why you wanna do that?"

"He paid us to do it, just like he paid us to go to this man's room and rob him."

"That didn't work out."

"Uh-uh."

"You think this would have worked out, too?"

"Don't know. He said the house was empty."

"He tell you this some old fat tourist?"

"Uh-huh."

"He wrong there, too. Tomorrow you be just another black criminal shot by a honky. You be in the papers. Your mama's gonna like that, you bein' dead and all." Lucius looked at me again. "You get what you want?"

I nodded. "More."

"You finished here?"

"Yes."

"I'll walk back to your car." He turned, stuffing the roll of bills into the back pocket of his jeans. "You boys stay put. I want to talk wit' you some more."

We went back to the Range Rover.

"Thank you," I said.

"Didn't do it for you. Did it for those boys. They not really bad. Oh, they bad enough, but they don't need to get any worse. This my neighborhood. Those my boys. Watched them grow up, watched their daddies leave and their mamas try an' cope. I stay. Been here all my life. Work two jobs.

Support my kids through college. Try to be the man in the neighborhood. It's too easy for those boys to be gang-bangers, dope dealers, do that shit. There ain't much else, as far as they know. But I know there is."

"You're a role model."

"I'm not much a role model, but it's me or the gang-bangers. You understand?"

I nodded. "Thank you again."

He shrugged. "One of these days those boys will get tired of me messin' up their fun. Probably shoot me. Then they'll have nobody lookin' after them. Just hope it's after I get my own kids out of here."

I offered my hand.

"Nah. Like I said. It wasn't for you." He put his hands in the pockets of his jeans and stepped away from the curb.

I drove away thinking that some people were luckier than they knew and hoping that the man at least got his wish. I didn't have much faith in the boys, but as long as they had Lucifer watching out for them, they might even make it. Someday they might shoot him, not knowing they were killing themselves as certain as they were killing him.

34

By the time I hit the freeway, I'd made the call and got what I needed. Stevenson's home was in an exclusive community in La Jolla on a mountain called Soledad, the neighborhood overlooking the Pacific coastline in both directions. Driving up Soledad Drive, I saw the dark expanse of Mission Bay, San Diego's recreational bay park, behind me, so big another city could fit inside its boundaries. Outlined in yellow lights, Mission Bay was huge. I remembered swimming across the bay at night as a young navy lieutenant. Sometimes I even swam the first two and a half miles of black water sober. I was always sober, swimming back.

Like those upper-class houses in Mexico, Stevenson's home was gated, surrounded by a high brick wall. Unlike the ones in Mexico, his wall wasn't topped by broken glass and razor wire. I parked the Range Rover at the curb and looked around. Like most exclusive neighborhoods, this one looked deserted, as if no one ever lived there, or even visited, like ground zero of a neutron bomb. I took a running leap at the wall and jumped over it.

I landed in a flower bed, crushing some tall green plants, and rolled onto a lawn. The grass was still damp from the rain and it smelled freshly cut. Stevenson's house stood about thirty feet from the wall. A pool reflected a yellow light on a stucco wall near the back of the lot. The hillside behind the house was steep and landscaped with ivy and short shrub trees, lighted by decorative paper lanterns. It was a party, without celebrants.

I crouched, waiting for the hue and cry that would follow any witness of my trespass. When none came, I went around the corner of the house. The big gold Lexus squatted in the driveway in front of the garage, its engine still ticking, cooling in place.

A pair of French doors opened to a solarium. They were unlocked, so I walked in.

I found Stevenson in his bedroom. He had a large leather suitcase opened on the bed, with suits and shirts scattered around the room on hangers.

"Going somewhere?"

Startled, Stevenson dropped the shirt in his hand as he saw me. "What are you doing here?"

"I ask myself that question every morning, and I just don't seem to get an intelligent answer."

Stevenson reached into a drawer in his nightstand and came up with a gun. He pointed it at my face, a Smith & Wesson Chief's Special, a little five-shot revolver favored by off-duty cops because it was so small and light.

"You're trespassing, Caine. Get out of here."

"You going to shoot me? I'm not armed."

"Got another one here." He gestured toward the nightstand. "It's registered to a dead man and reported stolen from his estate. I put it in your hand after I shoot you."

"Cute," I said. "I hate cute."

"You found the money."

"Yep," I said. "I know where it is."

"Where?"

"You know. You buried it."

"Buried it? Where?"

I shook my head. I'd told him too much. "No need to confirm what you already know. I'll get Claire's money back. That's why you hired me."

"If I knew where the money was, why would I hire you?"

Because you were told to, I thought. Because you would have been burned if you didn't. Perhaps because you knew you couldn't resist when Barbara and Claire forced you into it. "Why did you give a thousand dollars to a bunch of kids to burn down Claire's house?"

"Who said I did that?"

"The kids."

"That's a lie."

"Showed me the thousand. Kind of elaborate to make up a lie like that, just to frame a honky lawyer."

Stevenson shook his head. "It's a lie."

"Sure it is. These were the same kids you sent to my room to get me off the case. That didn't work. Still, we got a problem. I'm not leaving and you won't shoot me."

"I will."

We stood there looking at each other like two kids daring one another to fight. I'd pushed him into a corner but he held the gun and neither of us knew what to do next. I calculated the odds he might miss me with that short barrel. They weren't good. Three to one he'd hit me. I didn't like getting shot. It hurt.

The only thing I had going for me was his reluctance to shoot. I had to be careful not to push him too far. Until I had the gun.

"I'm not going to tell you again, Caine. Get out of my house." Stevenson shook the gun to emphasize his anger, the barrel pointing toward the bridge of my nose.

"Okay. But you'll have some explaining to do. I leave here, I call the cops. I've got you on arson for hire. Slam dunk. Then there's attempted murder, accessory to murder, a couple of other minor items. Then the bar association might be interested in your friends."

"Huh?"

"The Garcia woman. And her buddies, that Latino gang in Chula Vista. They live in your building. You stopped by there this afternoon but they weren't home."

"You followed me."

"It wasn't difficult. I've got the whole bunch of you. I just can't figure out what you were doing."

He shook his head again. "You can't leave now, Caine." He cocked the revolver.

I made sure I had my balance and could move when I needed to. Stevenson put both hands on the gun, aiming it straight-armed at my face. A .38 isn't a large caliber, but it's big enough. Six feet away and pointed at your head, the barrel looks enormous.

His hand shook as he pulled the trigger. I dove across the bed, rolling under the tongue of flame, landing on the balls of my feet. He fired again as I charged him. Something tugged at the collar of my jacket. I reached him as he fired the third bullet, kicked his feet out from under him, deflecting the gun with my elbow. Glass shattered in another room.

He still had the gun and the gun still had two rounds.

I stomped on his hand and the pistol went off again. The bullet ricocheted off a rock hearth and thumped into one of the pillows. Down feathers exploded over the bed, an indoor blizzard.

Stevenson still had the gun.

I broke his trigger finger and twisted the revolver away. He howled like a wounded animal and clubbed me on the head with his left hand. I saw stars. He clubbed at me again, his big fist curving in over my shoulder. I blocked his punch with my forearm. My whole arm went numb.

I kicked the revolver into the hall.

He hit me a one-two combination that jarred me to the soles of my feet. This guy knew how to box, even with a broken finger. He slammed me with two lefts, spaced so close together they felt like one big one, but I managed to turn my shoulder into them, protecting my face. I like getting hit in the face almost as much as I like getting shot.

"Joe," I said, breathing hard. "You're going to get hurt if you don't stop this."

His answer was a fast right-left-right-left that staggered me, driving me back against a bench. He hit me again with a solid right to my forehead and I fell backward over the bench.

He waited for me to get up, backing away to the center of the room, dancing on his toes like a prizefighter ordered back to his corner after a knockdown.

I couldn't believe it.

"One more time," I said, dragging myself to my feet. "Stop hitting me. You're ahead on points right now, but you don't know what you're getting into."

He came at me, faking a right, then a left, jabbing, faking, then committing himself to a big right.

I caught his arm, raised it toward the ceiling and turned so he was just behind me. Using my elbow, I broke a rib or two on his right side with a series of kites, then followed with another elbow kite to his right clavicle, shattering it. He fell to the floor and lay still, conscious, but not moving, immobilized by the pain.

My ears rang. There's nothing like a short-barreled pistol fired in an enclosed space to make your ears ring. My face felt hot and swollen.

I found the gun in the corridor, opened the chamber, and tilted it. One live round dropped into my palm, the other four empty shells remaining in the cylinder, expanded by their use.

I reloaded the remaining live cartridge and slipped the gun into the pocket of my leather jacket. It was mine now. Now that I knew Peters wasn't ever coming back.

A laptop computer in a black leather case lay on a table near the bathroom. I wondered briefly of its origins, then dismissed the thought. It didn't matter now.

A wayward round had broken the bathroom mirror, but there were enough pieces still glued to the wall to let me see my face. Under my beard my chin was raw and bleeding. My lip was cut. I had a mouse on my forehead that matched the cut from the edge of the door. In a day or so my face would look like a Technicolor nightmare. My arms would bruise up, too. I'd probably make small children cry for a couple of weeks. I was glad I wasn't young and movie-star handsome in the first place.

"Who is that other lawyer that fights? Shapiro? That O. J. defense guy? Is that what you fellows do in your spare time? Take boxing lessons?"

Stevenson was silent.

"You made a mistake when you backed off. You'd be tough to beat if there were rules. Just remember the only rule of street fighting. There are no rules." I bent over him, violating his space. He looked at me, pain etching permanent lines into his face. "You want to talk now?"

"No."

"Too bad. Now we talk."

"Need a doctor, Caine."

"Yeah, you do. You've got broken ribs and a broken collarbone. It hurts a lot, but those aren't serious injuries. That's why I broke them. You'll get over it, in time."

"Fuck you."

"What did you do with Paul Peters?"

Stevenson was silent.

"You know the alternative to doing this voluntarily?"

"You're going to call the police. I wish you would. You break into my house and—*aaaaaaaah!*" The big lawyer nearly leaped off the hardwood floor when I punched his shoulder. A jagged portion of the broken bone tented the skin, nearly penetrating it.

"Wrong. We don't call the police. I'll just sit here and play with the ends of your bones until you talk to me. Like this." I punched him again. It was more a slap than a punch, but it worked.

"No! No! *Aaaaaaaah!*"

"There's no Constitution here, Stevenson. I am not the police. I am not the courts. You've got no protection. You lost that when you pulled the trigger. I'm just the guy you're going to tell the truth to. We'll worry about rules of evidence later."

"You can't torture me!" He gasped, his breath coming hard. He'd lived his life in violation of society's rules, expecting protection under those same rules when caught. He was a lawyer. He knew the Byzantine labyrinth of the law, knew how to circumvent, delay, and prevent justice. He wasn't prepared for this. Even though he'd participated in years of violence, he wasn't prepared for me.

"This isn't torture," I assured him. "This is creative questioning. You don't have to hurt. You've got the control. Answer my question and nothing will happen. What did you do with Paul Peters?"

I reached for him, but he shrank away.

"He's dead!"

"I knew that," I said. "When? After Claire saw him in Calafia?"

"Yes. He had been hiding from us. He'd been having second thoughts and wanted to think it through. He hid the money. Nobody knew where it was. But after he saw Claire, he panicked and ran to Elena. He told her everything. Once she knew, she killed him. Or had him killed."

"Who killed him?"

"Her brother, Chico."

"Young kid, lives in your building in Chula Vista? That's her brother?"

"Yes. Of the seven million dollars, Peters gave us two million to start. He gave it to Elena, really. He thought they were going to start a new life together. It was a down payment."

He gasped, though I didn't touch him.

"Go on," I urged. "Tell me the rest."

"This isn't actionable. . . . You can't use any of this. . . ."

I raised my hand.

"Elena can get a man to do anything. Especially after she's gone to bed with him."

"Why?"

"She's, well . . . she's very well trained. She's also got herpes, and she tells them she's HIV positive, tells them she got it from a blood transfusion, some such story that makes her the victim. She can play the victim, let me tell you. She lets them know only after she's got them, tells them she just found out. She makes it a tragic romance. Just as she's found the love of her life, she's dying, and she's killing the only man she ever loved. She tells them she doesn't have any symptoms. They can't check, because it takes at least six months to show up once someone's infected. By then, it's over. She's got their money, and they're dead."

He clutched his side. "This hurts," he said.

I nodded. "It'll feel better in a week or so. Maybe two. Tell me more."

"Once she gets a man in this situation, he thinks he's dead.

He's a pariah. He can't go back to where he was, so then she loves him to death, keeps him from thinking about going back to his wife. Makes it impossible for him to go to bed with his wife again. She makes plans for their future together. Turns tragedy into a triumph."

"When did this start?"

"We thought it out years ago, after she came down with herpes," murmured Stevenson. Now that he started telling me, it was like he wanted to get it all out, confess the whole thing. Maybe the Catholics have it right. Confession is good for the soul, although it can also be detrimental to your health if you're not careful who you confess to.

"We had a similar thing going when she looked young, underage. It was a chicken trap. She played a teenage kid and seduced wealthy men. We had another partner then, her brother was too young. He would come in and discover them in the act. The target was always married, always successful, and always liquid enough to buy his way out of the problem. That's where I came in. They took it to their lawyer. I drew up the paperwork. Legal documents always scare people. They were good legal documents, too."

Stevenson almost smiled, proud of his craft.

"It never failed," he continued. "But it was small money. Then her partner died, and one of her targets gave her herpes. We never knew which one. About that time the AIDS scare came up. We knew we'd have to change direction."

"What happened to your old partner?"

"Died in a traffic accident. Chico took care of him when he started to get greedy. Her brother was coming up, too, and we didn't need the man anymore." His eyes were glassy, staring past me, looking at something a thousand yards distant.

"Since the mid-eighties?"

"Yeah. We've gone after the big money since then."

"How many?"

He shook his head, and winced, his face pale. Sweat ran down his cheeks. I felt his forehead. It was clammy. He was going into shock.

"Her victim doesn't know what hit him," he continued, the

words flowing as if he couldn't stop himself. "He can never sleep with his wife again. And he can never tell her. He believes he's dying. Elena made it seem like they would die together, a tragic couple facing life's cruelties. . . . Oh, shit!" Stevenson's face turned white as a wave of agony passed through him. He vomited.

Then he passed out.

35

I cleaned him up as well as I could so he wouldn't drown in his own fluids and then splashed water on him. That had no effect, so I looked in his medicine cabinet and found smelling salts. They did.

"You know where the money is?" I asked him when consciousness returned. It was time to focus on the problem.

"Buried."

"You know where?"

"Yeah. Me and Elena. We never told the boys. But you said you knew."

"I just took a wild guess and said that to see what you'd do. Where is Elena?"

"Don't know."

"Where were you going?"

"It's falling apart. I was getting out."

I considered that. It didn't make any sense. Trust a lawyer to lie. "Where does de la Peña fit?"

"He's the Mexican connection. We work both sides of the border. He protects us down there."

"That's all?"

"He's also enforcement, working with Chico."

"So he sent the two kids to Claire's house? To do what, clean the slate?"

"Yeah. He and Chico. After you snooped around with those San Diego cops, he thought you were onto him. He went around the bend. I gave you his number knowing he'd never talk to you. I never dreamed you'd get the San Diego cops involved."

"People underestimate me all the time," I said. "It's a gift."

"He sent the boys up to the house after you left. They were already in Chula Vista, waiting for the order. He'd already set that up when he found out a private detective was on the case, looking around. I didn't know about it. I didn't want Claire hurt."

"Nice to see you have ethics. Steal her money, kill her husband, ruin her company, destroy her life, but don't hurt her."

"Things just got carried away," said Stevenson.

"De la Peña was so hinky when I talked to him he didn't leave anything to the imagination. He sweated guilt." I remembered Ambrosio's reading of him on the way back from Ensenada.

"He's not bright," said Stevenson, gritting his teeth. "He's just powerful."

"That's a bad combination."

Stevenson grunted. "You know why I'm telling you all this?"

"Because nothing you say can be used against you?"

"No. Because right now Chico and the boys are after de la Peña. He's become a liability. He's a dead man, or soon will be. Once they get rid of him, they're going to dig up the money and vanish. It's too dangerous with him alive. If he knew where the money was, he'd kill all of us. That's why we never told him."

"What were your plans?"

"I'm joining them as soon as we get rid of you."

"You aren't going anywhere, Joe."

"Chico will be here soon. He'll take care of you, and then we'll head south to meet Elena. Once we dig up the money, we all vanish. There are places in Mexico and Central America that are lovely all year, where you can live like a king."

"That's your dream? That's why you kill people?"

"Well, it was more before, but it'll do now. You've limited my options."

I heard the front door open and pulled the revolver from my pocket.

"Chico! In here!" Stevenson shouted, then held his side as the force of the shout caused the ends of his broken ribs to rub together. The sound of footsteps echoed off hardwood floors.

"I'll see you, Caine." Stevenson smiled. "Don't send me a bill."

I saw a door near the bathroom and opened it. It led to a service corridor. Another door at the other end opened to the outside. I could see the lighted pool through a sidelight.

I ran through the hallway, crossed the backyard, and made it to the cover of trees on the steep slope at the back of the property and hugged the earth, facing the house. The little revolver with its single cartridge was next to useless, but it was something. I cursed myself for leaving the big Colt in my briefcase aboard *Olympia.* It wouldn't do me any good there. What was it I told Claire the first time I met her? Only people who made mistakes needed guns and I tried not to get into situations where guns were necessary? It sounded good at the time. Made me sound smug and smart and a little superior. Well, at least those who carried had their guns when they needed them and weren't hiding in the ivy in somebody's backyard armed only with a borrowed, nearly empty popgun.

Nothing happens the way you expect. The sound of four spaced gunshots came from the house. Then I heard the front door opening and closing and the wrought-iron gate slamming against the brick. A motor raced, tires chirped, and the sounds receded into the distance.

I approached the house, holding the little revolver in front of me. Nothing moved. No sound came from the house. I entered the way I'd exited and moved down the corridor to Stevenson's bedroom. I listened at the closed door for anything that might tell me someone was inside. I lay on the floor, cocked the gun, and pushed open the door until it swung wide.

Stevenson sprawled on his polished hardwood floor, his good left hand pointed toward me. He didn't move. I watched his chest, but there was no rise and fall. Keeping the gun aimed at his body, I got up and went into the bedroom to make sure.

He was dead. Four entry wounds circled his chest like a Catholic benediction. Father, Son, Holy Spirit. Amen.

Chico was cleaning house, getting rid of the nonessential members of the crew. Most likely he'd already shot de la Peña. It didn't matter to me. I wasn't building a case against these people and I didn't care if they lived or died. My job was getting the money back for Claire.

That would be Chico's next stop.

They'd dig it up and find it already gone. With Stevenson dead, they wouldn't know who took it or when. I smiled when I thought about it.

Sirens whined in the distance, coming closer. I wiped the revolver and put it in the lawyer's right hand.

Let the police chew on that one. Paraffin tests would show he had fired it. Slugs from the gun were all over the house. Let the cops figure out why it had been wiped clean of fingerprints. And let them wonder at his injuries.

I calmly walked through the front door and the gate, got into the Range Rover, and drove up the hill. There would be another route down Soledad, one the police couldn't block. In the dark it would be easy. I picked up the phone while I threaded the needle, looking for an avenue that would take me to the southbound interstate, toward Mexico.

36

"Thomas." We did not yet have a land line on the *Olympia.* The detective answered his cellular phone on the first ring.

"I've just left Stevenson's house. He's dead."

A profound silence greeted my statement. "Did you do it?" he finally asked, his voice flat and disapproving, the way he'd spoken when he didn't have a contract, when it bothered him that Claire had spent the night in my room.

"No."

"Farrell called. He told me the police just left Claire's house. They were looking for you."

It was too soon for anybody to make a connection between the lawyer's death and my presence at his house. "Why would they be looking for me?"

"Some official in Tijuana's been assassinated, a top cop down there. The Mexican police make you as the prime suspect."

De la Peña, I thought. It had to be de la Peña. Apparently Chico and his friends had taken care of their Mexican problem before going north to close out Stevenson's account. Thomas wasn't sympathetic to de la Peña, knowing his history, but he was a retired police officer, and cop killers weren't high on his list of favorite people, regardless of their motives.

I shook my head. This wasn't happening. Maybe I had fallen through the looking glass.

"I didn't do that one, either," I said. "Tell Farrell to be cautious. Stevenson paid a gang to torch Claire's house tonight.

It got shut off. I don't think they'll do it now, but there's an outside chance they'll follow through."

"You've been busy."

I was driving south, near the airport. An orange airliner floated above the freeway, lit up like a Christmas tree, flying so low I felt I could reach up and touch it, landing with roaring engines that overpowered the Range Rover's sound insulation as it passed overhead. The cluster of brightly lit office buildings stood beyond, a reminder of my first night in this city.

"Tell Claire it's almost over," I said, hoping I was right, deciding that I was. Regardless of what happened, she would be safe by morning. "Tell her she can go home tomorrow."

"How many more people are you going to kill tonight?"

"I didn't kill anybody, Ed. I don't expect to kill anybody, either." The qualifier wasn't lost on either of us. A totally innocent man would have said he won't kill anybody. I've never been that innocent. "Who were the cops that came to see Farrell? Did he know them?"

"They were your buddies, the ones who took you to Mexico. Sergeant Esparza and another Intelligence type. Esparza is steamed."

"If he thinks I did it, I can see why. He must think I used him."

"Uh-huh. Where are you?"

"Headed south on Interstate Five."

A stunned silence, interspersed by cellular crackle, was my only answer. "You're going back to Mexico?"

"That's where Claire's money is, Ed. Once I recover that, I'm coming home."

"The Mexican cops will kill you the moment they see you. You cross that border, you're dead."

"Why are they looking for me?"

"Turn on the radio. It's on the news. That *federal* you suspected? De la Peña? He was out walking his dog this evening. Somebody ran up behind him and put eight forty-five-caliber bullets in the back of his head and two more in his dog. An eyewitness put you at the scene. Described you, described the car you're driving, the jacket you're wearing. Either you did it, or you got a twin."

"It's a frame, Ed."

"Turn yourself in up here to the San Diego PD. That's the smart thing to do."

I thought I'd hidden the money well, but I wasn't certain. At best it would only slow them down. A thorough search might find traces of my passage. A metal detector would locate the footlockers buried below the sand. It wouldn't be difficult if they were motivated. And if five million American dollars was motivation enough to kill three or four people, it would be motivation to search a small beach. Thomas was right. The smart thing would be to turn myself over to the San Diego police and let the legal system straighten it out. In time I'd be released. I'd still have some explaining to do, but in time the truth would come out.

By then Elena and the boys would be gone. And maybe Claire's money, too.

"It's not smart," I told Thomas, "but it's the only thing I can do." That little voice I keep in the back of my head, the one who is smarter than I am, the one who tries to keep me on the right track and out of trouble, that little voice gave a big sigh and said, "Oh, shit."

"Stand by on this number, Ed. I may need your help later on."

"You're really going to go?"

"I found the money, but it's still there. I found those responsible. They're cleaning house, first de la Peña, then Stevenson. They're shutting down their operation. Shine a little light on them and they scurry, like cockroaches. I hid the money again, but it was only a temporary solution and if they really looked, they could find it. If they do that, Claire's in deep water and there's no way I can help her."

A California Highway Patrol car edged up beside me, gave me the once-over, and moved over, more interested in an old pickup truck with expired tags. His lights came on and the truck pulled over.

"Besides, remember what Frederick asked the boys at

Kolin? They were retreating as fast as their legs could carry them, away from an overwhelming force, and old Fred got in their way and asked them if they wanted to live forever?"

"What?"

A woman's voice said something behind him. I couldn't understand the words, but her tone was insistent. Ed Thomas answered, repeating the news of finding the money.

"It's the same question we used to ask ourselves in Vietnam. 'Hey, man, what the hell, you wanna live forever?' "

"You're a fool, Caine," said Thomas. "A ballsy fool, but still a fool." The woman's voice in the background asked questions, identifiable by rising inflections.

"It's one of those handicaps I've learned to live with," I said. "Stay tuned, Ed. It'll get done."

"There's somebody here who wants to speak with you."

"John?"

"I'm here."

"What is happening? Ed said you found the money but you don't have it."

I debated how much to say over the cellular airwaves. Even with digital, there's always someone listening in these days. "It's almost done, Claire. Just a couple of details to get right."

"Did you find the—"

"Did Paul ever speak of a real estate investment near Ensenada?"

"A little harbor down on the coast. Sand something. Baja Sand. Baja Sand Dunes. Baja Dunes!"

"Baja Dunes."

"That's where—"

"If something happens, take Ed and Hat and a metal detector. Check the beach directly in front of the first peak north of the harbor."

"But—"

"But nothing's going to happen. It'll be all right."

"Don't patronize me, John Caine. I know where it is. Should we come down?"

I liked the way she said 'we.' "No. Not yet. You may not like sitting and waiting, but this time it's best."

" 'Oink, oink,' said the pig."

"It's still too hot, Claire. If I fail, you've got the location."

"If you fail . . ."

"It'll get done."

"Good luck."

If what Thomas had said was accurate, I'd be better off getting rid of this car and getting another one. I couldn't rent. The San Diego police might be looking for me and they might have alerted all the rental agencies in town. Esparza would have figured it out and broadcast my identity on the American side of the border. The only question was whether he would share it with the Mexicans. If he really thought I'd killed de la Peña, he would. In a cocaine heartbeat.

They didn't have me by name in Mexico unless Esparza had told them after he ran the check. He'd been by the house. I wished I'd asked how long ago that had been.

One way to find out.

I punched in the numbers on the cell phone, watching the freeway signs. The border was less than five miles ahead.

"You have reached the office of—" I hung up on the voice-mail announcement. Sergeant Esparza was not in. I dug around in my wallet and found Ambrosio's business card. He had also given me a cellular number. I dialed it, hoping he had it close at hand.

"Ambrosio."

"This is Caine. Why is everyone looking for me?"

"Caine! Where the hell are you, man?"

"What's going on?"

"You know, Caine, you ask questions, and I ask questions, and then you ask questions again and nobody answers. It's better if you answer first."

"I don't think so," I said. "I just spoke with Thomas. Why are you looking for me?"

"Been to Mexico this afternoon?"

"You know I was there. I told Esparza before I went. Border patrol strip-searched me when I came back. Took my car apart looking for drugs. It's easy to check when I went either way."

"Did you go back?"

"No."

"Tijuana police want you for the murder of Teniente José Enrique de la Peña. We know he set you up for that border search. An hour or so after that, someone pops him. Somebody calls it in, tells the Tijuana police that a big blond, bearded gringo—just like you—ran up behind him on the street, caps him and his dog with a whole clip and a half, runs back and drives off. They all but name you."

"I didn't do it."

"Problem is, nobody knows where you were after you crossed the border. It's easy to turn around and head south again."

"It's a frame, Ambrosio. I need your help."

"I don't know that, Caine. I saw you once for what, maybe ten hours? You buy me lunch, tell me a bunch of stories, we take a ride together. You get us to introduce you to de la Peña. That's all I know about you. What you think, I'm some dumb, stupid Mexican?"

"Hey—"

"No. Hey, yourself! How do I know you're not some assassin, using us to ID your target? It's been done. Not to me, but it's been done."

"I haven't crossed the border yet, but I'm heading that way."

"It's better you come in here. Mexican cops, they'll shoot you down."

"I didn't do it."

"Doesn't matter. You're the one they'll shoot."

I had a perfect alibi for the de la Peña murder, except one witness was dead, a victim of another shooting, and the other was a gang of black youths, two of whom I'd beaten badly a week ago. That wasn't something I wanted to share with this police officer, who might feel compelled to do his job. Then there was Lucius, who might or might not speak up for me, a white man. The very act of sending the police onto his street, even to check out an alibi, might make Lucius angry. If he was angry, he would deny knowing me at all.

"Can I talk to Esparza?"

"Doesn't matter, Caine. He might shoot you himself, he's so pissed. Or he might turn you over to the Mexicans, let them use you for target practice. May not matter to him. He don't like being used any more than I do."

"Where's Esparza?"

"In Tijuana."

"Give me his cellular number. I want to talk to him."

"No can do, Caine. Better you come in here."

"Then I'll just have to do this on my own." I studied the road ahead. I had just passed the sign warning against firearms in Mexico, marking the final off-ramp before commitment. I drove past the off-ramp, toward the international gate and the unknown.

"Okay," I said to Ambrosio, feeling a pucker and a rush of adrenaline as I came up to the border and was waved through, watching the soldiers lounging against the barricades, their rifles slung. "Give my number to Esparza. Page him with it. Have him call me." I read off the Range Rover's telephone number and hit the END button.

37

Tijuana at night is like center ring of a gigantic circus. Wild patterns of neon, fluorescent, and incandescent lights cover every building on the main streets, money traps, designed to ensnare American dollars from across the line. From nightclubs to whorehouses, elegant restaurants to street vendors, anything is available for a fee, a fee considerably lower than could be found a few hundred yards to the north.

My stomach rumbled. It had been at least twelve hours since I'd eaten. Pungent food smells greeted me as I passed the street vendors and the restaurants, kick-starting an appetite and a hunger I hadn't recognized. Now it would have to wait.

I was going into battle. From my days in Vietnam, when the commanders offered steak and eggs before patrol, I'd eschewed the traditional meal before battle. I'd seen what happened to men with stomachs filled with food after a bullet sliced through the membranes. I'd always waited until I returned, even if it meant going hungry for days. The thought was that if I didn't return, I wouldn't need the meal, anyway.

If the Tijuana police were looking for me, they didn't show it. I passed two of their blue-and-white squad cars, the Range Rover receiving no more than a curious glance. Of course, I was headed into Mexico. The guards at the border, the ones watching those leaving the country, would be certain to have the description of the cop killer, alert to my departure.

The report had to be the work of the woman. Cagey like a fox, she missed few options. To Elena I was a loose end, something to be tied up before closing out the operation. If she could use me as a smoke screen for de la Peña's death, so much the better. I had to admire, even if I was on the receiving end of her vicious construct.

I transited the city without incident, not even getting a second glance from the police officers I passed. Esparza didn't call. Whether it was because the Range Rover's car phone wasn't compatible with the Tijuana cellular system or because he refused to converse with a suspected cop killer, I had no idea.

The first toll booth south of Tijuana is below the bullring, near the ocean. The attendant took my American money without pause, offering valid coin in change. The soldiers, ever present yet thankfully not vigilant, ignored me. I drove on.

In an hour I passed Baja Dunes, abandoned like a bad habit at a Baptist convention. As I drove by the empty sales office, my headlights exposed more tracks leading back into the dunes, toward the lagoon.

I turned off the paved road and drove down the sandy lane to the base of the mountain, parked the Range Rover under the same scrub tree, locked up and got out. I might never come back to it, regardless of how the night ended. The rich man's Jeep was a good, solid machine. It had served me well. Paul Peters must have hated leaving it. Just as he must have hated leaving his company, his houses, and his wife.

When my eyes adjusted to the dark, I started up the hill, fingering the Buck folding knife I always carried. That and my brain were my only weapons. Often it's been that way. In a life filled with opportunities for violence, I usually rejected the customary carrying of a gun. Oh, sure, I own one. I used to have more before they were swallowed by a hurricane along with the rest of my possessions.

I'd always figured I could sense when a gun was needed and kept it where I could get to it. This time was different. I was in an alien nation without authorization, and maybe a price on my head. I was in a country that regarded the private ownership of firearms, and particularly the old .45 ACP, the gun I favored, as an especially heinous crime, punishable by forty years in one of their penal institutions. With a charge for murder lodged against me, the man shot with a .45, I didn't want to risk having the gun with me if I were stopped.

I could have gone to the *Olympia* and retrieved the pistol, but I rejected that for a number of reasons. If the boat was under surveillance, I'd have other explanations to make to the law. The gun is registered to me anyway, easily traced back to its owner. If there was shooting to be done down here this night, I didn't want anything traced back to me.

I had the knife. That was enough. With the knife, and a little luck, I could get all the guns I needed.

I hoped a gun wouldn't be necessary. If I thought Elena's gang would give up the search and go away, I'd wait them out and pick up the money after they'd gone. That was the plan. The little voice inside my head mocked me, telling me it was a fool's game, echoing Thomas's sentiments. Elena and the boys had killed too many people to give up easily. They'd look, keep looking, find the tracks, and dig up the money. Then I'd have to stop them.

It didn't have to be that way, but that's the way I knew it was going to go. Unconsciously, I opened the Buck knife and felt its blade. Sharp enough to shave with, over thirty years old, it was one of the oldest Bucks made, the blade manufactured from the original case-hardened stainless steel that could cut half-inch bolts. The company changed the formula sometime in the seventies, went to a softer steel to meet consumer demand. Too many people complained the old knives took too long to sharpen. True. That was true. It did take a long time and a lot of sweat and skill to get one of the old Buck blades sharp, but once it had an edge, it kept it.

My Buck's been with me all my adult life, from Vietnam to Grenada, and after, traveling the world from Europe to Hong Kong. Its blade is short enough even the FAA thinks it isn't lethal. I fly with it, cross borders with it in my pocket, hand it to guards at security checks and have them cheerfully hand it back. Nobody gets upset over a pocketknife. It's an American tradition. But I'd killed with it before: dogs and snakes as well as people. I'm always armed.

When I reached the summit, I rested and watched. Two pair of truck headlights illuminated the corner of the slab where I'd stumbled onto Peters's secret. Covered by the night and the noise made by their work, I quickly descended the mountain on the same path I'd used earlier. Once in the dunes, I scurried toward the activity, careful not to be seen or heard. I found a patch of cover across the lagoon, providing concealment and a front-row seat.

I counted eight young men as they passed in and out of the headlights. I caught the moving orange glow of a cigarette inside the cab of one of the trucks, either Chico or Elena. From the frequency of trips the burning coal made up and down, I judged that the smoker was nervous.

One of the workers shouted. The truck door opened and Elena got out. She stalked forward, anticipation and anxiety focused in one small human being. The man who had shouted made room for her, gesturing toward the hole he had dug in the sand.

She bent down and picked up a chunk of concrete, one of the many small blocks I'd broken that afternoon. She threw it down, spitting out a vicious string of Spanish, insults spoken so fast I couldn't follow. The young man backed away, stung. She continued her condemnation, striking him with her small fists. He dropped his shovel and covered his face, allowing her to strike his body. She hit him until she tired. When she stopped, he peered at her from behind his hands and she roundhoused him with a good left, catching him behind the ear, knocking him down.

Every eye was attuned to the confrontation. I used the opportunity to get closer, skirting the edge of the lagoon, so I could hear their words.

"Fool!" Elena slapped the boy as he tried to get to his feet.

"I didn't know!"

"*Estúpido!* Who did this?" She looked at the group gathered around her, searching each face. No response greeted her question. The boys didn't even shrug.

"The only one who knew is dead. Did one of you take the money?"

Eight heads shook in unison. These young men had committed multiple murder over the last several hours. Now they looked like children caught with their hands in the cookie jar, confused and hurt at the unfairness of the accusation.

"Okay," she said. "Someone took the money. We'll look."

Elena issued orders in Spanish and English; apparently some of the gang spoke no English and others no Spanish. Elena was fluent in both, underscoring her undisputed leadership.

The one I knew as Chico, Elena's brother, spoke to her quietly. He had an Uzi slung over his shoulder and a big flashlight in his hand. When she nodded, he took two of the others and fanned out toward the west, toward me, searching the edge of the lagoon. I noted that the other two boys were similarly armed. A second group moved out, searching the east.

Chico may have been young, and he may have been a murderous criminal, and he may have had only a fuzzy idea what to do away from his mean streets, but he wasn't stupid. Elena was on the warpath. Getting away from her was the best thing to do.

Chico was also lucky. His group started toward my position, then shifted off to the south, beginning a grid search that would box me in if I didn't move. But if I did move, I would call attention to myself, or be caught in the other group's pattern.

With Chico and his people and the other group out searching for sign, only Elena and two of the gang remained with the trucks. Elena didn't look or act as if she were armed, and the other two young men didn't have anything showing, no long guns that I could see. They could have had pistols, but it didn't matter.

I closed in. This wasn't a part of my plan, but my plan was changing, shifting to meet the threat. They had forced the issue. Content to remain in place, I could have waited all night. Now they were searching for something, a sign, a mark, a trail. I'd done a pretty good job covering my tracks, but not perfect. If they were good, or if they were lucky, they'd find them. What I needed was a diversion.

I dodged one leg of Chico's patrol, slithering over a dune before one of the gangsters walked through the hollow I had occupied. I pressed myself to the sand, Buck knife in my hand, hoping he wouldn't see my tracks and follow. After a full minute I peered over the edge of the dune. The kid was gone.

I scrambled back over the top and followed.

This kid was a gang-banger, accustomed to city sidewalks and lights, not the uneven terrain of a dark, foreign beach. Like Chico, he didn't grasp the task at hand. Unlike Chico, he wasn't lucky.

He didn't hear me as I crept up behind him; he didn't feel the blow that felled him. It was almost too easy, the way we'd done it in training.

I let him live. He'd been no threat. I could have used the knife, but I wasn't in the mood for cold-blooded murder. I took his Uzi and the two extra magazines he kept in the hip pocket of his baggies. I didn't want to deal with him again, so I took his high-top shoelaces and tied him hand and foot like a roped goat. He had a bandanna and I stuffed it in his mouth and secured that around his head. To make certain his friends didn't find him too easily, I rolled him into an arroyo and covered him with brush and branches.

Sand clogged the breech of the Uzi. They're sturdy weapons, designed for desert warfare, but I didn't want the fatal embarrassment of discovering that it had jammed. I extended the steel buttstock and locked it in place. I had other plans for this gun.

The second gangster was just as easy. I found him standing near the ocean, his weapon slung. Both hands were at his crotch as he stood emptying his bladder, facing the ocean. A cold gentle breeze blew in off the sea, covering my approach.

"Hey!" I hissed.

He turned, urine still leaking, and I butt-stroked him. He collapsed and I caught him by the sling, gently lowering his body to the sand.

I'd hit him hard over the bridge of the nose, a little too hard. When I checked his vital signs, I found none. He was dead.

I shrugged. Anybody who pissed into the wind wasn't that high on the evolutionary scale, anyway.

Besides, he'd been a killer. Just because he was young didn't make a difference. The killers are getting younger every year, and less remorseful.

I checked his weapon. This one was clean. I dropped the first one I'd liberated, picked up his spare magazines, and loped off into the dunes.

Two down, six to go.

Plus Elena.

I'd never hit a woman before. Shot a few, but never hit one. Could I do it?

It didn't take much thought. I remembered Claire and the look on her face that first night, the accounting of her betrayal, her finding the courage to tell me the whole story as she knew it. I remembered the dead lawyer and his stories about Elena's voracious appetite for money, and her willingness to kill anyone or anything to get it.

Could I hit her? Could I hit a women?

Yeah. This one I could.

No problem.

38

Chico, the only remaining member of the southern patrol, wasn't difficult to find.

He was huffing along, shuffling his feet through the sand, so I heard him a long way off. At first I thought it was an animal in distress. Closer, when I could hear the sounds he made as he walked, I realized he was singing. Sort of. He mouthed tuneless, angry rap lyrics, miming those blasting into his ears from a micro-headset and CD player hanging on his belt. Only the rhythm betrayed its origin as music. Otherwise I would have thought him in pain.

Totally absorbed, Chico closed his eyes, planted his feet wide apart, and rendered a grand conclusion that might have impressed the late Tupac Shakur.

Until I hit him.

I took advantage of his distraction, rushed in and punched him hard over the solar plexus, about as hard as I've hit anyone in recent years, getting a lot of shoulder in the punch and considerable follow-through.

He doubled over, headphones falling to the sand.

I hit him again.

He fell over.

I made sure he was unconscious, then followed the headphone wire to the little pouch on his belt, found the CD player and turned it off, appreciating the silence once again.

A search of the little belt pouch turned up folding money, a Beretta .25 ACP automatic pistol with a full clip, an extra magazine for the pistol, Ford keys, and a plastic Baggie stuffed tight with marijuana. I tossed the pot and his Uzi into the lagoon.

He started to come to. The Beretta had a cartridge in the chamber, so I cocked it and held it to his head.

"Chico," I hissed.

"Wha?"

"Chico! You feel this?" I pressed the gun to his temple.

"Yeah."

"I've already killed the other two. You I need. But not very much. *Comprende?"*

"Yeah."

"Okay. I've got your Uzi, I've got your pistol. You and me, we're going for a ride. And you're going to be real quiet. *No tengo que enseñarle, no chapas malditas. Comprende, amigo?"*

"Stop with that Spanish shit, man. I speak English."

"Then you'll understand this. You do anything that calls attention to you and me and I shoot you. I can always get another hostage. I think your sister might not shoot you. Then again, she might."

"No."

"You bet your life on it?"

He was silent. I took that for thought. He could have gone to sleep.

"You with me, Chico?"

"Yeah."

"Okay. We're going back to the trucks. You got some keys here. Which truck belongs?"

"The white one."

I cuffed him across the face with the pistol, opening a gash on his cheek. He tried to raise his hand to feel the cut but I slashed the hand with the barrel. He winced when steel struck bone.

"They're both white, dickhead. Which one?"

"The one closest to the water," he said.

I looked. Of the two, the one closest to the water was farthest from our position. Nice.

"If you're wrong, *amigo,* you're dead. Better think on it. You get me in a world of hurt, I'll scatter your shit to the wind." For emphasis, I ground the barrel of the Beretta into the soft flesh over his temple.

"Ouch!"

"Shut up, Chico. I'll ask you once more. It's the last time, because we're going for it. Whichever truck you say, we'll take. If it's the wrong truck, it'll be a short night for you."

"The one near," he almost shouted. "That's mine."

"That's what I thought. Good boy. You finally got smart." I prodded him with the gun. He didn't take much prodding. "Take it easy. That's it. Nice and slow. I'll tell you when to run."

He had something more in him. I knew that. Chico was a natural born killer, like Billy the Kid or Charlie Manson. He wasn't about to give up this easily, no matter how hard I hit him. In some small ways he reminded me of me.

I counted on it.

He stayed with me until we got close to the trucks, then tried to shake me.

He'd had some training. *Some* training is dangerous.

He back-kicked where he thought my shin was, arcing his elbow backward simultaneously, aiming at my head. It was a good move, designed to cause pain and disorientation.

He fanned air.

I wasn't there, having felt him gear himself up for the move. I ducked out of the way as he reversed. When his elbow blew by me, I slammed into him, getting my forearms around his neck and squeezing, cutting off his circulation, blanking his brain. He instantly went limp. I scooped him up in a fireman carry and circled back toward the rear of the closest truck.

No one stopped us, because no one saw us. As I approached the truck, I saw the woman pacing the edge of the lagoon, nervously puffing another cigarette. The two gangsters who had stayed behind squatted in the lee of the truck's front bumper, trying to stay out of the chilling breeze, sharing a cigarette of their own. The syrupy sweet smell of marijuana wafted toward me in the cold evening air.

I needed Chico. I didn't want shooting. I wanted to divert them away from the beach. He was my ticket out. Elena wouldn't leave her brother, and she wouldn't shoot at him.

When the gang saw that one of their trucks was gone, they'd forget searching the beach for the money and chase me. Getting them away from the money was the reason for this exercise, after all. The disruption would change their plans and cause them some more pain. Once they were scattered, I could get Ed and Hatley to come down and retrieve the cash.

I edged to the driver's door, holding my breath.

I practiced a couple of times, going through it in my mind, making sure my footing was secure and my hands were where they should be, the key in my right hand. When I was comfortable with it, when my body felt as if it had performed the action a hundred times, I tossed Chico into the bed of the truck, opened the door, stuck the key in the ignition and turned it. The engine caught.

Cool relief flooded my body, an added mixture to the heated adrenaline flowing there.

I dropped the transmission into reverse and stomped the gas. The truck shuddered and shimmied backward into the night, crashing though scrub brush and small dunes, only the back-up lights illuminating my path.

I didn't like what I saw.

The truck bounced and nearly tipped. Chico's body rolled, catching on the wall at the last moment. I corrected, fighting the wheel, and braked, bringing the truck to a stop halfway up a big dune, listing at a thirty-degree angle. I felt around in the driver's compartment and found the four-wheel-drive lever, engaged it, and put the transmission into first gear.

Experimentally, I gave the Ford some gas. The wheels spun, then caught, and the truck moved forward. I turned on the lights, looking for a way out.

The windshield exploded, bullets and bits of glass rocketing through the cab, blowing out the rear window, piercing sheet metal, impacting in the seat beside me. I didn't have time to duck. I had my head turned, looking to the right. Something hit my ear, stinging. Glass, I thought. It had to be glass. A bullet would have gone right through and I wouldn't be thinking this. I wouldn't be thinking anything at all.

I ducked, too late, and pressed the pedal all the way to the floor, jerking the wheel to the right, sending the truck slaloming across one dune and behind another. I knew the road was somewhere ahead, but not certain how far. A second patrol searched the dunes. I was moving too fast for them to follow on foot, and they couldn't shoot at me if I kept the truck below the tops of the dunes.

It wasn't always possible. One arroyo ended and the truck churned up the end of the dune, nearly bottoming out at the crest, then fishtailed down the other side. Two or three bullets pounded the body as I hesitated, others vanishing harmlessly overhead, their passing marked by the distinctive sounds of angry bees.

A figure stepped out in front of the truck and leveled a gun, calling for me to stop. I swerved, hitting him solidly. He went down and both wheels went over him.

Suddenly the road was there, the double white sand tracks flashing in front of the truck's headlights, and then it was gone. I braked, backed up and found it again, straightened the front tires, and floored it.

Another figure aimed a long gun at the truck from the other side of the road. I ducked, but the round missed. His second shot came through the back of the cab, drilling through the fire wall, hitting something under the hood. The engine began making a screeching sound, as if it were mortally wounded. Red lights came on all over the panel, and the truck slowed perceptibly.

A third shot nicked me as it went by, numbing my right arm as it plowed into the dashboard.

Bright lights from the other truck came up over a rise behind me, moving faster, eating up the distance between us.

Something hammered the tailgate and the back of the cab. Something winked in the rearview mirror until the glass shattered, wanging off into the night. The engine chugged sluggishly, spiraling to a mechanical death. Smoke and fire licked from under the hood. Another burst of gunfire ripped into both rear tires and the truck sagged, then stopped, the fire intensifying, filling the cab with smoke, giving me some cover. I jumped out and ran into the brush along the side of the road.

Looking back toward the truck, I realized I'd made another mistake. Old Chico was having a hard ride, absorbing their bullets. I'd wanted him as a hostage to prevent shooting. Too late for that. Probably too late for Chico. His body slumped directly behind the driver's seat; it had shielded me from the incoming rounds.

Thanks, kid, I thought. You weren't good for much in this life, but in the end, you were good for something.

39

Flames reached the gas tank as I glanced back from the brushy slope. Burning debris blew high into the sky, lighting my patch of turf like an illuminating flare. My pursuers skidded to a halt fifty yards back, intimidated by the heat and fire. I kept running, circling back toward the beach. Doors slammed and eager footsteps followed.

I collided with the rifleman, bowling him over in the darkness. He'd been jogging toward me when we hit and the top of his head struck my chin. Shooting stars, as bright and as colorful as the truck explosion, caromed off the inside of my skull. Blood filled my mouth. I started to get up when somebody hit me hard from behind and the shooting stars found a way out through the hole in the top of my head. When they went away, only darkness remained.

My concussion was a kind where I could hear everything around me and was convinced I would have seen, too, had I the energy to open my eyes. But I was comfortable lying on the sand while blood and whatever else leaked from my skull, and I didn't want to move. I was aware of a group surrounding me, and somebody trying to bring me back. It surprised me that they didn't kill me immediately. Then I remembered why they wanted to wake me up. I knew something they wanted to know. And I was supposed to tell them.

Someone slapped my face.

"Caine. Wake up."

"Yama. Frazzit. Grrrrz." I tried talking to them but the words didn't sound right.

"Caine!"

"Funkzit."

"You hit him too hard!" I recognized Elena's voice.

"He'll come to. He's trying to talk."

"Filuper dup."

"Pour some water on him. I want that money."

"Muh-neee," I said.

Someone grabbed the front of my shirt, twisting it up under my chin. "Yeah, money," Elena said, her mouth near my ear like a lover, so close I could feel the moisture of her breath on my earlobe. "My money. Where is it?"

"Mo-ney," I repeated, marveling at the contours of the word and how my tongue worked with my lips and the top of my mouth to form the syllables.

She hit me hard, grinding a sandy fist into tender tissues near my eye. She straddled me, her skirt hiked to her waist, velvet thighs gripping my arms.

"Buried it," I managed to gasp, trying to save something.

"Where?"

"Can't tell you," I said, risking another pummeling. "Have to show you."

Her weight disappeared. "Pick him up!"

I opened my eyes. Boys sat on my arms, pinning each limb to the ground with a fierce energy. I felt like Gulliver. Another youth stood three meters in front of me, aiming a rifle at my head. Blood coursed down the front of his face from a gash near his hairline. That would be the marksman. He wore the blood like a badge of honor, letting it flow. The kid was tough, and he wanted the others to know just how tough he was.

"Put him in the truck."

They led me to the back of their pickup and covered me as I got in, treating me as if I were one of those dangerous jungle cats that would, if allowed, turn on them and rip them to pieces. The boy with the rifle slung it and produced a pistol, a .45, similar to my Gold Cup. He cocked it and aimed it at my face. I had no doubt he'd shoot me if I moved. He may have been young, but he was as deadly as a cobra.

"Where is my brother?" Elena demanded, her face a mix of fury and fear.

"I don't know," I replied. And it was true. Perhaps he was in hell. Her question told me she had not checked the wreckage, still burning brightly on the road behind us.

"He has not come back. Others are missing. What did you do?"

"Nothing." I had no problem lying to her. If she knew the truth, my life span would be shortened to microseconds.

She ordered two of the youths to go search for the missing members of their team. That limited my time. They would find the dead boy and raise the alarm. The still-burning truck would prevent their finding Chico, but only for a short time.

"*Ándale.* Let's go." Elena got into the driver's side and the others piled in the back, surrounding me. She drove like Mr. Toad, hitting every rut, bump, and pothole until we reached the lagoon. When the truck stopped, they hauled me out of the back, still under the close supervision of the kid with the high-powered rifle.

My head started to clear, but things still looked black and fuzzy around the edges as they marched me to the beach. I stumbled in a shallow hole and got a rifle stock in the kidneys for my carelessness. The butt stroke drove me to my knees and I put my hands out to catch my fall. Someone kicked my arms out from under me and I landed on my face. A quick learner, I remained on the ground.

"*Cuidado,*" Elena said. The little marksman had a talent for inflicting pain and no reluctance to use it.

"Hold him," she said. Hands grabbed me and pulled my arms apart. The rifleman stood three meters away, off to my right, but in position to shoot me and miss his companions.

"Here is the beach, Mr. Caine. Where is it?"

"Near the lagoon. At the sandbar."

"You have to show me. That's what you said."

"Can't show you from down here," I mumbled into the sand surrounding my mouth.

"Stand him up!"

The two boys helped me to my feet. I was careful not to stumble, and I watched the muzzle of the rifle all the way.

"Now, where is it?"

"This way," I said, leaning toward the lagoon, one boy giving ground, the other pulling back, both off balance. I noted the rifle barrel tracking my movement.

"Are you certain?"

With the rifle's point of aim dead between my eyes, I figured his reaction time would beat my ability to move out of the bullet's path. He was too far away, and his attention too keen. The two boys holding my arms would slow, but not stop me from breaking free. Only the rifleman kept me still.

"It's dark, but I think this is the place."

"If you make a mistake, other measures will ensure that you tell me." Elena searched my face and must have found evasion there, because she hit me, her fist balled, punching me right in the nose. It hurt, but she held her hand, squeezing the pain away with her left. "Asshole!" she screamed, and kicked me high on the inside of my thigh. "Hold him!"

The two youths holding my arms were unsure what to do as she continued beating me with her fists and kicking me with her hard leather shoes. I backed up and they retreated with me, a step at a time, as I tried evading the blows with my body.

I also tried keeping the rifleman in sight, but that was even harder with one eye closed, clotted with blood, and the other taking a pounding. When I spotted him, I noticed that he moved with us, trying to keep a bead on me while missing Elena. Because of her passionate animation, she stayed close and it seemed that he might not shoot, fearful of hitting her. It was a chance, slim, but still a chance, and I took the abuse and watched for an opening. The kid with the rifle didn't give me much.

The rhythm of Elena's fists started to slow, no longer a staccato drumming. It's hard work, hitting people for any length of time. That's why boxers train so long and so hard. That's why they train aerobically. Going fifteen rounds can be grueling. When she'd pounded me for two or three minutes, she stopped and stared, her chest heaving. One round and this lady was winded. The marksman raised the rifle to his shoulder when she stepped away, aiming at my head.

"Where is the money?" she demanded.

"In the sand."

She beat me again, this time with a renewed violence that was surprising in its vehemence. I took it, wondering which of us would last longer.

I leaned against the boy on my right, absorbing a vicious left-handed slap. When he gave way, I kept pushing until the kid on my left started pulling back. The instant he pulled, I reversed and went with him, putting all my weight behind it, catching the boy on my right off balance. As he started to fall, I grabbed his arm and turned.

I swung him into Elena as the rifle fired, its muzzle flash lighting up the night, the explosion not quite covering the sound of a bullet smacking into flesh and bone and the mortal gasp of a human life's last moment.

I rolled, catching a pair of legs, upending the body, then sprinted and dove into the surf as the rifle bolt clacked like dogs' teeth and the gun went off a second time.

40

Cold water brought all my senses to full alert, even more so than the pumping adrenaline from the near miss of rifle bullets fired from the beach. Fully clothed, I had to make this a short swim. My sodden clothing and fifty-degree water would kill me as surely as a bullet to the brain. But water was my element. I had only one chance and this was it.

I swam through the waves, eeling under white-water turbulence to get away from the incoming fire. Dark as it was, I didn't have to go far to become invisible. Once I found myself beyond the surf line, I started stroking parallel to the shore, using the combat swim I'd learned a lifetime ago to avoid making waves of my own.

Dark cliffs jutted into the Pacific about a quarter mile down the coast and I headed for them, looking for a way ashore. Big black boulders would hide my landing, but might cause me injury. Landing on beaches is always easier but increases your chances of getting shot. Landing on rocks doesn't leave footprints, either, and if you do it right, there's no trace of your passing. That's why SEALS always go in the hard way. We save the easy beaches for the marines.

I kept an eye on the beach, looking for Elena's crew, wondering if they still looked for me. I was the only one who knew where the money was buried, and Elena struck me as someone who was clearly focused on what she wanted.

I figured she'd send her remaining boys to look for the missing Chico and take the little marksman with her to hunt me. He was the best she had. He might even have had some experience at this sort of thing. That's what I would have done, given her situation. At the most, I'd have to face only two. Of course they were armed and I wasn't, except for the little .25 I'd taken from Chico and my Buck knife. I searched the beach, looking for sign of pursuit. They wouldn't use lights, and they would take care to avoid making tracks in the sand, so I watched the line of dunes just above the high-tide marks, watching for movement. I saw nothing.

By the time I reached the rocks I was shivering, my body core temperature lowered to dangerous levels, and I knew I had to get out of the water before I lost consciousness. The waves seemed higher here along the base of the cliffs and the rocks looked sharp and menacing. My hands and feet felt leaden, and I had to will my limbs to move. It would have been very easy to let go and sink. Too easy.

I entered the surf zone, timing my progress to match the waves, riding the combers into narrow gaps between the rocks, trying to avoid smashing my head or an elbow or a knee into a chunk of ancient sandstone. I made negligible headway, once even grounding my feet on the slippery bottom pebbles before being dragged out to sea again by powerful backwash, but kept at it. I didn't have a choice.

I felt the strong pull of a big wave before I saw it, turbulent water dragging me into the darkness and back out to sea. Helpless to do anything but travel with the rush of agitated violence, I was washed over the reef rocks into deep water. The leather jacket protected me from the worst of it, acting as both a shield and a sea anchor, but as I shot through the channel, I saw a wall of black water rushing to meet me, a massive breaker, its crest decorated with white wispy foam.

I took a deep breath and dove for the bottom but the wave broke on top of me—tons of roiling white water picked me up and smashed me among the rocks, tossing me like a rag doll. I curled into a ball and went with it, trying desperately to relax, hoping I wouldn't be crushed, or trapped below an underwater ledge. Hope was all I had.

For what seemed an eternity I was swept along until the surface felt nearer and the bottom scraped my knees and elbows, and the strength of the wave lessened and I understood I'd reached the shallows. Sometimes the hard way is the only way. I uncoiled, dropping my feet and reaching for handholds, and found both footing and something to grasp and forced my way from the water onto a rocky shelf below the cliff face. I lay there briefly, catching my breath and shivering, hoping to draw some heat from the cold hard stone, then climbed higher, above the surf line, onto truly dry land.

I was cold, soaked to the skin. My head felt light and weird, like it might float away at any moment. I checked my pockets and found I'd lost nothing in the swim to shore. My Buck knife remained in my trouser pocket and Chico's .25 automatic was still a nice little weight inside the sodden leather jacket. I pulled the pistol and charged it and began trudging back to the lagoon, watching for sign of Elena and the rifleman, hoping we wouldn't meet in the dark the way we had before.

I had covered half the distance when I heard them coming. Actually, I heard her coming, heard her complaining, whining, scraping her shoes on rocks, telling her companion to slow down, making a racket that would have awakened Chico and Tupac. Like her late brother, Elena was not at home away from her familiar paved cityscapes and bedrooms. Wilderness was alien to her.

I wondered if her companion suffered from the same deficiency.

The answer came in a way I didn't expect and it told me that maybe I was no longer at the top of my form, either.

"Drop the gun, old man," said a soft, calm voice behind me, muffled by an outcropping, the rifle barrel an exclamation point between my shoulder blades.

"If I drop the gun, it'll go off."

"Toss it into the water, where it will do no harm. Elena!"

I transferred the pistol to my left hand and complied, flinging Chico's little automatic far out into the surf. "You were here?"

"I can run faster than you can swim, old man. This was the only place where you would go, even though it was difficult. Elena waited over there behind those rocks and made noise when I gave her the signal. You were easy."

"Yeah."

The woman appeared on top of a boulder. She smiled when she saw me. "You didn't get far, did you?"

I shook my head. "Not far enough, I guess."

"Why don't you show me the money?"

"I don't think so."

"You will, I think. Paco, bring him to the beach. I want to find the money and get out of here tonight."

The rifleman struck me with the end of the barrel, another hard poke in the kidneys, and I started forward, slowly, so he wouldn't shoot. Suicide was not an option I favored, although I did not want these two to recover the money. Claire would find it if she had to dredge up the entire beach. And if Claire didn't get it, better someone anonymous, a lucky someone someday in the far future, than these two.

When we reached the beach, Elena turned and smiled. "You have two choices. One, you tell me voluntarily and everything goes easy for you. Two, Paco shoots you in both kneecaps and then I cut pieces off of you until you tell me. You will tell me, anyway. Let's make this quick, shall we? It will be easier on all of us."

The moon came out from behind the clouds and the wind kicked up, chilling me to the bone. Or was it the threat that made me shiver? This woman was centered on what she wanted. She was not grandstanding. I watched her face in the moonlight, a ribbon of silver light gracing the ocean behind her, and wondered how much longer I had on this old planet. I must have smiled, because Elena smiled back.

"You find this amusing?" she asked.

"No."

"Paco. Shoot him!"

The marksman raised his weapon, aiming at my right leg, sighting down the barrel, focusing on that one spot where the bullet would tear into me.

I leaped on him, deflecting the barrel with my left forearm and grabbing the stock, twisting and pulling simultaneously. The rifle discharged, the shot snapping Elena's back, driving her down into the sand as if she had been smashed by a giant hammer.

I kept twisting the rifle until I had possession, then reversed and clubbed him across the neck. He fell, rolled, and came up with his pistol, firing rapidly, both hands on the grips like they show in those dumb movies, shooting without aiming, instinctively blowing large chunks of lead downrange in my direction, filling the night with flashes of light and the repeated thunder of a large-caliber pistol.

He got off four rounds before I was able to cock the rifle and shoot him, aiming at the hollow in the front of his neck, just above his breastbone. He collapsed and lay still.

The front sight of the rifle didn't want to let go of him and I followed the barrel across the sand to where the bodies lay. The kid was dead, stilling gripping the .45. I pried the pistol from his stiff fingers, safed it, and stuck it in my soggy hip pocket. Then I looked at Elena.

I didn't need to check life signs on either one of them. A high-powered rifle at close range doesn't leave much room for question. I dumped the rifle in the sand, next to Paco, and checked for holes of my own, finding none. Paco was practiced and knew all the moves but he forgot to aim, missing me at ten feet. Good boy, Paco. The world needs more bad guys like you.

I started searching for the missing kid, the one Elena had sent to search for Chico.

Three shots, so close I knew I was dead, went off behind me, and even though I knew it was useless, my body reacted, diving for cover. Unhurt and amazed, I continued rolling until I found protection behind a small dune.

Three more shots exploded sand into my face, blinding me. I ducked and rolled, finding concealment behind a tiny creosote bush. Watching, I pulled Paco's .45, hoping he'd had enough sense to load the damn thing. I'd neglected to check the load and hadn't bothered searching the body for additional magazines. I pulled back the slide a quarter inch and found brass in the right place, ejected the clip and counted three more bullets.

I only needed one if I used it right.

The kid fired again, blasting the top of the dune I'd recently occupied. I tracked the muzzle flash, extending the

.45's front sight through the bush to avoid deflecting the bullet from its intended path. When the kid fired again, I saw his face in the reflected light of the gun's blast, centered his forehead on top of the black metal V, and carefully squeezed the trigger until the piece fired.

When the silence lasted long enough to assure me I'd hit my target, I got up and walked to where he lay on the sand, panting. I took his Uzi, slung it over my shoulder, and stood there watching while life left him, letting him see my face as he died. It was his right, letting him see the man who killed him.

It's pure Darwin out here in the bush. Only the fittest survive. That's why we train and train and train until we get it right. That's why I lived and others didn't. My body and the training I'd lived with had taken over when my brain refused to believe I was still alive.

The myth that guns are the stuff of heroes and that they solve problems is stupid. Kids buy into that. They see it on the streets. They also see it in movies and on television, where the people who make films pass on a message that might makes right, that society is so violent only fools don't carry guns. So the kids see the gangsters making the big bucks and they see their screen idols and rap stars carrying guns, and they conclude that they're idiots if they don't.

But carrying a gun does not make you Superman any more than it makes you invincible. Ask any of these armed young men who died along this dark Baja beach on this cold January night. There's always someone out there who's going to be luckier, or more trained, or deadlier than you. It's a risk every time you pull a piece. When you use deadly force, it brings in a dimension most of us would just as soon leave alone. And it makes the odds ever greater each time you use it.

These young men were unlucky this time. They ran into me.

I wondered who would stand over me and watch me die on some cruel coast someday when my luck eventually ran out. Probably be a kid like one of these, no smarter or wiser or more practiced. Just luckier. I'd had a good run of luck in my life, and it still seemed to be running. And all I could do was run with it until it ran its course and came to an end.

Like all things.

41

The rest of the night was spent in hard labor, dressing the setting I wanted the police to find, and hiding the money I hoped they wouldn't.

I found the body of the man I'd crushed with the truck, pausing only to confirm his death. It wasn't a man, just another kid with a gun who'd watched too many movies. I wished I could have felt bad about his death. Maybe someday, when the shakes passed and the adrenaline charge faded, I'd think about him as a kid and not a target, and I might consider it. And maybe not.

He'd made his choices and taken his chances, heading toward this sandy death from the moment he'd come squalling into this world. My choices had also placed me here, but at least I'd had the experience and ability and the luck to choose my own path to this beach. The kid was a follower. I doubted he had done anything in his life but go along, only in the end making a stand, a stupid, futile one, but at least a stand.

You try, you fail. Sometimes they let you try again. It's a tough world.

It took me some time to locate the gangster I'd knocked unconscious and rolled into a ditch. He was still out cold, but he was breathing. I cut the laces binding him and removed the gag, lightly slapping his face and rubbing his hands to arouse him. That, too, was part of my plan. Finding him, the authorities might be tempted to come to a conclusion that would shatter my construct.

"Wha . . . *dónde . . . ?*" He started coming around. I backed away, not wanting any more violence.

"Tienes inglés?"

"Solamente español," he said. This one spoke only Spanish, if he could be believed.

I told him his companions were all dead, and outlined his choices. They were simple: Get up and get the hell out; remain here and I'd kill him.

I saw clarity come into his eyes. The boy was one of the lucky ones, and he clearly understood either my halting border Spanish or the tone of my voice, but he got up and only paused to look around to get his bearings before making a run for the beach.

I watched him go, jogging along the sand in laceless boots, heading north, toward Tijuana. Because he claimed only Spanish, the chances were good he had relatives there and could find shelter by morning. He might even avoid a connection to this whole affair. The road to Tijuana was a long one, but it was his country. He might have been a killer, might even have been one of the boys who shot de la Peña and Stevenson, but to me it didn't matter.

Maybe he would return to the gangster world because that was the only thing he knew. And maybe he would think about this night, change his ways, enter school and become a teacher or a doctor.

And maybe pigs could fly.

I told myself I was getting soft and sentimental in my old age. Had this been war, his death would have been incidental and automatic, a detail to be stricken, a loose end to be cut. But my little war was over and the kid's life was spared. He would probably take the low road, seeking, like water, his own level. But John Caine didn't remove any chance of the better life. The boy lived to make his own choices, and better yet, he was no longer my responsibility.

When he disappeared, I paced the beach in measured strides, looking for the monuments that marked the buried money. Satisfied that we could still find the money, and convinced I'd left no trails leading to the site, I scrambled up the little mountain overlooking the lagoon and did not look back when I crested the peak and descended the other side.

The Range Rover sat like a faithful pony beneath the little tree. It started easily, the way her British engineers intended, and when I drove onto the Ensenada-Tijuana Highway, the engine accelerated beautifully. I felt bad about my plans for this car, but I didn't think Claire would mind if it was her only loss and she got her money back.

Remembering from an old map in my head, I found the Ensenada-Tecate Highway, a two-lane road leading inland and north. I didn't want to be found anywhere near Tijuana. If the police still looked for me, they would concentrate their search near San Diego. Tecate, about an hour east of the coast, seemed the better choice.

The sun rose over virgin mountains as I neared the border, its clear, clean light shining in my eyes. I found bottled water under the seat and drank a toast of Evian to the birth of a new day. It had been a close thing and I'd nearly been deprived of seeing this sunrise. Like the kid I'd set free, my life choices took me right out there onto the edge, sometimes dangling over it. Watching the sun brightening the tops of the pine trees, I wondered how long I could keep it up, how many more glorious sunsets and sunrises would come my way.

The answer was, and I thought it the proper one: *I don't know.* All I could do was strive, and thoroughly appreciate each day until I'd used up my allotment and they didn't give me any more.

Morning brought new danger, the Range Rover a bright, shiny target. I wanted to drive as close to the border as possible, abandon the car, and hotfoot it across the mountains into the United States. Thousands of people did it every day in this part of the world. My idea was to join up with a group heading north, tag along, watch what they did, and follow.

Of course, I was more than a foot taller than most of the *pollos,* the name given to the emigrants by the border dwellers, and the fact that I resembled them not at all might be a small handicap. But I could be charming when I chose, and nobody ever heard of *norteamericano* immigration on this side of the border. It just wasn't part of the game.

It was more difficult than I thought.

Finding the road north was not hard. Groups of people

carrying knapsacks and shopping bags strolled along the road, seeming to converge on the mouth of a wide gulch. I passed it twice, and when I discovered groups traveling the opposite direction, back toward that same canyon, I turned around, parked the Range Rover, and slung the Uzi under my jacket. I grabbed the Evian, took one last look at Paul Peters's car, and followed.

The arroyo had no paved road, only a small footpath worn smooth by thousands of pairs of shoes, sandals, and bare feet. The path was lined with trash, the leavings of a civilization on the move. This little path, no greater than three or four feet at its widest, was a main emigration thoroughfare for an entire people. Whatever caused the migration was not my concern, but the effects and its detritus were everywhere. Families, couples, and singles joined the parade, but I was not welcome.

When I tried to follow, they stopped and squatted, watching me from beneath the brims of straw cowboy hats, black eyes avoiding the gaze of the big *Yanqui* with the bulge beneath his leather jacket. They wouldn't move until I was out of sight. Wherever I approached, each group would repeat the action, squatting and staring at the dirt at their feet until I no longer violated their space.

I continued north. The path got steeper and the sides of the canyon more sharply defined. The air turned colder and thinner as we rose into the mountains. Patches of snow clung to shaded areas. A little stream now trickled through the bottom of the gulch, surrounded by pale green brush. I came upon several campsites. The occupants studiously avoided my presence until I was out of sight.

Sometime after noon the path divided, both forks heading north. I took the one angling east. The country looked rougher in that direction, a less likely place to encounter law enforcement.

I hiked without incident for two more hours, enjoying the scenery and wondering how far I was from the border, when I heard shouting ahead. I eased off the path and jogged parallel to it, moving carefully from bush to tree to bush, edging toward the sounds.

Clouds drifted in from the south, low and threatening. The temperature, already chilly because of the elevation, dropped another five degrees without the sun. I shivered when I removed my jacket to get at the Uzi, grateful I had a jacket, even if it was still sodden. Many of the emigrants I'd encountered on the path wore nothing heavier than thin flannel. If it rained or snowed, the wet cotton would not protect them from the cold.

I crept to the edge of a clearing, keeping low, inside the brush line. A line of ragged *pollos* faced a man wearing a filthy white ski mask with red piping around the mouth and eye holes. He pointed a blue-steel revolver, his arm extended like a classic marksman's, and he shouted orders, his words accentuated by the barrel of the gun. My Spanish isn't fluent, but I made out most of his words. He was an old-fashioned highwayman, and this was an old-fashioned robbery.

The bandit seemed to be alone. Lying still, I searched for an accomplice. Nobody moved within the clearing other than the participants. Nothing stirred around the edges except me.

I concentrated on the revolver, a small-frame pistol, most likely a .22. No fun to catch one of those, but it's not in the same league as the 9mm I carried. And he only had six rounds. Fully charged, each of my magazines held thirty.

But I didn't want any shooting. Looking around, searching the clearing, I soon found what I wanted. I backed off and silently made my way around the group until I lay behind them in a clump of weeds, facing the gunman.

The men and women had emptied their pockets and were now shedding their clothing. Something about it seemed strange, and it took me a moment to realize what it was. When they removed their pants, they revealed another pair underneath. They didn't carry many possessions. They were so poor they wore everything they owned.

When they tossed the clothing into a pile, the bandit went through the pockets and checked the lining. Several times he presented his back to his victims and they didn't move. Their passivity angered me. Had I been there, I'd have taken his head off the first time he turned away.

But I *was* here, and I couldn't let this pass.

When he turned again, I crawled forward, finding a position behind a granite boulder, six feet from the line of *pollos*. I watched him, and the next time he looked down at his feet, I was there, Uzi under his chin, lifting him off the ground with the gun's muzzle.

"Lo siento!"

"I'll bet you're sorry, pal," I said. *"Arriba las manos!"* I didn't know exactly what that meant, having learned it from *Butch Cassidy and the Sundance Kid,* but I thought I'd ordered him to raise his hands. He did, dropping the pistol, his hands shaking. I risked a glance at the *pollos*. Their hands were raised, too. They hadn't moved.

It started raining, a cold drizzle.

Keeping the Uzi pressed against the bandit's throat, I gestured with my free hand toward the pile of clothing. Not knowing how to say what I wanted to say was frustrating, but a couple of the men figured it out, looked meaningfully at each other, and bent down to sort out their belongings.

I gestured to the bandit's pants. Fumbling, he undid them, letting them drop to the ground. Unlike the *pollos,* he wore neither spare trousers nor underclothing. Standing there, his pants pooled around his ankles, white skinny legs already starting to pucker in the rain, and without his gun, he didn't look as fierce as before, and a nervous laugh bubbled from one of the *pollos*. It was funny, and it gave me an idea.

The immigrants joined in, pointing and laughing.

I backed away, pointing the gun barrel at his shirt, making signs to remove it. He complied, his hands shaking. Whether they shook from rage or fright or cold, I didn't know and didn't care. This man had been willing to rob a dozen people, to bully them with a gun, threatening them with deadly force. Would he have killed them? I didn't know that, either. It didn't matter, his intent made manifest by the aiming of the weapon.

When he had completely disrobed, he huddled naked in the clearing, facing the mocking group of men and women, his intended victims, trying to cover his shriveled penis and maintain his dignity. That's difficult to do when you're shivering so hard your knees knock. With the ski mask, he had seemed sinister. Without it, he was just another unshaven criminal, another pitiful example of the human condition. I wished my Spanish was good enough to force him to apologize, but I lacked the verbs. It wasn't important, anyway. Their laughter was enough.

"Ándale, cabrón!" I shouted, pointing his way down the mountain with the Uzi's barrel. Relief and disbelief flashed across his face in rapid sequence. He'd thought he was a dead man. That's what he would have done, had our roles been reversed. He'd have killed me.

But then, I was having a streak of soft lately.

The bandit gingerly stepped across the clearing toward the trail, carefully placing his feet on the cold, rocky ground. He walked slowly, hands cupping his sensitive parts, shoulders hunched and quivering. At the edge of the clearing he stopped, turned, and looked at me. It was brief. For an instant our eyes met. I don't know what he saw, but I saw only surrender. He was finished as a bandit. He might have been finished as a man.

Not my problem.

The immigrants were still too wary to approach me. I smiled at them, giving it my most ingratiating effort. They smiled back, as you would at a savage dog, or at a tiger you'd just seen slip out of its cage.

I realized the gun was still in my hand and put it under my jacket.

We stood facing each other, the *pollos* and me, but there was nothing to say and little means to say it. I waved and started up the trail toward the high country, toward the United States, where I belonged. They hesitated, unwilling to commit, and finally they followed, unsure of the man who had saved them, unsure if he was a good man or bad, unsure if they should follow him to an uncertain destination.

I didn't blame them. I knew the guy well and I still had those same doubts.

42

Texaco materialized through the tops of snow-frosted pine trees, the first sign of civilization that assured me I was back on American soil. It told me that my thirty hours of hiding, dodging Mexican police and United States Border Patrol agents, had ended.

I tried to brush some of the filth and snow from my clothes before entering the little redwood-sided café that stood in the clearing next to the gas station. A third building, a private home, was the only other visible structure. After a day and a half of cross-country scrambling through thick brush and forest, the little settlement looked familiar and comforting. Satisfied that I'd cleaned up the best I could, I went inside, sat at the end of the Formica counter and picked up a menu. Three other people sat at the counter. Nobody occupied a table.

The waitress, a plump, worn woman in her mid-fifties, leaned against the counter, talking to a slim, weathered man about her age wearing jeans, cowboy boots, and a plaid duffel coat. A white Stetson lay next to his elbow. Both had stopped their conversation and watched me when I came in the door. The café was warm, and the smell of coffee and hot grease enveloped me like a comfortable old friend.

The waitress picked up a small pad and a pencil and edged over to my place at the counter. "Coffee?" She sniffed. I probably smelled as bad as I looked.

"Please," I said. "Do you have steak and eggs?"

"Six ninety-five." Her voice was flat, unfriendly.

"And orange juice?"

"One ninety-five."

"Biscuits and gravy?"

"Comes with the steak."

"Can I use your rest room?"

She hesitated. "Over there," she said, pointing to a narrow corridor near the window that overlooked the gas station. "How do you want your steak?"

"Medium rare. Eggs over medium."

She stood still as I got up, rooted to her place behind the counter, waiting.

I took a fifty-dollar bill from my wallet and laid it on the counter.

"Been camping?" she asked as I went to the rest room.

"Something like that."

Inside the bathroom, I took off my jacket and shirt and hung them on the doorknob. The waitress's hesitation was probably justified. The man in the mirror didn't look like he could afford steak and eggs. He had a battered, dirty face, with enough scabs and bruises to have gone six rounds with Mike Tyson. The money changed my image. It established an ability to pay. Suddenly, I was a camper, not a homeless freeloader.

Using paper towels and the astringent liquid soap from the wall-mounted dispenser, I washed my face and hair and beard. The water in the sink ran gray for five minutes. It wasn't a shower, and I wished I had a toothbrush, but I felt better. At least I no longer resembled the Unabomber. Well, I thought, looking at the haggard, bearded stranger in the mirror, still ragged, but clean.

Coffee would work wonders.

Steak would be better.

Breakfast waited on the counter, my fifty beside it. It had been over ten years since I'd tried to pack so much cholesterol into my bloodstream in one morning, but it was my first meal in two days. I guess it tasted good. It went down so fast I didn't notice.

"My, we were hungry," the waitress said, coffeepot poised above my cup. "More coffee?"

"Please," I said. "This mountain air works up an appetite."

"That it does," she said. "That it does." She took the pot and went down the row, filling every cup.

Now that I felt almost human again, it was time to call Thomas.

"Excuse me," I asked her when she wandered back toward my corner. "Do you have a telephone?"

"Over at the Texaco." She pointed through the window. Across the parking lot an old-style booth stood next to an air pump. "It's snowin' again." Light flake fell, melting as it hit the pavement. Snow had fallen off and on all night as I'd pushed through the mountains after crossing the border. It had been welcome, covering my tracks. I didn't know if anyone followed. After the trouble at the border, I wasn't certain, one way or the other.

"Is it local?" she asked.

"San Diego."

"That's local enough. Here." She pulled a black, dial-type telephone from below the counter. "You look like you've had some trouble, but you don't look like you plan to make any. I can tell. It's warm inside." She refilled my cup and retreated to the other end of the counter, providing me privacy.

I called Thomas's cellular phone. It rang three times and I nearly hung up before he answered.

"Thomas."

"This is Caine. I'm back."

"Caine?"

"Yeah."

"Where have you been? Are you all right? Where are you?"

"Whoa, Ed. I'm fine. I've been in the wilderness. I made an unauthorized entry into the United States and I don't know where I am." I put the receiver against my chest and called to the waitress. "Excuse me, ma'am. Where am I?"

She put her hands on ample hips and shook her head. "Mountain Meadows. And that's Highway Ninety-four about a mile down the road. You mean you didn't drive?"

I shook my head. "Mountain Meadows. In the mountains east of San Diego. About a mile from Highway Ninety-four."

"I know where it is. Are you okay?"

"A little tired, but okay."

"Had two women riding me. Farrell and I finally went down there to look for you. There were a whole lot of *federales* and locals around, but you'd vanished."

"What did Esparza say?"

"Said you were clean for the de la Peña shooting, but he still wanted to talk to you. I guess you got them all." There was disapproval in his voice.

"I let one live."

"Esparza found a bunch of eyewitnesses that night that cleared you. Two young men dressed in gang clothing did it. But I guess you already know that."

I hadn't known that. "Tell Esparza I'll talk to him, but nobody else."

"He'll be happy to hear that. It'll take me about two hours to get there. It's raining again."

"It's snowing here, so take your time and be safe."

"Uh-huh. Somebody here wants to talk to you. I'll leave now."

I heard his voice rumble something away from the mouthpiece, but I couldn't make out the words.

"John! Is everything all right?"

"The money's safe."

"Well . . . that's wonderful, but you don't have it?"

"It's safe."

"When can we get it?"

"Soon. As soon as the dust settles."

"Soon," she repeated, as if the word were important, something to ponder. Then she said, "And you. Are you safe?" There wasn't much solicitude in the question; it was merely pro forma.

"No new holes. I'm tired. I walked the last thirty miles, most of it uphill. Walked all night and didn't sleep. But I'm fine. Honest."

"It's over?"

"Yeah, Claire. It's over. You can have your old life back.

All except your husband. That I can't get back for you. He's in a place where he can't be salvaged."

"You did it."

The lack of a response to my comments about old Paul surprised me. I hadn't said anything to get a response, had just blurted it out, but her lack of interest astounded me.

I yawned. Maybe I was too tired to understand much of anything. The food made me sleepy. Even coffee couldn't keep me awake. "No, Claire, you did it. If you hadn't hired me, it would have been somebody else doing the heavy lifting. But it was your pushing that did it, not taking no for an answer, believing in yourself, believing you were right when everybody else told you you were wrong."

"I wish I could believe that—"

"Believe it, Claire. You'll get your money back. You earned it."

"You said it's safe. It's still in Mexico?"

"Uh-huh. But nobody but me knows exactly where it is. Let me rest today. Maybe tomorrow we'll go get it."

"Barbara's here: She wants to speak with you."

"Thank you, Claire—"

"John. Are you all right? I, uh, we were worried sick about you. We heard so many conflicting stories, we didn't know which ones to believe."

"I'm fine. Just look a little worse for wear, but nothing that won't grow back or wash off."

"No jokes. You're sure you're okay?"

"I'm fine. Save me a glass of wine. Or two."

"You got a bottle if you want it, and it's champagne. The good stuff."

"Great. In the meantime I'll wait for Ed. Right here at the Mountain Meadows Cafe. The coffee's good. I'll see you in a few hours."

43

The next thing I remember was a gentle hand shaking my shoulder. My vision came into focus as I sat at the counter of the Mountain Meadows Cafe, my right forefinger through the handle of a blue mug.

"You want a warm-up for your coffee now?"

The merry face of the waitress, a coffeepot poised over my mug, the warmth of the café, and the hot grease smells coalesced and I came awake. Rush Limbaugh's voice whined over scratchy speakers. Ed Thomas leaned over from the left and said, "He'll take some coffee. I think his got cold."

The waitress laughed, joined by a couple of others in the café. It had been a great joke. This guy comes in out of the snow, orders breakfast, drops a fifty on the counter, makes a phone call, and then falls asleep, his hand still wrapped around his coffee mug. Man, that's funny! Didn't spill a drop! Didn't fall over. Just sat there for a couple of hours, sound asleep while people came and went. Someone turned on the radio. Commerce continued. Still, this guy slept!

I smiled.

"Guess I was tired."

"Guess you were. You settled up?"

My fifty still lay on the counter, untouched. I pushed it across to the waitress. "Keep it," I said. "For everything."

She opened her mouth to say something, but then just shook her head.

Ed hustled me out of the warm café and into his pickup. A gentle snow was falling, light, delicate flakes drifting down, hanging in the trees. It lay in scant piles on the earth; the snow that fell on the asphalt only made the road wet.

He studied my face. "You look like you've been hit more times than an anvil."

"Always lead with my best punch."

"I've got lots of questions, Caine, but my first one is, how in hell did you get way out here?"

"Long story, Ed."

"We've got two hours. I want to hear this."

"Drove most of it, a hundred miles east, way beyond Tecate where the terrain is steep and difficult, up into the hills near the border, then walked."

"Yeah, but we're thirty miles from the border."

"Couldn't find a place to make a phone call."

He shook his head, as if he had never heard such lunacy. "You thought the police were still after you?"

"I didn't know and didn't want to take the chance. I hid the money again. Nobody knows where it is but me. If they shot me . . ."

"Esparza cleared you that night. It would have been all right."

"I didn't know." I wasn't sure. If it was a mistake, it was one I could live with. I'd abandoned Claire's Range Rover. All it cost me was a day out of my life and a little walk in the woods. Measured against the alternative, I preferred this.

"How did you get across?"

"Joined some illegals."

"That was you?"

"What?"

"Was there a coyote?"

I nodded. "There was a smuggler."

"Said you saved their butts."

"I persuaded him to behave."

"Persuaded him to take off his clothes in the rain and then ran him down the mountain, from what the paper says."

"I'm very persuasive."

"Yeah. With a smile and an Uzi you can get almost anything you want." Thomas smiled and shook his head. "They called you *El Tigre*. That made the papers."

"Border patrol caught them, I guess?"

Ed smiled. "Sent them back. Flew them down to Guerrero, I heard. Way down into Mexico where it will be difficult and expensive for them to come back, a humane way to discourage them. Back home they'll tell the tale about the gringo with the submachine gun who saved their lives, stopped the coyote from robbing them and sent him back down the trail without his pants. You'll be legend down there, Caine. I can see them telling that story for years." Thomas laughed at that. "What the hell else did you do?"

"Left the group just this side of the border and struck out on my own. A couple of the young men tried to follow, but I discouraged them."

"I'll bet you did."

I thought of the families trying to get into this country. I couldn't blame them. I'd probably try, too. The people I'd met were not bad people. Still, not all of them come here to work, and not all of them are good people. Neither am I. But I was lucky enough to have been born here. That's a big part of life, I guess.

"Border patrol repeated the story. The *Union* printed it. Radio talk shows are yammering about it. Some member of Congress wants an investigation about safety of the illegals. It almost covered the little miniwar you had down there, *El Tigre.*"

"Ed, I—"

"Eight people, Caine. Esparza said you killed eight people. Nobody does it that easy. Not even you can do that and not let it get to you."

"They killed themselves."

"That's what Esparza said. But he said he knows you helped them on the way."

"He know that for a fact?"

"He can't prove it. But he knows you did it."

I nodded. It was cop talk.

"Way the Mexican police put it together, the gang had a disagreement."

"No evidence of anyone else at the scene?"

"Nope. You're home free."

"They killed themselves."

"Nobody disputes that."

"They killed de la Peña."

"Weapons turned up in one of the trucks. Two MAC-11's matched the bullets taken from the body. Open-and-shut case. Problem is, nobody can figure out why. They weren't political. They weren't in possession of drugs or money. Only guns."

"The why will have to remain a mystery," I said.

"Uh-huh. They won't hear it from me."

"Just like the whereabouts of Paul Peters."

"Didn't find him?"

The road descended into a long, broad valley, where the snow turned into rain. When it climbed again, the snow came back. Thomas took it slow and I was glad he did.

"Everybody said he was dead, but I don't know. Two people confessed to killing him, but they're both dead now. If he's alive, let him enjoy it. If he's not, let it rest."

"You think Claire will go with that?"

I thought about it. "Why not?"

"It'll be neater."

"And there's already a body. He's officially dead. I don't need to dig up, pardon the expression, another one."

"There's that," he said. We'd gone down into another valley, still lower, and the rain had stopped, but now there was an annoying mist that fogged the windshield if he didn't run his wipers and made them jump if he used them too much. Thomas cursed and adjusted the wipers. The road stretched out straight in front of us, a long toboggan ride into the little valley, bordered on both sides by avocado groves.

"I'm going to need you and Farrell for one more job; then you can do what you want."

"That's pretty choice, considering you work for me, I don't work for you. You going back to get the money?"

"We'll take *Olympia*."

"Money's still on the beach?"

"Close. Weather permitting, let's do it day after tomorrow." I needed rest, and I wanted to make a couple of telephone calls to ensure we'd get back in one piece. It was time to claim a favor.

"Your call, Caine. I say let's do it as soon as possible."

"Day after tomorrow."

Thomas nodded. "All right. One last job. After that you're heading back to Hawaii?"

"Yeah. Time to go home."

"Do me a favor?"

"Sure."

"Next time you're in San Diego and you've got work, call me. I'll give you a number to call. You'll like this guy. He's young enough to keep up with you."

44

Thomas dropped me off in front of Claire's house, claiming his wife had something planned at home and he didn't want to disappoint her. It was the first time he'd ever mentioned having a wife and it sparked my curiosity. I'd pictured him as a loner, one of those self-sufficient Old West gunslinger types. Now that a wife had been mentioned, I didn't find it difficult to enter her into the equation. Ed Thomas was too civilized a gentleman not to have a woman in his life.

And he was far too private even to speak her name to someone like John Caine.

I walked up the circular drive toward the house. It looked exactly as it did when I first arrived. Nothing had changed, except everything had changed.

Juanita answered my knock, a look of joy on her face that changed when she saw the condition of my face. "*Madre de Dios!*" she said. "Meester Caine! Joo're ogly!"

"My mother used to say that."

"No, I mean . . . jour face!"

"That's what she meant, too."

Juanita laughed, shaking her head. "Joo got beat up some more! That's what I meant to say!"

"Yeah. But here I am."

"Come in, come in," she said, pulling me in by the arm. "And joo messed up jour clothes again."

"Can't take me anywhere."

Laughing, she wagged a finger at me. "Joo don't take care of anything, do you?"

"No."

Juanita reached up and kissed me on the cheek. "They say you find the money. *Gracias,* Meester Caine."

"Por nada," I said, "for nothing."

"No, for Mees Claire. And for all the people who work for Mees Claire. Like me."

"You know what I mean."

"Jess. I do. Mees Claire is upstairs. Weeth Mees Barbara. Go. Now." Juanita gave me a little swat on the fanny. Merriment twinkled in her eyes.

"I'll be back," I said.

"Don't be so sure!"

My gear was still in the guest bedroom and I went there first to get a change of clothing. I was looking through my clothes when Claire appeared at the door, leaning against the jamb, arms crossed.

"Didn't Juanita tell you to come see me?"

"Thought I'd shower first. It's been days."

She smiled. Unlike her earlier smiles in this house, this was a warm one, no longer brittle. "That's that smell?" She uncrossed her arms. "You did it, didn't you."

"We'll go get the money in a couple of days. We'll all go. Aboard *Olympia.*"

"And?"

"And you can do whatever you want with it. It belongs to you. Nobody, no government, no court, no person can tell you otherwise. Besides, it's cash. All cash. I know, I looked. Two footlockers full of hundred-dollar bills. Nobody's ever disputed cash."

Claire colored, her cheeks pinking all the way to the tops of her high cheekbones.

"Cash?"

"Yep. I don't know if you want to involve Barbara, but I know a guy who'll exchange the cash for letters of credit or cashier's checks from a Geneva bank. He'll help you convert it into . . . I was going to say real money, but what money's more real than cash? I guess I should say 'usable' money. Not much you can do with that much cash these days."

"You know a Swiss banker?"

"Better than that," I said, thinking of ways Chawlie could help replace the money, imagining Barbara's alarm when she discovered what Chawlie really was. "He's not a good man, but he'll work with you. He owes me."

"That sounds like a threat."

"Just good business. He'll work with you. I promise."

"You always keep your promises, don't you?" She turned when Barbara entered, silently coming upon us as if she did not wish to disturb something. When she found nothing disturbed or disturbing, she looked relieved.

"You got hit in the face again," Barbara said, smiling, crossing the room. "That happens a lot, doesn't it?"

"Ladies?" I put my arms around each woman and kissed a blond and a brunet head of hair, smelling a different flowered scent with each kiss. "I have to take a shower."

"Yes," Claire said, wrinkling her nose and wriggling out from under my arm. "You do." Barbara remained in my embrace. In the mirror I saw a hint of a challenge in her expression as she looked at Claire.

"I'll be right out." I tried to move away from Barbara, but she was having none of it, moving closer to me, her body proclaiming its own allegiance.

"Take your time," she said, releasing me, but watching Claire.

Knowing when to retreat, I went into the bathroom and ran the water, leaving the door open. Barbara pushed Claire into the corridor and locked the door and came back and lounged on the bed, lying on her left side, watching me undress.

I got under the hot spray and did a better job than I was able to do in Mountain Meadows. Just standing under the shower made me feel better. I luxuriated, washing my hair, brushing my teeth, taking my time. After several days, this was more than a luxury, it was a need. Now I felt human, or at least as close as I ever felt.

The shower door opened and Barbara stepped in as I was rinsing my hair, my head down. I opened my eyes, saw bare legs and feet. She got behind me, put her arms around my waist and hugged me tightly, pressing her breasts against my back.

"I couldn't wait," she said, one hand reaching down, grasping me, cupping my already thickening flesh. "I hope you don't mind."

I turned around and nearly laughed, but her look was so vulnerable I didn't dare. It might have been a long time for her, the first time since her marriage ended, and she was fully aware of her gamble. This could end badly if it was not handled absolutely right.

"I'm not much of a catch."

"I'm not looking for a husband, John. I've had one. Look where it got me."

I laughed, enveloping her within my arms, wondering at her body, feeling the wonderful combination of suppleness and softness, of muscle covered by the ripe womanly flesh. It had been a long time for me, too.

"Come on," she said, looking into my eyes. Barbara took my hand and we found the bed without drying. She didn't let go of my hand, grasping it in her own in a strong grip that was nearly painful. When she lay down on the bed, she brought me directly down on top of her, holding me tightly against her.

"No," she said in response to my exploration of her body. "There's no time for that now." She moved under me and I found her ready.

Sometimes the act can be gentle. Sometimes it can be passionate. On the extreme end of the scale, it is violent, a force of nature, where bodies are merely the means to the end and the end is the total, absolute reduction of the persona into sexual climax. Some women can climax more than once. Some cannot do it at all. Barbara was way off the scale, and it didn't take long before I discovered that making love to her was akin to experiencing an earthquake. The earth didn't just move, it damn near exploded.

The first time she came it was urgent, and our lovemaking had all the refinement of a wrestling match. When she discovered I had not joined her, she kissed me and breathlessly asked me to hold on, if I could. I found I could do nothing else but hold on, her passion, if that's what it was, so great and so overwhelming I could not follow her anyway.

Barbara climaxed three times, each time more intense

than before. She pinned my head into the soft place between her neck and shoulder, holding me tightly with strong arms, thrusting and bucking her hips and legs, wrapping herself around me in her frenzied quest for fulfillment.

Whatever she was seeking, she eventually found it. On her fourth and fifth occasions, she cried out, a hair-raising, atavistic cry celebrating her survival. By then I understood that I was nothing more than a lever, a tool to be used to assist her on her way.

This was not lovemaking. It was pure sex, a seeking not of completion with another human being, but of self-absorption so deep I could not see the bottom. It was not the stuff of romance.

When it was over, she pulled away and lay panting, eyes closed, one hand thrown over her face. I touched her, but she pushed my hand away.

"You must think I'm awful," Barbara said into her hand, not facing me, not looking at me.

"No."

"What are you thinking?"

"I'm thinking you're one hell of a woman. I'm thinking it would take one hell of a man to keep up with you."

"Don't keep score."

"I wouldn't dare. It was . . . an experience."

"It was . . . this was just . . . I don't know. You helped me exorcise some demons."

"Are they gone?" We all have demons. I was surprised that Barbara's fears ran so deep. It had never shown before.

She nodded, opening her eyes. "I think so. Why?"

"You wanna try again? I mean I, uh . . ."

She looked, then put her hand on me, wrapping her fingers around me. Chuckling deep in her throat, she said, "Well, I'll be damned!"

"Please be gentle with me."

She laughed, rolled over, and kissed me. This time she allowed me to explore her body the way I wanted to explore it, the way a woman's body is meant to be explored. This time she responded the way I'd expected.

And this time, when the earth moved, it moved for both of us.

45

Three days later we dropped anchor beyond the surf line, about a hundred yards from a barely familiar Baja beach. The lagoon and the black mesas beyond looked different from the water. From here the land looked alien.

We didn't go the next day, partly because of the weather, but mostly because I couldn't get through to the man I wanted to speak to. When I did, I was glad I'd made the effort. Some things are worth waiting for, as Barbara had happily pointed out to me a couple of days earlier.

We'd all put Barbara on a plane back to San Francisco the night before, making her departure an occasion complete with confetti and streamers. People turned and stared, wondering at the commotion.

I knew she had to return to her job, but I didn't enjoy it any more than she did. We both still resonated with the discovery of what could be a new love. Barbara's gift of herself had been such a surprise I'd nearly missed recognizing it for what it really was. In the end I let her go only after she promised to come back before I left the Mainland.

Ed Thomas and I took the Avon inflatable to shore. Claire and Farrell remained aboard. To prevent potential immigration problems, we left Juanita back in San Diego, happier, I thought, and relieved. Strange as it may seem to me, some people are not sailors.

We brought two small folding shovels, the kind the army calls entrenchment tools. I carried my Buck knife. Other than that, Thomas and I were unarmed. Farrell had his six-shooter, the shotguns, the elephant rifle, and the 7mm Magnum sniper rifle on board *Olympia,* but we took no weapons ashore. We didn't expect trouble, and we were too old and tired to go looking for any. All we wanted was to pick up the money and go home. If we did have trouble, Farrell was there, watching over us like a guardian angel, an angel with killer eyes.

I found my monuments and markers immediately and within twenty minutes of digging, we found the footlockers. That was the easy part. Dragging them back to the Avon was harder. The hardest part was yet to come.

Getting out through the surf in a heavily laden inflatable boat isn't real easy, either, but I'd done it before and we made it, soaked by cold seawater, but intact. It didn't increase Thomas's sense of security when I inflated divers' buoys and secured them to each of the footlockers before we pushed off.

"Just in case," I told him.

"Yeah, sure," he grumbled in reply.

"We've gone to all this work, you want to lose them now?"

"Let's go, Caine."

The hardest work was transferring the heavy metal boxes from the dinghy to the *Olympia*. The seas were rougher than I'd hoped, but we'd prepared for that, too. Farrell used the forward boom as a cargo winch, hoisting each footlocker from the bouncing Avon to the deck of my schooner, not exactly a stable platform. It wasn't a task I'd want to do every day, and it took longer than we'd planned, but eventually we wrestled the two heavy containers aboard. We all knew what was at risk.

It took the four of us to carry the footlockers below. I winced a couple of times when we scratched my teak getting them through the hatch. We stashed the money boxes in the main salon under the table. They looked like pirate chests. I guess, in effect, they served the same purpose.

"If you don't sink us, Caine, I think we've recovered the lady's money." Thomas popped the top off an Edelweiss *Dunkel* and toasted me. "I do believe you know what you're doing."

"Coming from you, Ed, that's a compliment."

"Yes. It is."

"There's more of those," I said, meaning the beer. "I think we've all earned one."

Thomas passed them around and we clinked the bottles together in a mutual toast.

"Now our only worry is the Coast Guard." Thomas followed me up on deck and helped raise the anchor. "I don't care what you say, there's got to be something illegal about bringing that kind of cash into the country. Hell, there's probably some kind of law against having that kind of cash in the first place."

"I don't think they'll bother us," I said.

"Why's that?"

"Wait and see. Let's get the canvas up. Claire, can you handle the foresail?" We'd sailed down and I planned sailing back; it took about eight hours each way. We'd be home by early morning.

She could and she did handle the foresail, showing Thomas and Farrell how to unfurl *Olympia*'s full complement of canvas. This was my maiden voyage. The boat did everything she was supposed to.

The Mexican coastline looked brown and barren under the harsh winter sun, resembling the California coastline, save the gazillion-dollar homes. Baja was starting to get its share of those, too, what with American investment and the influx of new drug money, but it would be decades before its coastline looked anything like Southern California from Malibu to San Diego. Maybe it would never have the same prosperity. Until it did, there would always be the foot traffic of the small brown people coming north to seek their fortunes.

When the sun set, acres of glass reflected the pale peach-colored sky from a darkened shore.

Night falls quickly on the ocean. Dusk transforms to dark without effort. *Olympia* sailed on through the invisible barrier, marking one more day in our lives. This day would never come again. There would be other days, fewer for me than for others, more than for some. We never know when it will be our last sunrise, when the sunset we see now will be our final curtain. We never know what will become of us after it is over. It is a universal question, one of the greatest mysteries in our lives.

Paul Peters was there, wherever *there* was. So was Stevenson. So were de la Peña, Chico, Paco and Elena and the rest of their gang. Vanished. Unable to appreciate this fine sunset and anticipate another. Kate was there, too. It isn't only the bad ones who die.

The crew must have sensed my mood. In any case, they left me alone. I remained on deck, making sure it was my watch when we entered American waters.

The cockpit had a radar screen slaved to the master unit in the communications cabin below. I saw the blips approach from twenty miles out, knowing we were on their radar, as well. They came right at us, without hesitation. They knew we were there.

I went below and woke Thomas and asked him to wake Farrell and meet me on deck. Then I went into my cabin.

"It's time?" Claire lay on the bunk, her hands behind her head, staring at the bulkhead.

"We're here, in U.S. waters. Just an hour more. Maybe two. Come on deck. There's something I'd like you to see."

"How soon?"

"About ten minutes."

"I'll make some coffee."

"Farrell's already done it. He had the last watch and made it then."

After my encounter with Barbara the other evening, Claire had made an effort to be nice, but her pleasantness was forced. I eventually understood that I'd merely performed a recovery service for the lady, removing the big bad wolf from the door, giving her reason to go on. As it was the night I'd met her, I was the hired help, appreciated, well paid, but as much a friend of the woman as her gardener.

Well, there are worse jobs. Not everyone is a friend after something like this. I'd recovered the money and restored her life to her. It was only what she had hired me to do, nothing more, nothing less. Of the husband there was nothing, so in that I had failed, although we both knew he was dead. I watched Claire, and thought I knew what she was thinking. I could see her begin thoughts of the future, and to plan, now that the past was past and no longer controlled her.

"Penny for your thoughts, John," she said.

"They're not worth that much." Then I saw it. "There! See the lights?"

But it was wrong. The lights were approaching from the wrong direction.

"Ed! Hatley!"

Both men came on deck, Farrell with the long gun.

"We've got problems." I pointed toward the southern horizon. A Mexican patrol boat quickly approached, guns bristling, its intentions apparent. We were the target. "Everyone get below, and get those guns out of sight."

"We're in U.S. waters."

"That's right, Ed, but we've got the global positioning system and they don't. They can do anything they want and claim they had the right."

"You think they know about the money?"

"I think old de la Peña had partners, and they knew about it. Someone had to be watching the beach. It's just our luck they were a little slow relaying the information. Otherwise they'd have caught us on their side of the border."

The patrol boat plowed through the swells, white spray turning a luminescent green in the black night.

"What's your plan?"

"We've got one ace card, but I'm not sure where it is."

Thomas looked at me with an expression resembling a sneer. "You don't know where it is? Or what it is?"

"Where. Get below. You guys guard the money and Claire. When they come alongside, I'll play dumb."

Thomas shook his head. "Good role for you to play, Caine," he said, disgusted.

"And if they come aboard, we're in U.S. waters and it's piracy. Shoot to kill."

He peered out into the darkness. "They might have fifties aboard, huh?"

I nodded. "Most likely."

"We won't stand a chance."

"We've got the money. Fifties would sink us."

"Sure, and I believe in Santa Claus, too. Here's your gun." He handed me the Colt. I shoved it into the waistband of my Levi's.

"It'll be okay," I said, hoping I was right.

Then I was alone again, watching the radarscope, hoping for a miracle.

Claire came up from the cabin.

"Get below," I told her. "If there's shooting, we'll be first."

Her face, illuminated from below by the green radar screen, was bleak. "They take the money now, I might as well be dead."

"Don't think that way." I looked over the railing behind me. The patrol boat was two hundred yards to our stern and quickly closing.

"You're going to win, Claire. Believe it."

She closed her eyes. "I wish I could."

The boat was now a hundred yards back and beginning to slow to match our speed. I saw five men standing at the bow, making ready to board us. A searchlight reached out and found us. It remained focused on the cockpit as they glided in.

"Attention the *Olympia!* Stand by to be boarded!"

"Get below, Claire. I'm not letting them aboard."

She shook her head fiercely. "I'm staying here!"

"Attention the *Olympia!*"

"I heard you," I said through my own loud-hailer. "This is a documented United States vessel sailing peacefully in American waters. Any attempt to interfere with us is piracy!"

"You are in Mexican waters and you will be boarded or we will sink you!" The tinny voice got closer. We had about three minutes before it was Molly Over the Windmill.

"I think this is called a Mexican standoff," I said, watching the radar screen.

"What happens now?"

"Get below, Claire. They will not board us and they will not sink us, but you've got to give me some room to move up here. Okay? Trust me?"

She gave me the long look. She'd had little reason to trust any man lately.

"You promise?"

"Yep," I said, watching the radar.

Without a word, she leaned over and kissed me on the mouth and went below.

The Mexican patrol craft came alongside, matching our speed. Twin-barreled .50-caliber machine guns pointed at me. One spasm, one twitch of a nervous finger, and John Caine would join his ancestors. Two seamen reached for our railing, trying to jump aboard. I twitched the wheel and they nearly fell overboard into the froth between the boats.

"You will comply!" the officer snarled. He had a thick black mustache that made him look like Saddam Hussein.

"Sorry, pal, but you're on the wrong side of the fence. Turn around and go home!" I stood, my .45 in plain sight. I could feel the tension rise a few notches, just the way I'd planned.

"You are armed in Mexico! Throw down your weapons!"

I heard the whoop, whoop, whoop of a boat siren far away. I looked toward the western horizon. Coming toward us, lit up like New Orleans at Mardi Gras, were two United States Navy inshore patrol boats. Smaller than Coast Guard cutters, but far faster than anything else on the seas. Updated PT boats of World War II, they were originally designed and built for coastal defense and unconventional warfare. They had weapons that dwarfed the Mexican .50s.

"Turn around and go now, while you still have a chance!" I shouted across the water. "This is a documented U.S. vessel in United States waters."

Doubt crossed the face of the officer who resembled Saddam Hussein. Most likely he'd been told a story, a story that now wasn't standing up.

I watched the lights coming on, separating now, one heading south of us, the other moving toward the north to encircle our position. Armed to the teeth, these were warships with the ability to destroy even a ship in seconds. Were I a target, or a drug smuggler, or a Mexican warship threatening a peaceful pleasure craft, I'd have been petrified.

The Mexican patrol craft angled away from *Olympia,* gunned its engine, and ran south.

Ed Thomas poked his head out of the cabin in time to watch the pirate run away. He disappeared and then returned with Farrell and Claire.

"Are those friendlies?" he asked, his attention focused on the navy patrol boats.

"Like you wouldn't believe," I said.

In two minutes both craft had throttled back and were puttering alongside, matching our more sedate pace. A black face leaned out of the pilothouse of the warship on our port side, a big white smile appearing on the man's grizzled features.

"Here we were, running around the ocean like our hair was on fire, and we run into you! What you doin' out here, Commander? Admiral MacGruder sends his compliments."

"In all the oceans, in all the world, you just happen to sail into mine. Hello, Max. It's good to see you! And you can thank the admiral for me. How the hell have you been? I heard you were somewhere else."

"They keep me hopping, they surely do! Sent me back to the Balkans, then to the Middle East, and then home again. I'm home for a day and a half when the admiral asks me for a favor. So I take these kids out on a training mission. And here you are! It's amazing!"

"You know this guy?" Thomas looked at the warship and back to me, bewilderment and disbelief written on his face. "You're a commander?"

"Lieutenant commander. Retired. And this guy is my best friend in the world. Known him all my adult life."

"The United States Navy is escorting us into port?"

"Why not? Claire's a taxpayer."

"I guess so."

"I'm a taxpayer. *Olympia*'s a documented United States vessel. We're repatriating some United States currency that got stolen. After all, it's millions of dollars that won't go against the balance of payments on foreign debt. That's a good thing."

"These are navy ships."

"They just happen to be here. We just happened to be here. They're heading home after a short-term training mission. We're headed home after a pleasure sail. Leave it at that. Nobody's harmed. Everyone's happy."

"We almost had an international incident."

"Almost is the operative word. Nothing happened. Believe it."

He shook his head. "God damn it, Caine, if you don't keep coming up with surprises. God damn it."

"You upset?"

He laughed. "Hell, no. I've just never met anybody like you in my life. And I've met a lot of people."

"Is that good?"

"Maybe. Maybe not. But if I'd met you when I carried a badge, I'd probably have arrested you. Using the United States Navy as an escort service! Jesus Christ!" He laughed. It was a belly laugh, the most emotion he'd ever displayed. Farrell joined him, shaking his head and wiping his eyes. I don't know why, but I joined, too. It started as a chuckle, then real laughter, then progressed to great whoops, then knee-slapping, back-pounding guffaws, feeding upon itself until it went completely out of control. Young navy seamen came on deck of the warships to watch us, pointing and smiling. I caught Max's eye. He wore a huge grin, the best one I'd seen on him in a long, long time.

"Why don't you get us some more coffee, Ed?"

"Why the hell not?"

He kept laughing all the way down the ladder to the galley.

Claire looked at me, her face unreadable. "You are resourceful, I'll give you that."

"That's comforting."

"Barbara's right about you."

"What'd she say?"

"It was woman talk. You wouldn't understand."

"Oink, oink," I said, my voice soft, wondering what the two women had talked about, and how much detail they'd gone into. "Works both ways." Claire smiled and put her hand on my shoulder, a friendly pat, not a lover's touch.

"She said you were a free spirit, one of the last cowboys, that if you could settle down, you'd make a good partner, but you'd never settle down. It would be cruel, like putting a wolf in a cage. She said the best would be to be your friend. It would be good, knowing there's a friend like you out there, somewhere."

I nodded, following what made sense, but not following all of it. She was right. I didn't pretend to completely understand woman talk.

"Told you."

"But what she said, it was good, wasn't it?"

"Of course, you silly man. It was very good."

"Then I should just shut up, shouldn't I?"

"I think that would be a very good idea, John Caine."

46

Waiting is hard. I never liked it, although the military and my current occupation demanded it more often than not. I did it; I just never liked it.

Waiting for a woman is similar, although there's an anticipation that makes it easier. And waiting for a woman is as common as waiting in the military.

I'd checked the boat stores twice, I'd checked the rigging three times. I'd checked my fuel and water and the spare electronic parts. I spent time in the bilge, making sure the batteries and the pumps worked. *Olympia* had full tanks; her provisions were secure. Everything was set. All I lacked was my passenger.

She'd said she'd meet me at the yacht club at ten. In three weeks we'd be in Honolulu. I looked at my Rolex. It was ten-thirty.

Barefoot, wearing shorts and my old cutoff sweatshirt that said SKI THE VOLCANO, I paced back and forth along the dock, eager to cast off my lines. If she waited much longer, we'd have to go tomorrow.

"John!"

Barbara Klein stood at the top of the dock. At first something about her didn't register. When I watched her walk down the dock after taking off her high heels, it did. She wore a tailored business suit, a frilly silk blouse, high heels and nylon stockings. She carried a black leather purse over her shoulder. Not exactly yachting garb. A sour knot began to form in the pit of my stomach.

"Barbara, what's up?"

"John, I wanted to tell you last night, but I couldn't." Last night had been a night to remember, memorable in many ways. Now I had the feeling it would have to do for a time, only a cherished memory. Her ardor came back after the money's return, and I was the lucky beneficiary. Only occasionally did the arm's-length appraisal reappear. Then she would peer at me with warm brown eyes that told me everything and nothing at all. She was honest to a fault and answered all my questions, but she volunteered nothing unless asked. The one thing she never did was speak of a long-term relationship.

"Tell me what?"

"I can't come with you."

"Oh."

"Too much is happening for me to get away." She stood on the dock, looking up at me. "Can I come aboard?"

"I'm sorry. Sure." I reached down and she grabbed my wrist and I hauled her up and over the railing.

"Claire's business is really going again. What none of us knew was that during all the bad times, Adrian kept working. He'd started collaborating with a hardware genius, a garage tinkerer. You know, like Jobs and Wozniak? Anyway, Adrian was frustrated because of the money shortage, but he stayed with it, coaxed the guy along. He worked on the software part of the unit."

"What?"

"Adrian and this guy came up with a new product! It'll replace the personal computer, I think. It works with a telephone line, any kind! A pay phone, a cellular, anything, as long as it can access a phone line somewhere, somehow. It's a search engine for the Net, the Internet? And it's cheap! We can produce it for a whole lot less money than we could build a computer. Do you know what this means?"

"No." And my enthusiasm wasn't high. I'd seen the computer Adrian had used and thought it a great tool. This was beyond me.

"This puts Petersoft on the ground floor of a revolution. We could be IBM in ten years!"

"I understand. You've got to be here."

"Yes. I'm the godmother. I can't leave now."

She was right. She was senior management at the bank. It was her account, and it would be irresponsible to just leave now, to sail away to Hawaii when the future of the company was at stake.

"They demonstrated it this morning as a surprise! I've got financing to arrange. I've got to help Claire get production up and running. Someone's got to get the patents and the copyrights worked out. There's a whole world to conquer!"

I patted her cheek. "And you're just the guy to do it, too."

"Was that condescending?"

"No. It was accurate. Go get 'em! You've got the know-how, you have the company, you have the product. Don't let anything stop you."

"John, I—"

"This isn't sour grapes. I want you to go for it. You have the responsibility now."

She put both hands on my face. My bruises had faded. Only the deepest cuts remained, scabbed over. My face still looked battered, but then it always did.

"John. We couldn't have done it without you. We all owe you so much."

She made it sound like a good-citizenship award. "Go out and conquer the world, kid. That's what you have to do." I kissed her. She didn't kiss me back, and I felt a little foolish.

She stepped away from me and dug into her purse. "This morning the board voted to give you a reward of common stock in addition to your fee. Congratulations. You now own ten thousand shares of Petersoft. It's undervalued now, worth about twenty thousand dollars, but when the new product comes out, it could be worth millions." She handed me a brown envelope. I took it, but didn't open it.

"Thank you."

She kissed my cheek, a sisterly kiss. "Thank you, John. You saved a lot of lives. By the way, Claire says good-bye and thank you, and wants you to know you can keep the guns."

"Tell her thanks," I said, feeling a kind of self-pitying sadness swelling my chest. "You need a lift down?"

She grinned. "Yeah!"

I picked her up and carefully eased her over the transom to the dock.

"This isn't the end, you know. We'll be friends. I like the idea of John Caine out there, wherever you are, knowing I could call you if I ever needed help."

"I kind of like that, too."

"I warned myself you'd get emotionally involved."

"And you're not?"

"You know it was . . . it was just what it was."

"Exorcising demons."

"Yes. Aside from the others, you saved me. From a lot of things."

"They call me the exorcist."

"You okay?"

I nodded. I wasn't, but I wasn't going to tell her.

"Write to me?"

I nodded. "I'll send a postcard."

"Good-bye, John."

I waved, then put my hands in the pockets of my shorts. I didn't trust my voice.

"Good sailing."

"Thanks," I croaked.

I watched her walk up the gangway, watched those strong, smooth legs, those trim hips beneath the tight skirt. I watched the curve of her rear as she bent down to put on her shoes at the dock. I watched her walk away, not looking back, holding her head high, her back straight, moving toward a new life.

Sometimes you work so hard to win, and you do, and then you lose anyway.

Barbara was right. There was no reason to come to Hawaii with me. She had her responsibilities. And if you really thought about it, she didn't need a boat bum in her life. Not permanently. Oh, it was fun while it lasted. It always is.

I smiled a grim smile, realizing I'd been used, my body,

my penis, just a warm comforting piece of flesh to chase the shakes away. In a way it was my reward for finding the money, a pat on the head for the good puppy. I felt soiled and used, probably the way women have been feeling for centuries.

I'd thought something might happen, misreading her vulnerability while at the same time missing what was going on in my own vacant and vacuous head. Coming on the heels of Kate's death, I thought I was ready for something, and maybe I was. But a relationship with a Barbara Klein wasn't it.

But it was nice while it lasted, the fun and games with the beautiful woman. Deep down, I knew she'd tire of the game and want something permanent. I just never thought she'd be the one to pull the plug, or as quickly. She never gave me the chance to see if we could have something permanent.

Could I do that? Could I commit to permanence? I didn't know the answer to that one. And fortunately now, I wouldn't have to find out.

It's about choices. It's all about choices. This life I'd chosen, the one I'd embraced, it wasn't compatible with the corporate culture. Hell, I didn't even know where home was, except for a lovely chain of islands floating in the middle of the Pacific.

I glanced back to where Barbara had disappeared. A figure stood on the top of the dock, looking down at me.

"Thought you'd get away without seeing me?" Sergeant Gregorio Esparza came down the ramp, dressed as I'd first seen him, looking like a hard-edged college student with an attitude.

"Sergeant Esparza."

"Had a few questions, Caine."

"Come aboard. Want a beer?"

"Sure." The policeman leaped over the transom and found a comfortable cushion.

"I was just leaving," I said, handing him an Edelweiss. "So if you're running me out of town, save your breath."

"We thought about tar and feathers, but the Environmental Protection Agency would fine us for spreading the tar around and the animal rights activists would sue if we used real feathers."

"You see Mrs. Klein?"

He nodded. "I waited. Didn't want to interfere." He took a long drink, looked at the bottle, then took another. Most people, used to the horse pish we Americans call beer, are vastly surprised with their first taste of the real thing.

"This beer?"

"Austrian. I get it from a guy in Long Beach."

"Tastes like liquid bread."

That was as good a description as any I'd heard.

"Give me a name," said Esparza. "I won't arrest you."

"A bribe."

"Money, never. Beer, maybe. This beer, sure." He drank more of the Edelweiss. "Wasn't going to arrest you anyway, but maybe you could give me his name?"

"Sure," I said. "His name's Pa. He's a university professor who loves real beer; got the American concession and imports it himself." I went below, found my Day-Timer, and wrote Pa's telephone number. I brought another beer when I returned.

"I left messages. You don't return your phone calls when you don't want something."

Barbara and I had spent two weeks helping Claire put her life back together, starting with the company. Chawlie was, as I had predicted, unusually helpful, although we never would have succeeded without Barbara's guidance. She pointed us toward an excellent attorney who began unraveling Claire's legal and tax problems. With the cash in hand, she said, it wasn't difficult. Without it, she raised her hands in helpless supplication.

And when we met four of Chawlie's men at the airport to turn over two well-wrapped packages for bonded shipment to Honolulu, Barbara nearly had a heart attack, disbelieving they had come to help us. With guns all too visible, they stood silently behind Daniel, one of Chawlie's young nephews, as he negotiated the exchange. The entire operation lasted less than five minutes but felt like a lifetime.

And when we left the warehouse, she bombarded me with questions as to how I could know someone with access to that kind of money, with those kinds of thugs.

"Daniel is not a thug. He's a well-educated, polite young man."

"You know what I meant," she said.

"A friend of a friend."

"And what was his fee for making the exchange?"

"Nothing." Not even a fraction of a percentage point, the risk and the costs carried by my old friend, the lack not lost on the lady.

"So maybe he owes you something."

"Owed, my love, owed. I'm sure he's calling it even right now."

"So you'll do something to catch up?"

"Maybe, maybe not."

She remained silent, and then punched me in the arm. "I'll never understand men."

"You couldn't," I said. "You've never been a man."

And she hit me again.

Now this policeman was asking where I'd been.

"I was busy."

"Sure. It was only police business. A little murder. Or ten. How many, Caine?"

I shrugged.

"Okay. It's unclear. We've got it all worked out . . . just the way we were supposed to, I guess." He looked at me—no college student. "Is that the way we were supposed to work it out? The gang does de la Peña, then shoots it out with Stevenson, then the brother and sister factions fight to the death in Baja?"

"Isn't that what happened?"

"Officially. On both sides of the border. They apparently stole Mrs. Peters's Range Rover and used it to commit the crimes. Our investigation turned it up at Stevenson's house at the time of the shooting. Then it showed up stripped and abandoned in the mountains near Tecate."

"Then that's what happened. Is Peters dead?"

"Officially."

"Then that's it."

Esparza nodded. "So that's the way it is."

"Yep."

"And you're leaving town."

I looked around at my surroundings. San Diego's skies were blue, as blue as they had been since my arrival. But the weather was still cold, and the air seemed thin.

"It's time," I said. "I'm going home."

"I'll call your friend, Lieutenant Kahana, Kaha . . ."

"Kimo?"

"Yeah. I'll warn him you're coming."

"Thanks."

"You know what he said about you the first time I called him? He asked me if I knew why California has fires, floods, earthquakes, and riots and Hawaii has John Caine. He said California had first choice."

Esparza stood and shook my hand. "I wish I could say it's been a pleasure. Knew you were trouble the first time I met you. Glad to see I'm still a good judge of character." He looked around *Olympia,* taking in the extra stores and supplies. "You heading south? Through Mexico?"

"Sure. That okay?"

He nodded. "I talked to a few friends down there. Like I said, they have some good ones, too. They're not all like de la Peña. Nobody's looking for you. You should be all right."

"Say good-bye to Ambrosio and Manny for me."

"I will. Good sailing."

He hopped over the railing and bounded up the dock, looking once again like a college student.

I started *Olympia*'s engine, jumped down onto the dock, and cast off my lines. I motored out into the channel, past the submarine base, past North Island, past the tall, tan cliffs of Point Loma.

When I cleared the harbor I raised the sails and turned south, toward Mexico, toward Hawaii.

Toward home.

47

Diamond Head looked exactly the same since I'd last seen the craggy lava landmark, the gray-blue Ko'olau Mountains ranging beyond. Maybe the old volcano had got a little greener along its slopes. Waikiki still sheltered below its western flank, the high-rise hotels and the white sandy beaches as much a part of me as my own skin. It hadn't been all that long, but it felt like years since I'd been back. Honolulu looked serene and quiet from five miles offshore, a welcome sight.

A pod of dolphin swam escort duty, playing tag with *Olympia*'s shadow.

I'd had what the Chinese call an interesting month getting across the Pacific. I'd followed the Mexican coast down to the tip of Baja, skipping from one port to another, stopping for three glorious, wondrous days at Bahía de Los Angeles to watch the gray whales, and then paid for it by taking a nasty drubbing from a head wind all the way to Cabo, around the point and into the sheltered harbor known as La Paz, "The Peace." I spent a few nights in port replenishing supplies before setting course for Hawaii. It's almost due west from La Paz, and should have been an easy trip, but the currents and the winter storms conspired to frustrate my goal. *Olympia* and I were both a little bruised and battered from our voyage, both of us a little older and a little used up.

My blond hair and beard were nearly white from the sun and I'd made up for the tan I'd lost under San Diego's winter cloud cover.

I'd lost weight, and every part of my body hurt from the month of constant physical abuse. A boat this size is not meant to be sailed alone, even with special rigging. I'd done it because I didn't want anyone else aboard; I had thought about signing on a couple of ex-navy types I met in La Paz, then reconsidered it and made the rigging adjustments in port before setting out. The two looked like they could be trouble, and I'd had all the trouble I wanted.

Solitude was my reward.

Olympia had GPS, but Ed Alapai had taught me something about being a *ho'okele,* a Hawaiian wayfinder, the art of using the stars, the wind, and the currents to find your way across the Pacific. To an accomplished *ho'okele,* the surface of the ocean is a landscape to be read and understood. There's even a story about a blind navigator who could tell where he was by the taste of the water.

A haole, I didn't taste, but found navigating with the night sky almost as easy as using electronics. With A'a, the star I knew as Sirius, the brightest in the sky, on my starboard and Acrux of the Southern Cross, known to the Hawaiians as Mole Honua, on my port side, Hawaii lay dead ahead. Stars filled the heavens, horizon to horizon, old friends, the reliable panorama the ancients witnessed and recorded. Most days were sun-blasted bright and I enjoyed my solitary sail. But I loved the nights.

On the radio, Pearl Harbor gave me permission to enter after a short discussion about the name of my boat. For years, *Duchess* had gone in and out of the narrow entrance to the naval base and my name was on the list, but *Olympia* was not. I had to explain to the harbormaster that *Duchess* wasn't coming back. Ever. He finally got it, and I called the Rainbow Marina on the cellular to let them know my slip would be used again, to give them fair warning to get anyone out of there who might have pirated the vacancy during my absence.

In an hour I bid farewell to my dolphin escorts, dropped my sails, and entered Pearl Harbor under power. I could see the white USS *Arizona* memorial at Ford Island, the new bridge construction, and the lush, green mountains beyond, their peaks shrouded in billowy white clouds. Off to the west, the island gave me a rainbow welcome.

I was home.

I tied up at my slip at the end of the mauka dock. Henry, the Rainbow Marina's Filipino dockmaster, was there to meet me.

"When I hear your voice, I can't believe it! It's good to see you! This your boat?"

I tossed him the bowline. "Secure this, Henry. It's good to see you, too."

"You been gone a long time, yah?"

"It sure seems like it." I jumped down and tied off the stern line.

"*Olympia.* That's a good name. This bigger than your old boat. Prettier."

"She'll do."

"You live here again?"

"Yep. I'm home."

"I'll tell everybody. We'll have a party, once you get settled good."

"That'll be fine, Henry. Thank you."

"Good to have you back, John Caine. Thought you was gone for good, yah?"

"Yeah."

He laughed and went up the dock. I thought I heard him singing.

I went back aboard my boat. She needed work, some port time, some tender loving care.

So did I.

I had a little laundry, not much, but some, having spent most of the time wearing only a ratty pair of shorts. I had a few electronic parts to replace. I needed batteries, a couple of new sails, some hull work. Two portholes were missing glass due to one particularly dark and stormy night. And I needed a drink. The Marina Restaurant, above the boat docks, beckoned like an old friend. I collected what I needed and went below for my wallet.

"Hello, sailor!"

I heard the voice out on the dock, not certain I was hearing what I was hearing, not trusting my senses.

"John Caine!"

I stuck my head out of the cabin. Barbara Klein stood on the dock, dressed in a tight pink tank top and red short-shorts. She carried a bottle of Dom, and she looked magnificent.

"Aren't you going to invite me aboard?"

"Sure. Just let me put my tongue back in my mouth."

I reached down and she grabbed my wrist and I swung her aboard, just the way we'd done it before.

"What are you doing here?" It was all I could think to say.

"Well, I heard the fleet was in, so I came down to show my support. Love you navy guys."

"No, really. It's wonderful to see you, but why are you here?"

"Claire has her business back on track. She no longer needs me on a day-to-day basis. When I went back to San Francisco, I got all mopey and sad. I couldn't concentrate on my work, so my boss ordered me to take a vacation, and I thought, why not Hawaii?"

"And?"

"And so I hadn't been to Hawaii for years. Actually I came here on my honeymoon, but you don't want to hear about that. I wanted to see the place where you saved my son, and I wanted to see you."

"You wanted to see me?"

She rolled her eyes. "You're pretty thick, aren't you?"

"I have my moments."

"Which ones? Good or bad? I can't tell." She reached over and squeezed my hands. "Look, John, I have some time here. A couple of weeks. And I wanted to come see you in your own element. If you want me to go home, just say so."

"No."

"Okay. Thank you for asking me. I've been fine."

"How did you know where I would be?"

"Your friend Max kept track of you. You spoke with him on the ham radio and the satellite phone, he told us where you were, when to expect you in port."

She was silent, surveying *Olympia*'s battered condition. "You had a rough trip."

"It had its moments."

She looked up at me, intelligent brown eyes penetrating my gaze. "I'll bet. So what's it going to be? You up for this?"

"It's nice, seeing you. I thought I wouldn't again, and I missed you."

"You're going to show me around the island? Maybe see Maui? Kauai? I'd really love to see the volcano. Is it true you can't carry pork across the mountains at night without getting the gods angry? I want to try it. And I want to work on my tan."

"Sounds fine."

"You look like you could use some rest, too, sailor boy. What do you think?"

"Where are you staying?"

"We're checked into the Royal Hawaiian."

"We?"

"Got us a suite. Thought you might want a shower, a drink, or something."

"A shower was just what I had in mind," I said. "And the drink."

"And the something?"

I looked at her. She wasn't kidding. Here was the real prize at the end of the quest. A prize that only a fool would turn away from. "That sounds best."

She nodded, taking my hand, enfolding it between her two small, soft hands.

"Come on," she said.

Here's a preview of Charles Knief's latest book

THE EMERALD FLASH

Coming soon from St. Martin's Press

The first time I saw Margo Halliday she was stark naked, running for all she was worth down a Honolulu alley in the middle of the night.

A big man chased her. Every thirty feet or so he'd stop and fire a round from an automatic pistol. The woman was in more danger of stepping in broken glass than getting hit by a bullet. The big guy's heart wasn't in it. Unsteady on his feet, just tipsy enough to be overcautious, he would come to a complete stop, carefully aim way to the right or way to the left, and pull the trigger. He'd watch the bullet powder brick on either side of the alley, then start chasing her again. It reminded me of a cat chasing a mouse. A lot of fun for the cat, sure, if he felt sadistic, but the mouse would just as soon prefer to be otherwise occupied.

This time neither party appeared to be having fun. The man cried as he chased her, mouthing unitelligible words, tears streaking his cheeks, his nose running. He looked like a wounded man, the way a man can only be wounded by a woman. And for all his pain he looked grimly intent on inflicting pain of another kind on the source of his misery.

I'd just left the back room of Chawlie's Chinatown restaurant where he'd beaten me once again at *Go*. That made it about twenty-five gazillion to two, and I was very proud of those two.

The big man jogged past and I dropped him with a flying kick. He went down easy but refused to let go of the pistol, so I broke his wrist and he gave it up. All the fight went out of him.

He deflated like an octopus brought up on a lure and dumped into the bottom of a canoe, when it knew it was going to die.

I released the pistol's clip and eased back the slide. A bright brass 9mm cartridge popped out. The gun was a Glock, one of those new automatics that carried half a box of ammunition. Load it up in the morning and shoot all day. It was good for those unsure of their marksmanship, or for those loonies who imagined themselves facing hordes of enemy lurking between their homes and the corner 7-Eleven. The gun safed, I stuck it in my hip pocket.

"Is he dead?"

The naked woman had returned. She stood near the big man, who lay curled against Chawlie's back wall. Hip slung, she presented an explicit representation of female anatomy.

"Not unless he's had a heart attack." I squatted and felt the big neck. The slow, strong heartbeat was reassuring. "He's okay," I said, looking up. She had moved closer and my face was now in direct proximity to her sex.

I stood and pulled off my sleeveless SKI THE VOLCANO sweatshirt and handed it to her. The sides gapped, but if she kept her arms down it would cover her. She was not a particularly small woman, but it was an XXL.

She silently accepted the sweatshirt but held it against her thigh. She stood naked in the filthy Chinatown alley, as still and as beautiful as a Grecian statue. And as unremarkable. All flesh is equal, regardless of its age or condition. Her body was one I could admire as I would admire a work by a master sculpture, but like a statue, no heat radiated from it and I was not drawn to her.

"Put it on," I said.

"Oh." Her eyes focused suddenly. She had been far away, but she came back from wherever she'd been and shrugged the shirt over her head.

"Thank you," she said, her voice shaky. Now she looked scared.

"You know this guy?"

She nodded, her arms wrapped around her body, long fingers gripping the gray sweat cloth. "He's my husband. Or was. We're divorced. Have been for years. But he keeps coming around, making demands."

"Come on," I said, reaching for her. She flinched away.

"Where?"

"In here. It's a restaurant." I pointed to Chawlie's back door. "There are people in there. Other women. They'll take care of you. Get you some clothes. Then you can decide what to do."

She nodded again. "What about him?"

I looked down at the man. He still lay against the wall. I couldn't tell if he was unconscious or if he was faking. It didn't matter.

"What about him?"

"He's hurt," she said. "Shouldn't we do something for him?"

"Why?"

She thought about it. Then she nodded again and I knew she was going to be all right.

"John Caine. You only man I know who can walk out the door and come right back with naked woman." Chawlie whispered, his smile large and generous, his eyes twinkling.

We lounged at his bar sharing one more beer. His bar girls had taken charge of Margo, wrapping her in silk and taking her back to Chawlie's private quarters. Eventually one of the girls returned with much ceremony and giggling to present me with my sweatshirt.

"Anthony checked man in alley. His arm broken, he no move. Next time he look, man gone. You do him, eh?"

"He was chasing the woman and shooting at her with this." I pulled the automatic from my hip pocket and handed it to Chawlie.

"Grock."

"Yeah. A Grock. He was shooting, but he didn't mean to hit her. He aimed wide."

"This her husband?"

"Ex-husband."

Chawlie shook his head. The lack of clarity and the vagaries of haole relationships were alien to him. He offered me the gun.

"You keep it," I said. "I don't like those things."

He laughed. "You old-fashioned."

"A nine's too small," I said.

"You like what you like. Forty-five your gun." Chawlie examined the automatic again. "Expensive," he muttered, and put it away behind the bar. "You know this man? You recognize him?"

"Who? The woman's husband?"

"Yes."

"No. Do you?"

"Never saw him before," said Chawlie, sipping his Tsing Tao. "Just wondered. All you haoles look alike to me. Especially in the dark."

"Funny, Chawlie."

"You see bruises on young woman's face? Or you just looking at her tits?"

I hadn't seen any bruises, but it was dark in the alley.

"So what you going to do, John Caine? You going take young woman home, be her big hero? Hope to get lucky, or what?"

"Somebody's got to take her home."

"I send girls and a couple of my people. She feel safer that way, I think."

Chawlie was trying to get rid of me. That meant there was something he could use to his advantage. And he didn't want me involved.

That Chawlie would send the woman home with his girls was certain. He might be a criminal, he might break the law, but unlike most of those who craft the laws, he is a man of his word. Although I didn't know her name at the time, Margo Halliday was safer than she'd ever been in her life. Whatever advantage he might gain by assuming the responsibility for the woman's safety would not adversely affect her in any way.

"I'll take that hint," I said, sliding off the bar stool, "and go home."

"Leave by front door this time."

"Good night, old friend."

"Good night, John Caine. If you find any more strays tonight, you keep them."

That was the first time I'd ever seen Margo Halliday. It would not be the last.

The next time I was aware of her was seven months later, when news of the murder was the *Advertiser*'s lead story, her photograph prominently displayed on the front page, her feathers instantly recognizable, bringing back the events of that warm summer evening. Her ex-husband had been shot to death in her Hawaii Kai condominium. Police wasted no time in charging her with a variety of crimes, curiously excluding any of those indictments that can be brought when one human being takes the life of another. The crimes were all misdemeanors and minor felonies and she made bail with the help of a high-priced defense attorney from Bishop Street.

The paper reported the sanctioned police statement that they were investigating and would have further announcements. It didn't look good for the woman I'd briefly met in that dark, dirty alley.